By Blood, By Salt

Land of Exile Book 1

J. L. Odom

Cover art by Jeremy Adams

Cover Design by Kelly Carter

Map by Rhys Davies

ISBN: 979-8-9900244-0-3 (paperback)

ISBN: 979-8-9900244-1-0 (hardcover)

ISBN: 979-8-9900244-2-7 (ebook)

To Ellen Stackable and Jan O'Connor
For the books you brought and the history you taught
Thank you

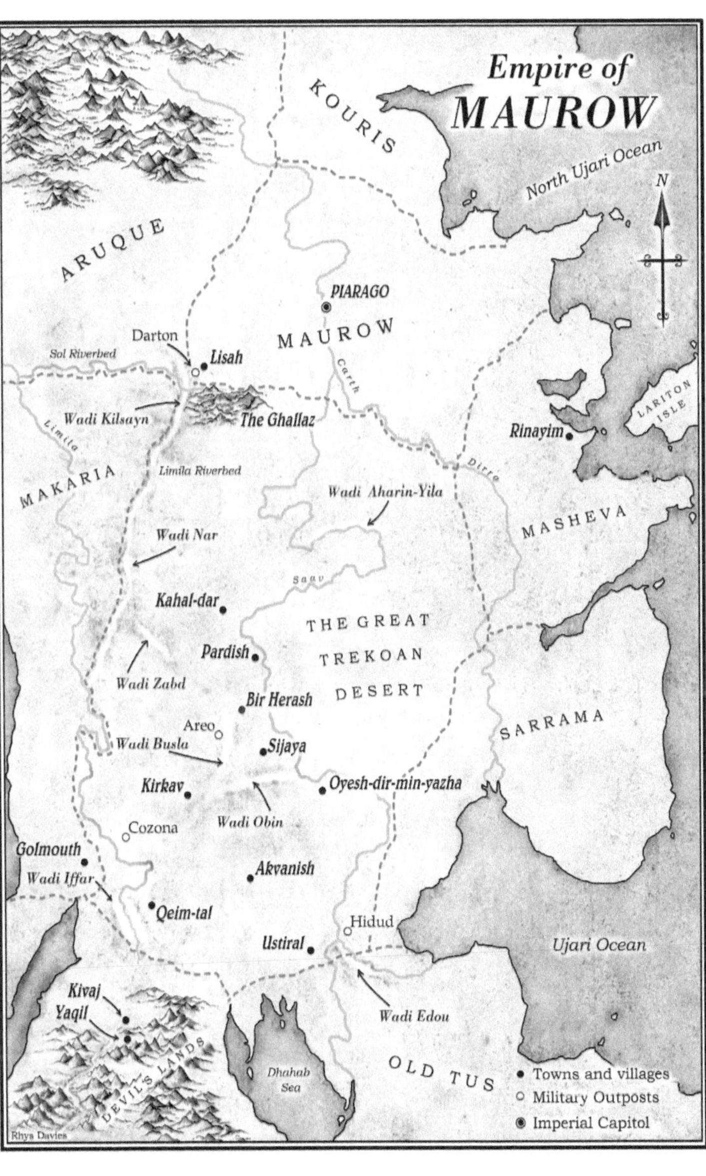

Empire of
MAUROW
KOURIS
North Ujari Ocean
N
ARUQUE
PIARAGO
MAUROW
Darton
Lisah
Sol Riverbed
Carth
Wadi Kilsayn
The Ghallaz
Limila
Rinayim
LARITON ISLE
MAKARIA
Limila Riverbed
Wadi Aharin-Yila
MASHEVA
Wadi Nar
Dirre
Saav
Kahal-dar
THE GREAT
Pardish
TREKOAN
Wadi Zabd
DESERT
Bir Herash
SARRAMA
Areo
Wadi Busla
Sijaya
Kirkav
Oyesh-dir-min-yazha
Cozona
Wadi Obin
Golmouth
Akvanish
Wadi Iffar
Qeim-tal
Hidud
Ustiral
Ujari Ocean
Kivaj
Yaqil
Wadi Edou
DEVIL'S LANDS
Dhahab Sea
OLD TUS
Towns and villages
Military Outposts
Imperial Capitol
Rhys Davies

1

The wind was warm and pungent as it dove down, twisted through the narrow alleys of South City, and pushed softly at Azetla's back. It was early in the year for the desert to be driving its scent up through the Imperial capital, but Azetla took comfort from it. He let it shepherd his smooth strides toward the northern half of the city, and he breathed in those little hints of home.

"Spare some blood, O jackal, spare some blood?" a boy chanted as Azetla passed. "Show us your filthy innards and throw yourself into the river!"

The pale boy was clearly pleased with himself as he rocked on his heels, trying with all his small might to provoke a reaction. With a hungry look on his face, the boy threw several pebbles at Azetla with a wild arm, but Azetla simply ducked out of the way and moved on. The child was a beggar and thin as a pike, but even had he been otherwise, it wouldn't have been worth the price of bread to respond. Especially not today.

The streets turned from dust to stone as Azetla walked beneath the archways of the central aqueduct and toward the capital colonnade. The columns were dressed with scarlet cloth. Soon, all of Piarago would have a violent tinge of red to it: wine and animal blood left at the feet of the temple statues, crimson dye splashed in the streets, and roses dumped into the river by the armful. Finally, there would be human blood flowing through a small gully in the stone floor of the colonnade; it was a blood-soaked Imperial victory that would be commemorated today, a day to honor the Maurowan goddess Serivash—she who, they claimed, drank the fruit of the veins like the fruit of the vine and was never, ever satisfied.

They called it the Red River festival, which Azetla thought had a deceptively innocent sound to it.

"You! Jackal! Come here."

A soldier posted in the colonnade entrance waved him over. Azetla hesitated a moment. The soldier had a weary demeanor, as if he had just come off watch only to be posted here. Probably not interested in making extra work for himself.

Azetla walked over and dipped his head in respect.

"Yes, sir?"

"Are you wanting to die today?"

"No, sir."

"Well are you a citizen at least?"

"No."

"Look, jackal, not the best idea, going into the colonnade just now," the soldier said. "If you've business there, keep it until tomorrow."

"I'll be careful, sir. And I know the law."

Azetla lifted his palms slightly and took a half-step back to emphasize his visible lack of even so much as a common cooking knife. He never brought anything that could be construed as a weapon when he ventured into North Piarago.

"Oh, all you jackals *know* the law. Knowing's not the thing, eh?" the soldier said, giving Azetla one last look of tired scrutiny before waving him on.

Azetla simply nodded and walked through. There was a time when all the urchin insults and soldierly suspicion could have fanned the small, dampered coal that was his temper, but he had long since learned to pick his battles.

Beyond the colonnade hall, Azetla stepped into the enormous stone square which it encased. The sun was peering over east Pirago through the columns and Azetla shaded his eyes against the onslaught of light. The square roiled with people and revelrous noise. Vendors peddled the traditional blood-cakes—their fillings thick and dark with pomegranates or cherries and the tangy scent of lemons. The hot-sweet smell of them warred with the far heavier smell of too many people pushed too closely together.

Azetla remembered that he thought the aroma of the blood-cakes horribly tempting the first time he smelled them, though he would never have considered putting one to his mouth. Now, the least whiff of them turned his stomach.

Some twelve years ago, he'd had one forced down his throat by a crowd of young revelers looking for a means to entertain themselves, and they gleefully held his mouth and nose shut so that he could barely breathe. The taste would always remind him of gagging on sweet red syrup and desperately trying to draw a breath, like one under water.

There were, of course, very few of his own people in the square, because they had the good sense to skitter to shadows when the city was in revelry. Azetla kept to the outer edge, folded his arms, and watched the Maurowan nobility mill and chatter and approve of one another. A few were quiet, desiring to appear devout and contemplative. Azetla recognized them all—he particularly noted the low-tiered nobles like Verris and Thearaty, trying to put on a high-blooded front. He kept his eyes on them right up until the moment the prisoners slated for execution were brought out to the sound of rabid cheers.

All of the condemned "criminals" were, whether of birth or descent, from the Imperial province of Masheva. The day commemorated a victory against suspected Mashevi conspirators, and thus Mashevi convicts were usually set aside for this festival, like one reserves the good wine.

"*Thieves, murderers, and traitors!*" the crier shouted. There were eighteen of them. The details of their crimes were expounded upon at excessive length. Some of the accusations were true. Others were manufactured, for it was an easy matter to condemn a Mashevi without evidence. Most of them were South City dwellers with little more than a sadhin tunic and sandals to their name, but some were men and women of stature. Merchants. Nobility. One was a physician.

Money and rank could not buy a Mashevi out of Serivash's teeth.

The first Mashevi brought forward for execution was one of noble blood, gray-headed and refined in manner. His crime—so said the crier—was that of fomenting rebellion and disloyalty to both Emperor Riada Sivolne and his proxy, Governor-King Keved Aver of Masheva. This accusation Azetla believed to be true. The elderly man's beard had been roughly shaved, and his eyes fixed to the ground as if to evade the din, the squalor, the scents, and the morbid glee of life observing imminent death.

He ought not to do that. He ought to hold his head up high. But he was afraid, as anyone would be, and fear sapped pride and life out of the blood. The choking-hot smell of blood-cakes hit Azetla afresh, and the miserable taste sat in his throat.

With due spectacle, the elderly Mashevi's head was pulled back and his throat neatly slit, vein to vein, blood quickly soaking the front of his white sadhin. Azetla bit down on a flinch; it was so like an animal slaughter.

One by one the others followed, each causing the faintest hitch in Azetla's breath. His were not sheltered eyes, but the whole spectacle was designed to be jarring. The executioners leaned each Mashevi forward at the severing, and the blood pooled and trickled into the rut in the center of the colonnade making its diminutive river to their goddess. Then the bodies were shunted to the side, like refuse.

Azetla stood still and silent as a statue at the farthest edge of the happy clamor. The whole atmosphere thrummed with their giddy sense of vindication. He had lived among them long enough and he knew what they saw. They saw justice being done. They saw it as curative as a physician's bloodletting, draining the evil out of the community that it should rise the stronger. They felt wholly and passionately justified.

When the last man's neck was cut open, Azetla let out a long, ragged breath. He dropped abruptly to one knee, scraped his hand along the ground as though scooping ash out of a dead fire, and brushed his calloused, brown fingers over his head. He mouthed the Mashevi death benediction with the quickness that came of having said it a thousand times.

He meant it no less for that.

One breath later, he rose quickly to his feet and turned to leave the colonnade before anyone could drive too keen a gaze toward him amid the crush. Eyes level, he shouldered his way through the pressing crowd, the smattering of taunts, and one failed, drunken attempt to knock him to the ground.

The festival tended to make the city's blood hot and foolish. Azetla had to slip around the fires, the fights, and the hungry-eyed city-soldiers.

For fourteen years now he had made this trek into the northern half of the city for the Red River festival. Each time he wondered if he could become inured to the sight of Serivash's river of death. One tends to acclimate. The senses coarsen. Guilt begins to fade.

He would keep coming every year, no matter that it was unwise for him to do so. He would keep watching, stone-silent, as that dark river cut through the colonnade. He would subject himself to it again and again until, by some miracle, the river's source was cut off once and for all.

Even if that day never came.

Even if his eyes grew cold and accustomed.

But he was not yet so far gone. He still needed to brace himself and close off his thoughts to get through it. And though he kept his head erect and his eyes attentive to every passing face, he felt as though he dragged each of the Mashevi bodies behind him as he walked southward. Not only the innocent, but also those whom justice had served perfectly well.

After all, he just stood and watched. He had done, and could do, nothing. So they clung to him a while.

When he reached the barracks, he performed all his tasks with slowness and meticulous concentration, as when one's hands are thawing from terrible cold. He donned his baldric and secured his weapons till they rested against him, both comfortable and comforting. He tied on his Imperial battalion cord until it hung at his shoulder just so.

Taking his ledgers in hand and writing out the fresh columns in Maurowan script, he packed the morning's sights away to a certain corner of his mind, cutting the weight of it off his shoulders. It was too much, it helped no one, and he had work to do.

For the first time since he was a boy, Lord Wesley Verris was disturbed by the sacrifice to Serivash. He was strangely bereft of all the satisfaction he had learned to enjoy on the Red River festival. A haze crept over him, though Wesley was surrounded by absolute merriment and the sweet, sharp blood-cake smell of victory.

When the knife was first drawn and set against the neck of some jackal criminal, Wesley felt a lurch in his gut. No longer did he see the gray head of a Mashevi, but his own. He saw himself standing in prison clothes on the execution dais, head pulled back, throat exposed to a just and final laceration.

The image collapsed, but the effect of it lingered. All his cheers and smiles had to be manufactured with great effort.

He ought to be gratified to see the jackals pay for their crimes. And he supposed he still was. Mashevis were seditious by nature and liked to bite at the Empire's ankles, like snakes. Well and good the criminals among them should die thus, to cheers. Well and good that the rest of them should see it and be warned.

This was all sensible and true. But it did absolutely nothing to comfort Wesley.

If he failed in what he set out to do, he would be counted among the jackals, a traitor and plague to the Empire. His throat would gape, and Serivash would drink him up.

But if he succeeded, he would be the Empire's savior. So, then. Eyes on the task at hand. One thing at a time.

Wesley took a deep breath.

As Serivash's bewitching river trickled down through the colonnade, Wesley soothed himself with the sight of it. He soothed himself with all he knew to be true. The Goddess would respect his shrewdness. The Empire herself—not the Emperor—was his master. All he was about to do was in her service. Those who disagreed were merely the sort who could not see the symptoms until a disease had already overtaken them. They didn't understand that the Empire's strength was eroding, her blood thinning, her whole future teetering in the hands of one capricious man: Emperor Riada Sivolne.

By the time the abuse of the jackal bodies commenced—nothing more than the mild insults of rocks and refuse—Wesley had managed to gather his focus and conjure the appropriate scorn for the pile of bodies before him. The jackals' contempt for the divinity of the Empire demanded this. Today, just a small portion of that blood was drained and swallowed by the Goddess of blood and love.

More to come.

"Honor and blood befall Serivash," he shouted in a chorus of his peers.

And honor to all her oldest and most voracious kin. Wesley felt in his bones that the greater Gods would favor him in the end. He would beseech, or he would bribe; he would prove his case to them.

As the fanfare dwindled and Serivash's river began to dry to a less festive brown, Wesley left. He had done his public duty, now to his private affairs.

He changed attire at his villa in North Piarago and came out looking as much like a common merchant as possible. With two of his armed serving-men shadowing him, he went on foot toward the winding, unfamiliar streets of South City.

When he cut down from the central road, unease settled over him, like the dust kicked up from the streets. He had stepped over some invisible line—nebulous and disputable as a provincial border—and seemed to have arrived somewhere other than his native city.

On first glance, he did not like it. It was dirtier, narrower, and more crowded than North City. Poorer, without a doubt. It was more like the desert on whose edge the city rested. North Piarago was full of sluices, drinking richly from the River Carth, and South Piarago took whatever muddy swill was left. A cacophony of southern languages hurtled through the parched air.

Wesley did not know any of the tribal tongues. He spoke formal Kourisad, like any educated man, but the southern languages promised him no influence, no gain. He had never touched them.

There was a chance, now that he thought of it, that this had been folly.

The southerners were *supposed* to be the easiest to deal with when the time came. Easy to manipulate, bribe, or ignore altogether. Wesley could conjure no more than vague caricatures of the southern deserts in his mind: the goatherd, the chieftain, the nomad, the date farmer.

Indeed, the most powerful chieftains in the south, the great Rokhs of Trekoa, were terribly intractable of late, and even the

Makarish Shaykhs could not always be relied upon. There was no way of knowing what they might do. Wesley had been working as though the whole of the south would follow him like a horse on a lead when, in fact, it may well kick and bray. Violently.

A dizzying thought.

Wesley was also cast off-balance as he passed through crowds unnoticed. He could not decide how he felt about it, but he kept lifting his hand to where his blood-rank and military insignia would have been, as if to assure himself that he was still a man to be acknowledged. Still of the old blood of ancient Maurow. Still worth something.

How these southerners would part like water if they knew that Wesley stood at the shoulder of the Emperor's own brother, James Sivolne. He had fought and finagled hard for that place. That mattered, even in South City.

His pale face and northern clothing did begin to stand out the further he walked through South City, though. Every now and then he earned a second glance. These were all Trekoan, Makarish, or Tusian provincials. Sarramai. Nagonans. And jackals, too. Citizens, some of them, but of a lesser status.

With no rank to clear paths for them, Wesley and his men had to shove their way through the sea of southerners, and it proved a harsh current. But Wesley learned to wedge with his shoulder. He did not want to miss his rendezvous, or to linger on the south streets any longer than he had to. The place made him feel that his city of Piarago was, perhaps, not quite his.

The battalion Captain with whom Wesley was to meet was an old and passing acquaintance, and Wesley had little idea of what would happen tonight. Captain Edmund Olan Hodge was of a very minor noble family, disappeared into a South City battalion in his youth, and had rarely showed his face in North Piarago. But Captain Hodge had recently sought to reintegrate into court society, and Wesley made very sure that *his* were the arms that welcomed him back.

There was always a chance of adding a military ally to his little cabal of lower nobles. He was in desperate want of those.

The Captain had told Wesley of some inn or drinking house near the military quarter where they were to cross paths. To Wesley's growing discomfort, the inn was far outside the old city walls, and in one of the poorest sectors. An open-walled room served as the entrance, where dozens of southerners sat, shouting at each other, smoking upright pipes, and sipping cups of what looked like mud.

Wesley hesitated at the doorless lintel, knowing only how little he knew of all that surrounded him. Throwing off his discomfort with a sharp shrug, he stepped onto the stone floor and tossed a substantial tip in coin to the waiting-boy at the front so that the boy would be attentive to his requests.

He eyed the room with mild disdain. The air was thick with the warmth of bodies, the haze of scented smoke, and loud, merry voices. He stepped past several Trekoans as they tugged at their linen robes and dropped to the cool stone floor. The Makarish sat in low, curved chairs, hands cupping tiny finjans. There were northerners too, like himself, but only a few.

Not one of the workers—though he could scarcely tell the servers from served—came to attend him. He was treated like nothing more than a dull, discolored piece of the shifting landscape. Also, he noticed that the waiting-boy had scurried away like a mouse. It occurred to him that the use of waiting-boys might be a northern practice and he had, in fact, just handed some wandering child an excellent payment for absolutely no reason at all.

At last, he caught a servant's attention with an exaggerated gesture, and had wine brought to him. He set one of his men out to observe in the alleyway, and the other to linger just inside the entrance. He told them to drink and chatter and glean what they could. Captain Hodge was nowhere to be seen.

So Wesley waited, doing his best to give no outward sign of his inward fidgeting.

That image flashed before his eyes again. The elderly, high-blooded jackal trying—and failing—to hold his countenance while the slaughtering knife was put to his neck. Wesley rubbed his hand gently across his own throat and severed the thought from his mind. He was being very careful. Very shrewd. He thought of the men of the ancient high council who had risked their lives to stop Emperor Iramun the Second when he went mad with divine power.

Was Wesley different than them? No. His blood was theirs.

Suddenly, amid all the various languages, Wesley heard the Maurowan tongue and he glanced up, seeking the source.

"No, no, no! Of course not!" some Makarish-looking man shouted. "I only meant to compare in the most honorable light. The holy cat will always land on the feet, ah? And if his back, we shall call the back the feet."

Half-hearted laughter.

"And always eats his kill, does he? The cat has the divine right to the mice..."

More laughter.

"So call yourself a rat and you're safe!"

Wesley's understanding of the words lagged far behind his hearing them, but a few more minutes of close attention revealed that they were talking about Emperor Riada Sivolne himself. Some impasse must have occurred across tribes to drive them to use the Maurowan language, and it was a slipshod, slangish Maurowan, which had traversed rather a long distance from Wesley's native tongue.

They mocked the Emperor with a strange mixture of contempt and awe. They had a careful, poetry-soaked way of approaching the matter—all slyness and metaphor—but one could eventually catch the underside of all their words.

They spoke of the Emperor as one might speak of a myth. Love a myth or loathe it, it was beyond your touch and, perhaps, beyond your comprehension. A myth could be bowed down to or toyed with. For these men, Emperor Riada Sivolne was so far from them, so great, he was not really flesh and bone. He might as well be a God.

Which was precisely the problem.

And what of James Sivolne, the younger brother? Wesley leaned to hear what they might say of the man whose ear Wesley *did* have. But James was not even worth their mentioning. For as Riada was uncommonly sharp—liable to gash any who touched him—James was soft as clay: all the potential in the world to become something, just in need of some strong guiding hands and a little fire to harden him. Almost anything could be wrought.

And Wesley was the one for the job. James Sivolne, rumored to be a mere bastard, but recorded in the books as a full Imperial son with requisite rights, accorded the divine blood of his lineage, and the perfect mixture of necessary fact and fiction.

To these southerners, James might as well not exist. But if Wesley had his way, this smoky coffee-room would be humming with praise and adoration for the Emperor's brother in a few months' time. If he had his way, that hum would swell and reach the wide streets and high towers of North City. If he had his way, Emperor Riada would regret how coolly he had discarded the family of Verris, and would hope for a crumb of merciful bread from those he had scorned.

And he would get *nothing*.

The conversation died out and most fell back to their own people, their own tongues. Wesley's eyes strained to see into the darkening street and, when someone stepped out of the fire-flecked evening, his shoulders lifted in hopes that it was Captain Hodge.

Instead, to Wesley's surprise and disgust, three Mashevi merchants entered the coffee-room. Jackals ought to know better than to stir about among decent people on the Red River festival. They did not receive the warm brotherly greetings of their fellow southerners, nor did they give any. But the innkeeper did not have to ask what they wanted. They were known, quietly.

Wesley felt a craving to stand and pour wine for both Serivash and his name-God, Ranoth, just to spite these people who would call his Gods "unholy," "unclean," or "false." They would destroy the great temples if they could, as they had done before Masheva succumbed to the Empire. Despite his fears and his vulnerable throat, Wesley was proud that he had gone to the ceremony today. One must be reminded. One must not grow accustomed. Just because they looked like the other tribal southerners, did not mean they *were* like them.

The jackals sat, calm and assured, flaunting their wealth and inexplicable sense of security. If Wesley had been wearing his rank, he could have done almost anything he liked to them. They ought to have worn the fear of that.

Instead, the Mashevis did as they pleased and spoke to one another in a rough language that seemed to live more in the throat than on the tongue. He was glad when their voices were drowned out by a burst of southern music: a sharp, wild drumbeat drizzled with the deep, melancholy quarter-tones of a Trekoan oud.

Wesley drew straight when, at last, he saw soldiers enter the inn. Twisted along each baldric was the blue, red, and black Imperial cord of Captain Hodge's Black Wren battalion. The soldiers were hailed with warm familiarity and Wesley breathed a sigh, half relief, half nerves.

There were only two of them, both calm and well-seasoned in manner. Different ranks and provinces both. One was Nagonan, dark as pitch and built like a man of the sea. Common enough. Every seventh man in the Imperial Army was Nagonan.

But the other impossibly—*unlawfully*—was a jackal, with a sword at his hip and a long-knife at the base of his baldric.

2

There was a brief moment in which the warm sound of southern tongues and the thick smells of tobacco smoke, garlic, and burning juniper all mingled together, pressing calm and comfort across Azetla's shoulders. The lamps were bright, the fire crackled, the music simmered, and the patrons of the Colha inn were accustomed to Azetla and tolerant of him. But his eyes instinctively worked their way across the room and all its contents, drawing the social landscape in his mind.

Azetla first noted his fellow Mashevis in the south corner of the inn. He gave them a nod of acknowledgment, but they only narrowed their eyes. Two of them pulled at the edge of their garments so that their hems lifted off the ground: a way to shun someone thought to be unclean.

And yet Azetla's body instinctively tilted toward them to hear the Mashevi language. It was even his very own dialect and he had a sudden craving to speak it, as if his mouth was parched, and the simplest greeting would have been cool water. A few words stirred on his tongue, but he never opened his mouth. He swallowed his language down his dry throat.

His countrymen kept no such silence. "It's people like that which bring all the misfortune to the rest of us," they muttered.

"They make the name jackal come true. *Armed*, even? Does he want to get us all killed? And we wonder how all this talk of 'goatherds' and the 'great' Samuel Aver is stirred up! If they would just keep their mouths shut and their fists in their pockets, we could be left in peace."

It was the sort of thing Azetla expected them to say, but he had seen eighteen Mashevis killed today and he was tired, so the words managed to slip through this time and jab at the old bruise. He held on to the ache for the smallest moment. Then he smoothed it away, that wrinkle in the cloth.

He scoured the room once more and, at last, lifted his eyebrows in surprise. There he was. Lord Verris had actually come. In person.

It had been Azetla's suggestion to Captain Hodge to make him come here, instead of going north, and both he and the Captain had expected him to make polite excuses.

But he hadn't. It bespoke a sharp eagerness on Verris' part—a willingness to make himself uncomfortable, which Azetla would never have otherwise supposed of someone like him. It added weight to some of Azetla's privately held suspicions and he considered the idea carefully, letting it sift and settle slowly into his mind.

Not long after, Joseph noticed him as well.

"*He's* giving you quite the devil's eye," Joseph said, elbowing Azetla in the ribs. "Northerner. The merchant there."

"He's not a merchant," Azetla replied quietly. "And the cord will speak for itself."

"I don't know about that," Joseph said with a half-smile.

Azetla brushed his fingers over his shoulder to ensure that the battalion cord rested as it should, not tucked beneath the fabric of his threadbare overshirt. It was the braided Black Wren colors that earned Joseph—and even Azetla—kind welcome in the Colha coffee-room. But Joseph was right. It wasn't going to get much from Verris.

"Besides, what do you mean 'he's not a merchant'?" Joseph asked, leaning against the stone support at the entryway. He waved at the worker, Farah, who lounged by the fire-pit. Farah only smiled and gestured for Joseph to wait.

"That's him," Azetla said, keeping his voice low so that Joseph had to lean forward to hear him. "Wesley Verris."

Joseph raised his eyebrows and tsked his tongue in friendly admonishment. "*Lord Colonel* Verris, minding your jackal mouth. Wants our battalion for a task, does he?"

"Something like that," Azetla replied, cutting his words carefully to size. "And he's a colonel in name only."

"You certain it's him?"

Azetla nodded. "I saw him at the ceremony this morning."

Joseph let out one long breath and threw his shoulders back. "You're an idiot for going there. One of these days it's going to go badly and neither the Captain nor I will be able to do anything about it."

Azetla did not answer, except with a loose shrug. Joseph always said that, but he had stopped trying to prevent Azetla from going north on the Red River festival, and Azetla was grateful for that. He still tried to convince Azetla to drink the requisite draught of wine in Serivash's honor—just for the look of the thing—but that would have been sacrilege. If a friend asked for him to drink to their health, he would do it any day except this one.

"I doubt his Lordship is in the mood for jackals," Joseph said.

Azetla held his expression steady. "No one ever is. He'll have to reconcile himself."

Joseph touched the back of his ear with his open palm as if he could not hear. "By blood. I can't understand a single word off that tongue of yours."

Azetla waved his hand dismissively at Joseph's antagonistic smile. It was an old joke, albeit one for which Azetla could not conjure any genuine amusement. Joseph had that crisp, respectable northern lilt—almost that of a high-blood, for he was a jeweler's son and had been raised with nobility for neighbors—while Azetla's southeastern accent lingered thick as sap on his tongue. The Maurowan language had always given him trouble; the words and grammar he had eventually mastered, but the native sound of it remained elusive.

"Farah!" Joseph shouted across the room. "We've dry throats and weary heads over here. If Papa Colha still pays you to work here, prove it to us!"

Farah finally meandered from the fire-pit, slower than cold honey, conversing with everyone as he went. At last he came and poured Joseph and himself a generous cup-full of wine.

"Nothing for the jackal, I assume, so as to slight the Goddess," Farah said with a cool smile as he nodded toward Azetla.

Joseph put his hand on Farah's shoulder. "You serve wine with so much water in it, and you worry about a slight to her?"

Farah scoffed and raised his own cup to Joseph's.

"Honor and blood befall her," they chanted together.

"And may Darubha's knife be ever red," Joseph added, using the name and incantation for Serivash's Nagonan likeness.

Azetla stood back in silence, arms folded as though he were bracing for a chill, and waited for them to finish. Joseph was Azetla's most trusted friend in the battalion, barring only Captain Hodge, and even he did not seem to realize that when he ritually asked for "blood to befall" the Maurowan goddess that, today, said blood had come from Azetla's people.

Joseph finished his watery wine and looked across the room at Verris, who shifted in his seat and snapped his eyes away from Azetla and Joseph like a man not sure if he was in the right place, not sure what to do.

"Is that room ready for the Captain, Farah?" Azetla asked.

Farah nodded as he turned to loiter by the fire again. "Stable side."

Azetla tilted his head in assent. "Well, come on. Let's put the high-blood at his ease."

Joseph picked up his cup and searched it for a last sip. "If we must."

As they wound their way through the bursts of drunken conversation, Azetla saw Lord Verris gesture at his serving-men; they held their distance. Though he appeared calm, Azetla could see that the man's relaxation was conscious and intently held.

Azetla tilted his head at Verris in a decidedly military form of greeting then leaned against a hard clay alcove in the wall, folding his arms and letting Joseph step forward as the man of senior rank. Joseph bowed, smiling and looking as bright and revelrous as any paid-in citizen should be on Serivash's holy day.

"My lord, Gods bless you and may honor and blood befall Serivash! Forgive us our boldness. I am Lead Sergeant Radabe of the Black Wren, and this is Azetla Rinayimi. The Captain will be here shortly and he sent us to ensure you are well and comfortable," Joseph said in a low, friendly voice.

Verris nodded softly, his eyes cutting toward Azetla as if trying to make sense of him. Azetla's name would be of no use to Verris, for there were thousands of "Rinayimis" in Piarago. It was not a family surname, but a regional one. It simply meant "from Rinayim," but it was the type of public moniker most Mashevis took on when living outside their holy city so as to remind others—and themselves—of where they belonged. That was why Azetla had spit it out when Captain Hodge first demanded a formal name of him, fourteen years ago. It was, at least, not a lie.

"We've spoken with the innkeeper," Joseph added, in the exact manner of a gracious host, "and there's a fire-lit room awaiting you and any words you may wish to have with the Captain."

"Very well," Verris said, giving Joseph a dismissive nod.

Azetla then felt the usual gaze of scrutiny fall upon him. Verris was a smart man, by reputation, and did not likely miss much.

Not the leather "jackal band" on Azetla's arm, nor the absence of a rank, nor that the way Azetla wore his sword showed that he was left-handed. That he had a sword at all was the real infraction.

Joseph stepped forward to re-enter Lord Verris' line of sight. "Shall we escort you to the room, my lord?"

"No," Verris said slowly, his eyes remaining on Azetla. He took a drink of his ale, and kept his forced calm. "I'll wait here. Besides, should it not be someone's lawful duty to disarm and report *that* one? He would be dead already if we were in North Piarago."

The friendly light in Joseph's eyes was abruptly snuffed out, and his smile pinched in bit by bit until it wasn't a smile anymore. Arms folded firmly against his ribcage, Azetla had to make a swift calculation.

He knew more about Verris than the man might like. His was an older, lesser family that had, for generations, been ever on the cusp of entry into the highest circles, but never *quite* given an invitation. And now they had begun to fall even past the hope which had strung them along.

After working for years to cultivate good standing with one of the southern magistrates, Azetla could access most court summaries and public proclamations. He could read the space between the words, filling in the gaps with his best guesses. But Verris was rarely mentioned in any Imperial documents—he was not associated with any recent law, proposition, or council. The Corra James Sivolne, to whom Verris was attached in a vaguely advisorial role, was mentioned still less.

They were fenced out of Riada's inner circle.

This made low-blood aspirers of the politicking crowd, such as Verris, overzealous and vindictive. But Verris still wanted to talk to the Captain, he had forgone his rank and title to do so, he was nervous, and he did not look as though he trusted his footing on southern ground.

For Azetla, that would do well. He gave a soft, subtle nod that he hoped appeared respectful.

"Then do your duty, if you feel you must, my lord," he said to Verris. He stood straight from the alcove and stepped forward. He pulled a coil of vellum from his satchel—calmly, non-threateningly, and with conscious use of his right hand so as not to offend—then gave it to Verris.

"Regardless, my papers have all the correct signatories, my lord. I am as lawful as I'm allowed to be," he said.

Verris sat, iron-eyed, and unrolled the vellum. He mouthed several of the words in a slight whisper as he scraped his gaze down the conscription record. It was a concise summary of the last many years of Azetla's life: illegal South City resident, common, non-ranked, and a debt-conscript with thirteen years served and seven owed. Not approved for citizenship, and no chance for such approval.

"There is nothing in here exempting you from the law, jackal," Verris said. "I can read it to you if you would like to know what it says."

Joseph's mouth twitched as he glanced at Azetla. The merriment flickered back into his eyes. "My lord—"

"No need, my lord," Azetla said. "I scribed it."

Verris' mouth tightened and Azetla could tell that he needed to be more conciliatory. He weighted his posture so that his shoulders lowered and his head tilted downward. Verris could collar Azetla if he wanted, drag him to a city magistrate, and—if he was feeling particularly ungenerous—contrive to have his throat preserved for next year's Red River festival. Or slit tonight. The Mashevi merchants in the corner knew this just as well as Azetla did. They sat rigid with apprehension, observing the exchange as if their own throats might somehow become involved, clinging to their corner like a fortress.

"What I mean to say, my lord, is that I usually act as scribe for the Captain," Azetla added.

Verris took a deep breath and a slow sip.

"That's all very well, but the fact that you can read and scribble does not alter the law. You are bearing weapons *within the city*—"

"We are outside the walls, my lord," Azetla said.

Verris smiled faintly. "You jackals love your minutia and technicalities, but they do not help you. I know for a fact that Mashevi conscripts are relegated to tack and wagons. Or am I simply supposed to ignore Captain Hodge's illicit practice of arming jackals?"

Azetla tensed, and so did Joseph. That was not a jab at them. That was directed at their Captain. Azetla tasted a sharp reply and swallowed it. Then, in a respectful voice, he took aim at Verris in the most careful, circumscribed way possible. For, though Azetla did not know the whole of why Verris had come to renew his old acquaintance with Captain Hodge, he knew the one part that was important.

"My lord, the Captain is a practical man and a veteran of battle. I am certain you understand: he is the kind of man who is willing to do something unorthodox if he believes it will better serve the battalion. The city. The Empire herself."

Verris' hands curled a little where they rested on his lap, but he showed no change in expression.

"I came to speak to the Captain," he said in a cool voice. "Not to his common subordinates."

"Of course, my lord." Joseph lowered his head. "We are honored to be in your service should you have need of anything."

They gave slight bows and left Verris to himself. Joseph went to check the Captain's meeting room. Azetla went to wait in the entrance.

Captain Hodge arrived not long after and clapped Azetla on the arm in greeting. It was no small thing to be greeted thus, in public, on the day of the Red River festival. The Captain would vouch for Azetla, if it came to that. He had to remind himself of this, to try and believe it for more than three minutes at a time.

Hodge had a festival manner about him as he lifted his head slightly to look at Azetla.

"So?" he said.

Azetla gestured toward Verris and spoke quietly. "He came."

The Captain glanced and gave a wave of greeting across the room with a faint smile.

"And what the devils is he about, do you think?"

"I can't say anything with absolute certainty…"

"Yes, yes. You say it every time, 'all conjecture.' And? Is it what we thought?"

"I believe so. Something to do with invading Sahr territory, at the very least," Azetla said. "He's keen for it."

That was the most he thought wise to say at the moment. As a rule, he told his Captain nearly everything.

Hodge nodded thoughtfully. He opened his mouth—to give the festival greeting of Serivash, Azetla imagined—but closed it again with a wry smile, gave a nod, and turned toward Verris.

<hr>

Wesley argued within himself regarding Hodge's jackal soldier. Something ought to be done, but he didn't want to draw undue attention. It was with relief that he watched Captain Hodge approach. The Captain looked relaxed and warm with welcome. Wesley made a point to appear the same.

"A good festival to you, Edmund, honor and blood befall Serivash," Wesley said, carefully looking for Hodge's response to the unwarranted familiarity of one's given name. The man barely seemed to notice.

"And you, Wesley!" He clapped his hand on Wesley's arm in much the same manner as he had the Mashevi. It galled. There should have been some disparity. A great deal of it, in fact.

Captain Hodge had aged since he had been at court. His hair was rife with gray, and the lines on his face were crags. He smiled, though, and they became friendly crags. He had exactly the carved, weathered look one would expect of a man who had commanded an old South City battalion for more than two decades.

Wesley didn't really know whether he liked Captain Hodge or not, but he perceived the man's valuable potential and, despite the fifteen years of age that separated them, they had a great deal in common as lower nobles of disregarded families.

The question was whether it was enough to make common cause.

"Come," Hodge said, extending a hand of greeting. "There are more comfortable places for us to gossip and chatter and drink—especially with you a fresh-made Colonel! Congratulations!"

Wesley smiled half-heartedly at Hodge. "Oh you heard about that, did you? Given to me like a false currency that I can never possibly spend, thanks be to our Emperor. I hope you don't find it insulting."

Hodge shook his head with a breath of a laugh, heaving his wide shoulders in a shrug. Clearly he did not care one way or the other what artificial ranks were being doled out these days, which was just as well; it was unlikely Hodge would ever be more than a captain, or have possession of a full regiment, because in his hands, it would actually have meaning.

The two men walked through the thick, hot room, past where the jackal and Nagonan now sat on the floor, savoring fresh drinks. Wesley decided to say nothing about the jackal just yet. He had no idea where he himself stood with Hodge, or what Hodge might know, or if antagonizing him about the Mashevi would poison the whole exchange. He didn't know anything yet.

Hodge led Wesley into a small lodging room that was warm and well-lit. The smell of livestock wafted in through the high window.

Hodge sat back in one of the chairs with a sigh and a shifting. He smiled.

"So this is about the Emperor wanting to have a go at the devils, is it?"

Wesley did everything in his power to hide his astonishment. His blood suddenly felt very thin, and very quick. He lowered himself slowly into the curved chair, doing his best not to look like someone who had just been boxed on the ears. "What do you mean exactly?"

Hodge smiled and opened his mouth to reply but paused when a serving-girl came in carrying a meze tray and arak.

"Thank you, Mali dear," Hodge said, nodding for the girl to leave. Her eyes fixed low as she slipped around Wesley and out of the room.

"Am I wrong? You came all the way to South City just to wish me a good holy day?" Hodge said. "If so, I feel duly complimented."

Wesley glanced toward the door then back at Hodge. "I did not think that the Emperor's plans had become common knowledge."

"I may not attend court much these days," Hodge said, "but I have men who keep their ears to the ground. My jackal out there, for one. You know how his kind can be. He's always gleaning second or third-hand knowledge off the ground and bringing it to our advantage, speculating and such." Hodge raised his eyebrows and looked, not at Wesley, but at the cloudy contents of his arak cup. "And he's usually right."

"Then what did your bloody jackal speculate about *me*?" Wesley said, raising his cup toward Hodge and muttering, "To Serivash, honor and blood befall her," under his breath. The arak was much stronger than he was expecting, but pleasing, and it burned all the way down.

"Ah, so that *did* bother you," Hodge said with a steely smile. "Stomach it, Wesley. Count him as mine and do not let it trouble you. He told me the Emperor means to send soldiers to capture the devils' land in the southwest and that you have taken an interest in the idea. That you favor it, even, which befuddles me no end."

Wesley gritted his teeth for a scant second. That was a lot for *anyone* to collect from the dusty ground, let alone a jackal. It was no less than everything that he had purposed to tell Hodge in the first place. Wesley took another careful sip of arak, and let the heat and haze of it soften him, calm him.

"Your jackal does good work. I don't approve, Edmund. Know that," Wesley said, lifting his chin. "But the Emperor doesn't necessarily want to conquer Sahr territory..."

"Well what *does* he want?"

"I'm not sure. You know how he keeps his own counsel, makes himself the sole point of success or failure. I do know that the Sahr devils raid further and further into Makaria, driving refugees north, clogging the cities with people and terrifying stories. The Emperor means to, well, *capture* them. I think. Or some of them. To use them for their powerful devilry, if such a thing can be done. Or perhaps to show that he does not fear them and that they are not devils at all..."

Wesley trailed off purposefully, watching Hodge.

The Captain scrutinized him for a moment. "Oh they're devils, Wesley, be sure of that. But why do you care? Even if those Sahr devils weren't inhuman, just brutes or savages, they certainly aren't worth lives. The land itself isn't worth the dust that covers it. Dry, dead, and empty. Besides," Hodge shook his head and narrowed his eyes, "I hadn't known that you were so much in the Emperor's confidence that he would tell you even this little of his plans."

"I'm not in his confidence, nor could I ever be, for my family has little of his favor. But I *also* have men who keep their ears to the ground. The truth is the Emperor will do what he wills regardless of you or I or—" *Slow down,* he told himself. "Or anything else. The important thing is to make good of what he does. For all of us."

Wesley peered into Hodge's mud-colored eyes, hoping to see that he understood: "for all of us" meant for the whole Empire.

For all those that the Imperial Sivolnes had arrogantly severed from influence. For those who knew that it was time for the Empire to be restored as a fallow grassland; with fire. Wesley strained to perceive a silent sympathy.

But he saw nothing.

"What good will it possibly do *you*?" Hodge said with genuine curiosity.

Wesley sighed and his shoulders fell slack with a mixture of relief and disappointment. Hodge may or may not be an ally, but he was far too long removed from the subtleties of court. So Wesley put forth the easy half-lie that would serve until Hodge could be made to understand that this was about so much more than some foolhardy campaign to catch or kill or use Sahr devils.

"If I begin to involve myself in military administration, perhaps the Emperor's generals will begin to see me as a real colonel rather than a farce of one. The rank was given as a gilt shackle, tying me to that which I cannot do, and precluding me from that which I can. So I must act."

"Then why come to me about it?"

"Because yours is one of the old battalions—you have more independence—and you are certain to be among those tasked to the devils' territory. If so, would you accept?" Wesley asked.

Hodge furrowed his eyebrows and flicked the rim of his cup.

"*Would* we? We will obey orders, certainly. It isn't up to us. I'm just holding out that we aren't decommissioned like the other old battalions. Yes, my jackal heard those rumors too, and that I take very seriously. A good campaign might keep us alive a little longer."

"And would you make accommodations for some additional company on such a campaign, if indeed it is to exist?"

Hodge scratched at the stubble on his chin and gave Wesley a tired smile. "You mean I will go confront those bloodthirsty devils for no sensible reason you or I know of, *and* you want me to take on outsiders? Well, they'd have to do things my way. Yourself included."

"I didn't say *I* would come."

Hodge raised his thick gray eyebrows. "Oh? Yes you will. Those colonels and generals want a man who has seen blood as they have. If you mean what you say, you'll come in a heartbeat. And if those jinn-devils show themselves to be nicely killable creatures, we'll put as many of them into the ground as we can, and keep some for prizes. If not? Well, the grave is where every man will go one day, ah? So long as this goes forward, and you really mean to give weight to your rank, I suggest you put both feet in the water...and make final supplication to the Gods while you're at it."

Hodge laughed as if death was an old joke and threw the last of the arak down his throat.

Wesley did not laugh. He *would* make supplication to the Gods. Not only because of the jinn-devils living in the southwestern hills—which he chose not to think about—but because even the slightest error would stir up far more deadly enemies right here in Piarago.

3

Mali Colha brought a skin of unmixed wine to the Captain and his North City guest and, once again, they fell silent at her approach. Captain Hodge smiled warmly, as he always did, but did not tease her. It was all rather strange. The privacy of their meeting. The tension that filled the other man's every limb. The fact that Azetla and Joseph had been sent ahead to meet him.

It wasn't really Mali's concern. High-bloods would do as they pleased.

The Colha inn had always been a hub for the Black Wren soldiers and, ever since her father's memory had begun to deteriorate, they had become Mali's duty. She took pride in them, and felt as though she belonged to the Black Wren and they to her. The battalion could be relied upon to swarm the place at night, and the Lord Captain usually took any high-blood guests here rather than at the barracks.

After weaving her way through a mess of wine-happy, talkative customers, Mali retreated to the kitchen. She leaned out into the alley to breathe the cool night air and feel alone. But the alley was almost as full as the inn, and though spring had scarcely begun, the wind already had a bit of summer to it.

Mali set new dough to rise, then wiped her hands on the edge of her headscarf. If the scarf fell, she let it fall. Southern though her surroundings were, she was mostly northern of descent and she did not feel the need to conform to southern customs.

"Sela, I'm taking my supper now," she told the Makarish hired woman. "Tell Papa if you need me."

Sela nodded as she skillfully shaved strips of spiced lamb over a bed of roasted onions and garlic. Mali's hunger was piqued at the smell, but the lamb was not for her. It was for those jackal merchants, for Captain Hodge, and for his North City guest. She could hope for what was left.

Quickly, Mali wrapped a red band of cloth at her waist; Mali had no great affection for Serivash—her name-goddess was the far gentler Lyrala—but she gave the Goddess of blood her due and wore her color. She prepared a platter with a large bowl of peppery chuva, strips of stale zaatar bread, and a few handfuls of dates. She kissed her father on the cheek as she entered the coffee-room—her gentle assurance to him that all was well—and made her way to Joseph and Azetla, who were talking on the floor near the fire.

Her father watched her, narrow-eyed, but said nothing. He spoke little these days. He knew routines, answered direct questions, and—once in a rare while—he still smiled with clear eyes and spoke with a clear voice.

"That cannot all be for you, Mali-dear," Joseph shouted over the din. He eyed the platter of chuva with a wide grin.

"Of course not."

She set the platter in their midst and sat with them. No one questioned this, for all knew that she was the keeper of this house now in all but name.

"I thought Khala was coming," Mali said.

Azetla waved toward the inn entrance, eyebrows pinned low. "So she claimed."

"She ought to have walked with us in the first place," Joseph said, grabbing a strip of bread.

Azetla was still looking at the entrance, fidgeting with the little wooden carving that hung around his neck. "I know."

He didn't touch the food.

Khala was the sort of person who did as she pleased and Azetla, pious jackal that he was, usually disapproved. Khala was not Masheva-born like him. She was not always wary and suspicious like he was. Moreover, she was a jackal woman out and about on the night of the Red River festival and she ought to have been here by now. Mali felt a tiny coil of worry in her own stomach, which surprised her. It had never occurred to her that someone like Khala—a clever, street-savvy jackal—required worry. It felt almost dishonorable to feel concern for any jackal on a day that called to mind all their treacheries.

But Azetla and Khala had become Mali's exceptions. Time and Captain Hodge had made it so.

Though the two jackals called one another brother and sister—and took on the necessary responsibilities and concerns therein—they were of no blood relation. They were street-kin, as the southern idiom went. They watched each other's backs.

"Khala said she would let Dersha or one of the others walk with her," Azetla said, finally turning and taking notice of the food. He still would not touch the platter, which irritated Mali. She knew he had certain cleansing and eating rituals, certain fast-days and the like, but sometimes she felt as though he refrained just to prove a point—whether to an audience or to himself, she could not say. She didn't have to give him *anything*. Not even a greeting. But here she was, showing him generosity, and the least the man could do was pretend to be grateful.

After a moment's pause, Azetla stood up and took the lid off the water jar on the far side of the fire. He poured half a ladle of water over each hand as he extended them over the outer hearth, water dripping down and steaming on the stones.

"Khala doesn't feel the need to do that when she's here," Mali said, thoroughly conscious of the censure in her tone. Khala never did *any* of the Mashevi rituals when Azetla wasn't around. She ate blood-cakes too, and made Mali swear by salt never to tell him.

"I know," Azetla said after he finished mouthing whatever it was Mashevis required of themselves before eating a meal. "But I wish she would."

As Azetla replaced the jar-stone, one of the Mashevis nearby spoke in a raised voice, and looked in Azetla's direction. Whatever the jackal said, it made Azetla's eyes snap toward them. He walked across and leaned over their table, looking so severe and imposing that it made Mali uneasy.

Whatever followed was an abrupt, taut conversation, in which Azetla did most of the talking.

Mali pinched the bread hard between her fingers, mashing it to crumbs. They were going to draw attention to themselves. *Today*, of all days. They were going to cause problems and she was going to have to deal with the consequences.

But, in a moment, Azetla broke the exchange and came back to the fire. Mali relaxed and reminded herself that Azetla was usually very, very careful. He sat back down and began eating with a healthy appetite and a belated expression of gratitude. Angling his body toward the entrance and keeping his eyes on it, he did not look at the other Mashevis again, and they were much quieter than before.

"What foolishness was that?" Joseph said.

Azetla shook his head and when he answered his voice was calm, though that didn't mean anything. His voice was always like that.

"It was about the sword," he said. "'It's unlawful and provocative and I'll warrant whatever trouble comes.' They've convinced themselves that Mashevis survive better silent and unarmed."

Well, don't they? Mali wanted to say. One could be forgiven for assuming an armed jackal had evil in mind since they had already gone so far as to break the law by carrying a weapon in the first place. Perhaps the Emperor was harsh toward the Mashevis, but he had reason for that; a group of them had orchestrated an assassination attempt on an emperor in the conquering age. They had caused many other troubles since.

Mali tried to look at the other jackals out of the corner of her eye. They were wealthy, by dress, and the cup they had used to wash *their* hands was etched silver, as was the catching-basin. "Well...it's good they're being cautious," she said.

Azetla gave a strange little half-laugh. "That's a way of putting it."

Mali narrowed her eyes, disliking his tone, but at long last Khala brushed in off the street. Relief overtook irritation. Khala immediately pushed back her headscarf, letting her dark hair fall as her copper-and-bead earrings chimed against her cheeks. Dersha—a half-Trekoan tackman who was certainly no more than nineteen or twenty years of age—strode in behind her, smiling cheerfully.

Kicking off her sandals, Khala dropped silkily onto the floor, folding her legs and bare feet under her. She put her elbows on her knees and rested her chin over her folded fingers. She was a year or two older than Mali, but the thinness of her face made her look older still. Beneath the cotton shift-dress, loose-fitted over her narrow frame, Khala's skin was an olive-brown shade, not quite as dark as Azetla's. She checked her sleeve as she always did, making sure it covered her jackal band.

"What kept you?" Azetla said.

"Me?" Khala said, sending a sideways smile at Dersha. "I know better than to walk through the Makarish quarter after dark on this fine red holiday. I was waiting on *him*."

Joseph handed Dersha a piece of bread. "What was so important then?"

"Oh apparently Dersha has a pretty pair of eyes in North City...and he couldn't manage to tear himself away from them," Khala said.

"That's *not* what happened," Dersha protested, looking hurriedly at Azetla and shaking his head. "There was a sewage overflow on the west side and I had to go the long way round, through the outskirts."

All Azetla did was raise his eyebrows faintly at Dersha, looking as close to amused as he ever did.

"Is this the same girl from several months ago?" Mali asked teasingly. A little arak in the blood and even rough soldiers became gushing poets.

"Yes." He lifted his chin, a little defiantly. Again, he glanced at Azetla, as if seeking approval. "I've no secrets. Azetla knows." Then he spoke more softly. "She's Trekoan, which will lighten my mother's eyes considerably, and she is a freewoman. A servant in one of the great families."

"Which family?" Joseph asked.

"Beranadon," Dersha said with considerable satisfaction.

Mali tsked with surprise. That was very old blood. Almost the same as serving the Emperor himself.

"Well I imagine a girl like that comes with lovely gossip in tow," Khala said, tapping the floor twice then flicking her hand upward. It was an old southern gesture demanding that one empty their hands and give whatever they have to the common pot. Now, it was for a different sort of morsel and Mali, keeping a soft smile, repeated the gesture.

And because Dersha was still a boy and because he was obviously relishing all the eyes on him—even Azetla was paying rather stoic attention—he yielded.

"Timaa said that the Lady Kathryn Beranadon and a Lord something-or-other Verris have been set together in the Emperor's eyes. It's not—"

"Keep your voice a little lower, Dersha," Azetla said, quiet and firm. He was sitting far straighter now than he had been a moment ago. "And what do you mean by that exactly?"

"He means marriage for them, although Timaa says he can't force it, and the Lady won't do it. It's a cruel insult to her blood."

Azetla and Joseph glanced at each other ever so briefly over Dersha's head.

"And I'm certain an insult is all it's meant to be," Azetla said dismissively.

The conversation veered to the amusing territory of Timaa's endless virtues, which Dersha spoke of very solemnly, and regarding which Khala and Mali indulged him for several minutes. When Dersha turned his talk toward battalion matters, however, a small glance from Azetla sapped the words from his mouth and he, quite abruptly, changed the subject.

All the battalion soldiers were attentive to Azetla that way. Certainly it was on behalf of Captain Hodge that they did so, but Mali did not understand why the Lord Captain permitted Azetla to represent him thus. She always wondered if the soldiers were secretly resentful. She sometimes was.

The room grew rowdier and Mali realized she had already lingered too long at her meal. She stood up reluctantly.

"By salt, Mali, I just got here!" Khala rose from the ground. "I won't be left to this rough crowd." She gestured at her street-brother and the other soldiers with false bashfulness.

"Just as well," Joseph said, waving Khala and Mali away in a lofty manner. "We didn't want you anyway."

Khala followed Mali to the kitchen fires, which probably meant she had something she wished to say. Mali began wrapping the old bread in cloth, and ladling hot water into a basin for washing. Sela had gone for the night, which was for the best; Sela did not like Khala very much and she did not like that Mali associated with her. She would not even condescend to be in the same room as Azetla, and often made Mali feel guilty for her tolerance.

"We were almost worried about you," Mali said, beginning to scrub. The water quickly turned yellow with oil and turmeric.

Khala tsked her tongue softly. "Honestly, I never have trouble on the Red River festival because *I* actually celebrate it. I don't make myself a pariah like Azetla does. I spent most the evening at the barracks, in fact…celebrating."

Mali paused in her work. "With whom? The soldiers you know are here."

Khala just smiled. It was a pretty smile, but sharp, and it made Mali feel young and naïve.

"Have you honored Serivash yet?" Khala asked, eyeing a half-empty wineskin mischievously.

"I haven't had the chance."

"Well, she keeps her promise; heats the blood, and loosens the tongue!"

Khala settled herself in the lintel along the alley and breathed in the festival air.

"There was a Makarish Lieutenant," she said after a moment, her smile ebbing. "Drunk as seven devils and handsome as ten of them, if you know the type. He mixed the wine for me and was liberal with his compliments. But then I realized: he couldn't tell I was Mashevi. He thought I was *Makarish* of all things. If that had happened to Azetla, he would have corrected them with a vengeance. But I was enjoying myself. So I didn't say anything."

Mali raised her eyebrows. She knew that the Makarish and the Mashevis had an especially vicious, bloody history. They were worse enemies to each other than the Mashevis were to the Empire, but Mali didn't know if it had to do with their god, their tribal alliances, or territorial disputes. One way or the other, the jackals and their intractable god made enemies of everyone wherever they went.

"He said something odd," Khala added, turning to Mali.

But instead of talking, Khala pulled her shawl tighter around her shoulders and ran her teeth against her lower lip.

"Well?"

"The man was in the drink, mind you," Khala knotted her head-scarf and then unknotted it, as if her hands needed something to do and she wrapped it so elegantly, Mali felt it was an art form. The Mashevi style was so much simpler. "Then in this one sudden moment he bent toward me, looked at me clear-eyed, and said, 'Those Sahr devils will come after us soon and I don't think Serivash will protect us. I think they'll ravage the ground beneath our feet till the Empire itself cracks open.'"

Mali felt a flash of fear hurry through her chest, just long enough to quicken her heartbeat. She stepped nearer to the fire, clinging instinctively to its light. Khala kept a quiet, pensive tone as she continued.

"I asked him *why* he thought that," she said. "And at first he mumbled about this and that, but finally he said it was because only Serivash loves blood as much as they do. They leave rivers of it wherever they go and maybe their tributaries have gone dry and they'll want to take hers."

"Was he a priest's relative...soothsayer? Possessed of the sight?" Mali whispered, clenching her hands around the drying cloth of her skirt.

Khala shook her head. "No, no, nothing like that."

A trickle of relief softened Mali's frame and loosed her hands. "Well then it was just the wine."

"Wine tells the truth as often as it tells lies. He was *South* Makarish, of the Nur tribe. Word has been coming by southern caravan, month after month, that those jinn-things are slipping about where their land borders Makaria, leaving the dead behind, mutilated to damnation. They don't keep any land they scourge though. They just empty it and render it useless. Like locusts. One day a South Makarish village was, the next day it was not, he said."

Khala said those words in such a soft, riveted way, the air felt eerily touched. Mali wanted her to change the subject or make a joke about typical Makarish exaggeration, lest she start to imagine she saw the shadows of devils in the dark street or in lambent flames. She didn't know which of the many jinn stories were to be believed, but she couldn't stand that any one of them should creep to her doorstep.

"But they do this every now and again, don't they?" Mali said. "And they've never gone too far beyond their own crags and dust. Never come anywhere near us. They can't, can they?"

Khala smiled dully. "That *is* the northern idea. Southerners are not so certain."

"Did he—"

To Mali's exasperation, her little sister cut through her words with an abrupt yell. Anna leapt off the stone steps, down which she had apparently been creeping, and burst into the kitchen hoping to startle and terrify. The hellion-of-a-girl waved an embroidered blue cloth at Khala. Her dull brown hair was a small chaos, looking more like a nest of sticks and straw than the top of a child's head as she danced back and forth in an evasive manner.

"Oh Anna, *give* that to me. That's the Zawishi cloth," Mali said, grabbing after the shawl that Anna held hostage.

"Only if Khala will tell me a *jinn story*," Anna replied. She raised her shoulders and hugged herself as if in delighted fear that speaking of them might summon their searing hot wind, bringing a Sahr devil straight to her.

"Are you certain you can bear it?" Khala said, eyes wide in mock fear.

Mali managed to slip the shawl out of Anna's hand. She folded it in a very careful fashion, rubbing her fingers along the thread as she did so. It had been her mother's and it could not be replaced.

"Mercy-be-peace-be," Mali muttered, brushing her lips against the outer seam. Anna echoed Mali half-heartedly, then began clamoring once again for gory tales.

"You can very well leave Khala alone," Mali said, giving Anna a hard flick on the knuckles.

Khala tsked and took Anna into her arms.

"It's all right. What kind of jinn story, Anna-le? A Sarramai one, where the Sahr devils dig out souls and play with them as they please? Or the Trekoan one where the holy man binds a Sahr devil to him with metal and prayers."

"None of those. A *real* one," Anna said, eyes blazing green.

"The real ones are not much fun to tell, little one. How about something else?"

Anna climbed into Khala's lap and began to play with her black braid, undoing it and then re-braiding it horribly until Khala looked as though she had just survived a careening dust-wind.

"The one about the old-old Mashevi King...and about Samuel Aver and his mother, the prophet-lady from the river," Anna said.

Khala sucked a breath in through her teeth, glancing at Mali. Mali shook her head.

"No, Anna-le. I can't tell stories like that *today*. Serivash wouldn't like it. She's a bit like the enemy in that story, and we don't want to make her angry."

Actually, it was the Maurowans—Mali's own people—who were the enemies that the Mashevi King in the story tried to defeat, and Maurowans whose anger Khala rightly feared. Khala always told the story in an entrancing way. She moved her hands and cadence about, drawing images in the mind's eye, until she almost made Mali forget that it was about jackals spilling Maurowan blood and trying to thwart the Empire in its very youth. That it was how the Red River festival came to be in the first place.

"You tell a rather colorful version of the truth anyway, Khala," said a thick, heavy voice from outside the kitchen fires.

Azetla was standing in the dim, shadowy part of the room and Mali instantly felt that he had been standing there nearly the whole time.

"No, you tell a cynical version," Khala retorted, not sounding terribly chastened. She retrieved her decimated braid from Anna's hands and spoke in a low voice. "Our King didn't pass the name

Samuel Aver to his eldest son for nothing. He knows what it means. He knows...that it's important to us and we cherish it."

Mali completely stopped her work. They shouldn't be talking like this. She cleared her throat loudly. "That's enough, I think."

Suddenly, Anna clambered out of Khala's lap and started for Azetla. For while Khala never failed to tell a story, Azetla never failed to tell a cold, hard truth.

"But, Azetla, today they said that the *really real* Samuel Aver is going to start a war against the Emperor soon, just like the old King Samuel Aver in the story. But that this time he is going to *win*, and we should all keep our eyes open."

Mali blanched, snapped her fingers at Anna, and looked sharply toward Azetla. All this talk of Mashevi kings was his fault—he and Khala always indulged Anna with their horrible histories—and it was his duty to set Anna aright. He was given such courtesy here; the least he could do was *stop* this, and quickly.

For a brief moment, Azetla was stone-still and there was an almost savage look in his eyes under the dull orange light. Mali felt anger rising hot in her chest.

But the lines of Azetla's face softened as he stepped properly into the room. He kneeled so as to adopt Anna's height and looked at her like the older brother Anna seemed to think he was.

"They who, Anna-le?" he said softly.

"Ghada and Nachshi."

Ah. The Mashevi children who worked at the dyers. Mali knew she should not have let Anna play with them. She was losing all sense of disparity.

"That's a wild tale they gave you," Azetla said, his voice still soft, his brow furrowed.

"I *told* them they were liars," Anna said, starting to sense that she had made everyone uncomfortable, and perhaps only vaguely aware that Azetla and Khala were no less jackals than those whose spilled blood she had been taught to cheer. Anna had attended the ceremony before. She had seen the red river. She knew.

But she didn't understand, Mali could see. She thought there were The Jackals, and then there were the people she knew. And she didn't connect the two. Sometimes Mali didn't either.

Anna looked at Azetla with incredible frustration.

"But then Ghada just said that Serivash was the liar, and the Emperor also, and that made me so angry I threw the dry chuva at them and left. But...but Serivash *is* very clever and she *does* lie sometimes."

The look on Azetla's face was entirely inscrutable, but then he conjured something resembling a smile and glanced at Mali. How should he answer about gods he did not believe and would not serve? Mali's Gods. With a silent gesture, he asked Mali to take the task.

Mali sighed uneasily and reached out for Anna as Azetla stood. She began to untangle her nest of hair, an action that usually distracted and calmed Anna.

"Serivash does as she wills and as is her right," Mali said curtly. "No one, jackal or otherwise, prevails against her. Don't worry about what Ghada and Nachshi say when they want to stir your blood—they don't know what they're talking about. Rather worry about what *I* say, which is that it's time for sleep. Go on up."

Anna bolted for Khala as if for refuge.

"No, you bit-of-nonsense. If you use all your fire today, you'll have none left for tomorrow," Khala said, kissing Anna on the head and rendering her back to Mali.

"*Now*, Anna," Mali said.

Anna moved slowly and defiantly up the stairs to the small living quarters above the kitchen.

"She is probably the only northern-blooded girl that knows Mashevi history as well as her own," Mali said, lips pursed. "That must stop."

"She's also the only girl who throws chuva at other children for saying what she has cheered for when it came in story form," Khala said.

"What was it you wanted?" Mali asked Azetla irritably.

He pulled something out of his satchel. "Captain's correspondence. A Laritoni courier will come by for this tomorrow—later in the day, I imagine."

Mali nodded, then took the coil of reed-paper and dutifully tucked it into her own skirt-pouch. For a few years now, the Captain had been sending and collecting personal correspondence through the Colha inn. At least, Mali assumed that's what it was. She would never have been so disrespectful as to look at the letters and she couldn't read anyway. The Captain had been corresponding a great deal more lately. This was the fourth such letter in the last two months.

Mali knew nothing of the purpose or recipients, but she had taken dozens of his letters from either his or Azetla's hand over the years and she regarded the task an honor. She was of personal service to a Lord of Maurow.

Azetla turned to leave.

"I didn't bring up the old stories, Azetla," Khala said suddenly. "The girl brought them up herself. I swear it by salt."

"I know," he said. "I heard."

"She wanted stories of devils. *All* the soldiers were talking of Sahr devils tonight. As though someone had put it in their mind. Why?"

Azetla lifted his eyebrows ever so slightly and gave another one of those smiles so faint, it scarcely counted. All he said was, "Rumors."

He left. Khala looked agitated and Mali felt the same. She drew in a long breath and wiped her hands hard against her skirt. The night air was becoming colder, and the sounds of reveling beyond the alleyway grew wilder and more sinister. Talking of Sahr devils on a holiday of blood was foolhardy. Mali wondered if the Makarish lieutenant was right. There were a hundred stories of Sahr devils and of what they did—half of them lies and myths, surely—but no version claimed them to be anything but wild, bloodthirsty, and profane. But for the last of these, that made them very like Serivash indeed.

Mali lit incense to the house-goddess Lyrala that she would grant comfort and sleep.

4

The hour was late and the streets hushed when Joseph and Azetla turned their feet southward to the barracks. Joseph had laughed and sung and seemed almost drunk at the inn, but the moment he stepped outside he had a long, steady stride and a thoughtful look on his face. He was able to go so easily from merriment to concentration, Azetla half envied him for it.

The Captain had not said anything about the meeting before he dismissed them and left for his home, wife, and children. A simple nod had sufficed to tell them what they needed to know.

"Well, you were right," Joseph said. "They want to send us to the devils' hills."

Azetla looked ahead through the dark. "So it would seem."

He watched the corners and narrow alleys for leftover revelers, some of whom would try to make rivers for Serivash out of the weak and unsuspecting. The Red River festival was a dangerous holiday after dark and he had to be attentive. It was more difficult than usual. Little Anna's words had jarred him, and sent his mind darting about, gleaning, scraping, sorting.

The troubling thing was that a rumor like that was being tossed so lightly out of the mouths of Mashevi children. And what would the effect of it be if it were widely believed or—worse—if it drifted all the way up to North City?

"Well, cheers for us," Joseph said, his voice laced with sarcasm. His hard grin was just visible between the moon's offerings and the scattered hazy lamplights. "And three cheers for you because as we all know 'the jinn hate the jackals and the jackals hate the jinn.'"

"Enough of that," Azetla said, waving Joseph's words away.

"Don't pretend you're not afraid of them."

"I don't know what they are so as to know *how* to feel," Azetla muttered. "But I don't like being frenzied by third-hand stories."

Azetla had never been to the border of the devils' lands in South Makaria and he did not know how to parse out the tales that wafted up from that place with its superstitious refugees. He didn't even know how to sort through the Mashevi tales about them, come to that. It had been a long time since there were many Mashevis living near Sahr territory so as to give those tales depth and points of fact.

But the infuriating ditty kept making its way back to Azetla's ears: "the jinn hate the jackals and the jackals hate the jinn." All anyone really meant by that was that the despised hate the despised, and the miserable seek to cause misery. Azetla wasn't even certain that the jinn of the proverb were the same as those in Sahr territory. Jinn was a broad term. Sahrs were a specific menace.

Azetla believed the proverb was nothing but a sinister northern concoction, tying two of Maurow's enemies in a knot, and exaggerating both to mythic proportions. It had no basis in either fact or history. Some Mashevis held that the saying existed simply because the jinn feared the God of Masheva, He being so fiercely holy and they so fiercely unholy. Even his name was too sacred to pronounce, while they were too blasphemous for words. Oil and water, night and day, each innately pressing the other back.

But those were stories, not histories. Rumor, not writ. The fear Khala hid so well when she asked about the Sahr devils was a fear native to Maurowan tales, not Mashevi ones. When Azetla was a boy, he had been taught that they were nothing more nor less than particularly violent pagans.

Joseph breathed a sigh into the silence.

"Well I don't know what to make of the whole thing," he said gruffly. His nostrils flared with an irritated breath. "Just because the land is unconquered doesn't mean it's worth conquering. Is there any point to it other than the Emperor's pride?"

Azetla laughed and didn't answer. He had told Joseph what he knew same as he told the Captain. He had not yet told them all that he suspected beyond that. Such things he liked to sift first, and he was still shaking the matter out and pressing it through the sieve.

In silence, they passed into the Mashevi quarter—one long, narrow alley that cut at an angle through the whole East Trekoan quarter. Wealthy Mashevis lived in the center of the city, not in this slum. This was for the abandoned and the castoffs. It was where Azetla had been caught—fourteen years old, unknowingly violating a minor edict, paying no tax, and having no citizenship—and made into a debt conscript. It was where Khala's mother had walked as a night-woman. And it was where the Maurowans culled much of their criminal prey for Serivash.

This year, however, Serivash had hungered for "higher" blood, and she had got it.

Azetla scanned every hollow crevice of the street. He had lived here but one year, surviving by the skin of his teeth, and it housed all but one of his worst memories. Just walking through it drew that clawing, desperate feeling across his skin like a sharp wind. He had come closer here to cursing his God than he ever had before or since, though he hadn't done it in the end. Too stubborn or too afraid, probably, rather than too righteous.

He hated this place. It had shown him who he really was, and he had not liked the knowledge. No one does at first.

At the mouth of the alley, there were two city-soldier patrols, canvassing the area for troublemakers. He did not recognize them.

The dark hid his own features, leaving only the outline of a soldier, and they paid him no mind as they passed by. All other Mashevis walked huddled against the building walls, eyes on the ground, mouths pinched shut.

Suddenly, out of the narrow dark, there was a flicker of torches and a chorus of shouts. Azetla's left hand slipped softly to the hilt of his sagam and he quickened his step toward the thrashing lights. He could already see it in his mind's eye as he had seen it a dozen times in truth: a violent scuffle that would leave some hapless Mashevi dead and some Maurowan or Makar citizen without consequence.

As he came closer, however, the street simmered over with bits of Mashevi-Maurowan slang, Mashevi names, and Mashevi invective. The torches and lamps did not still in the hands of their bearers, but their flickers were enough to see a jackal band on every forearm and the lion's head, so like the old wooden one at his neck, etched on the stone lintel around which they were all gathered. One youthful voice shouted a traditional protest against the Emperor in his native tongue. Another joined in. Most were angry, arguing, or threatening violence, although against whom Azetla was not yet sure.

There was not a single Maurowan among them, thank goodness. Azetla leaned back into the night and watched as he walked.

"What are they saying?" Joseph whispered, walking faster, looking toward the end of the alley.

"Things that are going to get them beaten or killed."

"Well, that's their affair and none of yours," Joseph said, trying with his stride and shoulder to shepherd Azetla away from the scuffle.

Azetla stopped cold and looked at Joseph. Of course it was his affair. Even when he was useless and helpless—even when he had to bite his tongue—it was always his affair. After thirteen years, Joseph should know better than to say that. He *did* know better, by salt. But sometimes Azetla was foolish like this; he had put his life in Joseph's hands so many times, he almost forgot that, to Joseph, he was only an odd exception, one who ought to try and slough his own people off like a bad habit.

But that was not new. That was Joseph. This was how it had always been.

Azetla remained carefully still, standing just outside of the small, violently moving swath of light.

"Let's *go*," Joseph said, straining to move on, though he did not leave Azetla's side.

Azetla pressed the fingertips of his left hand together in a curt gesture for silence, while he kept his eyes fixed on the crowd of twenty or so Mashevis. The cause of the commotion became apparent; there was a garland of blood thistles strung up beside the carved lintel—a lintel which led to the one gathering place for pious Mashevis in South City—and this had incensed the street's inhabitants.

The garland was for Serivash, the color for Mashevi blood. Moreover, it was an act of idolatry—an offense before the holy God of Masheva.

There were several men and women, driven back against the alley wall, shouting their defense as to why they had hung the garland; they thought it would offer them safety to join in the holiday and honor the northern goddess. But the rest were screaming at them, screaming like madmen. Screaming like someone had taken a knife to their innards.

"*Blasphemers!* Bloody traitors! How dare you honor that *disgusting* idol in our own street! By salt and the desert God, you deserve the slaughter dais more than those who died today!"

"We're not traitors!" one of the garland-hangers cried. "We want to be left *alone*. Why give them an excuse to set us apart? All of you will go to the dais if you keep denouncing Emperor and King, and the rest of us with you!"

The whole thing was a few hot words shy of turning into a riot. Then the city-soldiers would come, and that would be as dangerous for those who hung the garland as it was for those who wanted to tear it down.

There were deaths Azetla could not stop and there were those he could.

He made a swift assessment of their sobriety and strength then moved toward the crowd of Mashevis. Joseph grabbed him by the shoulder and jerked him back. "Don't, you idiot! You'll just get dragged down with them and it'll be far worse for you, because you're actually breaking the law. You're *armed*."

Azetla pried his shoulder sharply out of Joseph's grip and pushed him back. He did not even look to see whether Joseph's face held anger or worry, because it didn't matter: Azetla had his objective in sight.

"Gods and devils," Joseph growled, brushing his hands together as if washing them of the situation and of Azetla. He did not follow, but he did not leave.

Azetla hailed the Mashevis in their mutual language, pushing his voice over theirs and squaring his shoulders as he walked. Two pro-testors spat on the ground at his feet—perhaps because his precise Rinayimi accent was not to their liking—but some did not even understand him. They were probably citizens of Maurow, many generations removed from the land of their ancestors and of Azetla's birth. They railed against a governor-king under which they had never served, bellowing for justice for a land in which they had never lived, uttering phrases of a language they scarcely spoke.

And all it brought them was chaos and division.

Azetla ignored the spit of contempt from his Mashevi kindred same as he did those from foreigners and turned his mouth back to the language of the Empire so that all might hear him and under-stand.

"Brothers and sisters, this is neither the time nor the place! The city-soldiers will bash you against the walls and there is nothing I could do to stop it. So take the garland *down*, put your insults away, and go home. Keep yourselves safe."

The cluster of Mashevis who had placed the garland began shouting again but Azetla drew his sagam and there was a swift quieting.

The eldest of those who protested against the garland looked Azetla over and spat again, though he kept a few feet of distance, sizing Azetla up. "He is in the Maurowan army, brothers, look! He's no friend to us."

"I'm a debt-conscript," Azetla countered gently, though his jaw tightened till it ached.

"It still means that you fight for the same Emperor who grabs King Aver by the scruff of the neck, like a cur, and makes him do as he pleases," the bent old man said. He raised his eyes and had enough courage to look at Azetla with immense hatred.

"You traitors do as you like," the man said, gesturing at Azetla and the garland-hangers with disgust. "But we will not bow and commit idolatry like our King. Better to be like the goatherd than like *that* coward. We wait for Samuel Aver to take his father's place!"

Azetla felt a sudden faltering in his posture and expression, as if from a wave of exhaustion. His grip on himself almost slipped. So it wasn't just children in the streets. Talk was running amok, and no one was being strict or savvy with what they heard. Azetla rolled his jaw and raised his voice again. "I know as well as you that King Keved does not honor his authority, but neither he nor his son deserve your *lives*. Their names aren't worth dying for."

"The name Samuel Aver is worth dying for," said one of the younger ones. "Unless you're a garland-hanger yourself."

Azetla breathed out sharply. "Serve God, boy, and not some bloody prince who was simply given an old name that's probably better than he deserves."

Why was everyone waving the name Samuel Aver around like a smoking brand? It was stinging Azetla's throat. When it was convenient to regard the name as dead, so it was, along with its bearer. But suddenly the name was alive in the air, and any man might snatch it and try to make it do his will. That name was going to cost lives if it could not be reined in and channeled aright.

Azetla looked back, past Joseph, into the alley. The patrols would come again soon, and they would have drink in them, and they would be looking for any excuse to draw jackal blood.

Emptying all patience out of his voice, Azetla gestured with his sagam. "Enough! All of you! *Leave.*"

Don't give their goddess any more blood than she already has. Please. You don't even know what you're talking about. You don't even realize how little your death would mean. You could not even be a symbol. No son of the King would be able to help you or cover you with his name, no matter how you revere it.

Azetla tilted his sagam down as his words seemed to take effect. Most began to disperse.

But the younger boy, wild-eyed, slapped his hand against the stone and repeated the chant that had caught Azetla's ear in the first place: "*Keved the coward, Emperor's dog, eats the blood of his own! Serivash, blood in her teeth, drinks, drinks us down!*"

Azetla snatched the young man by the collar of his sadhin and lowered his voice to a raspy whisper. "There are much, much better days to die than this, little one, I swear it. You're done here."

He pushed the boy off, causing him to stumble backward. The others took the young man gently in hand and growled curses at Azetla. A few of the men raised their voices and shook out their hands at him—a gesture of cursing and shame—but they made no move to retaliate. Their eyes rested on his sagam, and on Joseph at the far end of the alley.

They knew what Azetla knew; they could not keep even a single Mashevi from being harassed or killed. They couldn't fight him any more than they could fight the patrols and rowdy citizens that hunted them, so they fought each other instead.

Azetla would not hesitate to make them bleed if it kept them from something far worse.

He pushed through, shoving them aside with the flat of his sagam, and tore down the last dangling fringe of thistles. He put it to the torch, which gave acrid smoke rather than fire.

"There. Nothing more to contend. Everyone leave. Now."

Only one man was stupid and drunk enough to make a run at him. Azetla knocked him back. He tried to do it gently, but he didn't, and the man hit the wall hard, gashing his jaw on the lintel.

"I said *leave*."

By now most had already disappeared and, slowly, slowly, the last few gathered themselves and began to depart, all the while looking at Azetla with such profound hatred that he desperately wished he could explain himself. He felt wrong in the stomach, like one does when the pleasantness of being drunk wears off and only the unevenness of it is left. The Mashevis were gone, and the alley went hollow and lifeless.

Joseph stepped beside him.

"When they're sober, maybe they'll thank you for it," Joseph said with false lightness.

Azetla almost laughed. They both knew that wasn't true, though it was kind of him to say it. He could never win among his own and, for the moment, there wasn't any point in trying. He had to walk steadily on, no matter what either side said. If he was pulled this way or that, it did none of them any good.

His people were still his. And he theirs. For years now he had been paying in blood, indignity, and servitude, and his people had no return yet for his loss. It was all a waste. But seven years debt pressed down on his head, and much worse besides; the only way out was through.

5

J ames Sivolne almost turned back. Several times. What had started out as mild nervousness stirred toward nausea when he heard
his brother's calm, clear voice issue from the court anteroom. All of
Emperor Riada's chief advisors would be present and James froze.
There was no place for him in there. Well, yes, he was technically
permitted at the Emperor's advisorial meetings, but so were flies and
cockroaches.

The dark red cloth of the portiere hung still, and the voices of
old-blooded Lords and Generals rumbled beneath Riada's. James'
teeth hurt from anxious clenching. He loosed his jaw, stretched
his mouth, and cursed Wesley for making him do this. At last, he
walked cautiously forward. He tried to remember Wesley's advice:
*Sift words, James, every last one of them. Turn them over like rocks
to see what's underneath. Your brother means three times what most
people hear.*

Sift words. James mouthed it like a prayer.

No servant or crier preceded him as he brushed through the
embroidered part in the linen door. Walking in unannounced was
more than he had ever done before.

James gave a slight bow of his head, befitting his high station, and
found himself smiling like an idiot. A nervous idiot. The Lords and

Generals narrowed their eyes at him, but Riada returned the smile coolly. James probably looked like he had wandered in by accident; his reputation bore up the possibility.

"Yes?" Riada said with patient amusement.

"I wondered if I might have a private word, Your Highness," James said.

Well, his voice still worked.

Belatedly, he thought to nod his respect to the esteemed personages about the room: Lord General Pall, Lord Noben, Allonesh the Great Priest of Serivash, and Riada's nephew and current successor, Lord Callan Umbreth. Immediately afterward he realized it might look as though he was nodding to dismiss them—an outrageous presumption by any measure—and another wave of anxiety washed over him. Riada raised his eyebrows at James and, slowly, his expression slid into vigilant place, the way a soldier's body does when he takes a fighting stance. Wesley had said that would happen and not to worry.

With a casual flick of the fingers, Riada dismissed his advisors. They seemed as surprised as James himself. He had expected to be put off—half hoped to, really—so it was with wide eyes and uneasy posture that he watched them rise from their chairs. They skirted around, each muttering "Your Highness," under his breath as he passed by. Emperor Riada's advisors were not accustomed to James being a relevant presence.

Riada relaxed into a chair and donned an easy manner, as if the two of them were old friends, which was as far from the truth as east from west. Though two years older than James, Riada looked younger. His clean-shaven face showed his features to be striking and thoroughly Imperial. Thoroughly *Sivolne*, and the quintessence of that great, ancient line which struck a bargain with the Gods themselves, sealing their authority over Maurow.

"Sit, then, James. You look ill-at-ease." Riada gestured to a chair.

James obeyed rather dazedly and began collecting his words. The wood backing of the chair felt unusually hard and straight and the angle of it forced him to crane his neck toward his brother. Wesley's words buzzed in his head, marring his focus. *Just speak plain and simple, don't overexplain yourself, but don't be coy.*

Bloody impossible advice.

"What brings you to me today?" Riada said. His tone was indulgent, but not with kindness. It was condescension. One is indulgent toward animals and small children.

James' eyes wavered from Riada's; he had never been able to meet that fierce gaze for more than a few moments at a time. That ancient bargain with the Gods was said to put a terrible brilliance in the Sivolne presence, and in Riada it was distilled to unbearable potency.

"The rumors," James breathed at last.

Riada's cool smile was unchanged. "Which rumors? You mean about my wanting to go to Sahr territory?"

James nodded. "And defeat the devils there, to take their land."

Riada laughed as though what James had said was charming in its stupidity.

"Where *do* you get your rumors, James? The common bazaar? I'm not going to fight over that dry, thorny place. It's not worth even a small army. No, no. What is the *real* problem with the Sahr devils?"

Caught off guard, James opened his mouth and could find no useful thing to put into it. Riada pressed his lips together in a taut smile, as if he was both glad James was too ignorant to answer, and held him in contempt for it. Thanks to Wesley, James had begun to notice that Riada did this all the time. He set little tests before James—of cleverness or observation—and then visibly enjoyed himself when James failed. It did not even anger James, exactly; it wearied him. It made him want to drink tea and go to sleep for hours.

He wished the Gods had given him better blood. He was supposed to have at least half of the old, Gods'-blessed blood, but it felt that he had none at all.

"People often flee before they even come, and those that flee bring with them poverty and more tribal conflict. But it's the appearance of the thing, not the thing itself, James. The people believe that land to be inviolable because they believe the Sahr creatures to be unkillable and soul-stealing. So they live in fear, and half-truths abound. It is the *stories* that need to be killed. The rest will follow."

James was tempted to nod as though he understood perfectly, but he really didn't. Wesley *had* told him to be plain. "Your Highness, I have no idea what you mean by that."

Another look of mixed pleasure and contempt rustled beneath Riada's otherwise cordial expression.

"Catch even one of them and kill it and you may as well have killed them all. One is proof of the nature of the rest," Riada said. The condescension in his tone softened. "I'll change the stories that are told about them. Sometimes that's all it takes."

Riada looked hard at James for several moments, making James feel as if his thoughts were being read. There was no question but that Riada's motivations were more complex than what he said, but James could not divine the dozen-and-two layers of meaning, and he didn't really want to try.

"It's a matter of practicality as well," Riada said at last, his tone turning dry and didactic. "There's trouble with the desert Rokhs, especially that Trekoan firebrand Bin-Zari. I'll not have any southern ground denied me, and if I have to get my hands on some devils to clear the path, so be it."

"Do come to the high council next week if you've taken an interest," Riada added. "I'll be announcing the venture to all who attend."

Gods and devils, there it was. The open door. May he not stumble through it.

"Well, I already *have* taken an interest," James said pointedly, his eyes falling from his brother's once again.

"Indeed? That's unusual of you," Riada said. "What sort of an interest?"

"I mean to go. To the devils' land."

Something happened then that had never happened in the twenty-seven years of James' life. Riada's eyes narrowed, and his fingers pressed slowly against the table. By Serivash and all her divine kin, the unflappable Emperor was *shocked*. James felt the alarm as if it were his own. He was even sympathetic to it, for he was almost as appalled by the announcement as Riada was, though he'd practiced saying it in his quarters a dozen times.

"*Go?*"

"I want to accompany whatever men you send. My role can be as circumscribed or ceremonial as you like. But I want to go. I'm little use to you. I know that—" James paused and lowered his head respectfully. "I know what my limits are and what cautions you are forced to take regarding me. But this is a thing I can do, and I begin to feel I must do *something*."

Riada's face was once again inscrutable. James simply wanted to hunch his shoulders, stare at his lap, and wait for this all to be over.

"And you think this, of all possible choices, is a good something to do? There are less dramatic tasks that can be done with your idle time. Half of the court is going to be scandalized at my sending anyone at all, much less my own brother."

He said the last word with a faint sarcastic emphasis.

"I understand, Your Highness. Even so," James said. He looked at Riada as steadily as he could. "I ask little of you, and I won't ask for more, I promise. If you don't like the result of it—if it causes problems for you—you can bloody send me to Lariton or Okiziu or wherever you like afterward."

Riada tapped his fingers on the thick oak table. He looked at James and kept looking at him. James tensed, fearing his nervousness would show through his skin.

"It's foolish."

"Maybe," James said, shrugging stiffly. "But if I make a fool of myself, it will have been from effort rather than idleness."

"I'll consider it," Riada said slowly. "But don't set your eyes too fiercely on the idea."

"Thank you, Your Highness, Gods uphold you," James breathed through the formal words.

He stood and, with another respectful bow, left the room. That was when he realized that his heart was thundering in his chest. He rushed back to his rooms, his breaths coming and going in shivers, half terror, half relief. The task was done and he was glad of it. All the tightness that had been building up in his stomach turned to water. He collapsed into a chair by the central window of his quarters. Knowing his moods very well, his serving-man immediately sent for valerian root tea and fresh water.

James let the warmth and light of midday fall on him like a balm.

The problem was, he was not a good liar. In fact, the only reason he had managed the conversation, despite its strategic purpose, was because each individual sentiment had been utterly true. He did feel useless. He did feel the need to act. And he really would ask nothing of Riada after this. James would be the one of whom all things were asked.

He shrank into his chair at this thought.

The tea arrived with a basin of fresh water and a tray of dates and olives. James let the tea steep, flushed his face with water, but the food he could not yet tolerate.

Wesley had warned that this would not be easy. James had to be prepared for a fight, if worst came to worst. But James clung to the idealized version of events: a sly, silent coup. He wished it could be done bloodlessly. Well, he wished it could be done without him altogether, but that chance was lost. It was too late for him to recant.

When Verris first broached the subject of ousting Riada, James had been stunned silent by the idea, so strong and foreign it was to him. He had no interest in the throne. He *never* had. He had not been made for it. If it had been given him outright, he would have balked. No, he would have gathered his feet and run like all hells in the other direction. He didn't have the full, blessed blood. The very idea of skirting around the divine pact seemed idiotic. Why take such a risk if there was no need?

Unlike so many bastards before him, James was recorded and treated as a full-born son. He had no need unmet and little was required of him. So what did it matter that his mother was some new-blooded unknown? He had always been content to take the benefits of one bloodline while the other precluded him from all responsibilities. It was perfect.

Then came Wesley, quiet and careful, and new thoughts trickled from his mouth into James' ear. The Imperial house of Sivolne was not without enemies, he warned, and there were many who wanted Riada set aside. More than James could imagine. And they would succeed, so long as *someone* bridged the gap between old and new. Otherwise it would be chaos and civil war.

"But the divine pact—" James argued.

"—was made by crafty men and could be unmade by the same. In any case, I think the Gods are grown as tired of that pact as the people themselves," Wesley had said. "Perhaps the Gods are ready for something new."

A thoroughly blasphemous idea when he first heard it. But perhaps James was not as content with his lot as he had believed, for the notion held a faint and faintly threatening attraction. As if, instead of being the muddied water surrounded by clear pools, *he* was the fresh spring that would keep the rest from going rank. A stirring idea indeed, and so savory to chew on.

Not something to actually *do* anything about, mind you. A fantasy.

But Wesley had such conviction and he slowly pulled James into its gravity. First James was unconvinced, then he was enraptured, and then he doubted, but though he lifted not a finger in Wesley's favor, he likewise did not lift one against him. In one of those cruel ironies, his failure to act on the conspiracy became the deciding action; he was in it up to the knees already.

He had been shamefully slow to realize this, yet he saw no way out but through. If he clung to the Sivolne house, he would fall with it. He would be dispatched easily and they would do what they wanted without him. They would find someone else.

The moment he gave his actual word, everything in James' carefully confined life began to change. The position of token figurehead had been prepared for him ahead of time. It had been meticulously carved and polished to seat him. And hold him fast.

One time he had considered dragging himself out. He could reveal all to Riada, dealing irreparable damage to the Emperor's enemies, and showing his value and loyalty. Two things had stopped him: first—and he could admit it to himself freely—he had feared taking action of *any* kind, in any direction. Second, he could not see the wisdom in betraying someone who saw value in him to someone who decidedly did not.

So the opposition won him—that was how he thought of it at first—and he knew now that he had been as cleanly caught and gutted as any fish. He was not as naïve as he once was, and he did not suppose that his fellow conspirators actually revered him, but they surely thought him useful. He felt a fool, but perhaps it mattered *whose* fool.

The only thing left to do was to take that folly and make something out of it.

His job was to bring his name to the fore and give it distinction. And what could be better than going southwest to face a Sahr devil?

To bring one back, even, as a prize? The whole plan was terrifying and utterly ludicrous, especially when he was alone with no one to soothe his fears. Yet, of all ideas, this one—and *only* this one—had been his own.

How he wished he had held his tongue when the thought came flitting in, half a joke. Now he could only hope for Riada to reject his request. Then, whatever else followed, it wouldn't be his fault.

"So?" A quiet, whispered voice snapped James out of his thoughts. He lifted his slumped frame and found that his tea sat cold in his hands. Wesley stepped through the inner doorway. "What came of it? What did the Emperor say?"

"I think he saw right through to my bones, Wesley," James said, shrugging his shoulders.

He threw the bitter tea down his throat in two swallows.

"But you say that every time you talk to him," Wesley said, taking a seat across from him.

"Because it seems that way every time. But I forget," James said miserably. "You think you know my brother better than I."

"Half the court knows him better than you. They watch every twitch of his finger as though their next breath depends on it. Because it does. Our blessing from the Gods is how very little the Emperor thinks of you."

"I'm glad for you that my poor reputation is so beneficial," James said, giving Wesley a faint glare. "And good, too, that you bring it so often to my attention."

Wesley smiled at the unusual bite in James' tone as though he was rather proud of it.

"I do so only to calm your nerves. The Emperor knows the way he and his father fashioned you to be. His notion of you. Not you, as such. Now what did he say?"

"He said he'll consider it."

Wesley nodded thoughtfully.

"Well, that's as much of an answer as can be expected. In the meantime, you'll need to put forth more effort at each high-blooded gathering."

James frowned and said nothing. These gatherings were one of the many reasons that he was deemed useless. He hadn't the lilt or charm of his peers. Listening to Riada, people became rapt, and their blood thrummed, whether with fear or devotion. Listening to James, their mouths tightened with boredom, and their hands clasped impatiently behind their backs. He'd seen it a thousand times.

"Don't let these things distress you, James," Wesley said calmly. "You're Corra to the Emperor. You *can* act with wit and dignity."

"Oh, can I?" James said, half slouched in his chair. "Even when Beranadon sends his daughter over to confuse and distract me like some conjurer with silk scarves?"

"Lady Kathryn is slyer than a conjurer and much lovelier than his scarves. Learn to keep pace with her and she'll not confuse you so. She is our ally."

"And our only deep pocket," James muttered under his breath.

"Each one gives as they can. You, your lineage. They, their coin. That Captain, his sword."

And you, your unblinking determination, James mused, which—Wesley would be loath to hear—was more like Riada's than not. It often overwhelmed James, Wesley driving him like a hard wind, angled in his favor, but always unrelenting.

But James would obey. He would go about at the gatherings between now and the high court assembly. He would try to charm even where he knew he was merely being endured. He would attempt witticisms at which he would fail, though no one would say as much. He would pretend not to be afraid of someone like Lady Kathryn Beranadon, a woman who could probably match minds with Riada himself if ever she got the chance.

And wouldn't she like the chance, James thought. Who would cling to James if Riada suddenly turned to them with the full light of his favor? That was why he tended to skirt far around her and her ilk, as he would large garden spiders. Hardly any of them were poisonous, he was told, and would benefit the garden as a whole. But frankly, his eyesight wasn't the best, and damned if he was going to get any closer than he had to.

If only he could just close his eyes and awake the day of high court, to hear whether or not he was to go to the devils. And if he *was* to go? Then he would only want to close his eyes again. But he wouldn't. Because Wesley would not let him.

James stood taut outside the entrance hall of the high court. Every few minutes he forgot to think, and his body relaxed. But, like the jolt of remembering a horrific dream, it would all come back to him, constricting his chest. He both wished that the time had not yet come, and he wished that it had already passed.

"Ready?" Wesley whispered to James, walking as though he would brush past him, and had only stopped to pay formal respects.

"Not remotely."

In fact, after a rush of impotent fury at Wesley for bringing him into this, he wished for all the world that he could go back to his quarters and lounge, and read, and linger, and not say another bloody word for the rest of his life.

Anyone who knew how to glean rumors off the court ground already knew what Riada was to say: soldiers would be sent to Sahr territory. But no one knew anything beyond that.

"What did they talk about in the first half of council?" James asked.

"The jackals, the rebellious tribal Rokhs, Bigharan trade routes—the usual problems," Wesley said. "The treasurer was very convincing as he lied about the marvelous state of the Imperial coffers. I half believed him."

James nodded distractedly. "You know, even if Riada honors our every request…well, Hodge's men have never actually encountered those devils in person, have they?" he said in a hollow voice.

"No one has bothered to try for many years. Superstitions held strong in days past. That kind of thinking predisposes one to failure," Wesley said with a stiff smile.

"Most people do still think they're devils. Imps. Jinn. Brutes. Whatever you like. The Southerners—"

"Southerners are wont to exaggerate, Your Highness," Verris said curtly. "Perhaps we would have long since handled these so-called devils *and* their territory had we not allowed ourselves to be daunted by southern folklore."

"I believe that speech as you believed the treasurer," James said, smiling with the thin-blooded determination of one who lacks both the conviction to step in and the courage to back out.

There was but a brief glance under the veil, a look in Wesley's eye that showed his own fears, his own superstitions, but confidence resumed when Lady Kathryn Beranadon approached with a gracious tilt of her head. The silver and blue cord of a woman of high court was tied at her shoulder; she was one of but a handful of women in all Maurow who could wear it. Her blood was high and old, and everyone knew she was the fresh strength of her ancient family. She and her kin had the whole Empire to gain and only their lives to lose.

"Good afternoon, Your Highness, Lord Verris," she said.

Cloth of vivid green and blue was draped with elegant perfection from her shoulders, and there were pearls woven into her copper-brown hair in a delicate imitation of the Nagonan style. Makarish kohl and northern crimson colored her eyes and mouth. She was a striking and classical Maurowan beauty, and knew it well. Honed it. Wielded it.

"My Lady," James said, shrinking inwardly. She terrified him.

"It is good to see you take an interest in high court, Your Highness," she said with subtle intonation and an even subtler smile.

James' jaw clenched. He knew she knew of all their plans, but he did not know how to play with courtly language, and circle the truth without touching it. He merely managed to nod and mutter some assent.

"So, do you think the Emperor will allow you out to test your paces?" she asked, leaning forward and looking at him with a warmth that did the trick of wine to the blood. "Or do you think he fears you'll gain too long a stride?"

James took a deep breath. A boyish part of him liked the way he sounded out of her mouth: a stallion ready to bolt and toss off any rider. It was flattery and drivel, but it was *attractive* drivel. Savory to the taste.

"I do not begin to know, Lady Kathryn," he said, his voice stronger this time. "Whatever the Emperor orders, I will do."

She smiled a little, then seemed to assess him. Whether she was pleased or disappointed, he did not know. She gave another small tilt of her head and then walked onward into the court amphitheater, to take her honored seat.

James was grateful she had not pressed him further, trying to tease some coded banter out of his mouth. She had the same wearying effect on him as all Riada's tests and subtle mocking. Kathryn, Riada—all of them—knew just how to give him a false sense of involvement in the conversation, drawing him with gentle questions. He began to think that what he said mattered. But then something always punctured this delusion, and he ended up feeling dizzy, tongue-tied, and lost.

He almost felt that way now as he walked the long way around the enclosed amphitheater toward the row of stone seats designated for the Imperial family. The imposing structure of the place seemed to scoff at him. The columns were too tall, the resonance of voice too clear. Riada, at the center, was too calm and astounding. He made the whole affair no easier than he had to. Over dreadful stone silence, Emperor Riada Sivolne announced a campaign to invade the devils' lands.

For a moment James forgot he was supposed to be a participant in this affair, and became mere audience, full of the excitement, hope, and awe that Riada's words unfailingly sparked. It was as though he did it with a snap of his fingers. The Gods' gift.

"All the tribes that fled from the Sahr creatures speak of fire and devilry and darkness. They speak as if the Empire, blessed by the Gods of Maurow and of Carth, is helpless against them. This is a lie that will not stand. We will *find* that fire and devilry and darkness," he said, "and we will destroy it, stamp out its very last coal, and put the ash to the wind. If we can strike bargains to our favor with the very Gods, we can seize these creatures and show them small. Show that they bleed. And die out.

"Whatever they may be, whatever their nature, Maurow cannot and will not be beholden to them in any way. There should be no place my people fear to set their feet.

"By this you will know my confidence in our purpose: I command my own brother, the Corra James, to lead the great Black Wren battalion into the southwest. I send my own blood on behalf of Maurow."

James started at the sound of his own name. Never had it been spoken so *loudly*, or with such purpose. His muscles felt like water as the whole contents of the imposing room lit their eyes on him in astonishment. James' meager sense of resolve nearly slipped to the ground as he stood and bowed to accept his brother's words.

Only as he began to raise his head again did he realize that only one battalion had been named. Hodge's battalion, yes, but no other. His brother was sending him to Sahr territory with only six hundred men. That was...that was tantamount to a backdoor execution.

Wasn't it?

James' thoughts were muddy. It almost didn't matter. He was going to the *devils*.

With one battalion.

He slowly straightened himself. Prayed that his knees would not buckle. Riada's eyes rested on him with all the weight of his power. "*This is what you asked of me*," he seemed to say in silence. He looked neither angry, nor glad, only frighteningly sure.

At rare, odd times in his youth, James had little blazes of panic—a mad need to do *something*. Something more than wake in the morning, go to bed at night, and avoid trouble. In the end he did nothing. Now that he had finally put his hand to a task, he could not look anyone straight in the eye and say he thought it wise. It was madness. But he had edged himself into this bloody current, and now he had to let it carry him.

6

As soon as the slyest suggestion of dawn touched the barracks walls, Azetla doused the torch next to his watch-post. It was time to wake the men. The older hands slept like the dead, but the newer ones would bolt from their pallets. Excitement or fear could work equally to keep a body awake even when it most needed sleep. Today the Black Wren was to set out toward the southwest hills to catch a devil and, in theory, one needed to be well-rested for that sort of thing.

It had been less than a fortnight since word came from high council down to Captain Hodge. Apparently the Emperor—or was it Verris?—was quite eager. The soldiers harbored a more sober enthusiasm.

Some of the men were convinced that they would encounter grotesque beasts. Long teeth. Longer strides. The rest held firm to the notion that the Sahrs were either demons, jinn, or something worse for which none of them cared to invent a name.

Tackman Dersha was particularly confident in his conjecture, for he had soaked in the stories from the Trekoan half of his family. "They're jinn. Through and through. They'll steal your soul through the hot wind, under the blood suns. Everybody knows that."

But a few—Azetla among them—suspected that the Sahr devils were nothing more than violent and secretive South Makarish savages. Not that he ruled out their being jinn entirely. It was always possible. Just as there were holy things in the world, there were unholy things. But chattering about it so as to tingle one's spine and lace tight one's nerves wasn't really to any purpose. Azetla let all the talk about what and if and maybe flow around him, and he held his own thoughts securely under his tongue.

The battalion was quick to its feet. By the time Azetla had finished his prayers, the men were already gathered for morning rations. Before he could take his own portion of dense burghul mush—made somewhat palatable with cloves and cinnamon—Captain Hodge stepped through the inner gate and beckoned Azetla with a small jerk of his head. Azetla abandoned his place amid the huddle and followed the Captain.

They walked in silence until they reached the Captain's headquarters. Hodge turned toward Azetla and narrowed his eyes at him, arms folded loosely across his chest.

"Got some outsiders coming with us," he said.

"I assumed as much," Azetla replied, hands clasped behind his back in a posture of respect.

The Captain let out a short, half-irritated laugh.

"Of course you did. Did you manage to assume *who*?"

Azetla said nothing. Yes, he knew who.

Hodge's mouth stretched tight. "The Corra James and Lord Verris will not only be coming with us, but the Corra is given command of the battalion."

"Command?" Azetla said, gently raising his eyebrows. "You mean *honorary* command."

"Obviously. But he's still the Emperor's brother, and Verris technically outranks me. You *do* realize what this means?"

Azetla smiled half-heartedly.

"It means I'm a jackal."

"Well you're always that whether I like it or not." Hodge smiled. "But yes, you'll have to *act* like one. What, you think I'm any happier about it than you? You think I want the bloody Corra looking over my shoulder everywhere I go? And Verris did *not* like seeing you as emissary last month. He'll like you a lot less if he realizes the extent of your position here."

The Captain paused, unfolded his arms, and pressed his palms together.

"I want you to go about your same duties. I just need you to do it in such a fashion that the outsiders and whoever else they bring with them can't be offended by it. I'll talk to Radabe, Brody, and Sarrez to make sure they understand the situation."

Azetla nodded briskly. "Yes, sir."

This had happened a few times before; some outsider accompanied the battalion and made life very tapered and tedious for Azetla. He had earned his way up to Hodge's right hand, but circumstances like this made him feel reined backward with a cold, hard bit.

"Also," Hodge continued, "we're supposed to march through North City—the Emperor wants a send-off with pomp and ceremony, so—"

"Understood. I'll stay back and join the march when it comes back through South City," Azetla said calmly. He was happy to oblige on that point.

Captain Hodge scowled at him.

"This is how it bloody is and you've no right to take offense at it."

"I didn't say a word, sir."

Hodge breathed out through his nose like a bull. "You never do. But I know what you're thinking."

Azetla lowered his head toward his Captain—who did not at all know what he was thinking—with genuine deference.

"It's all right. I know how it has to be. But they *will* figure it out eventually. Especially if we come to arms."

Hodge gave Azetla a sharp look—a thousand abrupt concerns clicking in his eyes—and he sighed. "The devils will tear my soul to shreds because of *you*, you bloody jackal."

"No they won't," Azetla said with a twitch of a smile. "Because according to the Emperor we're going to catch one and kill it. And that's all there is to it."

The Captain gave a raw laugh and dismissed Azetla, telling him to send the others as he found them. Azetla nodded and left. Even though he hated the way he would be forced to talk around everything, soften his manner, and act like a low tackman, he could do most of his work just as well while keeping to the shadows. It was as much for the Captain's safety as for Azetla's because, really, they were both breaking the law. The Captain deserved that much from him.

By both birth and official record, Azetla was authorized neither rank, nor billet, nor sword. He was to dig privies, clean tack, and carry supplies. Nothing more. But Captain Hodge was a ruthlessly practical man, and he did not see the point in wasting a body that could read, strategize, and command simply because it belonged to a Mashevi. Muck work or scribe work, Azetla did whatever was put to him. Because Azetla had once taken a severe wound to aid the Captain in battle, Hodge began to trust him very early on. Far more slowly, Azetla had come to trust the Captain as well. As best he could.

Azetla's wound had healed, the trust had strengthened, and now the Black Wren had the strange habit of putting a Mashevi in a position of higher command, which was precisely where all good Maurowans knew a Mashevi should never be.

Hodge had given him almost absolute authority in the battalion when and wherever he could safely afford to do so. The only question remaining was whether he would have the sheer audacity to give Azetla the whole battalion when the time came. Azetla had been working toward the commandership the same way he did every other task—with firm and gentle precision—but nothing was promised.

For all his quiet tenacity, his was a precarious situation. This mission to Sahr territory might push it past what he could sustain.

He ate his breakfast quickly and sorted through his satchel: supply ledger, maps, rosters, scrolls of notes, vellum, and ink. All these he kept and organized for Captain Hodge. Hodge could read and write, but it was wearisome for him because of some queer trick the letters were wont to play on his eyes. They didn't organize themselves properly, he said. He had Azetla conduct all his scribing, even his personal correspondence with his wife and relatives. That was the Captain's shrewdness: he knew what he could and could not do.

As Azetla and Joseph began checking the supply wagons, half a dozen North City officers—the first of the outsiders—arrived.

"Here to bestow upon our humble battalion all the convenience of a second left foot," Joseph muttered, ready to slip the ledgers out of Azetla's hands should any of the high-bloods offer them a suspicious look.

Azetla kept his eyes fixed on the charcoal marks and tucked his right arm, with its telling jackal band, against his body.

They did not look. Azetla carried on with his work. He had noted, however, that three of them were Makarish. That was no help. It took all of Azetla's will not to assume the worst of any Makar—so old and bad was the blood between their peoples—and sometimes he failed even at that. They would disdain him at first glance, and he didn't exactly mind returning the favor, only he had to keep quiet about it and they didn't. Azetla hated them as a rule, and he had only broken that rule a handful of times.

"We should have Sarrez escort them around," Azetla said in a low voice. "Keep them occupied."

Joseph nodded with a smile. "He can pretend to be scandalized about you, and they'll feel safe."

Lieutenant Nimer Sarrez was one for whom Azetla had broken the Makarish rule. The nature of the Black Wren battalion forced such exceptions. Sarrez was a North Makar, from a tribe that had largely assimilated into Maurowan culture. He and Azetla held each other at a respectful arm's distance, but there was no contempt between them. Not anymore.

Upon Azetla's instruction, Sarrez managed his newly arrived kinsman with a deft hand, making them feel important while keeping them from interfering with anything of substance.

Azetla was relieved when the battalion finally gathered, formed, and marched off to make a goodly military spectacle in North City. They would have drums and trumpets and fanfare, and Azetla would have a brief rest. Since he had been on night watch, he had only a few hours' sleep to go on.

But there was something he had to do first.

The barracks were empty and quiet. The sun was already blazing a trail from the east, though the air was still cool. Masheva lay east. His home city of Rinayim lay east. In a certain strange way, it was as though his very soul lay east, stretched almost to the breaking point. No one else knew, unless they had paid terribly close attention over the years, that today was the beginning of a weeklong holy festival among Mashevis.

Azetla couldn't celebrate it in the prescribed way, nor could he do so publicly, but here, alone, he could drink the few small sips of mixed wine that Joseph had saved for him and eat the small handful of honey-dates he had set aside for the occasion. There ought to be lamb and sharp-sour rimash herbs. There ought to be salted dak-bread, no work-of-the-hands, and a recounting of ancient stories. Beautiful chants of thanks to God, peppered with the shouts of children whose attention wandered during the long, repetitious verses.

But none of that was possible.

So Azetla said the traditional prayers and songs in a careful, lonely hush, offering honors to the God of Masheva, of the desert, and of everything.

He repeated one of the prayers twice because the first time it fell off his tongue without a thought. Sometimes it was difficult to bring meaning into the words he had memorized since before known memory. They had been placed in his mouth, like the salt of vows, before he even understood what half of them meant. They had just been sounds on a small child's tongue, though he had always thought them savory and vibrant.

Now? Sometimes they tasted like the raw strength of truth and holiness. Other times they only tasted like ash, dead and dry. He never stopped saying them, though. It was duty. It was memory. It was—he hoped—holy. Calm and gratitude fell over him, despite everything.

When he finished, Azetla sat at the west barracks gate, nearest the main road, and waited for the cheers and drums to draw him to his feet. When he could hear that they had passed the old city wall, Azetla took long strides to meet them where the road turned along the River Carth. By the time they reached the outskirts, he had melted into his place in the formation, greeting Joseph with a nod of his head. Joseph rapped him hard on the shoulder.

"You've been deprived, Azetla. It was a sight. I think they were about to make love to us all in the passion of the moment, and then pronounce us king of something or other," he said.

"I don't doubt it."

Riada had whipped the city into a frenzy over the past few days; he had always been very invested in the look of a thing quite as much as its nature. And this mission was made to look important and grand, while actually being ill-prepared for success.

Riada was playing some game here. Sacrificing lives as symbols, as he was wont to do.

Azetla unclenched his jaw. He looked out beyond the marching line to the desert before him with its violent interruptions of rocky earth. The fierce brown terrain reached up into rugged hills and dipped down into riverbeds. It twisted and curved and cut and broke and stretched out under the sky. For a place that offered few colors more dramatic than the occasional streak of dull red, it affixed eyes to itself in uncanny fashion.

All noise dwindled to clinking metal, horse hooves on rock-strewn ground, and the occasional order to halt and drink water. Time passed quickly as the sun traveled overhead.

Azetla began to feel a strange, light-shouldered sense of freedom stirring up with the south wind, in spite of the destination. He breathed easy as Piarago disappeared behind and found solace in the coarse russet world around him. It both ached and allured beneath the fierce sun. At dusk, it turned seductive, drawing the gaze into the last yellowed light. Different from the hilly scrub desert and salty shores of Masheva, yes, but there was a certain taste in the air that made Azetla feel the old craving for home. He held the feeling close, curling his fist against himself as if the desire was a material thing inside his hand. Then he loosed his fingers and let his arm go slack. He left the fleeting thought in the dust at his heels.

It took Wesley nearly a fortnight to gain his bearings in Captain Hodge's world.

He had always thought of himself as capable and resilient, but the first several days of travel drained the lifeblood out of him. He accomplished nothing but the ground underfoot. All that should have been at the front of his mind—the Sahr devils, James' reputation, the *jackal*—fell hazily beneath his concern. The swelling desert heat and a perpetually parched throat seemed to dull his will and wits. He thought about water half the day long, even though he and the Corra were privileged for all rations. The ground was hard at night, the sun like fire in the day, and Wesley had to work hard simply to learn the standard flag signals and march commands so that he would not look a fool.

Hodge kept what Wesley found to be a cruel pace, though his men thought nothing of it. Sometimes the gap between halts was so long that the formation of men began to reek of piss under the heat. It wasn't until the beginning of the second week that they began to parallel the River Limila and could wash at night again.

James bore it unexpectedly well. He collapsed off his horse like a sack of grain at night, but he never breathed a word of complaint. Nothing was required of either of them, except to do a formal walk-about each night to "inspect" the camp. This was pure tradition, and of no practical use whatsoever. At the beginning, Wesley had been relieved that Hodge never troubled him with questions or briefs or tasks of command.

But by the twelfth day, he began to acclimate. The aches, chafing, and discontented stomach gradually faded. He began to feel as if he was waking from a stupor, having lost two weeks of observation, of ingratiating himself, of discovering whether or not Hodge was an ally, or at least buyable.

The first thing he realized was that there was no kindness in the way they left him alone. Only indifference. Battalion activities flowed smoothly past him, like river water parting gently round a rock, paying it no mind, disturbing it nowise. The officers that Wesley brought with him were likewise given all manner of deference and absolutely no authority.

The Black Wren soldiers were like a pack of wolves; their hierarchy was complex, subtle, and resistant to outsiders in the extreme. All these old battalions were so tribe-like and insular, it was like breaking iron to get through to the inner circle.

The sense of being as a foreigner in his native Empire, of being kept just to the outside, being overlooked—it all rushed in at him afresh. The old anger stirred, but had no sensible place to land. What could he do? Go to Hodge, waving his empty Colonel's rank, and demand to be given authority and tasks? *What* authority? *What* task? He had earned neither.

Wesley watched the soldiers with hawk's eyes, searching for any crevice into which he might wedge his fingers so as to climb, any joint in the body of the battalion that he might calmly, sensibly manipulate to his favor.

Once he began looking in earnest, it only took him a few days to find it. Wesley felt the most sating fury rise in his chest when his eyes could at last see how matters really stood in the Black Wren. A perfect, lawful direction for all his anger showed itself bright and clear.

For Captain Hodge was not a meticulous man, but the Black Wren was meticulously ordered. Captain Hodge found reading and writing laborious, but the Black Wren kept perfect rosters, and co-pious records. Hodge was charismatic and had excellent sense, but the soldiers seemed to have firmer ground under their feet than mere hero worship.

And the jackal *was* the problem. How could Wesley have ever thought otherwise? Somehow, without rank, he acted almost as the vice commander of the battalion. Quietly, subtly, but there it was. A glance or a twitch of the jackal's fingers was enough to acquire immediate obedience from anyone. Even the officers.

In a strange, gnawing way, it reminded Wesley of Emperor Riada, the man who did not bluster or yell, but simply looked at you until you crumbled. Yet the similarity should not have surprised him. Emperor Riada loathed the jackals with a unique ferocity, but what he did not know—what he could not bear to understand—was that he was *just like them*. Just as arrogant. Just as self-reliant. Just as isolated in his thoughts and habits. Just as tethered to one single point of failure.

For while the jackals leaned solely on their desert god in all the world, spitting upon all others as worthless, Riada's own brilliance was the only thing he truly worshipped. To himself, he sacrificed. To himself, he entrusted all. To himself, must go all questions, and all hopes.

The jackals held themselves as unique, set apart, divinely blessed—the sheer conceit of it was stunning, really—but there was no question that Riada was exactly the same.

They were each other's mirror image. No wonder they hated each other so desperately.

Wesley bit his tongue and let his thoughts steep until they reached Golmouth. The battalion paused briefly outside the city, resupplying and permitting the adherents of Thaytal to offer their petitions to that goat-god of Golmouth. Everything smelled of camphor and balsam incense for hours after.

Then, the last real city before Sahr territory disappeared behind them. A low, quiet dread trickled into Wesley's blood, and he would have taken any distraction to suppress it. Dealing with the jackal would almost be a boon.

Little light remained when Captain Hodge finally gave the halt order on the twenty-first night of travel. The long lines slowed until the whole rippling battalion came to a quiet stop. At a shout, the men dispersed in swift, complex movements. Fires for food. Canopies for officers. Supply verification. Relief trenches. Night watch. Patrols. A steady stream of jars, goatskins, and buckets carried in from the Limila riverbank.

And the jackal was the directing arm, guiding currents this way and that.

A few goats were coerced from a nearby Makarish tribe and, when all was settled and pots were simmering, Wesley and James took their formal walkabout. Usually James would nod in approval of he knew not what and then each section leader would bow and that was that. Nobody took it very seriously.

Tonight, Wesley noted the jackal. He stood when he was supposed to stand, sat when he was given leave to sit, gave every respectful gesture, and generally tried to make himself as invisible and inoffensive as possible. But Wesley could see now. When Wesley instructed the men to take their ease, he saw the slight tilt of the jackal's head which let the soldiers know that, yes, they may sit and eat now.

"It's become tedious, how much they disdain our presence here," Wesley said offhandedly when they returned to the Corra's tent.

He thought it best to broach the matter softly. James became skittish if one demanded opinions and action of him.

"I think it is more disinterest than disdain," James replied, looking longingly at the thick pallet his man-at-arms had prepared for him. "It's a very southern trait, isn't it? Just nod your way past the interference and ignore it. But if it's causing problems—"

"It will, eventually. You need their regard, not just their dutiful salutes. You do realize we have to *court them*. And we all know that, when courting, one rarely relies on charm alone, but also certain acceptable levels of coercion. And, really, what is a bride-price except a bribe?"

James raised a hand and waved it loosely at Wesley, narrowing his eyes.

"What the devil are you getting at? I'm too tired to guess."

"You'll have marked some improprieties as regards the law, I'm certain," Wesley said.

"I suppose. They're informal. Can't make head nor tail of the way they handle rank. And there's a jackal roaming about," James responded, shrugging his shoulders as if the Mashevi was simply a wayward goat.

"Exactly," Wesley said. He felt a grim satisfaction as he spoke. "He's their most prominent discrepancy. I think we might...point it out."

James' eyebrows snapped down and he shifted uncomfortably.

"Are you sure that's wise? Just now you want to criticize them? We are dependent upon them for our safety! Do you remember *where* we're going? If—" James cut himself off and shook his head. "Better to have done that first thing or not at all."

"You misunderstand, Your Highness. There is a prudent way to address the matter and I have no desire to offend them to our own detriment. I merely want Hodge to understand that we see. We know. Then, if we use that rightly, we might be able to reach a sort of...forced mutual respect," Wesley said, using a gentle, instructive voice.

"Forced mutual respect?" James repeated with disapproval. "That doesn't strike me as good timber."

"It's strong if built right. Like I said: the bride-price makes the marriage. Love may only come after. We have to start where we can. They have skills and a reputation you desperately need to appropriate."

James nodded reluctantly and stared at the ground for a moment. He looked exhausted and pressed his fingers into his neck as if rubbing an ache.

"Honestly, Wesley, I don't care what the jackal does so long as he does it at the Captain's behest," he said in a weary voice. "We're almost there, and I don't want trouble."

The tone of James' voice brushed against the nerve of Wesley's own fear. He did not like it being drawn to the front of his mind and he worked quickly to ignore it.

"I think you do not see my purpose, Your Highness. It isn't about the jackal. Or even control. It's about gaining loyalty, using your voice, making yourself *matter*. But are you not at least offended on behalf of yourself, or on behalf of the law?" Wesley pressed. "Even if the jackal had as holy and bright a soul as the Seer of Carth—and we know that cannot be—the law is the law. Unless Your Highness thinks it is a law that needs changing?"

James' mouth went flat.

"Of course not," he sighed heavily. "Do what you think you must but, Wesley, don't..."

Wesley crossed his arms and waited respectfully. James kneaded his neck again.

"I know I don't understand military matters, but just watching them...I think they hold resilience in highest regard not...not clawing and haranguing for recognition," James' eyes darted away from Wesley.

Had James not acted like an embarrassed child, Wesley would not even have realized that the comment was a censure, and he would not have felt the sting of it.

"I promise you, Your Highness. I will not harangue them," he said, smiling stiffly, some tender muscle in his soul smarting from the slap. "And it is about more than recognition. It is about seeing this through, properly."

Wesley was not rash or retaliatory. His strategies were of a scholarly cadence. They had, he felt, a thinking man's lilt. He did not prefer that his future should rest between the crafty fingers of a jackal, yet he also needed to make sure that he would have any future to speak of.

He bowed with purpose firm in mind and departed the Corra's tent.

7

Azetla could still half hear the movement of the men all around him, but it was fading. Just a short rest before he woke for second watch. He felt sleep coming heavy over him like a cloak, despite the cooling air and the thinness of his pallet. He was almost dead to the world when the edge of a hobnail boot rammed into the back of his ribs—hard enough to send a sharp breath through his teeth as he jerked his shoulders from his pallet.

Two outsider Lieutenants from the Corra's entourage stood, staring at him. A Kourisad and a Makar.

"We would like a word with you, Mashevi," the northern one said.

Azetla looked up at them, lopsided from the bruise, hands resting against the dusty ground. Slowly, he stood and adopted the proper stance of a subordinate, hands clasped behind his back, chest tilted forward. He knew the northern one was Lord Lieutenant Brighton. The Makar was Lord Lieutenant Haqir. Azetla had noticed them watching him over the past few days, as if upon instruction. That, he had expected.

This, he had not.

He lowered his eyes for one respectful moment. "Of course, my lords."

"We'll have a name of you," Brighton said.

"Azetla."

"Azetla *what*?"

He hesitated before answering. "Of Rinayim...Rinayimi."

The Makar lifted his head in satisfaction, glancing at Brighton.

"Didn't I tell you?" Haqir said with a sharp smile. "City of sedition. A deaf man could hear it in the way he talks."

Azetla stood in calm, straight-backed silence, conceiving a reply and cutting it off.

Brighton looked Azetla over as if there were something hidden in his appearance that would explain him. "What are your exact duties here, jackal?"

"My duties consist of whatever His Highness the Corra instructs, sir," Azetla replied.

Brighton smiled faintly. "You know what I mean, jackal."

"I keep the ledgers, the maps, and the ration lists. And I assist the senior officers of the battalion when and however needed," Azetla said, forming each word with care.

"Without rank?" the Lieutenant gestured toward his own panel.

"As you see, sir."

"But *with* weapons," Lieutenant Haqir added. He did not smile.

"My lords, we are neither in Piarago, nor in its outposts, nor in any of the six cities and three port villages where weapons are expressly forbidden to me," Azetla said.

He knew the Imperial law down to the letter. He knew how to skirt it. And he knew how to use it.

"You are here as an *active* soldier, and that is prohibited no matter where you go," Haqir pressed.

Azetla's reply came quick as the snap of a bowstring, ready-drawn.

"I am a papered soldier, my lord, and thus a combatant only insofar as it is needed to protect these men—appointed by your Emperor—and to further the purposes which they carry out in his very name. Would you have me stand useless and a burden when you, your officers, or the very Corra are in harm's way?"

Haqir's eyes widened and he raised his shoulders. Azetla sensed the tense shift in the air. He could feel it in his own squared and lengthened posture. He could see it in the appalled looks on the two Lieutenants' faces.

Then he felt it in the surprisingly sharp slap the Makar threw across his face.

Azetla rolled his jaw slightly, smothering the small angry fire that woke up in his stomach. The slap stung, but that wasn't its purpose. A slap was for shock and shame, not pain. One slaps recalcitrant children. Subordinates. Slaves.

There was no good way to respond. He could not retaliate. Nor could he cower. His men, still and attentive on their own pallets, did not deserve that from him.

So Azetla kept level and silent, and bit, bit, bit into the skin of his cheek at a soft rhythm.

"Remember to whom you speak, jackal," Haqir said.

Out of the corner of his eye, Azetla saw Joseph slip away to apprise the Captain of the situation. The rest of the men sat quiet, waiting. Perhaps some were angry on Azetla's behalf, but they too could say nothing. In the tiny world of the Black Wren, Azetla was trusted and obeyed. In the presence of outsiders, he was only a jackal, and always must be.

"What do you need of me, my lords?" Azetla said in an impassive voice.

"One simple matter comes to our attention," Brighton said. "*You* keep the ledgers. And we're not on them. Not in the companies. Not in command. Not in duties. We are marked as 'a protected party,' not as combat officers. We are *not* your wards! We were chosen to come by Lord Verris and the Corra himself."

"Forgive me, but the exclusion is a courtesy, my lords. We deemed it unjust to throw you to the companies without knowing the men or our methods. The Captain knows your lordships will be with us only briefly. He did not wish to unnecessarily burden you."

"He had no right—" Haqir began in a furious voice.

But Azetla's overrode his.

"He *does* have the right. The Captain can confer or withhold status in his own battalion."

That brought another swift slap from Haqir; it was much harder than the last one, making Azetla's eyes clamp shut in surprise.

"From what position do you claim the right to *speak* this way, jackal?" Haqir said.

The silence among the men was excruciating, and Haqir's voice rose high and dispersed well across the sea of soldiers.

"From none, my lord," Azetla said quietly, leveling himself once again and setting his breaths to a long, slow, specific rhythm. He was not being careful enough. Either that or they were hell-bent on finding fault, so as to justify that which they already planned to do. "Which begs the question as to why you came to *me*?"

Lieutenant Brighton flashed a quick look at his Makarish compatriot, then turned back to Azetla. "Because we are not here to observe, but to take part."

"You must speak to the Captain, my lords," Azetla said again.

"But don't you speak for him?" Brighton said.

A dozen pairs of eyes dropped, horrified, to the ground. Azetla's careful demeanor failed him completely for the space of a breath.

"You think it's not obvious? Just because we're outsiders—as you call us—doesn't mean we're fools," Haqir said. "Jackal, we've every right to run you through with your own sword, by the formal custom. We've been far too tolerant already and our patience has worn out."

Panic hit Azetla in the chest. He held his tongue lest he misuse it again, and his mind began to feel for a way out, as if through pitch black. These high-bloods could say "kill the jackal," and it would be done. Even Captain Hodge was still beholden to law and rank when it took him by the throat.

If he was made to offer his sword for his own neck—the lawful death for convicted soldiers—the men would have to watch, whether with anger, shame, or satisfaction. Like he watched the Red River festival. The unwritten rule held firm. Yes, he *was* the second in command. Everyone knew it, lived by it.

And it didn't matter one bit.

He looked level at Haqir and Brighton, certain that no acquiescence on his part would change their intent. Why give it?

"So be it, my lords, complain to the Captain as you please. For our own part, we have work to do."

"By blood!" Haqir gasped, glancing at Brighton to share contempt. "These jackals have no shame. You deserve *everything* that will be done to you."

"Then I'll speak to the Captain, if you do not wish to," Azetla said in a flat, bland voice.

"I think not," Brighton said. "Given the circumstances, your Captain is culpable and cannot be trusted."

Now the men did rumble, and a few stood up. *Bully our jackal, we must allow it, but do not* touch *our Captain.* That was a step too far.

"My Lords, our Captain is a man of honor and he can account for himself by the law," Azetla said.

Neither replied. They exchanged a look, their hands dropping to hilt. Azetla's breath caught and his posture broke to brace; a long step back, the right shoulder instinctively angled the way it would have been if he was bearing a shield. But he was empty-handed. His sword was at his feet, next to his pallet, and he didn't dare use it.

Suddenly, all eyes leapt southward: The Corra James Sivolne and Lord Wesley Verris approached, hastily announced. The two officers stilled, hands poised to draw.

Captain Hodge was not far behind the Corra, taking desperate strides as though he feared he might not arrive in time. Hodge shot Azetla a look. Only then did Azetla's eyes tip toward the ground and hold fast downward, as they ought to have done since the beginning.

Azetla was not the only one who would feel the consequences of this.

"Is something amiss Lord Brighton? Lord Haqir?" Verris said, calm and smooth as lake water. "Why are we almost at arms?"

The Corra James, ostensibly in command of the situation, kept silent.

"You see, Lord Colonel," Haqir said, gesturing sharply at Azetla.

"Explain," Verris said.

"It is as we suspected. This jackal—is it not enough that he carries a sword? He carries the ledgers and orders too and, by them, excludes us. Captain Hodge has clearly permitted this, Colonel."

Verris glanced at the Captain with what seemed to Azetla to be a decidedly feigned expression of dismay. "Lord Captain?"

Captain Hodge's gray head and eagle eyes jerked from Azetla, across the tops of the many soldiers' heads, at last fixing on Verris.

"Azetla can write. He's dutiful and scrupulous. So I assign him the books. *I* assign. It's nothing worth concern. You *knew* we had a Mashevi, Lord Verris. We spoke of this."

Verris inclined his head with respect. "Of scribal work and such, yes, but it seems you have allotted him a position of authority—that you would bypass my officers entirely in favor of a jackal. You can see how they might find an insult in that, if it is true."

"I use each man as suits the battalion's needs, Lord Colonel Verris," Hodge replied thickly. It was not like him to be so formal. That was worry speaking. "He's been under my command for over a decade. If—"

"But this is not a mere softening of regulation. This is a serious violation of Maurowan law. All but treachery." Verris gestured lightly toward Azetla as though he were a display. "But I'm sure you feel that your reasons bear up under law."

"I do," Hodge said in a growl, his broad shoulders tightening.

Verris narrowed his eyes at the Captain.

"Tell me then, how did your men celebrate the Red River festival? How do they justify themselves before Serivash? Do you tell the story of how many the jackals killed and how they defiled the River Carth with our bodies? How they ground the statues of Serivash and Sharitha to powder? Does the jackal *partake* in your festivities? Or do you let him worship his lone desert God in defiance of all that is ours?"

Captain Hodge's gaze held steady, but he spoke not a word. No one did. The Maurowan beliefs about Mashevis were held with a similarly orthodox fervor as their beliefs about their own gods. And heresy in the matter of jackals was dangerous.

"I assume your intentions are honorable Captain Hodge, but the laws have purpose and the house of Sivolne does not make them arbitrarily," Verris said.

"The house of Sivolne does not fight in battle, my lord," Hodge replied.

For the first time, James Sivolne opened his mouth.

"We don't doubt your character, Captain. Not in a thousand years. Only *his*," the Corra said.

"I vouch for his character. He's been among us since he was a child. This battalion has reared him entirely. I trust him with my life, Your Highness. And as we are almost in Sahr territory, I have entrusted him with *yours* as well."

Azetla tensed at the Captain's lack of neutrality. It stung, somehow. Hurt his throat. Hodge shouldn't have said that. Proud and territorial though the Captain was, he had never defended Azetla to another high-blood before, and never so bluntly. It didn't...it wasn't even going to help. Only now he couldn't unsay it.

Hodge could lose his battalion so as to not lose a jackal. Azetla's eyes fixed hard on the ground and he could not manage to lift them. For once, he wished that Hodge knew how to play court. How to say what he meant without actually saying it.

"What His Highness the Corra is too gracious to say is that having a jackal in such a position confuses my men, confuses order, confuses *allegiance*," Verris said. "There are some things that cannot be tolerated and the Corra must know that you are loyal."

Captain Hodge balked as if he too had been slapped. "My lord, Your Highness, we are loyal down to the bone and blood. Whatever the talk of 'rebellious' old battalions, we always serve Maurow. My men have spilled blood—I have *lost* men—for our Maurow. And the jackal is one of us, so I ask that you leave him to his work."

Azetla lifted his head again to see an odd expression pass over Verris' face. "Come here, Mashevi," he said, flicking his hand in Azetla's direction.

Azetla stepped out from among the officers, stood before Verris, and grasped his hands once again behind his back. He tipped his eyes downward, but only just so far as to meet with Verris'. He could have sunk his frame down to appear submissive, but it was far past mattering, he hated doing it, and it was a falsehood. For a foolish moment, he relished the way proximity forced Verris to look up to meet his eyes. Such a man did not like being made to feel small.

"By Emperor Riada's laws," Verris began slowly. "I should have him killed this very moment. It would be seen as right and just. We don't like to train our enemies to fight us, and a jackal like this is proof of the danger."

A jackal like this? *If only I really was the threat you think I am,* Azetla thought.

Give it time.

Captain Hodge looked from Verris to Azetla, and back again. Desperation began to pull at the edges of his mouth. There was some sly, threatening gambit being thrown here and, all at once, Azetla saw it. He was nothing more than a piece being leveraged against his own Captain.

"I would not sanction it, Lord Colonel," Hodge said, his voice gravel.

"You don't need to, Lord Captain."

Hodge dropped whatever formality he had maintained for the sake of the men, all of them rapt, shoulders raised taut.

"Wesley, I know that—" Hodge began.

But Verris cut him off with a calm, but sharp gesture.

"You misunderstand me, Edmund. I spoke of what the Emperor says, but we are nigh beyond the reach of our Empire, and he and the Corra are not one and the same, honor befall them both. You must defer to His Highness the Corra's judgment on the matter. His word shall stand, whatever it may be. Your Highness?"

He cued the Corra to speak a second time, which he seemed disinclined to do. James glanced around for several moments, apparently ignorant of the anxiety he stacked up around him with each second of hesitant silence. He looked at both of the outsider Lieutenants.

"Would it satisfy your grievance to ensure that you are given your rightful places in the marching order? And will you trust myself and the Colonel to deal with the Mashevi as we see fit?" James asked.

Confusion clouded the righteous fury in their faces, but both bowed because he was the Emperor's brother, if nothing else.

"Yes, Your Highness."

"The Mashevi is under our eye," the Corra said, more firmly now, though his words sounded...practiced. "If I believe him treacherous, I will act. Otherwise, we must walk as a whole while we are in the devils' lands, and I think it would be wise to trust the Captain's usage of his own men. We must honor him thus."

Haqir and Brighton once again nodded, seeming rather dazed, as if a trick had been played on them. As if they had been promised quite a different outcome for the task to which they had been set.

The Corra beckoned Hodge and the two outsiders, doing what *should* have been done all along: escorting high-blood conflict away from the common camp. None of this should have happened in front of the men. But Azetla was convinced that not a word had been spoken, nor an action taken other than exactly what Verris intended.

Wordlessly, Azetla and Joseph walked to the high-blood part of camp. The Captain would want to talk to them both after, as his right and his left hand.

They waited an hour for Hodge to return from James' tent. Not much was said until then. Perhaps Joseph would rather have eased the air with talk or jokes, but Azetla took it as a kindness that he let the quiet hold fast.

The battalion had come under scrutiny before, but never from so high a domain or at such close proximity. No fulfilled debt or costly citizenship could keep Azetla from being a flaw in the eyes of outsiders, regardless of his true place within the battalion. It made him feel a liar and a hypocrite.

He had always been drawn to rules, laws, and logic. In Masheva, among the traditional and pious, laws were as fine art and silk—to be loved, admired, caressed, and methodically cared for. Precise truth and efficacy sewn together—these appealed to Azetla's blood. It was why the ledgers had been slipped into his hands in the first place all those years ago and why he was trusted to keep the men in good order.

Yet Azetla remained a walking infraction of Maurowan law. And he shouldn't even *care*. It was beyond reason to want to be on the right side of a law that was chiseled directly against him. But it made things unsound, unsteady. He would begin to think all was well, he would almost feel at home—he shouldn't—and then some outsider would come to remind him of the truth with a slap across the face.

At least it kept him from atrophy, from being the frog in boiling water. It was too easy for all of this to feel normal and natural. The skin goes numb. Insults and threats are mere weather, to be slogged through.

"Where's Brody? And Sarrez?" Captain Hodge said as he strode suddenly into his tent, exhausted and bewildered.

"We told Sarrez to rest—he had first watch command—and Brody's commanding second. He'll be by to brief you later," Azetla said.

"Did I *tell* you to hand off your tasks?" the Captain snapped.

"You didn't tell me not to, sir. I'll stay awake and verify everything. But we've had Brody for a year now and he's competent. I thought it best to keep out of sight for the rest of the evening."

Hodge dug the heel of his palm against his temple, nodding in frustration. He scraped his hand over his grizzled face and dropped it to his side.

"Brody will do well enough. But I want you to keep to *your* work, Azetla. We're half a step away from Sahr territory."

"Joseph can—"

"*Just*...keep to your work."

Azetla narrowed his eyes and glanced at Joseph.

"What did they say, sir?" Joseph said.

"We have to integrate their officers," Hodge said. He gave Azetla a sharp look. "I know, Azetla, I *know*. It was going to happen eventually. I just don't bloody..." His voice trailed off and so did his gaze.

Joseph and Azetla kept quiet, letting their Captain gather his thoughts.

"We'll put each one with someone at least court-superior to them. As best we can," he said at last. "They're beholden to that sort of thing."

"Put that Makarish idiot with Sarrez," Joseph said with a flash of anger. "He'll keep him from knocking men around. But I meant what did they say about *Azetla*?"

Hodge shook his head, uncertain. "It was very strange." He looked at Azetla. "The Corra was surprisingly generous about you.

He said they'll tell their officers not to antagonize you. You're allowed your duties, and I mine but..."

"But it seemed less than earnest?" Azetla said quietly. He already knew the answer.

"Something like that. They kept on about how shocked they were, how offended, and how unlawful you are. And they swear they will not harm you—they didn't say 'for now' but I heard it—and they 'deeply respect my authority' and honor befall me and all that formal rot. Like they were trying to convict me and acquit me in the same damn breath."

Azetla sighed, feeling the day's exhaustion suddenly wash over him. "They were. The whole thing was a show."

Hodge raised an eyebrow. "Oh?"

"They wanted you to know that they are aware of our...shortcomings," Azetla smiled grimly, "and how very benevolent and gracious they are to overlook them. It puts you in their debt. You have their lenience regarding something for which you ought to have their censure, or worse. That's why they didn't mind the impropriety of debating the matter in front of all the men; they had you insulted so that they could mount a 'rescue' and the men would *see* it done. Let me guess, they'll publicly reprimand those two officers?"

"Yes."

"To make the men happy, to ingratiate themselves. But they won't let you forget what they have over your head."

"Gods and devils." Captain Hodge thought a moment, moving his jaw as if he were chewing. "Does that mean that the knife is still at your neck? Or did they only pretend to be offended?"

"I think the offense is genuine and the amnesty entirely contingent," Azetla said slowly.

"Upon?"

"Our being of value to them."

Hodge nodded thoughtfully. "Then perhaps when we have accomplished our mission—Shouma and Sharitha grant us success—it might be best if you disappeared. For your own safety."

Azetla's mouth opened in astonishment. An hour ago, the Captain had defended Azetla so fearlessly, it had shocked his senses. Now he would discard him that easily. Make the problem go away.

"You want me to desert, sir?" he said in a hollow voice. But then the hollow suddenly filled out with anger he was allowed to show, here if nowhere else. "And go where? With *what*? Debt left on my conscription and nothing to show for thirteen years' work?"

"How can it be deserting if you're not supposed to be a combatant or to have duties in the first place?" Hodge said with a hard smile.

A sharp look passed between Azetla and his Captain. All that was unspoken on the matter of Azetla's position and future in the battalion bristled in that look. Hodge *knew* Azetla wanted the battalion, and he had set Azetla in place to take it; but Hodge couldn't say it out loud, couldn't put it in stone, or on paper—couldn't swear to his own hurt. Because it could all go away at the snap of some Imperial fingers.

Joseph laughed, trying to make light of the matter, to treat the Captain's words as a joke, and Hodge himself gave a tight half-laugh in return. But Azetla had no stomach for it. Everyone, even the best of them, hedged their bets when it came to him and expected him to take it as a matter of course. He rolled his jaw, unable to say to the Captain precisely what he wished, so all he said was, "I won't leave."

"Yes. You will if I order you to."

The words had a searing, final quality to them and, had anyone but Joseph been in the room, Azetla would have had to take them. But it was only the three of them. Azetla could use his whole voice and stand his full height.

"Captain, you know damn well that I'm not going anywhere except where the battalion goes. Throwing me to them and throwing me out a debt-criminal—these are no different to me," he said. He took a deep breath. "I'll manage myself with the high-bloods, I swear by salt."

"Oh you will, will you?" Hodge lifted his thick gray eyebrows sharply, his voice all grit. Azetla stared back at him, and neither gave any ground.

Azetla knew his own mind. He would not yield here, not even for his own safety. It had been Hodge's choice to cultivate him as he had, and Azetla was going to use every last freedom he had been given to its furthest boundary. He would use them until they were forcibly stripped from him.

The hardness in Hodge's face began to fade, worry supplanting it.

With the edge of his thumb, Azetla began to tap a thoughtless rhythm against the little lion's head he wore around his neck. An old habit of his which had worn the face to an indistinct sheen, and which often helped to calm him.

Soon his mind was quiet enough to work reason into emotion, like leaven into bread.

The Captain should never have suggested that Azetla leave, but he was tired and scrambling. Azetla wanted to hear his Captain take it back, to be ashamed of the words. What good to be safe, but paralyzed, unable to move or act or be? But Captain Hodge, for all his qualities, tended to look to the near rather than the far. Azetla could not afford to do that.

Azetla took a long, deep breath and forced his hands to fall loose at his side, not into fists.

"Regardless of what I do, or what they want to do, sir, the Corra is not going to lose interest in us, should we be so blessed as to succeed here. He wants southern *and* military allegiance, and if he has us, he gets a bit of both," Azetla said. "That's what this is all about."

"I don't understand. Lord Verris has no reason to question our loyalty," Hodge said.

"I don't think it's your general loyalty he wants. It's your specific loyalty. To the Corra," Azetla said.

"You mean as opposed to the Emperor?" Joseph said, turning a quiet and critical gaze toward Azetla.

Hodge narrowed his eyes as he fiddled with his knife hilt.

"The Corra is such a...a quiet, *submissive* man," the Captain muttered, with faint disgust. He knelt and jabbed the fire coals with the knife's tip, and seemed to find it satisfying. "He would never go against his brother. He barely dares to speak without Verris' permission."

Azetla shrugged slightly, a gesture that belied his confidence in the conjecture. "That may be precisely the line of thinking upon which Lord Verris is relying. And *him* you know to be capable. Weren't you at court with him?"

"I was at court with a lot of people, but I wish the court-mouths would stay in their arena and leave me to mine," Hodge growled, staring at the fire with stony eyes. "You two go on. Send in Brody if you see him."

One quarter hour after the end of second watch, Azetla sank to his pallet on the ground, muscles worn with tension. He took a few slow breaths as he blinked at the sky, the stars screaming bright in the clear desert black. He found himself mouthing a fervent, memorized prayer of thanks to his God, in Mashevi, pressing at the small wooden lion's head at his chest. It was a cheap, crudely carved bit of nothing, an old-fashioned, oft-disdained religious token. But it was of home, of his people, and of his God.

Azetla was losing count of how many times he'd been slipped out from under the knife. This being the least of them. He wondered if, in spite of everything he'd done and failed to do, the God of his people had not yet forgotten him.

8

Azetla slept deep that night, but woke early and wary.

Today's march would take them into the shallows of Sahr territory. That knowledge altered the air of their morning routine, bringing an unnatural silence among them in the gray-brown morning. They passed two small Makarish villages and a few goatherds, heads and faces covered to protect from the sun's heavy hand. After that, nothing. By the next day, the landscape had subtly changed under their steps. What had been an open, variable desert, laden with date palms and a soft, fine dust, had become wayward hills and crags with nettled shrubs that were a nuisance underfoot.

The land ached with emptiness. It drew raspy breaths across its rocks. Sharp, fallow, and rainless, it whispered with every crumbling pile of well-stones and barren grazing path that it had been abandoned. By people, certainly, but perhaps by the divine as well. It made Azetla's chest constrict as with a death, or a haunting. He had not realized how desolate South Makaria was. Most Makarish of the far south had migrated north or east to Trekoa before their camps were ever attacked by the devils, chiefly because of the terrible drought that plagued the area. Many thought the Sahr devils were to blame for that too.

It was yet another reason people thought them devils; how could human flesh survive so long under so severe a famine? Even Azetla had no answer for that. If any land was wild and cruel enough to hold jinn to the earth, this would be it.

Jinn was a useless word, anyway. So was "devil." Everyone took their own meaning, overlaid with their own beliefs. Made of fire, or made of magic. Dangerous by accident, or dangerous by power and malice. Possible to contain or possess, or as evasive as the wind. Imps, jumping about like dust in the wind, and just as quickly dispersed.

But surely the Sahr devils were no imps. The blood they spilled was real. Azetla had studied the Imperial campaign histories, and there were some brutal facts to be sifted out of all the fairytales. There was certainly the question as to whether this mission was meant to succeed at all. Riada had *wanted* this, but he always had contingent plans, layers of them, so that even when he lost, he won.

By the third day in outer Sahr territory, the hills grew taller and sharper. The ground pushed out scrawny plants that bit at the ankles and slapped at the knees. The pace slowed on the unfamiliar ground. The officers' horses had to pick their way through with tedious care as there was no path soft or wide enough for them. Most dismounted because of the way the rocks loomed above, like turrets.

That day brought their last sighting of South Makarish life: a goatherd with three emaciated agrimi goats. The herder paralleled the battalion for an hour or so, watching the soldiers through the folds of cloth wrapped thickly about his head. After that, the only evidence of any people, past or present, was the faint shadow of grazing circles on the softer hills far eastward.

The battalion formation fissured on the Sahr ground. As the hills cut more and more jagged before them until they were mere juts of rock, the vegetation thinned to thorns and spikes. The soldiers felt their disadvantage as they hugged the banks of the River Limila tributaries, which were lank and muddy. If the battalion was to be attacked by so much as a small raiding party they would find themselves fighting in the corridors between hills.

The terrain set itself hard against them.

Azetla finally stepped out of his place in the formation and fell in stride next to Captain Hodge's mount. It was where he belonged when danger was imminent and, though they looked on with contempt, none of the Corra's officers stopped him.

"Might have to send scouts just to find a good piece of ground for us," the Captain said after several minutes of the strange silence that had ruled the whole day. He glanced at Azetla out of the corner of his eye.

Azetla took his time in thought.

"So?" Hodge pressed.

The ground needed to be high and wide. And there needed to be more than one route of escape.

"That's all we *can* do. Daylight patrols only. And we shouldn't go any further than tonight's encampment either, regardless of what we find. The terrain is too unfamiliar, and we're stumbling all over it. We saw that goatherd this morning, so we can't be *too* far outside the realm of the living yet. We have to set ourselves up for a hasty retreat."

The Captain nodded with a long breath that said their minds were aligned in this matter.

They picked a camp while it was still light and sent several patrols on short circuits. Azetla selected the direction of the routes. Four groups of four, skilled, stealthy men armed with signal horns.

Two groups came back at dusk with nothing to report.

The third came not long after. The land is empty, they said. Empty as absolute death.

Azetla waited for the fourth patrol. He stood for an hour at the south end of camp, looking out at the blackened terrain, straining, straining to see what he wanted to see. But they did not come. Azetla decided to constrict the watch radius; they should assume the worst, just to be safe. Azetla told the Captain at once.

The patrol's absence, stretching out minute by minute, infected the camp atmosphere. It could almost be tasted on the tongue, and sensed thick in the lungs at every breath—not the right, grounded fear of battle, but that deep, dark dread of the numinous—of cold mists, sounds in the night, ghosts, and insanity.

It was possible—quite possible—that the patrol had nestled themselves into a safe place to hole up for the night and keep from becoming lost; rainless clouds had stolen across the sky and made the night black as a rook's wings. There were many other possibilities besides—an injury, a snake bite, a fall. Azetla waited until the middle of first watch, his eyes burning from trying to see through the dark. Part of him wanted to wait all the way through dawn for the last patrol, but he did not have duty that night, and it was Captain Hodge who always insisted, "If you give up sleep for the sake of worry and nothing else, you're a damn fool and I don't trust you."

Azetla had learned to skirt worry and go to sleep. Head to pallet, thoughts poured out, breaths steady.

He was wakened out of a dead sleep at the end of third watch. The shout in his ear and hand on his shoulder caused him to bolt upright before his eyes took in a thing.

"There's been an attack, but..." The watch officer, Lieutenant Sarrez, shook his head. "Collory is waking the Captain."

"But *what*? Tell me," Azetla said in a gruff voice, strapping on his weapons. "Was it the fourth patrol?"

"No, still no sign of them. But we've two dead *here*. That we know of. And it doesn't make any sense. Just...come see."

Sarrez led Azetla to the northeastern watch-post. Joseph was already there, turning over a body.

"Second Sergeant Dhebbo. The other is Lieutenant Kholse," Joseph announced.

The two soldiers lay within earshot of one another, throats slit cleanly. They had been discovered thus by their replacements as they came to take up third watch. Had they cried out, they would have easily been heard, which meant they had not been afforded the chance.

"I want more guards for the Captain," Azetla said.

If someone or something could come this close to camp and not be noticed, it could do much worse than that.

"And for the Corra. The Colonel?" Sarrez added.

Azetla nodded briskly.

"Wake them as well, and make them ready, but don't trouble them with the full account yet." Azetla glanced around and closed his eyes, picturing the whole encampment and the surrounding terrain in his mind's eye. "I don't think we can condense the camp much more than this, but we can double the watch. Somehow they...they got too far away from one another," he said, his voice rough in his own ears. "This should not have happened."

"I don't know how they were separated at all," Sarrez said, shaking his head.

Azetla ticked the edge of his thumb against his wooden lion's head, tucked carefully beneath his shirt. "I want a head count *now*, and two more men at each interval. Not earshot, close enough to *see*. Risk more fires. They already know we're here."

Sarrez nodded and went to task.

Within an hour, Azetla's men found four more bodies, already half cold. Two Lieutenants, a Senior Sergeant, and a young tackman, each having gone to different fringes of the watch-line to piss or crouch. Three of them had their throats slit like the others, but the fourth—the smallest in size—had his face ground against the dirt and rocks. He was dead of two deep stab wounds—one through the side of the neck and the other into the lung from behind. He alone appeared to have struggled. The boy's name was Piri; he was a debt-conscript like Azetla, and he'd been in the battalion less than a year.

Soon the whole camp was awake, waiting wide-eyed and taut-shouldered for daylight, ears strained for any and every sound. But the hours passed fruitlessly, carrying no hint of what it was that had slipped out of the dark and snuffed out six lives.

They saw nothing. Heard nothing.

The air changed around them, though. The dash of long black snakes and the rustle of sand foxes quickened the men's heartbeats as they never would have before. A thick, hot desert wind began to pour over the land when dawn came at long last. The Uhsar wind, the Trekoans called it. It was the wrong month for the Uhsar, and that was regarded by most as a very bad omen. It stirred the dust and choked the breath as if in alliance with whatever or whoever had attacked them.

Lord Verris, visibly unnerved, advised a ritual tribute to Serivash and Shouma; for blood and war. Each man was to prick a drop of blood for the Goddess and put it upon their shield or shoulder.

"Those that wish to do it may, but I will not command it," the Captain said.

"The power is in the unity of it," Verris said, glancing over at Azetla, who stood—as he now must—next to the Captain. "You make all your men vulnerable for the sake of one?"

"He is not the only one," the Captain growled. "But you may lead the tribute for those who honor the Goddess. I will."

Many a prayer and incantation were said that next night to many a god, from the pious and the indifferent alike. Dried blood spotted many shoulders. Even in the devils' land, the gods must have some sway, the men said. But Azetla heard an uncertainty in their voices, as if they could never be sure their gods were paying attention, or that their strength could reach so horribly far from Maurow, the center of their world.

At daybreak, they honored the dead by covering them in dust, rocks, and brush. They moved west to a place where the land flattened slightly after a rise—the least vulnerable Azetla could find.

It was midday when a scout finally found the fourth patrol. They were discovered in a jumble, like refuse. Two with slit throats, two others with stab wounds. The disrespect bestowed on the bodies was unsettling, especially to all the southerners, who would never leave even enemy dead for carrion. That was a sure way to curse one's self and one's tribe.

Dersha began to inspect the bodies. He crouched, wincing forward. Immediately, he leapt back in horror rubbing his hands across his clothes, as if scraping away evil, shouting Trekoan incantations against blasphemy, unholiness, and jinn. His revulsion contaminated the air, which hummed now with muttered prayers.

Azetla was silent, and not without fear. Slowly, he knelt in order to see what had so horrified Dersha. The tongues of each man from the fourth patrol were cut out and their eyes gouged from their skulls. No Trekoan or Makar would *ever* mar an enemy body thus unless they wanted divine wrath following them to the grave and beyond. Azetla knew this. Everyone knew this. This was one of the firmly shared beliefs among southerners.

The men were now convinced it was the work of a Sahr devil and, until evidence proved otherwise, Azetla could not gainsay them. He had rarely seen any marring of the dead, and that only in a distant northeastern province. The sight made him deeply uneasy. He wanted to cover their faces.

Laritonyans and Kourisads graciously dealt with the bodies so that the southerners wouldn't have to touch the tainted corpses. They tried to show the bodies the honor that had been so pointedly stripped of them. Azetla wondered whether the mutilation was threat, wanton cruelty, or ritualistic. The last thought nauseated him. *Devil, devil, devil,* his mind said, against his very will.

Night came again. Azetla stood watch command. The sky had cleared, and the moon showed with eerie brightness all the razored patterns of rock and shadow to the south. Azetla sifted his thoughts in the quiet. He refused to be certain of what had attacked them. But, they *had* avoided direct assault. Maybe they were few.

He hoped and prayed that it was true, but he had to plan as though it wasn't. He had to plan as though these were probing attacks. Rain before the flood.

Second watch turned to third. Third to fourth. Nothing.

In the morning, a few close patrols finally found a better shot of land to rest upon, and the battalion moved hurriedly through the early morning to set up their positions. All morning long there was hot, calming quiet. Some were lulled by it. The sun was high, blistering, and blinding, and the terrain defied their attempts to take the best of it. There was no *good* ground here. Only an eagle or an ibex could navigate the heights.

Azetla's searching eyes fixed on the gray spines and crooked trunk of a smokethorn tree. That seemed like a place a patrol could actually reach. Maybe. Not much cover, but a little, and good, clear sight in all directions. Perhaps if—

He heard a horribly familiar sound, and sucked in a breath, for that was all he had time to do.

The whistling arrow missed Azetla by less than a handbreadth, causing his whole body to rise taut as if yanked by a rope. As his left hand snapped to hilt, Lieutenant Connell took the second arrow in the bowels. Another cut into Sergeant Baze's throat.

The battalion jolted to action, rushing to assault the source of the arrows. But it was pointless.

The attack was over almost before it had started. Three plain, iron-tipped arrows, two men badly wounded. Could have been three. Azetla's heart was still pounding as he glanced back at the arrow shaft that had almost found its place in his ribs.

Arrows. Azetla's thoughts scattered for a moment, but he gathered them together quickly. Bows were not common weapons in the desert. There was little quality wood to be found, and woodcraft did not age well in the dry heat. Southerners had learned to use bows over time, but the weapon was not native to the region.

The attackers had fled long before the men reached the high finger of rock and earth out of which the smokethorn grew. There was no dust on the stones to show either print of foot or hoof. Azetla didn't believe it—he firmly told himself he didn't believe it—but it was as if the stories were true and these jinn were borne on the wind itself.

The battalion physician set to work on Connell, while Azetla sent out patrols to clear the area and set new lookouts, higher above. Four soldiers carried Baze's body—he died within minutes—over to a rocky burial. Azetla's jaw clenched as he caught sight of the woven sash Baze wore under his baldric because his wife "had sewn luck into it." Carried a bag of bird bones for luck too.

Azetla turned and picked up the arrow that had sought him, studying it. It was commonplace, to be found anywhere in Trekoa, Makaria, or Maurow. Useless. Told him *nothing.* He dropped it in disgust. He had never gleaned so little from a battlefield in his life. He felt as vulnerable as he did when he walked through the north streets of Piarago, which worried him; in Piarago he could not fight back.

Here, he must.

9

That night, after placing lookouts with ram's horns on the clefts, Captain Hodge called the senior men together. The Corra and the Colonel were not invited, but they took their attendance as assumed. The Captain could not deny them. He went through the motions to satisfy them, and the real meeting began after they had departed.

"Probing attacks. Still a possibility," Joseph said, although there was considerable doubt in his tone. "Which looks bad for us. If they have even half our numbers, the terrain will obey them and not us. Unless numbers don't matter to *them*."

Azetla narrowed his eyes, kneading his thoughts out before he spoke.

"I'm not entirely convinced that's what the enemy is doing," he said slowly. "If it were a probing attack they would at least sustain it long enough to see how strong we actually *are*, to test our lines, or to drive us to the ground they would have us die in. This enemy is gone before it even has a chance to threaten a breach, much less see how we reply to one."

Captain Hodge was quiet. There was an iron worry in his eyes, and he was looking off into the middle distance rather than at anyone in particular. It wasn't as though he hadn't lost men before. But they had always taken some blood back for what was stolen from them.

"It's almost as though the attackers were simply amusing themselves to no real purpose, like the devils in tales. Bored, aimless, or *mindless*," Sarrez said. He set his arms akimbo as if to force his body to a confident posture despite himself.

Azetla nodded at Sarrez's words.

"That was what I thought at first, but for one thing: most of our losses have been *of rank*. Seven of them officers. The rest were of senior common positions with years of authority under their belts and decorative rank panels. Tackman Piri was the only one who wasn't ranked and he appeared almost a mistaken kill. Not a clean one, anyhow."

"They aimed for you today, and you don't wear rank."

"Then either I'm wrong or the enemy is *very* observant."

"You keep saying 'enemy' as if we were dealing with something natural. Do you think this is anything other than the Sahr devils?" Joseph said. "Because I don't."

"I think it *is* Sahr devils," Azetla said slowly. "But whether or not they are natural is unknown, and beside the point. The one plain fact is that they're our enemy now."

Hodge took a deep breath and everyone turned to hear him. "We'll keep this piece of ground for ourselves so long as we're rationed—I think we have almost a week's worth—"

"Eight days at full rations, ten if we moderate," Azetla said. "Unless the tributary goes completely dry. Which it might."

Hodge nodded and continued. "We'll have to send out several more search patrols. It's either that or go back to Golmouth, and wait to make a new plan. Or cry mercy to the Emperor for failure. When and if we move, we do as we did in Susllai," Hodge added, dragging his hand across his stubbled, gray face.

In Susllai there were greener, softer heights, but they still forced the officers to go afoot and turn good horses into living armor.

Under such circumstances, Captain Hodge would not so much as walk to the food pot without his bay gelding serving as a wall for him. The men would move in packs, and each man in each patrol would have a ram's horn and keep only to runnable paths.

So they stayed. They kept watch and patrolled throughout the scorching, still day. They had sight from almost every angle, and men emplaced on the ridges as lookouts. Three retreat routes were planned, should they be needed. No signals or shouts passed through the parched air. They breathed in a crouching, tight-chested silence.

Hours passed, blank and eerie. Nothing but a few half-heard sounds that could have been anything. The land was brittle, crackling of its own accord.

Azetla wrapped his head in the Makarish style to keep the sun from striking him down, and many others did the same. He kept his eyes on the horizon of rocks as he worked his way from watchman to watchman, from west to east. The men gnawed, dry-throated, at their midday rations. The heat of afternoon bore down against them, making their worried eyes heavy and their words thick and tired.

The sun began to crawl away, leaving dusky light to confuse the eyes.

Then, a sound almost like a bird's cry. A single high yell, cut off abruptly. An instant later, one quiet arrow flew under the low sun, out from between the rocks. Azetla did not see where it struck, because he was already moving forward. More arrows followed, each one darting out moments after the other. The attack lasted just long enough for the men to fruitlessly gather form and mount a belated assault.

But, at last, there was a gain. Though he saw nothing and could not retaliate, Azetla now believed there was only *one* attacker. Always one single arrow at a time. There was no test of force and no hint of coordinated maneuver. Just careful and isolated aim. The enemy was taking each opportunity like a street thief, grabbing what blood it could steal, gone before the victim's head is turned, content to take a little here and a little there. As if Azetla's men were a game. The higher the rank, the more the prize, never mind that it could only take a few bites at a time.

Azetla felt his stomach turn with uncertainty. It was parching his throat, draining his patience, and pecking at his usually well-ordered thoughts. Of the six iron-tips the attacker sent, three struck, which was more than reason should allow for from distance and cover. One officer in the thigh, a senior sergeant through the ribs, and a new tackman in the meat of his arm, which he had flung across his chest.

But in the end, it was much, much worse than that.

Five watchmen, who had been placed as high, safe, and clear-sighted as Azetla could possibly manage, were found dead. It seemed almost certain they were killed before the arrows had flown. Three throats were slit, though this time the enemy had not spared the time to mutilate the corpses. One of the men was dashed down the east side of the ridge, leaving him a strange mass of flesh and broken bones. The last had been stabbed through the side of his jaw and torn open by several deep jabs to the stomach. He must have been the last and fought the hardest. He must have been the one who tried to shout warning.

The enemy had slaughtered their watch in daylight, and used their own lookout to fire down on them.

Azetla and several others searched the whole area and found nothing. The attacker was so quick. Quick enough to kill five and only let one half-shout hit the air. Quick enough to slither away like a snake into some hole.

Lieutenant Porter died within minutes. The battalion physician had tried to address the leg wound, but he found his hands hopelessly awash in the hideous gush that came of striking one of the "bloodrivers"—as the Trekoans called them—within the thigh.

It was almost a mercy the vein was struck. The Sergeant with the chest wound lasted several long hours and he was lucid nearly the entire time. It was an awful thing for a man to writhe there and watch himself die, feeling every last bit of it. Sergeant Arrick had hated Azetla, but he was of the Black Wren, he was a good soldier, and it was a sickening sight.

The Captain's horse had taken a scraping wound from the last iron-tip. There was no longer any doubt that the attacker understood rank. Rank panels had been removed after the first assault. But the attacker must have a good memory, and at some point, it must have gotten close enough to see in daylight. Azetla simply did not understand *how*.

Captain Hodge soon grabbed Azetla and pulled him aside. There was a skittering and straining in his eyes that was so terribly out of character for him. It worried Azetla more than all the tales of jinn stacked one on top of the other. His Captain was not a man easily shaken.

"What is it?" Hodge demanded, his voice low with anger. "Tell me."

Azetla was taken aback.

"What is *what*?"

"Stop it. Stop being cautious. I know you. You hold your tongue until you're sure, but you *always* have an idea. You said you think there's only *one* of...*it*...so what else? Tell me more than that. You always see *something*. Know *something*. Tell me what we're dealing with."

Azetla's mouth fell open, his eyes wide.

"Sir...other than what I've told you, *I have no idea*. None. I wish I did. I..." Azetla pressed out a long breath, rummaging through his mind as if he might find something he hadn't realized yet. "I don't know yet. A savage. A devil. A ruse. *I don't know*."

The Captain closed his eyes briefly as if realizing, all of a sudden, that what he expected of Azetla was not rationally possible. His voice calmed. "I just hoped you would have something more. A clear assessment. Because I don't bloody have one."

"I've told you all I can guess. All I know."

Captain Hodge rubbed his hands together and looked at the row of bodies, receiving their rites and a coarse, but honorable burial. A pyre was not permitted in the field of battle.

"Of course," he said quietly. "Just that fool thought. 'The jinn hate the jackals and the jack—'"

"It's just a saying, sir," Azetla said sharply. "I do think our problem is as much a matter of terrain as of devilry. We're at the mercy of the ground itself, no matter what the enemy is."

The Captain nodded, shaking away the tension. He seemed returned to himself, though it was as if he handed Azetla the apprehension he shook off. It troubled Azetla to see that desperate look in his Captain's eye, even though it had lasted only a moment.

As the sun slipped below the horizon, the soldiers that were not on watch spent the dusk hour chanting to the miniature copper or stone likenesses of their household gods. The thin, pungent smoke of many censers stung the eyes. There was a palpable fear in the air, and this was their way of excising it. Azetla sat on his pallet and watched quietly. Critically.

It was strange to see how dread of the otherworld could shiver the spines of so many honestly brave men. Let them face an army, or let them be tortured to death, but do not let their souls be tampered with, sullied, *destroyed*. Bodily fear and soul fear were such utterly different things.

Azetla still did not know if the Sahrs were real devils, but if they were, he was even more doubtful of the effect so many little stone gods might have on them. Stone-limbed lies, his mother had always called them.

In the old days, Mashevis did not tolerate foreign gods in any measure. The old kings banned the syncretistic temples of Maurowan gods. They belittled them. They had smashed their many likenesses to pieces.

Now it was the God of Masheva who was mocked and belittled, and though he had no likeness to destroy, the temple built for him had been burned long ago, the repair of it forbidden. It rested, a ruin. A holy one, but a ruin nonetheless. Much like Azetla's people. Or Azetla himself. But better that than bowing to the unholy grandeur of the Maurowan temples and their silk-storied, copper-covered gods—gods that were beautiful in form, empty of virtue, and held knives behind their backs that were peculiarly attracted to Mashevi throats.

All their incense Azetla held as a waste, all their gods he held as disgusting and worthless. He did not have to say this; it could be read from him. There were retreats he had been forced to make as a Mashevi, but there were fortresses he would never relinquish. And the Mashevi God was, even as the Maurowans claimed in contempt, a jealous God.

When the chants and incense dwindled, Azetla lifted his head and whispered his own memorized words of prayer. After the first stanza, little Dersha made his way out from among the others, and joined him. His mother was from the East Trekoan Atamlaq tribe, which had adopted Mashevi practices centuries ago. It shocked Azetla the first time the boy came alongside him. He was so used to being isolated that he had felt defensive and suspicious. But Dersha took the words seriously, and Azetla had slowly softened.

Sometimes there was greater resonance and comfort in the prayer when there was more than one voice.

Though Dersha spoke the prayer in South City slang, and Azetla recited classical Mashevi, they were the same words. The two of them together muddied their hands with spare drops of water and Azetla believed they were heard.

A few of the outsider officers watched with disdain, but Azetla could not bring himself to care. He would have done his prayers and rituals regardless—even had he believed not a word of them or preferred some other god—if only as some sort of desperate attempt to keep ties and stoke hope.

But he did believe the words.

"What do you think the Sahr devils *are*, Azetla?" Dersha said after they had finished their prayers.

Azetla laughed tiredly. They all desperately wanted him to know what he could not possibly know. But then, perhaps there was precedent for that.

"I don't know."

"What if they can't be found? Or if they can be? What will we do if we actually *see* one?"

Azetla looked at the boy, who wasn't really a boy anymore now that he had seen bloodshed and attack. His matted hair was tar-black and his teeth were in some kind of disagreement regarding which direction they should go. Thin and beardless, he looked young to bear a sword, though he was fully nineteen. Older than Azetla had been in his first battle.

"We'll catch it."

"Not *kill* it?"

"Well, I think we're supposed to trust the Emperor to do that for us when we return."

Dersha shook his head with derision. Azetla ought to have been more careful than to let the boy glean this hatred of the Emperor from him, but Dersha was so attentive and imitative. Whenever Azetla let some fraction of his contempt for Riada slip out of his mouth, Dersha hurried to take it up.

Azetla could have smiled at the boy. Instead he told Dersha to go to sleep, and trust God. Then he told himself the same thing.

The watch raised the alarm three times that night. But the attacker was frightened off or it was never there in the first place. Patrols came up empty-handed. The air felt dead and dry as bones as Azetla walked from one end of the camp to the other. He found an old Mashevi ditty in his mouth—a child's prayer-song that had an addictive rhythm to it. He didn't mean to whisper it, but it kept falling onto his tongue. Now he knew that soul fear was lurking round him, begging entrance, because he breathed those holy songs, in compulsive rhythm, as if they were charms of luck against that which comes out of the darkness. It wasn't true, but he wanted it to be.

Azetla let the little song swim through his mind, and cross over his tongue a few times, but then he made his mind quiet. The words were spoken. Now it was up to the One who heard.

When watch ended, Azetla went to receive word from the Captain.

"Did the last patrols find *anything*?" he asked Hodge as the Captain chewed a coffee bean for lack of spare water to boil.

Hodge shook his head tiredly.

"Nothing we can work with. They found some chobi leaf sprouting on a flat. Looked like it might have been cultivated..." He shook his head again, then stood, stepping out of his tent and into the guard of his men. "Azetla...I've had...a different thought."

"What?"

"Well. That the Emperor has sent his brother down here to dispose of him. That's mad. Isn't it?" The Captain's voice was scraped, hard, and weighted by sleeplessness.

"Actually it's very possible," Azetla said in a quiet voice. "The Corra did volunteer for this position, sir, as I understand. But perhaps, instead of denying him, Riada granted him his request without granting him the proper means."

"We aren't means enough?" Hodge said with a troubled smile.

Azetla did not answer. A soldier's piercing whistle shrieked from the south post, raising the alarm yet again.

Shouts followed, echoing from one watch-post to another. Azetla drew his sword and looked southward. Hodge took a sharp turn and began giving orders.

There came the wind-whipped sound of the arrow and the dull thud of it digging into flesh. The Captain's orders froze in his mouth. He collapsed to one knee, iron-tip buried deep in his back shoulder-blade, angled down into his gut.

There was one instant of sheer horror before the natural blood-rush of battle took over Azetla's body.

"Get him to shelter *now*!" he barked.

He ran hard, left hand at the low, ready, but came to an abrupt stop when he reached the base of the ridge.

It was then that he, and everyone, saw the source of the arrow. The archer crouched watchfully on the extreme edge of the eastern ridge—a precarious place that seemed impossible to reach. The assailant slung its bow in a languid motion and stood tall, its indistinct frame swaying with a spit of wind coming over the rocks.

It *wanted* to be seen.

Suddenly, it was clambering across the ridge, sure-footed as a mountain goat and lithe as a caracal, lower and lower as the ridge angled toward the flats. With the late morning sun behind it, fixing one's eyes on its position proved difficult; it was just a swift gray shadow obscured by glaring light. The eyes hurt trying to track it.

Azetla grabbed one of the lagging archers by the shoulder and dragged him forward to his position, while Joseph's squad began to advance toward the far end of the ridge.

"Shoot ahead and low," he shouted.

The archer let loose his first, while the other archers gathered and drew.

The first arrow flew awry of the attacker, accomplishing nothing. The way it moved—swift, sharp, and unreliable—seemed to deceive the eyes. Other arrows chased it, the last of which came very close to striking the enemy's feet, unbalancing it just as it nearly reached the bottom. The enemy wavered and tried to recover itself, but failed. It slipped on the rocks and tumbled violently down until it slumped, lifeless, at the bottom of the ridge.

The men froze. It was as though, the moment the enemy hit the ground, every throat was caught, and all sound was siphoned out of that long, miserable crag. The attacker lay still as death and the men stood still in shock.

Azetla tried to see, to analyze, to prepare. But there was nothing for it. He took the first step and gestured at his men: close in.

To his eyes, it looked like a human body and nothing more. But he did not trust his eyes right now.

"Careful, at the ready," Joseph told the younger tackmen who carried ropes to bind it.

They drew close until a dozen or so men surrounded the attacker, which bled from its scraped palms and elbows. It did not move.

Azetla drew his sagam and pressed the blade of it against the attacker's sprawled left arm. He dragged a long, shallow gash into its skin, down to the elbow. The creature's body gave a mild spasm, but its eyes did not open, and it did not cry out. It merely curled against the ground, face burrowed into the dust.

"There," Azetla said gruffly. "It's still alive. Ropes."

Owens and Dersha crouched to tie the creature at its wrists.

"Joseph, Sarrez: the watch, lookouts, camp boundary. Now. There could still be more."

The two soldiers were away in an instant.

Dersha muttered a Trekoan prayer as he handled the creature, visibly afraid of its unholiness and his proximity to it.

"Limp as the dead, God-have-mercy," he said as he tried to turn it from stomach to back.

It looked like nothing anyone would ever lose so many men to capture. Azetla stared half a moment, confused, uncertain.

The eyes opened. The body shot to life.

The arm that had been curled against its stomach struck out, digging a knife into Owens' thigh and ripping it out with an equally vicious motion. It thrust up from its knees and barreled into Dersha, driving the knife into him with the whole weight of its body. Azetla didn't even have time to watch the boy crumble down. He had the Sahr's arm in his grip, then he inexplicably lost it. Its knife nicked a tackman's shoulder as it tried to thrash out of the dozen grips that were now pressing it down like an avalanche.

It barely took the space of two breaths to contain it. Two horrible, bloody breaths.

A sergeant had its wrist firmly; he jerked the knife out of its hand with a sharp twist. A tackman had it locked by the elbow, another at the shoulder, and Azetla stood toe-to-toe, sagam at its gut. At his gesture, Collory came behind and put a knife at its neck. Fierce-eyed and wordless, the attacker stilled. Its gaze wandered across the faces of its captors in a slow, collecting way.

Dersha was heaving against the bloody ground, unable to rise. Eyes on the enemy, the kill order rested hot between Azetla's teeth. There was a livid fire in his chest, and it was burning him up to hold in the command.

He bit down hard on the words. Swallowed them.

"Alive" was what had been demanded. Alive it would be, by salt.

As they tied it up—almost tight enough to cut off the flow of blood—it buckled to its knees. Soon it sank entirely in their hands, as though its body had melted to water. Its weight became that of the dead, and it was too much doused in the tint and texture of blood for aught to be made of its appearance. As it collapsed, the clear and searching look in its eyes faded until it disappeared altogether, like a candle burned to the end of its wick.

When Azetla turned to Dersha, he was already unconscious. He probably would not wake. Azetla put pressure to the wound anyway, until someone came with bandaging. It was useless, *useless*, and he knew it.

The men asked him where to put the attacker. Azetla pointed to the water cart. He helped the men drag the captive across the rocks, like a dead animal with glazed eyes, and he hoped it felt every sharp stab of its own terrain.

10

James froze in his tent during the attack, his hand clutching at the hilt of an ornamental sword that he had not once used. He had never even tested the weight of it in a practice ring. Would that even *matter* if the devils burned through the ranks of soldiers, all the way to him? Did swords or skilled hands mean anything at all to jinn?

These thoughts galloped through his head, only settling into comprehensible form several minutes after, and much too late at that. James never so much as scraped a slit of his sword out of the scabbard. It all happened so dizzyingly fast and he only had time for his blood to pulse with fear and his hands to shake before he and Verris were told it was all over.

The Black Wren had caught *something*.

Before James chanced to see or ask anything, the whole encampment was in a swift, silent welter of activity that he did not remotely comprehend. Verris tried to interpret it for him, but he did not seem terribly sure of himself. Verris had drawn his sword when the alarm sounded and stood guard over James along with the others, but he was terrified. His voice still shook a little, though he tried to hide it.

Slowly, James began to grasp the hurried movements of the soldiers. His own tent was packed away before him. Lead Sergeant Radabe led the perimeter defense while Lieutenant Sarrez was set to command guard over Verris, the wounded, and James himself. With astounding quickness, snakehole fires were doused, equipment was assembled, and the marching formation coalesced in a northward direction. As soon as it was whole, it began to move.

It took James a moment to realize what this actually meant: whatever they had caught, it had satisfied them. Or, at least, given them sufficient excuse for retreat.

James had no notion of protesting. None whatsoever. He would have poured out much more than a drop of blood to the Gods so as to get out of Sahr territory as quickly as possible.

He felt all but invisible as the soldiers pushed out. He was glad that no one feigned to pay him heed just now. He didn't know what he should be doing and even Verris, for all his pride, was not fool enough to pretend that his rank was anything but a bright piece of embroidered cloth attached at the right shoulder of his tunic. He asked questions, but never tried to give an order.

James knew he could not do as Verris had asked and "assert some authority" while still permitting the men to do as they must. He didn't know what the creature covered in blood and rope was—jinn, beast, or savage. He didn't know how far outside of the devils' lands they must go before they were safe.

The only fact that was clear at present was that the Rinayim-born jackal was in full command. Even James could see it now. The danger had forced the real nature of his role in the battalion completely out of hiding. It happened without a word being said, easy as touching flame to pitch and watching it spread in silence. There was no more pretending among the men or from the jackal himself now that the Captain was wounded. The jackal gave orders. He looked high-bloods in the eyes. They were swift to obey.

No one seemed to care what the consequences of this might be.

Captain Hodge was borne on a stretcher made of tent canvas and stripped pikes. The men who carried him tried to move smoothly over the narrow path so as not to jar his body, but it was difficult and the pace was rushed. Despite their efforts, he began choking on his own blood not long after departure. The jackal hovered near his Captain, looking hard and furiously at the man's blood-drenched bandage and paled skin. He compulsively—and uselessly—reached out to steady the stretcher as he walked alongside it.

James felt queasy and tired and anxious. He could see what the jackal saw; Hodge would be dead before the sun rose next morning. The half-Trekoan boy—James hadn't the faintest idea of his name—would last longer. A few days, perhaps, because he had rallied briefly and that was unlucky for him. Most of the other soldiers had been blessed enough to die quick deaths.

The comforting rhythm of the march had settled into James' blood and his mind gone rather quiet when he heard the Mashevi's voice cut through the rumble of the march.

"Banners down!" he shouted. The signalmen passed the order. Every standard of battalion, company, house, or tribe was lowered, as were the signal flags. The officers covered their ranks and tucked away their pommel cloths. The men quieted until nothing could be heard but footsteps and the brush of cloth and leather. It was eerie how close to silent so many moving men could suddenly be. They had even slowed, and James slowed with them, confused.

The Mashevi walked through the narrow corridors of the formation to Captain Hodge's mount. The look on his face put a pain in James' chest. It was a hard look to mistake; it was that of a man trying desperately to maintain decorum when all he wanted to do was drop to the ground, head in hands. But the Mashevi's countenance and steps held steady.

The Mashevi untied the pommel cloth, which represented Hodge's house, and pulled the baldric from his saddlebag. With painful precision and care, he draped the implements over what James now realized was Captain Edmund Hodge's dead body. The porters of the stretcher had become as men taking a Lord and his trappings to a pyre, and their bearing reflected it. The jackal and

Lead Sergeant Radabe walked on either side of the stretcher: jackal on the left, Lead Sergeant on the right.

The pace eventually recovered, but the long, hard march toward dusk was completed in a funerary hush. James was in awe. He had known little enough of Captain Hodge—naught but what he saw in these last weeks, and what Verris had told him—but he felt that he now knew who the man was. This was a reverence earned, and unforced. It was a fearless, filial honor, so unlike that which was paid to Riada and theoretically owed to James himself.

It made James feel weak. Deficient. Would he ever be seen thus? Could he ever inspire this depth of loyalty? Could he lead thus? Could he ever be something other than Verris' construction?

By the Gods, and by every drop of James' blood, he had to learn how. And the heavy, tiring truth was he didn't *want* to. He dreaded it down to his very bones.

After all, Hodge may have been loved and honored—but he was also dead.

When the Black Wren made camp late that night, Azetla finally took a long, full look at the assailant. It lay in the water cart like a dead creature. It did not look at anyone, nor did it make a sound. Not when a tackman dashed water over its head. Not when soldiers touched copper to its skin to allay or confirm their private superstitions. Not when Azetla brought a torch one handsbreadth from its face, so that he could get a clear look.

At first glance, there was nothing inhuman about it. It wore threadbare southern flax-cloth and shabby goatskin leather. It had no armor. On its neck it wore something akin to a Trekoan slave band: a thin, limned leather collar that was complimented with one on the left wrist and the left foot. It was covered in blood, both from its own wounds and from those it had killed.

It had skin the color of cinnamon bark, just like any South Makar, and a tangled length of black-brown hair. The face was clean of beard or scruff, as though it was either very young, or female. There were tribal tattoos on the shoulder and the right hand. The hands themselves were scraped, calloused, and common as anything.

It looked like a ragged no one, an unbelievable nothing. But that did not signify much. A Sahr it may well be, but Sahr devils could easily be other than all that was believed of them.

Most things were.

To Azetla, it did not even matter. Let it be any of a hundred things; it had attacked, it had slaughtered, it had taken Azetla's closest ally from him, and now it was captured. That was what could be known.

And there it was, lifeless. It didn't seem to notice or care about any of its injuries, as apathetic toward its own blood as it was toward everything else. So *much* had been lost for this creature, this thing that was not even horrific enough in form to justify their fear of it.

What a waste.

Good soldiers. Little Dersha. And the Captain.

It wasn't only Hodge as a commander, or Hodge as a comrade-in-arms. It was all the hope Azetla had put in him. He had been Azetla's advocate. His chance. It was almost impossible that anyone would ever give him that much ground under his feet again. Azetla had lost his Captain, and—cold, cruel thought—his only real protection.

Sarrez walked into the ring of firelight near the water cart. Azetla took in a stiff breath and raised his shoulders.

"Watch is set," he said. "Radabe is almost done. He'll be by shortly."

Azetla nodded, his jaw iron, eyes still fastened to the creature in the cart.

"Still breathing, is it?" Sarrez asked with contempt in his voice.

Yes, it breathed, but that was all. He wanted it to bloody wake up, *look him in the eye*, and account for itself. Let it stand up so that he could bring it down, so that he could make some kind of sense of it. He needed to know what he was dealing with.

"It'll be pus and rot soon," Sarrez said.

Azetla tapped his cedar lion sharply and nodded.

"Send for Detalos," he said.

The battalion physician came quickly, but stood at a wary distance until Azetla told him what to do. "Wash its wounds with water and whatever else you have on hand. Bandage it too, and...examine it."

Together, they rinsed the creature, flushing the wounds with arak. The Sahr tautened and twitched when the alcohol was thrown onto each raw, red scrape or gash, but that was all it did.

Detalos was uneasy with the task. He touched it as though fearful of infection, whispering to the goat-god of Golmouth all the while. Soon, he blanched. He gestured for Azetla to take a look. On the Sahr's back, where the flax was torn, there were long, thick scars, forming a crude pattern. At the outer edge of its shoulder on either side, heavy indentations of slightly discolored skin ran in a straight line. The scars continued straight across the tops of the shoulders and—when the physician dared for half a moment to peel the cloth back and look—they cut down the length of the spine.

Azetla had never seen or heard of ritual marring among southerners. Other far-flung places of the world, yes, but in the south it was seen as a vile practice.

"By blood," Sarrez muttered under his breath. Azetla could see the conclusion forming in Sarrez's eyes: this is something unnatural.

They watched the physician circle the Sahr, nervously, doing his job with utmost reluctance, reciting his findings with uncertainty. Finally, Azetla told Detalos he could go; the murmuring incantations grew aggravating. Azetla continued the examination himself.

The Sahr's actual height was difficult to ascertain, crumpled as it was, but it was not thickly built. The muscles were strong and taut beneath its shoulders, but they were not quite those of a grown man.

Detalos had suggested this was due to it being a female of its kind, and Azetla was inclined to agree. Azetla did not know what, if anything, that meant. All in all, its wounds turned out to be slight, its breaths remained steady, its expression empty. Again, he found himself desperately trying to read a blank page.

"Azetla, I have to report back soon," Sarrez said. "I can't keep Lord Verris and the Corra happy for much longer. I've run out of polite, respectful ways to tell them to keep quiet and do as we say."

Azetla nodded. "I'll take care of that. Nothing from the scouts?"

"Not yet," Sarrez said, instinctively holding himself in defensive posture as he looked at the Sahr.

"I wish we could just kill it," Azetla said quietly.

"No knowing that we even *can*. But we have to keep something for our loss, Azetla."

"I know."

Azetla drew in a slow breath and leaned closer to the Sahr.

"But there's a chance we may have nothing as it is," he said. "Sarrez...what do you think?"

Sarrez did not even answer. He just shook his head and shrugged.

They both stood quiet. Azetla narrowed his eyes, searching, scouring, hoping to find some reasonable, clear column in which to set this Sahr. He hesitated a moment, then snatched up one of the Sahr's tied hands, pulling the creature in his direction. It tensed a little, animal-like. An animal that was either too tired or too smart to fight, but which instinctively recoiled from a foreign hand.

"Azetla! Gods and devils, stop *provoking* it! Are you mad?"

"Look at this," Azetla said. "Do you know which tribe does this?"

Faint black marks curled up the back of the Sahr devil's right wrist and hand, trickling over its thumb, like the tattoos of the South Makarish.

Sarrez glanced warily at the markings. He frowned and shrugged away from the Sahr slightly.

"I saw that, yes, but the Sahr is *not* Makarish. Few tribes mark themselves that way anymore," Sarrez said. "Shimlai, or Uoloya maybe. I'm not sure. But that mark on the upper arm, though. That's Trekoan. Those slave bands. Those are Trekoan too."

"That's what Nasla told me. Saqirani tribe, he thought."

Azetla released the Sahr devil's hand. Its fingers twitched, and it slumped back to where it had been, eyes staring hazily ahead at nothing.

Sarrez shook his shoulders back as if shaking off a sense of horror.

"Why is it marked like every damn thing? It's not Trekoan *or* Makarish. Maybe not human at all," he said through his teeth.

"It can bleed. We know that much," Azetla said.

"Maybe devils bleed, then. We don't know *anything*."

Azetla granted that with a heavy breath. He folded his arms across his chest and glanced at the guards set to watch the Sahr.

"Come get me if it so much as makes a sound. Canty is the watch officer. Collory is second. I'm at the north watch."

⚬⎯⎯ ⅏ ⎯⎯⚬

Wesley had been too slow to act and now he didn't know what to do. Without request or warning, the Mashevi simply walked up to the Corra's tent, bowed, and gave courtesy. Then he ignored Wesley and spoke directly to James.

"Your Highness, forgive me for not having approached you sooner, but it was a matter of protocol. We will do as you say, Your Highness, and I must put the question to you now."

The Mashevi clasped his hands behind his back and waited, his gaze respectfully tilted downward, his shoulders sloped as if to camouflage his frame and all the authority he carried upon it.

"What question?" James said, wide-eyed, before Wesley could chance to intervene.

"Do we take our captive for a true Sahr—as most of my men hold—and continue our retreat? Or do we go back and try again? Is there a certain number we must acquire? We must go by your word, Your Highness, for indeed this is your mission."

Wesley clenched his teeth and stepped forward, hurrying to relieve James and take the conversation in hand, for James would give what he ought not give, and approve what he did not understand. There was no overt sarcasm in the Mashevi's voice, but Wesley *felt* it from him. The jackal was not asking, he was telling in disguise. Wesley did not believe for one minute that he cared what the Corra thought about anything.

But James seemed to think he did. His eyes were wide, his lips parted, as though he were mesmerized by the mere asking. And that was dangerous.

"Your Highness, this jackal is—" Wesley began.

"Your men think it is a devil?" James said, still looking at the jackal.

"Yes, Your Highness, they do."

"This is a matter—" Wesley tried once again, but James took no notice of him.

"And you?" James asked, utterly transfixed.

"I think it is a native of the land out of which it came, Your Highness. I know nothing beyond that, but I can tell you what I would advise."

"And what is that?" James asked eagerly, sounding so naïve and trusting it pained Wesley.

Gods and devils. He was giving the jackal *legitimacy* by responding to him thus. Oh and the jackal knew it full well.

"I would take it to the Emperor," the jackal said. "I would tell him all that happened in plain words, and let him cut its throat in whatsoever manner he chooses, Your Highness."

Well. That was the right answer, only it had come from the wrong bloody mouth.

James glanced at Wesley for approval. Slow and stiff, Wesley nodded. How could he counter what he himself had intended to say?

A scant minute later, James had issued the formal order with something vaguely resembling authority. March on. The task is accomplished. We have our jinn.

11

The battalion was on its feet again well before first light. Sarrez managed the high-bloods, since he was best suited to them, and Joseph had command of the rear guard. Azetla set a hard pace and kept his eye on the prisoner, which remained silent and motionless in its cart.

As dawn broke to herald a hot day, a warning signal arose from the rear guard but was quickly allayed. Azetla fell back to hear the report.

"A stray horse. Riderless," Joseph said. "Very suspicious, obviously. The men are retrieving it now."

The horse was a tall Trekoan-bred buckskin dun, with a West Trekoan-style sword attached to its South Trekoan saddle. Makarish-made reins. Sarramai saddlebags. Strong, well-cared for, and entirely inexplicable. It was hard not to associate the equine anomaly with the devilish one tied up in the cart.

Azetla had the horse taken straight to the Sahr so that he could see how one or the other of the creatures might respond.

He wondered if he imagined the faint jolt of tension in the Sahr devil's shoulders when he brought the horse near it, or the wakefulness in its eyes as it kept them fixed on the wooden slats, never allowing them to look up at the horse's head which was hanging and snuffling over it.

But the horse gave its compatriot away easily. It smelled the prisoner in the cart then whinnied sharply and tossed his head. It pressed its nose against the Sahr devil's ribs, lively with affectionate recognition. At last, it was wrangled away and put under the care of the head groomsman. Saqirani and Janbari horses like this were walking wealth. A man could live comfortably for a year with the price of a Saqirani-bred horse, and a battalion could eat well for some weeks by the same.

The delay was brief, and the battalion pushed on through the heat of the day. They did not stop when dark fell, but walked steadily on under the three-quarters moon as the ground grew kinder beneath their feet. They held the pace until dawn, when the city of Golmouth came into view beyond Wadi Iffar. It was only a dark brown haze on the horizon, but the sight of it seemed to cast safety over the other soldiers like a soft net.

Not over Azetla, though.

Once the battalion was truly safe, Azetla would no longer be. Lord Verris and the Corra had been tolerant only because they had been vulnerable. Each day north diminished that vulnerability. Arriving in Piarago would erase it entirely.

Azetla had no idea what he was going to do.

He remembered the Captain ordering him to leave the battalion once the mission was completed. To keep safe. He felt an abrupt flash of anger break above the low-simmering, task-oriented irritation in which he had been walking all day.

Anger at a dead man for having suggested such a thing.

Anger at a dead man for being dead.

Anger at things over which Hodge could have had no control.

And then, as with a fever breaking, it wasn't anger anymore—just that soft, useful bristle of frustration, with something heavy and hollow lying underneath.

Exhaustion smote them all when they took camp in the shadow of Golmouth. Azetla did not lay down on his pallet until all was in order and he did not particularly remember laying down at all, so abruptly did sleep take him.

The following night, the soldiers finally made a belated funeral blaze for the dead. It was as like a pyre as could be managed. Though only two bodies burned in it—Dersha and Captain Hodge—the pyre stood for all who rested under piles of rock in Sahr territory.

The men relished fresh rations of wine and arak that night. They relished the memory of their Captain in loud voices and low song. The songs were mostly southern, the pyre and rites were a remnant of old North Maurowan custom, and the poetic homages were Black Wren tradition.

Azetla did not drink that night. He listened respectfully to all the northern rites, but did not partake. Afterward, he sat amid the men, the watchfire blazing uncomfortably against the right side of his face, the night sky beyond him a soft, soft black.

The Captain was a man utterly without fear, one of the younger ones said.

No, Azetla thought. He was better than that. A man who leads others must, without a doubt, bite the fear and taste it—just a little. It reminds his body that his mind is responsible for more than his own skin. Hodge had told him that and Azetla had found the truth of it on every battlefield.

But let them give their eulogies. Let them mythologize a man not two days dead. If it helped them.

Azetla would not. He kept having to unclench his teeth. That strange, seething anger kept returning till it could be tasted in his mouth, and felt in his ribcage. He tried to focus on the words around him.

The men told stories now. Some absurdly embellished. Out of their mouths, the Captain was an even greater man than he had been in life. He was bold. He was honorable. Brilliant. Flawless. Matchless. Fearless. Practically a god.

Azetla hated it. He couldn't stand when dead men were made out to be better and holier than men could be, leaving everyone after them blindly beholden to the legend. He had seen it become a deadly thing, foolish and horrible acts done in the name of men far less worthy than Hodge. Azetla preferred the mottled truth.

Captain Hodge had a temper and a profound disregard for protocol. He never played politics, and was not the most tactful man. He was—had been, rather—brilliant in the moment of disaster, but did not always perceive the larger scale of events. Ruthlessly protective of his men, yes, but somewhat neglectful of everything else. And he had been better than a father to a stiff, taciturn Mashevi boy that he had never wanted in the first place.

That was Captain Hodge.

And suddenly Azetla was so exhausted, he could barely keep his eyes open. Every thought he had staved off tumbled over him all at once. The words were starting to haze over his head, and he wished they were in Mashevi. As he pressed out his pallet, his focused control seemed to fall out of his hands.

What replaced it—trickling in slowly as he brushed gravel out from under the canvas—shocked and overwhelmed him. Cold, plain bereavement began hollowing out his chest, jabbing at his ribs, and stinging in his eyes. He was thankful his back was turned to the fire and lively faces. He wiped his hands hard across his eyes, as if that would make any difference.

The foolish, arrogant Mashevi boy who had come into the Black Wren over a decade ago could never have guessed that it would matter to him whether or not this Maurowan Captain died. He might even have wished him dead, in the beginning.

Now Hodge was *gone*. All his kindness toward Azetla, all his trust, all the times he looked him in the eyes as an equal—all of it was gone.

And this was Azetla's fault. In a way. He had done what he had to do.

Azetla had *pushed* Hodge toward Verris knowing that Verris was a man of no trivial aims. There were others like him, but Verris had been the easiest and most advantageous to access. The hungriest. That connection was supposed to have provided information. Small opportunities. Azetla had pressed and plied, and had done it slowly and shrewdly. He had used all his thin stores of subtlety. Of course, the Captain had listened, because he had trusted Azetla.

Whether or not he should have was a question Azetla preferred not to think about.

But now Azetla owed a dead man a debt he could never repay. That thought pulled a little of the anger back to the surface, but not enough to feed itself. It petered out almost instantly. He was too tired, too full of other thoughts, and too sick of sifting through them. The soldiers' voices dwindled and faded about him.

He woke sharply with a salt taste in his mouth, eyes reddish and dry. His chest still ached, as though his body intended to remind him of loss even when his mind had not yet thought of it. The eastern sky was a dull gray-yellow, and a few of the men had already begun to stir. With a slow, stretching stride, Azetla walked over to the dead watchfire and—hesitating only a moment—he grayed his head with a handful of ash.

He had never done traditional Mashevi mourning for a foreigner. It was a strange thing for him to do, and strangely calming. It was, if nothing else, the truth.

"Time to make it walk," Azetla said, looking over at the Sahr. "We need the cart for resupply."

Obediently, young Corporal Nuss looped out some slack in its bonds while Azetla cut the ropes from its feet. They kept the restraints on its neck and hands tight. It still hung half limp as Azetla pulled it out of the cart and let it sink to the ground.

"Well. If it wants to be dragged, it can be dragged," he said.

It sat still on the rocky ground, shoulders hunched, as the men filled casks from the nearest cistern. Azetla instructed one of the men to dash some water over the Sahr to rinse the coating of dust and its own muck, and then had Detalos clean and dress its wounds again. None of this elicited a response. Sometimes Azetla thought he saw its eyes move, but he was not sure. It breathed, so it was alive, and sometimes it adjusted itself, shifting a shoulder or stretching its neck. That was all.

Once the cart-horse took its first step, however, the creature rose noiselessly to its feet and began to walk an even stride. It was fast enough to keep the rope from pulling on its arms and nimble enough to pick its way over rocks or divots on the rough Golmouth road. Its eyes were slightly wakened to the task of movement. But it still did not respond to shouts, orders, or threats, no matter the language used.

Food and water for the creature was another matter. The first day or two they grudgingly forced water down its throat and no one minded watching it sputter and cough. Eventually, they set a bowl of water by it and waited until it slowly wrangled the vessel up to its mouth with its tied hands. They did the same with scraps of food.

Azetla had Detalos inspect it intermittently. Twice a day, the Sahr devil was taken to the River Limila and dragged to waist-deep water, permitted to do whatever it must, then plunged under a few times for good measure. They felt reasonably confident that it swallowed enough water in the process, and it kept the Sahr from reeking. It also fostered many a vulgar joke, as the dousing and proximity caused those who had not yet noticed to perceive its sex.

They would have killed it twenty times over if Azetla had let them, or beat it, or worse. He gave it no kindness, spared it no difficulty, but he did protect it from active harm. There were protocols for live prisoners, and Azetla had always been rigid about such matters. Moreover, he agreed with Sarrez: it served no one, least of all Captain Hodge, to come back empty-handed.

It remained, by all appearances, apathetic. Maybe it would simply atrophy like many animals in captivity. Or perhaps it was simply very patient.

Patience was a valuable weapon, Azetla knew.

From the crumbly South Makarish hills to the groomed roads of North Makaria on the border of old Maurow, it gave no meaningful evidence of itself. The men walked a hard pace. So did the Sahr. The men talked. The Sahr never made a sound. No hiss, no howl. No twisting about. It walked a calm, smooth stride as though that was the only work it was ever made to do in all its life. Try as Azetla might, he could glean nothing from it.

They were nearing Piarago now, anyhow. The Sahr would be handed over to Riada, to be disposed of as he pleased. But Azetla still did not know what would happen to *him*. He stood to lose his battalion. His sword. Maybe his life.

Joseph said that he should obey their dead Captain's orders and "*run*." But Azetla reminded Joseph that the Captain had, in almost the same breath, bid him "keep to his tasks."

It was thus that Azetla—as much subject to his own system of order as anyone else—found himself serving Sahr guard duty during the last night of the return journey, alongside Sergeant Isilia. By dusk tomorrow they would be marching through Piarago. Azetla shifted his shoulders. He combed through his plans for one contingency and another. None satisfied him.

Azetla glanced at the cart a few meters to his left. The Sahr stared, as if unseeing, at its own feet. There was just enough slack in its rope for it to slide down and sit, but instead it stood, leaning slightly against the cart, blinking its eyes only rarely and slowly, like something that was losing consciousness.

"Gods and devils," Isilia muttered. "What do we have, Azetla? Oh it's been half dead these days, but it moved like a snake that first time, you remember. Like a bloody spirit."

"I don't know. I really don't," Azetla folded his arms and glanced west. "Look lively, here they come."

Lord Verris and the Corra James approached for their formal rounds. Isilia and Azetla lowered their heads in deference.

"All is safe and secure, my lord, Your Highness," Isilia said.

"Sergeant, I want to be certain that the camp is in order. Go on patrol," Verris said crisply, though he looked at Azetla while he said it.

Isilia stared in confusion. "My lord?"

Azetla tipped his eyes at Isilia, giving the Sergeant leave to go wherever and do whatever he pleased. This was nothing to do with order, or a meaningless patrol. This was to do with him.

Isilia threw Azetla a nervous look and departed. Lord Verris waited, glancing out at so many pallets that held so many sleepers as if to ensure that they were still, quiet, and well out of hearing.

He gave Azetla a dry smile.

"You know, for a man brash enough to take command in full view of His Highness the Emperor's brother, you could probably exempt yourself from night watch and digging privy trenches."

"I've never had the right to do that, my lord. Nor the need," Azetla said calmly. "What is it you wish to speak to me about?"

"Not I, Mashevi. His Highness, the Corra, wishes to speak with you."

Verris gestured toward James Sivolne who stepped forward, looking characteristically uneasy. His fingers fidgeted against his palms and his eyes searched over Azetla, as if looking for sympathy.

"Your Captain..." James cleared his throat and lifted his chin with a slight jerk. "There is a chance that your Captain will be replaced from among the ranks of the Emperor's Army, rather than from within like under the old system. If Riada's Generals are given the task, whoever they choose is not likely to tolerate your presence here. His favorites usually like to match his hatred for Mashevis, as I've noticed," James said, in a bewilderingly casual tone. "And he does not entirely trust the old battalions."

"I'm aware," Azetla said flatly. He paused a moment, but made himself finish the sentence properly, with a slow nod, "...your Highness. Men like Lord Captain Hodge are difficult to replace, and the Black Wren will not be what it was with any such man as Emperor Riada would choose."

James nodded in a loose way, his expression pinching as with a thorny thought.

"Well, there is no guarantee—the Emperor will do as he pleases—but perhaps the Colonel and I will manage to take hold of the Black Wren. If it were put to you, who among your men would you place in Hodge's position?" James asked.

"I am already in his position, so, once you discard me, you mean?" Azetla said in a quiet voice. This made James visibly uncomfortable. "I would put forth Lead Sergeant Joseph Radabe, Your Highness. Without question."

"He's a common-blooded man," Verris interjected.

"I gave a plain answer for a plain question from the Corra, my lord," Azetla said, glancing over at Verris. "I would put Lieutenant Sarrez as his second."

James fidgeted, narrowing his eyes. "You speak as though we've already slit your throat and tossed you into the river."

"I speak as though Emperor Riada will supersede you regardless, and this battalion will be doled out piecemeal until it is useless to you, Your Highness. Moreover, I speak as though we're a day's march from Piarago and Captain Hodge is dead," Azetla said. It took work to hold his voice steady. "Let us not be coy about what that means."

His heart beat a little faster than it should, and no manufactured coolness of voice or manner could slow it down. He was blunt—dangerously so—because he did not have any way around it. There was no one to rely on, and no place to lie in wait until this trouble passed over. He had to do something *now*. He had to convince them that he was useful. That they needed him. Which they didn't. Nearly everything he could say would make him seem pleading and put him even more at their mercy. He needed a subtlety beyond his present capacity. He needed a thousand things he did not have at hand.

All he could think to do was say the plain truth with level eyes and a clear voice.

"I have earned my place, whether I wear a rank panel or not. I know you can cut me out of it, but it will leave a mark. Every loss does, and we've already had too many."

James glanced rather nervously at Lord Verris, pressed his lips together, and stepped closer to Azetla.

"I am not a military man, Mashevi, but I do believe it would leave a mark. In fact, I'm not certain we would retain the good will of the Black Wren if we were to do what really *ought* to be done..." James gave what Azetla supposed was meant to be a poignant look. Then his expression lapsed and he gave a half-shrug. "There are only a handful of your men who would be glad to get rid of their jackal. Far fewer than I would have thought."

Azetla bricked in his surprise. What was this? Verris didn't seem to know either. His gaze narrowed, his posture straining under the Corra's words as though they were not quite what he had expected, or not quite what he had planted in the Corra's mouth beforehand.

"What His Highness means to say is—" Verris began.

To Azetla's profound shock, the Corra held up his hand for silence. It was an unusually Sivolne gesture, and accomplished with a very Sivolne irritation.

"I'm tired, jackal...which you'll understand. Sore, through and through. I really don't want to play parries and jabs right now, and I can tell you don't either. So know this: for the time being neither

I nor the Colonel shall make official note of there being a Mashevi soldiering in the Black Wren. Nor will we yet inhibit whatever authority your own have seen fit to give you. I will let your Captain's judgment hold until I find reason to disagree with him," James said, with a bizarre laxity of tone that indicated he might not fully realize the gravity of his own words. Verris had almost turned to stone. James did not seem to notice. "You cannot deem that ungenerous."

Azetla couldn't deem it anything at present. But he did have confidence in James' utter inability to be coy or coercive.

"To your health and honor, Your Highness," Azetla said slowly, with a bow of assent.

The Corra glanced at Verris—some doubtfulness returned to his countenance—but he said nothing more before leaving the post. Verris remained with Azetla.

"The Corra has high ideals," he said.

That was a fine high-blood way of saying the Corra was utterly naïve, which Azetla knew full well.

"I respect high ideals, my lord."

"But they have to be offset by reality, don't they?" Verris said. "As with your Captain, you are only as safe as he makes you, as long as he wishes to."

Azetla looked Verris in the eyes.

"Health and honor, my lord," he said in as bland a tone as he could manage.

Lord Verris stepped back to take his leave. "I think you understand me very well, jackal."

When he had gone, Azetla let out a long breath and ran his hand over his face. Through force of habit, he felt for the little cedar lion's head. He tapped it pensively with the side of his thumb. He ran his eyes across the encampment, as if thoroughness and dutifulness would give him something to hold onto.

This time, it did.

The Sahr was watching Verris walk through the low forest of pallets and sound sleepers, its posture altering before Azetla's eyes. The listless slump melted off. When Verris was no longer visible, it tilted its head and looked at Azetla.

"You know Mashevi, the only reason I'm still alive is because your desert god has a cruel sense of humor, and I'm starting to think the same is true of you. I mean, they keep *snapping* at you, but they never quite bite, do they?"

12

The Sahr spoke just loud enough to be heard by Azetla, but not by any of the sleepers strewn just across the clearing.

Azetla stood rooted to the spot.

It spoke in Maurowan.

Clear, classical Maurowan with no trace of the south on its tongue. *Azetla* could not speak Maurowan like that, even after all these years.

Slowly, steadily, Azetla walked toward the Sahr till it was forced to tilt its head upward to keep looking at him.

It was an entirely different creature now, its dark eyes full of life as they had not been these many days, its posture relaxed and untroubled. A horrified amazement shivered over Azetla's skin.

Of course. Of *course*. It had been playing dead in every possible way.

The Sahr did not seem bothered by Azetla's looming over it or by his prolonged, half-involuntary silence. It gave a faint, cool smile.

"Yes, Mashevi, *it speaks*," the creature said, slow and sly. "When it wants to."

Azetla narrowed his eyes.

"And, yes, I am a '*Sahr*.'" It spoke the last word with derision, exaggerating the nasally North Piaragoan pronunciation. It breathed a slight laugh after the word. "Insofar as that's what northerners call us. But I don't know if I am what you think a 'Sahr' is."

Azetla scoured the creature's face for something he could understand.

"Why did you keep silent like an animal until *now*?" Azetla asked, noticing that its fingers twitched rhythmically against the ropes. He did not know if it was truth, myth, or the darkness of the night speaking, but he did not like to see it moving like that. He did not like the idea that, once it had decided to waken its eyes and mouth, there might be more to follow.

"It didn't serve my purposes to speak, Mashevi."

Azetla went rigid. His jaw locked tight. *That* time it had mimicked his own accent—taken the handful of words he had just spoken and turned the exact Rinayimi lilt of them back against him. The Sahr savored his reaction with a slight, smug curve of its mouth.

"Just because my eyes have been lowered this whole time doesn't mean I haven't seen anything. You pretend that all this talk of devils and unholiness is for simpletons and has nothing to do with you. But I've heard you mutter your little incantation of protection when you pass me by."

And then it lowered its voice and spoke one of his prayers. Azetla almost stepped back as if he'd been pushed by a gush of heat from a furnace. It said his own words, in his own tongue, as if it had stolen them straight out of his throat: "God of Masheva, protect us from the things that come out of the darkness, the deepest darkness."

He had muttered it several times in its hearing, unthinkingly, at a child's sing-song rhythm. No one else understood his tongue and he had let his prayers slip out as they pleased.

It was a few moments before Azetla could calm the twisting in his stomach and think clearly. The Sahr did not mind waiting. And watching.

"You don't even understand the words you've just spoken," he said, in Mashevi. "And they don't belong to you."

Its gaze was steady. It said nothing. He tried not to be too eager in taking that as a confirmation, but he suspected that it could not actually *speak* Mashevi. It had only recited it. Uncommonly well. Just as its Maurowan was uncommonly clear, with a curated North City lilt.

"Then how does it serve your purposes to speak all of a sudden?" Azetla said in Maurowan. "Is there something you're expecting to know from me?"

The Sahr shook its head gently. "Not really. You're under threat the same as I am; is there anything you want to know from *me*?"

Azetla rolled his jaw at the gall of the thing. He glanced around to perceive only silence and stillness in the distant sleepers. He kept his voice low.

"Why were you alone?"

"What difference does that make to you?" it said.

The question did not seem to be the one it had wanted from him.

"No tribe? No clan? Not even one accomplice?" he pressed.

Now it was the Sahr's turn to narrow its eyes and take its time.

"I guard my territory how I choose," it said at length.

"You mean alone and unsuccessfully?"

Out from its mouth jumped a quiet, vinegary laugh that was about as merry as death.

"Where are you, Mashevi? Not on my ground. And for that matter"—its eyes slid across the landscape and back toward him—"you're not on your ground either. *Easterner*. You haven't killed me or any of my own. Not one. Set *that* on your scales."

The crisp North City lilt of its Maurowan had weakened and something a little harder to categorize edged into its place. Something more of the south desert, perhaps, though it was too faint to be sure, like a scent caught in the wind and carried swiftly off.

"I see," Azetla said. He hoped to imply that he understood far more from the Sahr's words than he actually did. That he had reached conclusions he hadn't even begun to work out.

"Know this, Mashevi: my people are more like their worst reputation than unlike it. The Makarish tell the nearest truths." It paused, gauging how he listened, measuring his response. He tried desperately to leave it empty-handed.

The Sahr leaned forward, its rope pulling taut. "Knowing that, did you for one moment consider what would have happened if I had just...let you pass through? That would have been an easy thing to do."

Azetla breathed sharply out through his nose and shook his head.

"You do realize I'm not going to believe a word you say, don't you?" he said.

"I know," it said with a lopsided shrug. "But that doesn't mean I'm not going to say it. You will hear what you are willing to hear, and know what you are willing to know. That's up to you."

The words frustrated Azetla because he couldn't quite grasp them. The Sahr seemed to *mean* something that it presumed Azetla easily understood. He did not understand. Not at all. And it made him feel unsteady on his feet. He was accustomed to being the one to lean back, understand everything, say nothing, and wait for others to meander toward conclusions he had long since drawn.

He said nothing now, albeit for the opposite reason. There was real fear clawing at him. Not of devilry and unholiness, but of finding himself in the dark. Fear of blindness. So much happened around him that he could not possibly control or influence. But at least, when a blow came, he could always see it coming. And brace for it.

And maybe that was the answer.

Perhaps the Sahr was doing no more and no less than he had done tonight when faced with Verris' threats. It was saying whatever it could—maybe the truth, maybe only the scraps of it one might safely part with—and seeing how it fell on enemy ears, seeing what could be grasped. So it too could brace.

Maybe.

No great comfort, that. But suddenly the dark around Azetla was not pure pitch.

"Very well. So you turned us around before we breached too far into Sahr territory. Let us pretend I take you at your word…that this was your intent. But you showed yourself to us. You all but dared us to kill you. Why?"

The Sahr gave an inexplicably clear smile, entirely out of place for a creature half starved, wounded, and tied to a wagon.

"First of all, I don't think I can be killed by you. By any of you. Just a theory, mind you, but with good evidence thus far. But more to the point, how many more would I have had to kill for you to deem the cost not worth any potential gain?"

"I *don't* think the cost was worth the gain," Azetla said, under his breath. "And Emperor's orders or no, we may yet have the honor of killing you."

"Be that as it may," the Sahr said coolly. "I didn't watch you pass, you haven't killed me yet, and here I am."

It stared at him, cold and hard and pressing. It wanted something from him. An idea. A reaction. He tried to perceive its aim, as if through a haze, and almost thought he caught hold of it. Glancing compulsively out across the camp again, he confirmed that none stirred. The deep night lay quiet over the men, but the air around Azetla was vivid and restless.

He held a long time against the siege of the Sahr's silence, and to some satisfaction. Its posture began to exhibit strain. Of physical exhaustion, of uncertainty, of disappointment, he did not know. But it was a bit of light to see by.

"Well?" he said, starting to feel the steadiness of tactical clarity. "So you're here, with everyone else thinking you're a mute, empty shell of a devil. You think it matters to me to know you can speak? You think you've given me something for which you might demand a return? I don't care if you can speak Classical Maurowan, or parrot

Mashevi words. I don't care what devilish tongue you call native, and I don't care what they're going to do with you."

The Sahr clicked its tongue. "Oh *jackal*, yes you do. Figuring out what they're going to do is all that matters to you right now. You've got their threats jabbing you in the back, their laws tying you against the sharp edge…and the question of what they might do with *me* is not so far from the question of what they're going to do with you."

Azetla would have been happy, at that exact moment, to break its jaw. *Jackal*, it had said in Makarish. He knew the word in almost any language, like a horse knows the sight of any whip or spur, however decoratively wrought.

But now he knew what it wanted from him. Now he could think clearly.

The Sahr had never been a chief part of his strategy for this mission. The outcome had mattered to Azetla for the battalion's sake, so that the Black Wren would not be decommissioned, so that opportunities might be seized from the endeavor. The so-called devils were but an obstacle to overcome. An absolute unknown. But now, as the Sahr itself said, here it was. A factor literally demanding to be taken into account.

"I think you have no great affection for their Emperor," the Sahr continued. "And it would probably mean something to him to know that I am not deaf and mute. Don't you think? I can open my mouth and speak in front of anyone. At any time. For any purpose."

It was brazenly haggling now, *itself* the sole currency available. It raised its wrists, chafed and crossed against each other with rope, and indicated its Trekoan slave band and Makarish tattoos.

"I can say anything I want to. I'm Trekoan. I'm Makarish. I'm Sarramai. I'm whatever it is that your rulers neither need nor want. I can make it so that you go home empty-handed, no matter what happens to me."

There was a mismatch between the calm indifference in its posture and what Azetla suspected was really going on. If it truly felt itself cornered, just like him, then it was desperate, just like him. Terrified. Scrambling, scraping, searching for any chance.

Not a whit of this showed in its eyes or voice, however.

"You want to make me feel favored by this knowledge about you, and then you want me to worry that this favor might be withdrawn and reallocated?" Azetla said, almost smiling. "Never mind how I feel about the Emperor: if he drags you about in front of crowds before he tears you apart, that harms me none. I am looking at the matter of twenty-four dead soldiers. A dead *Captain*."

He could not help clenching his teeth over that last word.

The Sahr looked steadily back at him. He could almost hear the thousand thoughts shuffling behind its eyes, though he caught not a one of them. The dark was creeping back over him.

"That's true," it said. "A dead Captain. At my hand. I can say nothing to that."

It nodded, looking at the huddle of sleepers down across the way, not at Azetla.

"He is gone, and now everyone looks to *you*, Mashevi. Curious how that comes to—"

Azetla threw a hard fist into the creature's mouth.

His was a steady-soft anger, deep in the gut. Not the kind that flared against his will. He did not need to lose his temper to bloody a devil. And he had not. He didn't even change the set of his mouth. He watched calmly as the Sahr faltered. Its frame tilted and it slumped back against the cart, same as anyone's would have. It was all the Sahr could do to keep its head up. It coughed briefly on blood that trickled inside its mouth, reddening its teeth and lips.

It winced only a little as it righted its posture.

"Never mention Captain Hodge again. His name does not belong in your mouth," Azetla said.

The Sahr laughed. More a thick, smiling breath, really. It spat blood, rolled its jaw, and coughed out another muddled laugh.

"Such patience, by blood. I *really* thought you would want to finish me for that. It was the best I could do. But what can I expect?" The Sahr tossed its head skyward then settled its eyes back on Azetla. "All manner of snapping, but the bite doesn't come."

It clicked its blooded tongue, spat red, and dipped its head down to try and wipe its mouth with its shoulder sleeve. Azetla watched it with equal parts curiosity and contempt.

Suddenly, the Sahr's head ticked straight and it glanced west. In a slow, smooth motion, it lowered itself to the ground and leaned back against the single water cask that had been set there for it—a meager courtesy that Azetla rather regretted. The Sahr's expression waned, its shoulders slacked, its face turned away from the camplight and into the shadow of the water cart.

Azetla narrowed his eyes in confusion, but then he heard the sounds of leather and metal and unconcerned footfalls. Isilia returned to his post with a loud greeting.

The Sahr slept. Or pretended to. It was hard not to look for the flickering life in its face, where before all had been limp and empty.

Isilia did not mark Azetla's severe quietness after that, for he was always quiet and always severe. But Azetla's mind was raucous. He did feel a lingering satisfaction in his stinging knuckles. It was almost a comfort.

So the Sahr wanted Azetla to think it was useful to him.

That didn't mean it was the truth. Or a lie.

It didn't mean much of anything yet.

Azetla breathed not a word of this to anyone and, until the light came clearer still, he didn't intend to. He knew patience and he knew caution, those lonely old friends of his.

13

"Halt, halt, halt!"

The words echoed through the formation, startling Wesley out of a pensive daze. The order ran past him, on toward the rear guard. "Halt, halt, halt!" they shouted in run-together Maurowan, Makarish, and Trekoan. All their orders were tripled in language thus, according to older custom, and it lent a strange sing-song quality to even the most dire commands. It had sounded like gibberish to Wesley at the beginning, but he was accustomed to it now.

He did not, however, have any idea why they were stopping. They were scant hours from Piarago, and he was anxious to arrive. He shifted in his saddle and called across the central command line to the Makarish officer that had obviously been assigned to "manage" him, and lingered ever at his elbow.

"Lieutenant, what is this about?"

"I'll find out right away, my lord," Lieutenant Sarrez said.

He would go forward, speak to the jackal, and return. Always respectful in every particular, Lieutenant Sarrez tended to elide the source of the orders he conveyed. Not because anyone could possibly be ignorant of who stood in authority over the Black Wren, but rather because the man seemed to have a sense of delicacy. Why cast light on such unpleasant—and temporary—facts?

Before Sarrez returned, the marching line began to break around Wesley and reorganize into a parade formation. The flowing movement of the men ebbed until they were as still as water in a deep pool. Center line, Wesley now saw the Imperial banner of gold, green, and crimson whipping wildly in the hot wind, leading some sixty armored horsemen.

He did not wonder long who rode within the thick walls of cavalry. The figure could not be seen, was not marked. But, sheltered behind soldiers, shields, and banners, then withdrawn to a hastily erected tent, the Emperor of Maurow had certainly come.

Come to take his prize out of the hands of those who had won it. These soldiers could have no idea who had descended upon them, no idea how close they were to the beating heart of Maurow's power.

James was immediately summoned to the tent.

Wesley was not.

Dismounting, Wesley rushed through the parade column. He went straight to the water cart to which the all-important loot was tied.

The Sahr sat on the ground with its usual slump, its lifeless expression. The jackal stood over it, quietly giving instructions to his men. Water and midday rations for the Imperial cavalry, attendance to the needs of the tent, at-ease order for the Black Wren. The jackal saw Wesley, nodded respectfully, and continued his work without a word.

Always walking around Wesley like a stone in the pathway. Always eager to make him feel superfluous.

Well not this time.

"My officers will escort the devil to the tent," Wesley said, looking past Azetla and addressing himself to the young Lieutenant beside him. The Lieutenant glanced subtly at the jackal. A faint nod from Azetla encouraged the man to respond.

"Forgive me, my lord, but they have yet to request anything but the Corra himself. They've not even told us who has come, or why. The command entourage left their horses," he gestured to the animals, "and said nothing to us."

Wesley looked nervously at the meeting tent, the cloth billowing out and sucking in as the wind scurried about in fickle fashion. James was in there, by himself, saying only the Gods knew what, balking and shrugging his way through this crucial moment. Wesley desperately needed to be in there.

"They will ask. My men will take it. And I will accompany," he said, more to assure himself than to inform anyone else.

Azetla took no notice. He scrutinized one of the Imperial horses, tracing his fingers along the tack with a scowl on his face. Then, seemingly satisfied, he came back to the water cart and looked down at the Sahr devil with a similar expression.

"Here they come, Lord Verris," he said, glancing up toward the tent. "Do you wish to help me with the ropes?"

His eyebrows coolly raised, his tone sly, somehow.

Wesley did not want to touch the Sahr devil, nor breathe the air around it. He had meant for his officers to manage it for him. But he could not afford to say no *now*.

Bloody jackal.

Wesley grabbed aimlessly at a taut bit of rope while Azetla loosened the knots that tied the Sahr to the wagon. He set the lead firmly into Wesley's hands. Wesley shivered, though the Sahr still sat slack.

"Yours, my lord." Azetla bowed.

How a man could lower his head with such condescension, Wesley did not know, but the jackal certainly managed it.

"You do enjoy acting as though you know what is going on, jackal, but this time you don't," Wesley said, squaring his shoulders.

"I know who is in that tent, my lord," Azetla replied quietly. "And there is little question as to his purpose. He will have you forfeit your victory."

The coarse rope fibers needled into Wesley's hand as he held tight. Without waiting for a response, Azetla pulled the Sahr to a stand. It leaned against the wind and looked at its feet.

Four Imperial guardsmen approached, bearing shackles. Azetla watched with a vivid expression on his face while they chained its feet, as though he knew something Wesley did not.

Wesley clung fiercely to the rope and started for the tent. The Imperial officers gripped the Sahr devil by the shoulders and followed. Half walking, half dragged, the Sahr stumbled along, so that the chain caught on rocks and roots every few steps, exasperating the officers. It seemed even more languid and useless now than it had throughout the whole journey.

And this dross was supposed to be the gold. It was the sole currency of the day, and it deeply mattered into whose pocket it finally fell, and whose image should be stamped upon it. With a deep breath, Wesley pushed through the tent flap, leading in the captive.

Emperor Riada Sivolne did not acknowledge Wesley's presence at all; his eyes fixed solely on the Sahr with all their native strength and fire. The officers tried to hold the Sahr devil upright for their sovereign, like a tapestry or an article of clothing. But it was an ungainly effort for, at first, the Sahr refused to lock its knees and bear its own weight.

Wesley observed the Emperor observing the Sahr. The question struck him like a slap: what if the Sahr was *nothing*? What then? Who could prove anything, when the damned creature barely seemed alive?

Whatever Emperor Riada declared would become fact, regardless of what Wesley thought or claimed. Regardless even of the truth. The Emperor's silence gripped the tent room until Wesley felt that he was unpardonably loud even in his very breaths.

At last, the Emperor's voice came swift and sharp, cutting through the silence. "James, what sort of fool do you think I am?"

James' eyes widened. "Your Highness?"

"This could be any wretched Makar that you pulled out of a village or quarry," the Emperor said coolly. "Explain yourself."

"It is a devil! You must *see* it, Your Highness!"

"I can see it, it's scarcely an arm's-length from me."

"Forgive me, Your Highness, I...don't even know how to explain it to you, but it *is* some devil or other. It came upon us in Sahr territory, killing silently without anyone knowing how. Men just falling where they stood. Ask the soldiers! Twenty-four skilled men of the Black Wren were lost at the hands of this lone creature, and we scarcely *saw* it. It killed their Captain while he was under heavy guard," James said desperately.

Well thank the Gods that James had no doubts for once. He spoke with raw, innocent conviction, which lent unexpected force to his tone. Emperor Riada raised his eyebrows gently at his younger brother and looked back toward the creature in question, as though willing to reconsider. He folded his arms and walked about it as one walks about an item for purchase. He carefully avoided touching it, though he did ask one of the officers to lift its head that he might look at its face.

"It doesn't look like it was worth keeping alive; indeed, it doesn't even look like something worth killing. It is nothing," the Emperor declared.

All at once the creature lifted its head and squared its shoulders. Everyone in the room—the very atmosphere—seemed to flinch and focus. The creature planted its feet firm against the ground, and stood its height. Then, cocking its head at an angle, it looked the Emperor of Maurow in the eyes.

The Emperor paused in surprise, then leaned closer, like one drawn by a sudden glow of light in a dark corridor. Wesley held his breath. Everyone stood still, and all that could be heard was the tent canvas, taking its beating from the wind outside.

The Sahr smiled. That's what Wesley thought he saw.

Then, sudden as a fire going out, the Emperor of Maurow was struck hard in the chest by the Sahr's foot irons. The metal clipped his mouth, and he reeled back, stumbling against the rocky ground. The officers that held the Sahr faltered along with it as its feet dropped back to the ground. Dazed, they did not seem to realize that the ferocity of their grip had given the Sahr all the anchor it needed to bloody the Emperor of all Maurow.

Wesley rushed forward and pulled Emperor Riada away and to his feet, as a loyal Lord and Colonel might do. His heart was racing but he was almost too bewildered to be afraid. The Sahr had not freed itself, nor had it done anything otherworldly, but it *felt* as though it had done both.

The officers drove the Sahr into the dust with sharp blows. They put a horse-whip around its neck. It was still now. Stiff as bones. The eyes were ravenously alive, though, swallowing everything in sight.

Emperor Riada touched his mouth and rubbed a smear of blood between his fingers. He pressed his other hand against his chest. He was eerily quiet and the expression on his face was not one of anger, but of calculation. Intrigue. Maybe a drop of fear, but no more than that. He looked at the Sahr for a long time. When he spoke, he hissed from the pain in his jaw.

"Has it said anything of interest to you?" He turned to James. He sounded so calm.

James was breathing rapidly, his face filled with horror. Wesley did not dare speak without permission, so James was left unaided, stripped of succor beneath his brother's cold eye.

"Said anything?" James repeated, dazed.

Riada directed his eyes toward Wesley, at last giving him leave to speak with a flick of his fingers.

"Forgive me, Your Imperial Highness," Wesley said with a deep bow. "This creature cannot speak. Or has not spoken. Nothing even approaching an intelligible sound. The men have tried to anger it, cajole it into speech, to make it cry out. It seems to understand nothing of any tongue, not even Trekoan or Makarish."

Emperor Riada gave Wesley a dismissive glance, as though he spoke to a fool. As though Wesley could be supposed to have no more insight than James. The Emperor set his eyes back upon the Sahr with a sort of hunger, and a terrible certainty; his retreat to thought conjured a fresh silence, for no one could do or say anything until he ordered it.

His expression grew brighter and more intense until, at last, he spoke.

"Find a holding place for this creature in South City, out of the way, *outside* the old walls. I don't want it seen, and I don't want it in my city until our priests can assure us it brings no curse with it. I'll arrange for it to be dealt with as soon as possible."

James finally loosed his jaw. "What will you—?"

The Emperor ignored his brother and looked at Wesley.

"None of these men are to enter the city."

"Your Highness?" Wesley said, clearing his throat so that he would not sound as skittish as he felt.

"I had planned to send the Red Dome brigade to Trekoa a few months from now, but instead you will take *this* battalion to Trekoa," Emperor Riada said. "I don't want them stirring up tall tales about the Sahr while I decide what it is and what will be done with it. Any man who fancies a jaunt in the city to his wife or a whore will be paid a noose in full."

"Yes, Your Highness," Wesley replied. This was exactly what he had feared.

The Emperor wiped the back of his hand carefully against the cut at the corner of his mouth, stared at the smear of red, and smiled to himself.

"Your Highness," James said quietly. "I...I thought it was to be killed right away in the colonnade. As a symbol...an example, like the jackals. We were to show the people what a Sahr is and how we do not fear them. I don't understand."

"For the Gods' sake, we could catch a lion, kill it in the square, and say it was a Sahr devil. That would be no more or less believable than this. Doubt would remain. No, I think there's some other blood to be drawn out of this stone." Emperor Riada looked at the Sahr and it looked at him. "Have you ever considered that the Sahr devils have kept their ground for all this time? That is a nigh miraculous feat, isn't it?"

He leaned nearer to the Sahr. It was now held such that it could not move, could not adjust head or foot. Could barely breathe.

"The Sahrs have the whole desert in terror. They have *never* been taken. That is a story that should be understood before it is entirely unmade."

And it's a story you bloody well don't want James to be known for, Wesley thought bitterly. All of this would be for nothing if Wesley couldn't think his way around it. The Emperor had such uncanny intuition for these things; he understood not only how a tale should be told, but how it would spread, mutate, or dissipate. How it would be countered, how it would be revived, and how it could be made so permanent a fixture in the mind and soul, that even one's own eyes could not tolerate its contradiction.

Wherever Wesley tried to affix James to the Sahr's capture, the Emperor would extract him. And Wesley was not so foolish a man to think that he could come out ahead. He might lose far more than all he had laid down as wager.

"Your Highness..." James said, slow to see into the future, still trying to navigate the mere present. "The Sahr responds to *nothing*, it cannot speak so as to explain itself or its kind; it is not human."

"You have no eyes, James. *You* look at it. Of course it can speak. The language of fiends, perhaps, but those are not animal eyes. As to whether or not it is human? Well…" Riada looked the Sahr over again and smiled slightly through his bruised jaw. "It's a question for me and my priests to determine. It hardly matters to you. Simply do as I said."

He leaned toward the Sahr and spoke quietly. "I'm not afraid of devil's magic, so long as it can be fashioned into an arrow and shot in the direction of my choosing."

The Sahr devil's eyes were clear and focused, but the words did not seem to penetrate.

"Anything to say, devil?" Riada said calmly as the guards angled it toward him. "No?"

It looked at the Emperor dispassionately.

"When I next see it, this sort of nonsense," he indicated his red, swelling cheek, "will not do."

The young officer with the horse-whip tightened his hold on the creature as if that solved the problem. Emperor Riada strode out, refusing to give the Sahr a wide berth, but walking past it close enough to touch. The Corra followed his brother. Wesley told the officers to return the Sahr to the water cart.

Strangely, once he had calmed down, and once the residue of the Emperor's presence vacated the room, Wesley found himself grateful for the devil's inexplicable burst of violence and vitality.

It proved they had something the Emperor valued. A true token for James, if only it could be wrested from Emperor Riada's grasp.

14

Azetla caught a glimpse of Riada as he left. Bruises and blood. Then the Sahr was dragged back to its water cart. Bruises there too, and eyes awake for all to see. Azetla felt a cool satisfaction as he turned to resume the march.

But he was not allowed to give the order. Lord Verris summoned him to the tent.

"I would have called for one of your officers but he would just convey whatever I said directly to you and I have no patience for roundabout dealings at the moment. So pay attention to what I say now, jackal, and recognize the Corra's liberality toward you as a *very* contingent gift," Verris said.

"You have made that clear, my lord."

Verris narrowed his eyes and continued. "The Black Wren will not be returning to Piarago. You'll have to send men to Tarthus to resupply."

"My lord, that's three days southwest of here."

"Yes, and en route to Areo outpost, which is where you and your men have just been assigned. None of your men will enter the city tonight or *at all*. I will hold you personally responsible should that order be disobeyed by so much as one homesick soldier."

Verris paused, arms folded, driving his gaze at Azetla, as though daring him to protest. Of course, Azetla could not.

"Yes, sir," he said.

"More to the point, we require a holding place for the Sahr in South City. As far away from the thoroughfare as possible. Subtle. Unimportant. Stocked with no one and nothing that matters. Outskirts."

"My Lord, there is no place that can guarantee the silence that I suspect has been demanded. Any entry into the outer city creates the possibility of rumor," Azetla said.

"Just do as I say, jackal." Verris paused and smiled slightly. "The Colha Inn where I first met with your Captain is in a poor, uneducated district, far away from everything of import, and your battalion has clout there. You'll arrange it."

"I thought none of us were to enter the city, my lord."

"*You*, I'll risk. Go without the cord and baldric."

Azetla clasped and unclasped his hands behind his back. It did him little good to show his frustration to Verris, when this was all Riada's doing.

Riada was almost never rash. He was careful and meticulous. He thought long before he spoke, shared little, and then took action. It dizzied those who could not follow him, and there were only a few things that could tempt him to recklessness, such as his hatred of Mashevis.

That would not be the case with the Sahr. Here he would be all sense and caution. Riada would not bring the Sahr inside his city walls until he could be sure he was not inviting evil upon his city. He took his ancestors' pact with the northern gods seriously and when one's gods are as capricious as devils themselves, nothing can be safe, and sure, and true. Riada understood the importance of sacred ground, ancient boundaries, and symbols. That much Azetla knew and understood.

The difference was that Azetla believed Riada's gods were empty and mute and false, while Riada believed Azetla's God was merely "ineffective." A river that flowed too thin to bestow any riches upon the banks. A river that could be diverted and made to disappear into the swollen ranks of Maurow's gods.

What was sacred to Azetla was violable to Riada, and so also the reverse. Of neutral ground, there remained none. And now, after all this time, Riada's hand came, reaching down into Azetla's little world, twisting it around, and dragging it where he wanted it to go. And Azetla could offer even less resistance than a horse with a bit in its mouth.

"Of course, my lord," Azetla said. He hesitated, pressing a word between his teeth, weighing a strategy. "The Emperor will not be gainsaid, naturally."

Verris gave Azetla an odd, cold smile.

"Listen, jackal, I have neither the time nor the patience for anything but quiet obedience. Make the arrangements and report back to me."

Verris raised a hand to dismiss him.

"I will do as you ask, my lord," Azetla said calmly. "But it's in your best interest not to think we're all blind here."

Verris' palm curled to a fist. "What is that supposed to mean?"

"Anyone with eyes can see that the Corra joined us for reasons having little to do with the Sahr devil, my lord. It is a mere means to an end for the Corra. And also for His Highness, the Emperor." Azetla paused, drew in one slow breath, and threw his gambit. "Rather different ends, though."

He had struck flint. He could tell by the fearful spark in Verris' eyes.

Verris forced a cavalier tone. "Devil take you jackal, you speak utter nonsense."

"Perhaps I do, my lord. I simply mean to say that my battalion would not like to see its costly victory...misappropriated. The Corra may not be a soldier, but he was *there*. With us. That is not lost on my men. The Emperor, on the other hand, has decommissioned nearly all our sister battalions, one by one, and the threat of the same has been dangling over our heads for years. That too is not lost on us."

Verris stared at Azetla, his eyes wide. There was terror there, and desperation. Both were quickly shaken off and replaced by a dismissive mannerism.

"You have your orders, jackal," Verris said at last. "An Imperial detail will arrive at dusk to escort the Corra and his captive to the outskirts. Have the inn cleared and prepared. You'll remain with the Corra and the Sahr until I say otherwise. Now tell your men to make ready. I want them to leave as soon as possible."

"Yes, my lord." Azetla nodded.

Verris' mouth pinched tight, as if the very timbre of Azetla's voice galled him.

"And do not for one moment presume that you know my mind, jackal."

"And if I knew the Emperor's mind?" Azetla said.

"No one alive knows that man's mind," Verris rasped.

Azetla looked steadily at Verris until he saw the doubt bubble up on his face. Then Azetla bowed lightly.

"Health and honor, my lord."

He turned and left the tent.

The heat of the day seemed to weight Azetla down as he walked out and gathered the senior soldiers of the battalion. The new orders fell like a lash against his men. Areo outpost was at least a twelve-day journey from the outskirts of Piarago, and somewhat far afield of Maurow's trade-route towns in the south. Azetla had never been there, nor had the battalion. It was nowhere and nothing to them.

Everything Azetla relied on was being stripped from him, bit by bit. The usual recourses were thrown into the wind and he had precious little control over anything that was happening. He felt like he was making wild bets, blindly thrashing about in hopes of striking a foothold.

A visceral memory surfaced from his childhood, bearing with it a taste of sheer panic such as he had only known twice in his life.

He was swimming off the Mashevi shores of Khenim, when a swift current pulled him to where his feet could no longer touch the ground, out into the tall waves. They broke over him relentlessly, pulling him further and further out. He could never catch his breath or strengthen his stroke before the next wall of water came to pummel him. He became certain he was going to die.

It was as a miracle when his heel brushed against sand once again, and it had given him the hope and strength he needed to keep fighting back to shore. He crawled once he reached the shallows then lay down in exhaustion till his sisters and cousins surrounded him. He was sick with seawater the rest of the day, and wiser ever after.

Just some ground underfoot, that was what he needed. Any little bit of ground.

Azetla left the battalion in the capable hands of Joseph and Sarrez. He brushed aside any shame at what he was about to do. There was no way out of it. He had to turn the small, lively Colha inn into a cage to house a devil.

He took the ramshackle back-ways, and wore only his sagam for protection. When he reached the inn, he entered quietly through the side alley, stepping out of the street and over the threshold. The only person who saw him come in was Mali, and thank God. She was precisely who he wanted. Colha would not have known or understood what to do. Mali was a little less northern than her father, a little more tolerant of Mashevis, and a great deal sounder of mind. Most importantly, she was of a thorough nature.

Before she had the chance to offer her ever-tentative greeting, Azetla put her to work.

15

Mali did everything Azetla asked as though she were a tackman in his battalion and he a man of rank. Azetla had always acted for Lord Captain Hodge, and to obey him had become instinct.

But the Lord Captain was dead now, so her compliance felt strange when she thought about it after. Who did Azetla speak for now?

Mali was not even given time to think or mourn the Captain who had been her family's benefactor. His battalion had kept them on their feet, especially through the past few years of her father's deterioration of mind. He sometimes called her "daughter" in the southern custom, telling her how much she reminded him of his own daughter. Mali could have cried, if Azetla had given her half a chance. But he was full of orders, practicalities, and details, one stacked on top of the other, no room to think too long on anything.

Khala—who had come to borrow oil for her lamp—was sent to the upstairs room, to remain sequestered with Anna and Mali's papa. The inn was to be cleared out, all custom turned away, the doors blacked. Such instructions were more than enough to stir up fear, but it turned to dread when Azetla told her to prepare a room to harbor a prisoner.

Mali didn't ask what sort of prisoner. She didn't want to know. And she already knew.

Two hours and several angry customers later, the inn was empty such as Mali hadn't seen since her mother had died, when black cloth had been draped over the doorways for three days' mourning.

Soon, a well-regaled escort arrived outside: ten North City soldiers with cords and baldrics concealed, the Corra himself, and a captive, the nature of which Mali was left to assume. She could not see much of the prisoner, both because her eyes were fixed to the ground out of respect for the Corra and because the soldiers stood around it like a wall. If it was a devil, she didn't see what good the guards would do.

So the Black Wren had caught something. And lost the Captain doing it.

Mali pinned down her nerves, though her fingers fiddled restlessly and her skin felt tight and agitated. She wanted to escape to the upstairs room, and felt a sudden, shameful resentment against her father for being unequal to this task. All these high, strange, unknown things must fall on her shoulders alone.

Standing at the entrance, Mali bowed low at the Corra's entry and kept the posture for several moments. She wasn't sure what to do after. Azetla had not told her that the Corra would be here. She had not prepared for this.

"Is there a suitable room, girl?" the Corra asked.

For what? Gods of Carth, for the *Corra*? Did he mean to *stay* here? She had thought he came only to ensure the storage of his prisoner and would then go home to the Gray Eagle.

"A far too humble room, Your Highness, but clean and ready," she said, trying to put forth her voice with good strength. She felt so feeble-tongued.

"Good. Show me to it, then show the guards where to take our prisoner."

"Of course, Your Highness."

The Corra did not really look at her except when she indicated where he should go. She kept her eyes chiefly on the ground, lips pressed together. When the Corra stepped in the room, she locked her hands, white-knuckled, at her waist. The Corra seemed oblivious to her anxiety and nodded casually at her when she told him that food would be brought and a bath drawn as quickly as possible. She bowed deeply again—the Corra neither noticed nor acknowledged this—and departed. Once outside of the room she drew several uneven breaths and rubbed her hands against her shift as if to flatten her feelings, soothe her blood till it flowed calmly.

When she showed the guards to the old tanner's room—the inn had been built around a tannery from before the city grew so far beyond its walls—she stole a glimpse of the prisoner. A southerner, by appearance. Bruised face. Tattooed hand like the South Makars of the old stories. A woman. Or were such distinctions meaningless among Sahr devils? It flashed its coal eyes at her once, and she shrank backward.

Mali was glad to excuse herself quickly. Head down, mouth shut, she entered the Corra's room a second time to serve him his meal, then slipped back to the kitchen to find Azetla leaning in the alley entrance, watching the street with wary eyes.

"Azetla, the prisoner...is it...?"

"Yes," he said softly.

"Ah," Mali breathed. The idea of a Sahr, so close—in her *home*—made her almost dizzy. She walked to the west-facing alcove and threw a precious bit of incense into the censer. As soon as the coals touched powder, the tiny copper form of Lyrala almost disappeared within the amber-scented smoke. Mali lifted her palms, pressing the heels of them to her forehead. When she looked back, she saw Azetla's face pinched against the fragrance, his body angled as far away from the censer as possible.

Mali might have taken offense, but she didn't have the strength for it. Rather, she felt how dangerous it was for him to disregard all gods but one that was formless and ineffable. Only one pair of hands to cast yourself upon in times of danger, and nothing to look at with your eyes or name with your tongue.

Azetla still faced the alleyway, his posture awkwardly slumped. He seemed mired in thought, and Mali would not unmake his silence. Sitting down on the narrow clay steps, she waited, thinking Azetla would soon tell her what else she ought to do. Or relieve her. Though the sun was only just falling, the nerve-wracking weight of the day pressed suddenly down upon Mali and her eyelids grew heavy.

"There's one other thing I have to do, Mali," Azetla said quietly, at which point she realized he was standing right next to her, leaning over to wake her up. She had fallen asleep, apparently, and he had let her. It was almost full dark now. He had scrubbed his face, head, and hands and rinsed out his shirt.

"I'll be back, but you still need to black the alleyway door," he said, stepping toward the alley.

"What? I thought you said you weren't to be noticed."

"I won't be."

He had parchment folded in his hand and ink on his fingers. Suddenly, Mali remembered her duties. Duties owed to Captain Hodge, which only Azetla could now receive.

"Wait. I have something for you." She walked upstairs as stealthily as she could—only Khala was still awake—and retrieved a coil of reed-paper from the walnut box upstairs.

"For the Captain, I assume," she said as she handed it to Azetla. "A Laritoni brought it last week. There was no seal to begin with. I suppose you should have it."

Abruptly, Azetla pulled himself taut, his eyes widening, then he dropped his gaze to the ground. Slowly, he reached out for the coil and when his hand curled around it, his eyes closed. Mali wondered if he too would have liked to feel his mourning now, if only he had the chance.

"His family doesn't even know yet," he said, "Won't know, for some time. I can't tell them."

Mali felt the latent tears sting her eyes. She wanted to cover her face. And she wanted Azetla gone. She felt a bitterness toward him that she could not even fully understand.

"How many did you lose?" she whispered.

"Twenty-four. Of those you know best…Dersha, Baze, and Piri."

Mali pulled her shawl across her mouth; a southern gesture, impossible for her not to do. It was instinctive. "Mercy-be-peace-be. Mercy-be-peace-be."

Azetla looked back at her out of the alley. His expression was hard as stone in the dark. He seemed to gnaw on his words before he got them out.

"I'm sorry for all this," he said. His voice sounded sucked dry.

Then he was gone.

Mali collapsed back onto the steps. She still needed to black the door, but she didn't want to move.

She had always been so proud to be of use to Lord Captain Hodge. Proud of the high-blood favor and connection. But he was gone. Gods help him. Gods give him deep rest.

Now she was thrust into the service of…whom? Lieutenant Sarrez? The *Corra*?

Azetla.

She thought of the ink on his left hand, the parchment in his grip, and the coil she had given him. A troubling notion entered her mind. What if it was Azetla's bidding she had been doing all along? She never knew what the letters said. She never knew where they went, or where they came from.

The Captain had trusted him, though. Utterly. Whatever evils she could believe of jackals—of Azetla—she knew he loved the Captain. It seemed impossible that he would deceive him. With a sigh of forced relief, Mali brushed the idea away. It pricked at her once or twice more as she hung the curtain, unplaited her hair, and ebbed the fires, but sleep closed off all thoughts almost the moment she lay down.

James ate his hot northern fare with relish, glad to be under a roof, but wishing that it was his own. But Wesley had insisted, *don't let your quarry out of your sight. Protect your victory as long as you can.* James wished Wesley would have taken pity on him, and absolved him of this particular duty.

No such luck.

He did let his mind go slack, though, and kept his thoughts small.

He gloried in the crude amenities of the little inn, where once he would have scoffed at them. A bed, oil lamps, a small pitcher and basin whose water was crystal clear…these seemed like riches untold after nearly two months of hard travel. Wesley had his worries and his strategies, but James had hot water and a cake of soap.

James' clothing had a thick coat of dust on it. His skin too. He had eaten like a boor. His muscles ached from horseback. He looked common, probably, and disheveled. He thought of how fastidious Riada was about trappings and appearances, and laughed to himself for weary hopelessness.

But, for once, James felt as though he knew something Riada did not know, albeit very little of that "something." Ah, Riada of the lean build, the fierce look, and the swift mind; the image of the divine mandate. But James had seen blood and field and a caught devil. He had traversed the Makarish desert. He had been to Sahr territory. And lived.

He might not be made of much, but he wasn't made of nothing.

For a few fine minutes, James was calm and content. When he was told the hot water was ready, he rose quickly as if to a trumpet's call and lingered long in the bathing room, allowing the hot water to relax his muscles and the soaps and oils to soak into his sunned and dusted skin.

But the hard thoughts ate through the soft wall of comfort, and the worry that always accompanied him when he had to face Riada began to stir in his stomach. His hands dragged as he dressed himself.

This matter *wasn't* finished. And it wasn't just the Sahr. This was just a small maneuver in what was to be a large, unending succession of them. If he actually became Emperor, only death would end it. James sat down slowly on the lumped, woolen mattress.

But—he forced the thought—if the Sahr wasn't the *end* of it, it was at least the beginning. He would do exactly what Wesley said. He took a deep breath and steeled himself to sound like a Corra of Maurow.

"Well, Uttar," he said to his serving-man. "Let's go look in on the devil, shall we?"

Uttar blanched, but followed.

The guards outside his room began their bowings and mutterings. James impatiently waved away their obeisance; it was hardly fair, he knew, but he felt irritated at them for initiating the exchange of honors, which he was then supposed to receive and acknowledge. They weren't allowed *not* to do it, but he had no appetite for the hassle.

Uttar trailed him in a quiet scuffle. That vexed James too. The man's fear scraped against James' own, as if to make a grating sound in the ears. James would have liked someone at his back, goading him forward, but Uttar lagged, and James was starting to feel that he might change his mind before he made it into the room.

The common area was dark but for the one lamp the guards had between them, so James traced the wall with his hand as his eyes adjusted, and followed the scraps of light coming from the south end of the room. He found himself in the kitchen and gave a start when he saw a figure, half shadowed and indistinct.

It was the jackal, by himself in the dull light of a banked oven.

James had come upon him in the midst of prayers or some such. The jackal was on his knees, sitting back against his heels. He poured water over his hands, one at a time, mouthing something all the while. He noted James' approach out of the corner of his eye, but did not allow himself to be interrupted. Disrespectful behavior, yes, but James didn't feel like demanding from the jackal what he scorned from his guards. Let him do his all-important mutterings.

Beside the jackal sat a bowl of chuva and a strip of bread, and at one point the jackal raised the bread with quiet words. Then he was done. Not an elaborate to-do, by any means, but the jackal had not hurried. Now his food was blessed or sacralized or whatever it needed to be.

The Mashevi relinquished his posture of prayer slowly, like someone aching and weary who must rise from bed far too early in the morning. But rise he did. He turned and bowed his head to James as he must but, when he lifted it, he looked at James directly.

"Your Highness," he said.

The bow was short and shallow. Wesley would demand James take insult from this, but he could not cajole himself into it. There were times where feeling offense was, perhaps, the laziest tack, but for James it often required effort to produce and maintain. Formalities rankled him for reasons of neither pride nor humility; it was all so tedious and unintuitive.

"Why are you still here?" James asked.

"Lord Verris did not give me leave to depart, Your Highness," the jackal said.

James nodded as he looked around the room. "Well, sit, then. Eat. I'll not be bothered."

The jackal took James at his word. He sat smoothly against the lintel of the wide door and began to eat that most ubiquitous of peasant food: charred bread and peppered bean paste.

"Azla, is it?" James said.

The jackal swallowed the bite that was in his mouth.

"Azetla, Your Highness," he said, giving James a wry look.

Well they couldn't expect him to remember their names, especially when they came from all four winds and a thousand tongues.

James looked at the man with curiosity. For all of Verris' effusive ire—"*bloody subversive, arrogant, sinister jackal!*"—the man looked like nothing more or less than a typical specimen of Mashevi, in both manner and appearance. Then again, James had not known very many Mashevis, so that wasn't saying much.

This jackal ate quietly. Calm, but alert, regarding James only in his periphery.

"I thought to look in on the Sahr devil," James said, with a gesture in some direction approximating the tannery room. "Will it be a great ordeal for me to do so?"

"No, Your Highness. It was asleep when last I saw it. Or feigning to be. The guards have charge of it, and I'm certain they will rouse it for you if you wish them to."

James shook his head slowly. "No, no. I don't—that won't be necessary."

"What were you hoping to see, Your Highness?"

"I'm not quite sure."

James sighed, his arms hanging loose at his sides, too easily thwarted from his objective. He stood still in thought and hesitation.

"Your Highness?" the jackal said. He had finished his meager meal, but made no move to stand and adopt a formal posture. In fact, he merely rested his elbows casually on his knees and looked at James with all the calm informality that James naturally preferred. As though he was a man who understood one's taste in atmosphere, as a good servant knows the exact temperature the water ought to be for washing. "You do know that, until your brother says otherwise, you are still officially the commander of my battalion?"

James blinked in confusion. "But that...that doesn't mean anything. It would have to be in writing in order for it to..."

"It is in writing, Your Highness."

"I thought…"

"I wrote it. You, Lord Verris, and all your officers, fully integrated into the battalion ledgers, and just an hour ago delivered to the magistrate and barracks by a courier."

"Why—"

"I did precisely as I was instructed to do the night you and Lord Verris decided to prove a point to Captain Hodge by threatening to kill me."

The jackal's voice was just as even and cool as before, but there was something harshly alight in his face now, as though wind had blown over ash showing a bit of burning crimson underneath.

James tensed and fidgeted.

"That was about the laws of Maurow," he said haltingly.

"No it wasn't."

"I've let you keep your position thus far…"

"Thus far and no farther?"

James' shoulders rose and he had an instinct to draw back, though the jackal had not so much as moved a hair or raised his voice. He had misread the jackal's informality; it was not that of a servant, but that of an authority.

"Do not take my tolerance as a license for disrespect," James said, squaring himself. "You're in sore need of my favor, yet you invite reprisal."

James had little real power in Maurow, but he could snap his fingers at the Imperial guards and this man would lay dead at his feet. He had to remind himself of that because, at the moment, he was feeling cornered by someone who had no power or right to do anything.

"Has Lord Verris taught you that the only way to guide is by threats? That won't serve in the end," the jackal said. "You could have me killed for carrying a sword. You could have me killed for omitting a deference you don't even *want*. You could have me killed whether I did your every bidding, or defied you. I know that every morning when I wake up and every night when I go to sleep. I don't need to be told. Have you considered a different tactic?"

Now James could only stare mute and wide-eyed for, try as he might, he could not stop himself from hearing what the jackal said. His words made such simple sense.

"You do not need to grab my battalion by the scruff of the neck, nor me by mine, to hold our attention. There are better ways to have us. I can hold my battalion together from the inside, if you can hold us together from the outside. Do you understand, Your Highness?"

James fumbled, as with numb, clumsy hands, to put his own thoughts together. He had no one to tell him what he must think. All he knew was that these words were sharp and dangerous. He at least had the presence of mind to send Uttar back to his quarters with a curt wave of his hand. It took him an embarrassingly long time to work an answer out of his mouth.

"What you have made in writing, jackal, the Emperor can unmake with little more than a word," he said, stepping forward and speaking in a lowered voice.

"But the word has not yet been spoken, and the work of it would take more than a moment. I can be of service to you, Your Highness, but not if you flash a knife at me every time you remember I'm a *jackal*. Just because that's how your brother deals with us, does not mean you must."

James pressed his tongue against the back of his teeth and wished by all the Gods that Wesley was here. He would take hold of the situation. He would sort fact from fiction. He would not allow this jackal to push him into deep, troubling waters like this.

"Listen, Azetla...Azetla?"

The jackal gave a gentle nod.

"You have been brazenly candid, so let me be likewise: What is *your* aim in all this?"

At that, Azetla shook his head with a faint, exhausted smile. James was sure he had never seen this man smile in all of the last two months. "I would be even more straightforward, Your Highness, if I thought that I could survive it. My aim? To keep my battalion and my position in it."

"And you think *I* can accomplish that for you?" James was sorely tempted to laugh.

"Perhaps not. But I'm better off putting myself at your mercy than at your brother's."

"Why? Because you see me as weak and innocuous?" James said bitterly.

The jackal did not answer right away, which was its own answer.

"Your hatred for Mashevis has never seemed quite as thorough or as blind as the Emperor's," he said at last, his accent growing thicker as though the Maurowan words were heavy in his mouth.

And what vile words they were. That was a few steps shy of calling him a jackal-lover, and how *dare* he! Now there was real offense which required no effort whatsoever to manufacture, but came rushing in of its own accord. It gave James the confidence of anger.

"Don't presume to know me nor how I feel about *anyone* or *anything*, jackal. I have met your King. I found him to be a coward and a flatterer. I have met Samuel Aver, that great, famous name to which you are all so beholden, and he was as vicious as winter and arrogant as death—"

Slowly, Azetla stood and stepped forward, which caused James' burst of confidence to shrivel at the edges. He felt he did a very good job not to take a step back.

"You think to anger me by saying that, Your Highness, but I know that those are your brother's words," he said, his voice gentle, as if to compensate for the unavoidable imposition of merely being a soldier, standing, and strong. "I also know them to be true. If you mean to prove your contempt for my people by citing your contempt for the royal family, well...suffice it to say that I am under no illusions regarding our King, his apostasy, and the corruption of his holy office."

James raised his eyebrows. "By which you mean his obedience to my brother."

Azetla did not say anything.

"Ah, you're one of those," James said with a grim smile. There was always some little Mashevi faction trying to rebel against their King. A few years back it was the coastal fishermen. Then it was a small religious sect, named after an old prophet. Lately, Riada said, it was to do with a "goatherd" faction or something like that. There was a new one every day, it seemed. "You'd like to slit your own King's throat, wouldn't you?"

"No, Your Highness," Azetla said, his jaw working. "Doesn't matter if I hate him. He is still our King and only God may make him otherwise. Not me."

James didn't know what to believe. He wasn't accustomed to trusting his own judgment. But if he *did*? If James followed his own intuition? He would say that this Azetla was no fool. Possibly dangerous. And more than a little desperate. Afraid for his very life, in fact, and that for good reason.

This jackal had put himself at risk, talking to James as he had. He had asked for his help. Relinquished himself to James' mercy. Just James. No proxy. No Wesley. That fact worked a strange magic on James and ran him down an unfamiliar pathway, around his usual fear and trembling, to a pool of good nerve. James was on his own. That was it.

"I will try to keep your battalion intact. And to keep you as you are, though I can give you no assurance," he said.

Azetla gave James a strange look.

"Then, Your Highness, would you swear by salt?"

"What?" James laughed, genuinely amused. "That means nothing to me."

"It means something to me."

"I'm accustomed to swear by my name-God, Sharitha."

"Then I withdraw the request. Do not swear at all."

James was taken aback. Wesley *was* right: blisteringly arrogant. But this did not shake him as it would have Wesley.

"Very well. I believe a man's word is what it is. I swear by your Mashevi salt."

Azetla closed his eyes for several moments. When he opened them, James thought he saw a flash of real fear in those eyes. It fled so quickly that it might have just been a trick of the light.

"The Sahr can speak, Your Highness. Fluent, articulate Maurowan and, I think, other tongues as well."

James' heart beat fast. "How do you know this?"

"It spoke, hoping to coerce me by offering a token."

"What token?"

Azetla narrowed his eyes. "The very information I'm telling you now."

James shook his head with disbelief. Yet he believed it. "Is it—"

"I don't know what it is, Your Highness. But don't be so quick to relinquish it to your brother. Devil or not, it is..." Azetla pressed his lips together. "I do not think it is to be trifled with."

So Riada was right. Every bloody time.

"That jinn kicked my brother in the teeth, made him bleed—he wasn't frightened, by the way, only *fascinated*—and all the while I kept insisting it was deaf and dumb."

A little fire lit up in Azetla's eyes, but all he said was, "Well it isn't."

James didn't know what to do. His rush of confidence sagged, like a drug wearing off. He had an idea—well, he had fifty scattered threads worth of an idea—and he needed a wiser head than his own.

"Very well, Mashevi. I'll take you at your word. Now. Go back to the encampment. Bring Colonel Verris. Then return with him," James said.

Azetla's shoulders tensed. "Would it not be better for me to remain with the Black Wren—"

"You'll return with Lord Verris," James said firmly.

He was the Corra. He remembered that sometimes.

All expression faded from Azetla's face. "Your orders, my honor."

James felt a high, nervous energy; he almost enjoyed it as he wrote the message for Azetla to take to Wesley. He knew this was not his strength. He knew he may have just made every possible mistake in dealing with this jackal. So be it. Wesley would undoubtedly tell him. Wesley had managed to lure him into this arena almost against his will and James had limped along after him, not trusting himself to do otherwise, gently tempted by the idea of being needed.

Now James had a burgeoning curiosity to see if he could make a decision and it be the right one, against all odds. If he could do it once, perhaps he could do it again. And again. Then there would be a chance that, if Wesley ever let go of his hand in this current, James might actually be able to swim.

Learn by doing, the sages said.

Learn by doing.

16

Three hours out, three hours back, and Azetla's eyes burned with sleeplessness. The moon was gone by the time he and Lord Verris reached the furthest outskirts and the clouds had scuttled in, leaving the night inky and thick.

Lord Verris had scarce said a word the whole way, but he watched Azetla closely. Watched while Azetla wearily mounted a borrowed horse, watched to see if he would balk, as most foot-soldiers would if forced upon a mount, as if looking for some point of failure to manipulate. Azetla stared steadily north, for he truly had no idea what was going to happen. He had shot so many arrows in the dark—been so much more reckless than was his wont—and he didn't know what would strike, or what would be turned back against him.

Azetla signaled halt and dismount. The alleys narrowed. Lord Verris handed his reins to his serving-man and walked at Azetla's shoulder. Azetla could almost feel him seething in the dark.

"What are you finagling for jackal?" Verris said at a whisper.

"I told his Highness, the Corra, exactly—"

"Stop that. Try again. I'm not as easily satisfied as he."

"I don't think you realize how bold I made to begin with, my lord. Asking that you refrain from threatening me is, in my position, an extravagant request."

"Do not mock me, jackal."

"My lord, forgive me, I have spoken to the Corra. That should be enough."

Verris scoffed.

"You want leverage for some religious faction back home?"

"I have not been to Masheva in fourteen years, my lord."

"Citizenship then?" Verris said in a wry voice for, of course, the cost of citizenship for one not born to it was more than someone in Azetla's position could afford in a lifetime.

"I would not take that if offered in gilded writing," Azetla said through his teeth.

Under other circumstances that was too honest an answer, but now the truth must serve. Many would kill for the glorious, honored status of Imperial citizen, for the safety it offered. But even if it could save Azetla's life, he would not touch it.

And it *couldn't* save his life. Pay and bribe, bow and scrape, flatter and beg, and you could still end up on the dais at the Red River festival.

There were no more words exchanged between the two—the honorary Colonel and the unofficial commander of the Black Wren—until they reached the inn. The Corra was asleep, so Verris demanded to be escorted to the old tanner's room to see the Sahr devil "and to know whether or not you are a liar, jackal."

The Imperial guards leapt to attention to greet Verris. Two additional lamps were lit, and the Sahr was prodded awake by one of the guards, who stepped back from it quickly, though all it did was open its eyes blearily and stare at the ground.

The Sahr was tied firmly to a wooden tanner's post about the thickness of a man's curled fist. Its feet were knotted to each other, but not to anything else. The guards claimed that they had been instructed *not* to chain its feet, due to the nature of the Emperor's injury. Mostly it had slept. When it was awake, it had acknowledged nothing they either said or did, though they confessed to having been rather leery of touching it. All this they reported to Verris, while Azetla stood near the wall.

He shook his head with disdain.

"You ought to chain the feet *to* the post," he said to the guards at last. "Or just use rope. I doubt the intent of the order was to give it more freedom of movement."

"Ours is not the battalion that let it give the Emperor a blooding," the senior guard said, shooting Azetla a black look.

"Do as you please. But better it can't swing its head from one side to the other," Azetla replied. "And I'd gag it."

At that moment, the Sahr clicked its tongue loudly. The guard turned, confused. The Sahr's eyes lifted, focused. Its posture tautened. It looked at Azetla with some unreadable expression and then turned to the guard and clicked its tongue at him again. The guard stiffened. The Sahr clicked its tongue a third time and smiled.

"What did you *do*, jackal? It didn't so much as lift its own head till you got here," the guard said.

Worry entered the man's eyes. They had received the Sahr lifeless, and had believed the lie of its blank stare, just as Azetla had. The subordinate guards looked at their Lieutenant.

"Just secure it and ignore it. It's only trying to goad you," Azetla said.

He was beginning to think that this was its queer way of raising its hackles—of feigning to be more or stronger than it was. It kept at its soft target, looking brightly at the nervous guard. It seemed to enjoy the man's nervousness. To pull strength from it.

"No matter," the guard said with forced calm. "If it moves again, I'll send it to sleep." He set his palm against the Imperial dagger, his eyes skittering back and forth from the Sahr's hands to its face.

"I don't think that will make any difference," Azetla said quietly, but the guard did not even acknowledge him.

Verris clung to the entrance of the room, unsure what to make of the whole affair.

The Sahr gave another faint smile to the guard and then made a soft tsking sound. It was so inane, so meaningless, and so gallingly *nothing*. Perfect bait for rattled nerves.

The guard's mouth pinched, but he steeled himself and made good on his word. He pulled out his dagger and used the hilt to quiet the Sahr with a swift blow.

The Sahr's reaction to the pain was muted. No hiss or yelp or wrenching of the jaw. Only a slight recoil. It closed its eyes briefly then set them hard on the guard's face. Again, the galling sliver of a smile, absent mirth and full of mockery; the guard raised his hand to bring a second, more effective strike.

Azetla saw it ahead of time. He was too slow to stop it. And he didn't really want to.

The Sahr yanked its head, dodging the blow by a mere hair, so that the guard scraped his fist against the wood. In the same breath, it writhed away as far as the meager slack in the ropes would allow and pushed itself to a stand, splinters from the post burrowing into its arms and wrists. But the devil was *fast*. The guard tried to retrieve his balance, teetering close enough to feel the breath of the thing as he swung back wildly.

Then—so quick it fooled the eye—it pitched the guard to the ground with its roped feet and a shoulder thrust. Azetla was surprised it didn't sprain its own wrist, so sharp was the motion. The man's jaw hit the stone floor with an ugly sound. The Sahr dropped down along the post, arms scraped with raw wood, and rammed one knee onto the guard's chest and the other on his neck, holding itself in an awkwardly balanced crouch.

Azetla drew less than two breaths during this time. The Sahr's triumph lasted less than one.

Azetla had already emptied the space between them. He snatched the Imperial guard out from under the Sahr in the very instant of its victory. Pressing the Sahr into the post with one hand on its neck, he set a knife against its ribs. Its breaths were rapid with effort, its taunting manner dropped completely.

"Lord Verris, if it pleases you to wake the Corra now, I beg you to do so," Azetla said.

This time, Lord Verris did not hesitate or contend.

"Do whatever the jackal says," he whispered to the man in the doorway as he left to fetch his Corra.

"Go take care of your man, then come back with your Corra," Azetla said to the guards. "You're not needed at present."

Silently, they helped their senior officer along, slipping through the wide doorway, letting the cloth partition fall, and closing the outer door.

As soon as the room was empty, Azetla relaxed his grip and stood slowly. The Sahr slumped back with a slight grimace. But when it looked up at him, it was with satisfaction.

"They came that close to me half a dozen times while you were gone, prodding and snapping," it said. "But this time he came at the right angle. That was lucky."

Azetla said nothing. He did not care one way or the other about the bruises and jittery nerves of an Imperial guard. What mattered was that the Sahr had gotten exactly what it wanted. It had framed *him* as the catalyst for its sudden outburst, whether to play on their fear, or to corner him into some action or other, he did not know.

Slowly, carefully, it scraped upward against the post until it stood. It was a hand shy of Azetla's height.

"Thus far they've given me water and food and allowed me to live," it said. "And you've fared similarly."

Again, Azetla held his tongue. He would not make the same mistake as the guard and let it goad him. He walked the two steps to the wall, leaned against it, and watched.

Its eyebrows lowered faintly. There was a noticeable scar that cut through the right brow, marring it and pinching the skin between the bridge of its nose and its right eye. The guard's hilt had given it a fresh cut on its temple, and the cheek was swollen. It kept trying to lift its shoulder to wipe the blood off and keep it from trickling down its neck or into its eye, but it couldn't quite manage it. For one moment, Azetla thought, it looked well and truly tired.

"What does your Emperor really want with me?" it said at last. Azetla didn't know if the resignation in its voice was real, or simply meant to pacify.

"Not my Emperor," Azetla said. *And, in any case, the Emperor wants all you will give, whatever dignity you have thus far managed to keep intact, your absolute capitulation, and then he'll despise you for the very humiliation he drove you to. Any Mashevi could know that.*

The Sahr's eyes shifted away from Azetla's face, and its expression became clouded. He could see its jaw working, chewing on some thought. Just as the concentration on its face began to concern him, its expression went dull, its posture limp. Azetla turned to see Lord Verris and a bleary-eyed James. He straightened himself and bowed his head.

"Honor, Your Highness," he said. "And, Sahr, there's no point in doing that anymore. I told the Corra that you can speak."

He felt a cool, savory satisfaction when he saw by the rapid blinking of its eyes and twitch of its mouth that the Sahr was startled at his choice. It thought it had him mapped out. And it bloody well didn't.

"Has it said anything?" the Corra asked, looking the creature over from as much distance as the small room allowed.

"A great deal, Your Highness. But it thinks silence is safety and speech is leverage."

He had the Sahr's real attention now. The indifference melted off, and it was listening with every muscle in its body.

"Speech or no, the devil is Riada's now. That is the real issue at hand," James said, raising his shoulders in discomfort. He looked warily at the Sahr. "Does it understand *everything* we're saying?"

"Yes, Your Highness. Every word. There *is* an alternate route, I believe: consider what the Emperor wants out of all this."

James looked rather unsure as he spoke. "He wanted proof that we could take the territory and protect the outlying provinces from the devils. Test the waters, and such. Show his strength."

Azetla looked from James to Verris as from student to teacher.

"He wants it said that Emperor Riada Sivolne fears nothing. Mortal or immortal. God or devil. Jackal or jinn," Lord Verris said quietly.

Azetla had to speak now, forcefully, or he would not get another chance. He walked toward the Sahr and tilted his head in its direction. "Then deny him that. Even if you gain nothing, neither does he."

"How dare you speak like that?" Verris barked, his eyes fear-flecked. "You think because we've given you clemency thus far that it's your business to tell us how to manage our affairs? To presume our intentions? All honor to the Emperor."

Azetla set his jaw like iron. He was the only one desperate enough to hint at the whole truth of which this Sahr was a small fraction. They would go on talking as though this was simply a matter of giving James his due—of fairness and earned praise—but Azetla knew that their objectives ran far wilder than that. Wild enough to put many lives in danger.

And it was that to which he must speak, without ever saying it.

"What are you suggesting anyhow?" James said with a deep sigh. His eyes were still on the Sahr.

"It is no disrespect to the Emperor to say that it was you, not he, who went to the devils' territory. Sahr or no Sahr, that is still true. So, of course, you must faithfully do as the Emperor commands: send the Black Wren on its way to the Trekoan outpost. We will manage."

"But withhold the one thing. The tale he means to construct out of this." Azetla reached over and pulled the Sahr's head back by the jaw and put his knife to its throat. He felt its pulse go mad when the metal touched its skin, though its expression held fast and its muscles scarcely tensed. It looked up at him from the crooked angle, silent.

"Wouldn't that be a terrible waste?" James said, distraught. "After everything."

"The whole endeavor was wasteful to begin with, Your Highness. This is dabbling with fire and devilry. The Emperor may not fear that, but those not of his so-called 'divine' blood should take care. What more do you think you can possibly get from it?"

"The same as the Emperor can get," Verris growled. "Is that not so, Your Highness?"

But the Corra seemed too distracted by the Sahr's absolute stillness under the knife's edge. "Why doesn't it cry out? Why won't it *speak*?"

Azetla looked again at its face. It was not blank like in the water cart, but it was not full of the provocative vigor of even ten minutes ago. Perhaps it was not a matter of the Sahr being "unkillable" as it had taunted, but that it simply didn't care if it was killed. One person doesn't attack a battalion of six hundred unless they were other than a person, or wholly ready to die.

Eager to die, actually.

"How do I even know what to do with it if I take it?" James said, clutching his palms together and shifting his stance again and again. "What sort of devil can be *caught*?"

Azetla did not answer because he did not know. However he did believe that, if he pulled his knife back now, the blade would go through the skin, sever the veins, and the Sahr would bleed same as anything with a throat. Its breath would stop, and it would crumple to the ground.

James cautiously stepped closer to look at the Sahr in full. "What *is* it, really?"

The Sahr gave a cut-off laugh—it could not move very much for the knife—and it could only look at James sidelong. "Oh, northerner, even I don't really know the answer to that."

James gave a start. Verris did not, but his eyes flashed wide.

"Let...let it go, jackal," James breathed out.

With careful control, Azetla released the Sahr from his grip and sheathed his knife.

The Sahr rested back against the tanner's pole. All eyes were on it.

"It goes with you, Wesley. It goes to Areo," James said, his unsteady voice cutting through the silence.

"Your Highness?" Verris said.

"Why can't we, while still honoring the Emperor, be good stewards of our achievement?" James said. His voice shook only a little. Azetla could hear how hard he was working to shore himself up, to say what he meant without saying *all* he meant. "You were right, Wesley. We take the responsibility. And the jackal is right. We keep the tale of the victory in hand until we can tell it ourselves."

Verris began speaking in a careful, didactic tone. "There is no means for us to do so without incurrin—"

"Yes there is, Your Highness," Azetla cut in with his commander's voice. The one that told his soldiers that he was speaking with the Captain's words.

Before Verris could stop him, James gave a wary nod, and Azetla took it.

"My battalion must depart for Areo outpost *immediately*. This very morning. And you, Your Highness, should leave now as well. You go to the Gray Eagle. Be seen by everyone. By your brother. Then, whatever happens here, you will not be a part of it. Lord Verris will be said to have left with the battalion, just as he was ordered to do.

"But he will remain here, to see it through. As soon as his Highness and the battalion are a day or so distanced from here, and as soon as your dabblers—"

"—*Priests*," Verris interjected.

Azetla checked himself. He had been talking firm and fast, and had accidentally used the derisive Mashevi term. He pressed his lips together and forced an acquiescing nod. "As soon as the Sahr has been *seen*, you, Lord Verris, your officers, and the assigned guards will take the Sahr to rejoin the battalion."

"But how will that be explained to my brother?" James asked.

"It will not be explicable. Which is the point. Goat and lamb's blood will make this place look like something slaughtered its way out," Azetla said, glancing at the Sahr who drank every word in, but showed no thought. "And the Emperor will reach whatsoever conclusion he chooses. The important thing is, you will not have been present for any of it."

Verris' face was alight with calculation. "The guards?"

"They're not the Emperor's personal guard, they're upper court guard, and you are a colonel, are you not?"

"And the people of this inn?" Verris pressed.

Azetla let out a sharp breath through his nose, hesitating. "They...will have to come with us. Else they'll be liable."

James was nodding at each statement, looking as though he was far past thought or analysis. He had made his decision and was all but trembling with the fervor of it.

But Verris fixed Azetla with a hunter's eye.

"You're very quick with a plan," he said.

"If you had desired me to kill the Sahr, my lord, I would have had a plan for that too. Forgive me if my duties have taught me to prepare for contingencies ahead of time."

James was still staring at the Sahr as a sum he could not begin to calculate. But when he turned to Verris, it was with a decisive nod.

"Very well, Your Highness. I'll send a courier immediately."

Without a word, Azetla also started for the door to accompany the message back to the battalion.

"Oh no, jackal, you'll be staying here with me," Verris called out.

And that was the rope. He could almost feel it around his neck, jerking him back.

"There's no need for that, my lord," he replied.

"Yes there damn well is. Besides, you're our liaison," Verris said, stepping past Azetla, into the doorway.

"For what, my lord?"

"For *that*," Verris said, gesturing toward the Sahr. "You are responsible for it, jackal. And you are not yet sanctioned; remember that."

The rope cinched tight. God of Masheva, they would just as soon tie him to the same post as the Sahr. He made his voice empty, his posture loose.

"Very well, my lord."

The high-bloods departed, leaving him alone with the Sahr. Alone and livid.

They already had him by the throat, but now they would separate him from his battalion too? He felt like he was standing on a height, the wind blustering, with nothing to steady his feet. And he could see the whole jagged way down to the pinprick he would be at the bottom if he lost his balance for even a moment.

For a moment he thought all his risk and all his carefully aimed words had accomplished something for him. But he only bought more risk. His exhaustion broke suddenly over him and he would have laid his head directly on the ground if let.

"Was that what you *wanted* to happen, easterner?" the Sahr said.

Azetla had no words for that bloody thing. No game, no effort, no wit. He was spent. He walked across the room and sat against the wall nearest the door. His eyes burned and begged to be closed.

"Mashevi, don't you think—"

Azetla looked at it. "Stop. And devil, if you so much as twitch in a way I don't like—"

Its dust-dry voice scraped over his. "You'll what? Hold that knife to my throat again?"

All he wanted was for it to shut its bloody mouth. He glanced around for something to gag it with. But the room was empty.

When Azetla did not respond, the Sahr's posture collapsed with a slow, released breath. "You know you're not the first to put a knife to my throat, or to pry some bargain out of what I am, or to beg the Gods to curse me. And thus far nothing's come of it all but..." Its eyelids lowered, and it smiled a vicious little smile to itself. "Nothing but *nothing*."

It was quiet a moment.

"Anyhow, if the Gods can't kill me by their best efforts, you certainly can't."

Something in Azetla was pulled taut by what it said, but he severed it. The rest of his thoughts sank and burrowed in his stomach; his battalion would depart without him. He was trussed by Verris to this devil. He had no ally. And no way out.

17

Her sleep was shallow and uncomfortable. Almost useless. She opened her eyes to no purpose; it was blacker than night in the windowless room. She knew the terrain of the place from before, but there was nothing to do with it. She pulled in a deep breath through her nostrils. This had been a tannery, once. The sour odor of it had soaked into the northern wood, and been scrubbed over with the harsh tang of lye.

Drifting heavy through the cracks in the doorway was the smell of a fresh-made fire, but not the light of it.

She could hear the easterner breathing. His breaths were of a sleeping rhythm. When he was awake he breathed sharply, through his nose, giving a sound of fierce concentration or tamped-down anger. Even his throaty accent sounded like anger carefully locked away, which was why she had tried to find the latches to unhinge that anger to her benefit.

Not much luck there.

It would be easier if she were in her desert, on ground she knew.

She moved her tongue around in her mouth. Her throat felt chalk dry, so that it hurt to swallow. They wouldn't give her water till morning and they never gave much. Enough to tantalize, never to sate. Understandable. Thirst was distracting; the mind grew erratic, scratching desperately about.

It had seemed so simple at first: they were going to kill her, weren't they? But they kept not doing it. And the easterner wanted to so *badly*.

Yet this was what always happened. The Gods of Shihra were given an opportunity to take their vengeance against her—if they had any will left in their rotting bones—and the God of the desert was challenged to show his face for or against her.

And *nothing*. Divine silence was much worse than divine wrath. Nobody seemed to realize that.

It ought to make her laugh. Laugh until she choked.

Once she had been so naïve as to seek the Gods' favor. Then, perhaps, mere acknowledgment of existence, that scant token they gave to all who breathed. Now, all that was left—all that she could possibly incur—was ire, and even *that* she could not get. The fire in her, the burning will that kept her on her feet, was going out, and here she was making herself sick and dizzy with all the breath from her own lungs trying to wake that fire up.

She smiled in the dark and shook her head. What did she think would happen? She had been beating at her Gods long enough. She knew their backs were turned, stony against her fist.

Oh but it had looked like an answer at first. The arrival of the northern battalion in her native hills had been of such uncanny timing. She wondered if that bloody easterner's God—the vicious meddler—had finally thrown her a lure. Perhaps, since her own Gods were silent and dead, the God of the desert was still awake and weary enough of her blasphemy to do something. Anything. So she tracked the intruders, like a scent laid out by the divine.

Perhaps she should have gone the Ghoshri route instead. Then she wouldn't have needed to gut several of her own people to get out. Or she could have skirted southeast toward the Makarish Uoloya tribe, but she would probably have had to draw some blood to get past there as well. The number of places that would tolerate her was dwindling.

She hadn't even washed the fight off her skin that morning. She had been three hours from good water, moving slowly and deliberately, for each step she took out of her hills was one she would not be allowed to retrace. She savored every stride of the cut-throat terrain. She left her horse in the west valley so as to climb the last high ridge of what the northerners called "Sahr." Streaked with sweat-salt and dry blood, she had leaned against the wind and parted her lips to taste the sere gusts of air.

It used to be a comfort. Sharp edges and sheer expanse. Blistering heat rising up from the ground as if from fire. The wide, ruthless threat of it all. It made her feel as though she was the brightest burning thing in the whole earth, and with sheer will she could bring all the Gods to heel. She would let the wind all but knock her down.

But not this time. Her desert withdrew from her, quietly taunting as if with a turned back that she had nowhere left to go. Either that desert God was carefully stripping her to bones and breaking off all her paths, or she was doing it herself. It was hard to tell. She didn't know how to do anything else until she got the answer she wanted.

Then she had seen them, moving south, blackening the lowlands with men and horses: a northern battalion, looking for a fight. A precious, perfect, beautiful distraction from the shrinking ground under her feet. There was some feral hope in it too; the idea of standing her native ground, in spite of everything, was an intoxicating one.

So she had walked alongside them, as a goatherd, accompanied by a stolen flock, watching and listening. She climbed high. Waited. And then she began to bleed the battalion. Drop by drop. Each day she watched to see if they would gather their bodies and their useful superstitions and run.

But they refused. So she gave them what they came for before they could get too close to home. Now she was farther north than she had ever been, mapping new ground with every step and glance. The difficulty was not in gathering her surroundings, or in crafting a plan; the difficulty was waking the fire in her gut enough to even *want* to.

She stretched out her legs until they touched the nearest wall then, setting her jaw, she struck her heels hard into the creaking wood a few times.

She heard shifting shoulders against the wall.

"Stop that," the easterner growled from the corner of the room.

He woke easy, and the guards just peered their heads in each time. Since she could scarcely sleep, she decided to make his rest jagged as well. Everyone was always easier to read when they were tired.

He started to settle back into half sleep and she let him for the moment. Small bands of dark blue light began to manifest through the cracks in the pitch-mortar between planks. His breathing began to soften.

She kicked the loose wood again, as hard as she could. He took in a sharp breath.

"Better stay awake this time, easterner. It's all but morning," she said, leaning back and curling her fingers against the thick rope on her wrists. "You've Corras and Colonels to appease."

She needed these ropes off, but the doing of it required patience, precision, and a certain brand of cooperation from this easterner. It was not yet clear whether he would give it. She would not say she had misread him, exactly, but rather that aiming at his obvious vulnerabilities had produced confusing results.

Not that it wasn't fascinating to watch how exquisitely *nervous* he made the northerners, and how delicate a balancing act he managed. He was supposed to be the easiest path—pariahs usually were—but he had turned out to be more convoluted terrain than she expected. Mashevis were new ground for her. She was wary of them, not for their own sake, but for the sake of their ruthless God.

The easterner didn't seem to think she was jinn, either, which complicated matters. Even her own people, from within their carefully constructed reputation as devils, believed her to be a corrupted, foul *shikk*, too unholy to sanction.

She heard flint and saw sparks. A wick took flame and the easterner took shape in the dark, lamp in hand. Heavy shadows under his eyes, tired posture, grave expression. He looked at her briefly, but did not speak. Rarely did. He left the room, requesting a short relief from one of the northern guards. As the pale-skinned, pale-headed soldier took the Mashevi's place in the corner, she slumped and let her mind drift. She closed her eyes and listened to the guard's nervous breathing, the heavy northern accents that came muffled through the door, and she drew in the smell of sumac and rice just starting to burn somewhere nearby. There were times to provoke and times to play dead.

⚓

"Where's Azetla—the Mashevi?" Joseph asked the courier as he offered him water and food.

The man shook his head. "They kept him for something."

Like one informed of a fatal illness, Joseph nodded gravely. He had his marching orders, and dawn was already blazing. The battalion packed up the camp at Joseph's word and Sarrez set the Black Wren in the unlikely and unwanted direction of central Trekoa. There was pervasive bitterness and confusion about the drastic change in orders. They marched in quiet discontent.

Joseph was *furious* at Azetla for getting himself cornered like this. He wanted to wring his neck. How could he have been so stupid?

Everything was wrong. Everything.

193

Joseph kept silent and somber as the dead for the first hour of the journey toward Trekoa. It was a version of himself that few of his men ever saw and none of them liked. No easy grins. No teasing or jokes or affectionate antagonism. The younger soldiers skirted him warily, and he was glad of it.

In some frustrating, idiotic way, Joseph felt he was to blame for what could happen to Azetla. He had encouraged the Captain to use Azetla from the first. When Joseph had been given leave to go bury his wife and child after the Lavender Plague, the Captain asked if Azetla should stand in Joseph's place. And Joseph said *yes*. Yes, he was a jackal, and, yes, he was irksome with his rituals and his ledgers and his lack of levity. But he had such a talent for taking all of the work and none of the prestige. It suited everyone nicely.

Azetla was a mark of Joseph's savvy. And he was his friend.

He wondered if they would let him bury the body. It might well come to that.

"You worry the men, being so silent," Sarrez said, dismounting and walking alongside Joseph. "They're used to it from Azetla, but not from you."

"They'll survive it," he said with a grimace. "What the devils is going on here, Nimer?"

"I wish I knew."

Absent from their mouths, but understood by both, was the fact that Azetla would have known. Probably did know.

"Well. There'll be word of some kind soon enough," Sarrez said in the bland tone of a man who doesn't at all believe what he's saying.

"From who? You're almost the highest blood we have here now and they didn't tell you anything."

They were both quiet again.

"At least now we can throw back arak and toss those bloody ledgers and regulations to the wind," Joseph said with a half-hearted smile. How he hated those ledgers at first. So tedious. So unlike

Hodge's casual and instinctive style. So obnoxiously precise. And effective. Now Joseph lived by them.

"Oh right, of course," Sarrez said without smiling at all.

"Well, we *can* pray that they kill that devil in the foulest manner possible," Joseph said suddenly as he prepared to signal a halt.

"I wish they'd given us the job of it, by blood."

"Don't we all," Joseph replied.

Sarrez glanced around at the rutted Maurowan road. "Our jackal will manage, I'm sure."

"Ah. You really shouldn't call him jackal, Sarrez. He hates that."

"You call him that all the time."

"Only to irritate him. It's different when it's from *your* mouth. Carries all that old, bad blood, whether you mean it to or not."

"I don't."

"I know that," Joseph said. "But I'm not sure he does."

He called the halt and they consulted their maps. After Tarthus and resupply, they would be subject to rougher roads, and to the territory of the most powerful Trekoan Rokh, Imal Bin-Zari. Officially, Rokh Bin-Zari was a subject of Maurow, but desert rumor said he scorned all northern emissaries and did entirely as he pleased. He would not *attack* Maurowan soldiers, but he would never assist them, and was always happy to trouble or waylay them.

Joseph furled the map with frustration. Azetla should be here.

But it was not the absence of Azetla's leadership that set him on edge. Joseph was Lead Sergeant. He knew what to do. It was what the absence signified. Something was going on under the surface and Azetla had gone and gleaned too much. Colonel Verris might make good on his threats. He could put a sword through Azetla or make him commander. He could throw him in prison or put him to work. Lord Colonel Verris could do anything he wanted.

And Joseph couldn't do a bloody thing about any of it.

It was with a queasy feeling that he realized they could slit Azetla's throat to Serivash right in front of his eyes and, unless he wanted the same for himself, all he could do in response was bow his head and say, "at your service, my lord."

James gathered himself at a calm pace so as not to arouse suspicion. He was ready to see home. Ready for its regularity and comforts, for the kindly feeling of irrelevance he should not miss, but did, and for the morning game of Arratul with his old nursemaid. Blind though she now was, she never failed to tell him how handsome he was. Such utter nonsense, and such simple sweetness.

Wesley came to the inn room just as Uttar left to ready James' horse.

"No cause for worry," James said, feeling surprisingly unburdened. He had made a choice, and now he was choosing not to think about it. "I'll be safely visible at the Gray Eagle within the hour."

Wesley took a deep, ominous breath.

"There is one more thing, Your Highness. You must send a courier to Colonel Everson at Areo. *Now*, and with a Trekoan guide to assure it arrives before the Black Wren does."

James nodded easily. "To what effect?"

"An execution order."

"I don't—"

"For the jackal."

James' shoulders tensed.

"But...I thought we meant to *keep* him. I thought that's what you meant by all this."

"We will keep him only as long as we need him. But once we reach Areo, I believe we'll be able to do without him. And you'll be safer for it, Your Highness. You know this. We can hardly rely on Maurow's enemies to strengthen her. We'll make sensible use of him and I'll hold my tongue until he can be safely discarded."

"I didn't…" James faltered. "I just thought he could be an ally. He *hates* Riada."

Wesley's face drew tight.

"Of course he does and of course he would say as much. But a Mashevi hates Riada because what he really hates is *Maurow*. Don't you understand? A jackal would say anything to get what he wants."

"To live?" James said bitterly.

Wesley shot James a critical look. "You can never know in which direction or manner a jackal might be seditious and this particular one is…" Verris trailed off, pressing his lips together and shaking his head. "In any case, I mean to protect you and all your endeavors, Your Highness. So it has to be done: *as soon* as I arrive at Areo, before he has any chance to ingratiate himself with the men there, or influence them. Tell Colonel Everson that it must be quietly done. No fanfare, no theatrics."

"I…I don't like it."

"You don't have to like it, Your Highness, only—"

"But you don't think that seems a harsh sentence for a man who simply—"

"Who simply broke numerous laws? Carries a sword? Wields dangerous amounts of authority over a whole battalion? Now, consider. Are the men of the Black Wren yours or his?"

"His," James said in a small voice.

"And if we're not careful, he may do with them as he pleases. They must become *yours*."

James rubbed his hands over his face with a long, exhausted sigh.

"This is exactly what we've talked about, Your Highness. You must be more wary, more suspicious. You can't waver just because some jackal feigned to need your help, and forced you to make a decision."

"You mean the same way you did, Wesley?"

A flash of anger crossed Wesley's face. "I tell you the *truth*."

"I think he did too."

The lines of Wesley's anger faded, his voice softened. "Your brother is wrong about many things, but not about jackals, Your Highness. He goaded me, you know. The jackal. Made it sound like he knew more about our intentions than could possibly be true...or *safe*. You must trust me. He wheedled you. Acknowledge it, so to be the wiser."

The words left a pit in James' stomach. He closed his eyes and conceded with a nod. It was all he knew how to do. He had given his word to the jackal and now his word was made null. Something in him sagged down and he felt the stupor of his old apathy crawl over him, with no pleasing ignorance to accompany it.

"I'll write the order," he said in a low, muttering voice.

"Take heart, Your Highness." Verris turned toward the door. "Not every good decision pleases the palette."

James held the bronze pen in his hand a long while before he wrote the order.

But write it, he did.

18

Wesley sat across from the jackal in a cramped room. He was growing stiff in the only chair, while the jackal leaned, arms folded, against the stone shelf. They could both hear the group of priests, shamans, and augurs shuffling down the inn corridor to inspect the Sahr devil and declare it one thing or another, authorizing it to enter city walls or not. Why it had taken them a day and a half to come, Wesley did not know, but there seemed to be scores of them.

Riada was nothing if not thorough. And it was taking an arduous amount of time.

Wesley wished he could hear their divinings, but he was supposed to be long gone, on his way to Areo with the Black Wren. He couldn't risk being seen.

He looked at Azetla. The jackal made no attempt to veil his distaste as the temple scents wafted through the door. Sweet garlands, livestock, lavender incense, and the juice of berries which the priests wore on their hands to signify the blood they must sometimes spill. The jackal's expression, like someone smelling rot, irritated Wesley.

"So much for your disgust if they manage to give a real answer," he said.

"My lord?" Azetla answered in a tired voice, without bothering to look at Wesley or formalize his posture.

"If the priests of every God declare in one voice that the creature is surely a devil or surely not, will your contempt against the Gods still hold? Or do you only trust your own voice?"

Just like Riada.

Now the jackal did tilt his head and set his eyes on Wesley.

"I would not believe what your dabblers said, even if I fell so despicably far as to believe in your gods. My lord," he said in a flat, hard voice. "But not because I trust my own voice."

"You can't use that desert god as an excuse for your arrogance. Maurow accepts all Gods, all practices, even yours. It is you who shun and reject, not us."

Azetla closed his eyes briefly, then turned his gaze back to the corner of the room. There was hardly any other place to look, so small was the space. He was quiet for a long time.

"Yours mix the sacred and profane—*imitate* the sacred with the profane—until everything is muddled, and you can't possibly know the difference anymore," he said at last, quiet with untouchable certainty.

"What does that even mean?" Wesley muttered, exasperated. He was sick of this suffocatingly small room, sick of the way the jackal made him feel like he couldn't quite *see*. Somehow knowing that an execution knife was being made ready for this jackal did not soothe him. Rather, every word the man said felt more and more like grit in the throat, a bad taste in the mouth.

"You mimic your old practice of human sacrifice in the ritualized way you kill us on the Red River festival," the jackal said. "A half-hearted thing, really. You skirt your own gods' demands for clean and innocent blood, by feeding them what *you* deem to be vile and worthless. Your gods are mere nature and clay to you, and you bend them to your need."

Wesley stood, struggling to keep his voice low. "And your people don't do the same? I know that—"

Suddenly the inn girl, Mali, entered.

"They are gone, my lord," she said. Before Wesley could ask, she added, "They told me very little. Not what they think. Not what they plan to do. All I know is that the priestess of Lyrala took it as bad omen that they could not pour the vorstin for purification. The Sahr moved suddenly. The bottle fell and broke. It remained silent."

Wesley dismissed the girl with an abrupt gesture. Then he and the jackal went to the Sahr which sat and looked at them placidly.

"It could have opened its bloody mouth at least, and told them what they wanted to hear," Wesley said.

The Sahr smiled faintly. "But wouldn't a devil always tell you only and exactly what you want to hear? Why would you believe it?"

Wesley flinched a little. He was still not used to its voice. Its impossibly precise North City timbre.

"Why the wakeful mouth *now*, jinn-thing?"

It clicked its tongue. "Because I know when a gambit is bled dry."

"My Lord, the Emperor won't wait much longer to decide. We must move quickly," Azetla said, stepping between Wesley and the Sahr. "I've readied everything."

"And these inn people of yours," Wesley said. "They're compliant?"

Azetla glanced down and back. "Yes, my lord. I've explained it to them. They are prepared. And those guards out there? Are *they* compliant? Will they believe they are acting on the Emperor's orders?"

"I have arranged it so," Wesley said, strength and sharpness coming back to him, circling his anger toward the jackal, smoothing down its edges. "It *will* be an encumbrance, bringing the inn folk with us."

"Unless you have the stomach for the alternative, that is irrelevant, my lord."

Wesley raised his eyebrows and looked at Azetla with warning.

"Oh? Then on your head be it," he said softly. "If I find reason to distrust even one of them, I assure you I will have a very strong stomach indeed. Now, I leave that devil and the handiwork of its 'escape' to you."

For there was an emperor to deceive. Riada's prize must elude him and—this was the crucial part—there must be no one to blame.

The inn was ready—goat's blood, lamb's blood and all—and there was only one left who was not prepared: the reason the Colha family was being torn from their home, and the spoke around which everything now turned.

The Sahr sat back against the wood pole, eyes closed, fingers tapping softly at the wood.

"Stand up," Azetla said.

It ignored him. Azetla walked over and pulled it to its feet.

It remained standing of its own volition, but leaned against the post, as though—just maybe—weary at the prospect of once again being dragged around until rope burned its ankles and wrists half to the bone and its own smell began to choke its nostrils. It had been in captivity for a full month and looked it.

"If you—" it began, voice dry and sandy.

"I have less than no patience left for you, Sahr. Keep your tongue behind your teeth and this will be far better for both of us."

At that, he slipped out his knife and pushed the Sahr hard against the post, driving his arm against it and keeping it firmly in place. It sucked in a tight breath, bracing.

Keeping his grasp, Azetla crouched down and cut its feet loose. Then its hands. Last of all the rope around its neck, looking it dead in the eye as he did so. He carefully did not hold his breath as he stepped back.

The Sahr stared at him like he was a madman. Without haste, Azetla drew his sagam and held it low. It took one step, but then immediately fell back against the post for support. It glanced at its raw wrists and scraped arms with critical eyes. Gently, slowly, it rolled its wrists and kneaded its shoulders. It stood straight again, pressing its fingers against its palms over and over, rocking smoothly on its heels.

So far, so good. It *should* be atrophied, cotton-mouthed, off-balance, and its muscles stiff from lack of mobility. It kept its eyes on Azetla the whole time, looking more wary now than it ever had when it was tied hand and foot.

Still slow, it began to walk away from the post, pacing the room, testing its stride, limping at first, then regaining steadiness.

"Why?" it said, glancing at the ropes he had cut from it.

"The guards are bringing water and a basin—clean linen—and you're going to make yourself look and smell a bit more human. We don't need festering wounds," Azetla said. "We need you on your feet."

It did not respond but kept working away the stiffness in its body.

When the basin of water was brought, however, the Sahr did move quickly. It dropped straight to one knee and drew water up to its mouth several times over. Azetla stood against the doorframe and kept watch.

"Hurry," he said.

It drank a few more mouthfuls, then scrubbed its face. It removed the worn, half-fitted leathering, but left the ragged under-tunic hanging on its body, as though it had some southern sense of propriety. It was as exact and methodical about the task of washing as it had been about stretching its muscles, starting with all the cuts, scrapes, and raw skin. With brisk efficiency, it rinsed the layers of dirt and sweat out of its skin and out of the stiff cloth that covered its frame.

Filthy brown-red-tinged water drained out across the stone as it washed. With coarse scrubbing, it worked the grit out of its hair. The air inside the stone room was morning-cool and the water cold; the

Sahr's body shuddered involuntarily. When it finished, some of the sores bled anew from the scouring. It had been quick, quiet, and not remotely gentle to itself.

That was enough for Azetla. He handed it the clean linen Mali had provided. It hesitated only a moment before taking it.

Its bruises were more visible now that it was clean and it had dark shadows of hunger and exhaustion under its eyes. Its sturdy frame was leaner than it ought to be. He caught a brief glimpse of the heavy scars on its shoulders when it traded its ragged shirt for the clean linen. Then it brushed off the soft goat leather and donned it. Lastly, it took a grimy strip of cloth and knotted its hair in some deft, inexplicable way.

The guards were supposed to rap the stone when they were ready to bind it again, but he couldn't hear them in the corridor, so he kept his sagam drawn. He watched and waited. Livened by cleanliness and sated from thirst, the Sahr's eyes moved over every stone and dust mote the way the gleaner's hands raked slowly through the harvested fields to find the remains.

"My Trekoan knife," it said.

"What about it?"

It clicked its tongue at him. "You have it."

Azetla held a ready stance in case it suddenly dove for the concealed weapon.

"I'll need it back eventually," it said.

Azetla almost laughed at the gall of it. It only wanted to provoke. He let his sagam occupy the space between them, and it did not challenge the distance. At last, he heard the guard. He did not say "enter," but sheathed his sagam.

He had brought old strips of cloth, which Khala had given him, to wrap around the Sahr's wrists to protect the raw skin from fresh ropes. He disliked offering even this paltry comfort—one he had *always* given prisoners when their wrists looked like that—but made himself do it anyway. It was his own rule. A standard, not to be ignored on behalf of a Sahr.

With a rough hand, he wrapped the cloth about its wrists, feeling foolish the whole time. The Sahr gave him a look he well recognized. It was the one all prisoners gave when they began to suspect that their captors could possibly be softened. Tricked. Overcome.

The look was fleeting, though.

"I think you know better than that," he said, grasping it hard by the shoulder.

It looked at him, said nothing, and gave a slanted shrug. It was strangely calm.

It kept that calm even as the guards came in with fresh ropes to lash its hands together. He was ready for it to resist being bound again, but it kept still as the knots were cinched.

Only when they began to herd it through the door, did it suddenly make trouble. With just the cumbersome weight of its body, it rammed one guard into the lintel and shouldered the other in the chest, causing both of them to trip and scramble.

Then, just as suddenly, it was soft and compliant again.

The guards gave it a few sound blows—they would have beaten it senseless if Azetla had let them—but neither of them were hurt in any real way, just shocked into taking greater care.

The Sahr flashed a curious look at Azetla. He got the distinct impression that this irrational behavior had nothing whatsoever to do with rebellion or hope of escape. It was just testing the boundaries, gauging how the guards reacted. How Azetla reacted. And, almost, it seemed as though it was trying to break itself against those boundaries where it found them. And for that, Azetla had no explanation.

Now, at last, Azetla could go back to the Black Wren. Back to Joseph and Sarrez and the chance of someone at his back when the worst came.

The dark thought did occur to him that even a week or a fortnight might be enough for some to forget why they had ever tolerated a Mashevi in the first place. Fear and uncertainty can make
for short memories, and some had long hated him. The Black Wren
might already be much less safe—less home—than he left it.

Mali worked feverishly to ready herself, her father, and Anna for
departure. Better to work than think about what was happening.
Khala had tried to help, in her way. But this was not her home, these
were not her possessions, and her life had never been as rooted and
solid as Mali's. Mashevis were used to roaming in and out of cities
and provinces, or being ordered in and out of them by others. Khala
was used to being herded and shoved by city-soldiers to one place or
another for no known reason.

But Mali was Maurowan, and even her Makarish grandmother
had been a born citizen. She was the daughter of an innkeeper who
was the son of an innkeeper, on through three more generations on
her father's side. When she stopped and let the thoughts run free,
her stomach lurched and her hands shook until she clasped them
one to another.

The nature of the ruse required the inn to be damaged and
spattered in the blood a Sahr would have ostensibly spilled to escape.
Seeing her home this way made her feel gutted and blooded right
along with it. Mali took what was necessary and what was sacred,
but there was only one small cart for the journey, and it could only
be packed so deftly. Most of her life would be left behind.

Anna, in her half understanding, was wicked with excitement.
Mali's father was amenable to everything, given that Mali had convinced him they were going to visit her elder sister in the northern
outskirts, and that he would see his grandchildren. The lie tasted
like dust in her mouth, but for once she prayed that his weakening

mind would serve her well, and he would forget what she told him. Mali clutched his hand every few minutes to reassure him. Anna, she reined in by the neck and set to task.

Khala had the work of watering and victualing the Imperial guards, which she did with smiles and clever chatter—something in which she had always surpassed Mali—and the guards smiled and chattered back. She knew how to pretend all was well. She knew how to lie through her teeth without seeming the least bit bothered. Mali did not.

On the marked hour, Mali waited, tight-chested, for Azetla to come out to the street with the last and unholiest piece of cargo. With the curiosity of dread, she watched the Sahr step smoothly out onto the dust and cobble. It had the same restraints as before; hands tied in front this time, and guards set at either elbow. But it carried itself...*free*. As if the ropes were a courtesy to an audience, not of any real meaning.

Azetla had said not to be fearful. Mali tried to comply.

Azetla knotted a small sack of dry chuva to the Sahr's hands with twine. The loose cloth sank over the rope so that it looked like any common no one trudging through the back streets with a burden, and so its hands were weighted down. This did not comfort Mali, but Azetla didn't seem much concerned with anyone's comfort. He was in what Khala derisively referred to as "his aiming mind." His eyes were secured to a target and other matters and people could have no place in his thoughts.

The Sahr scoured each and every one of them with its gaze. The eyes seemed to *drink*, slow and strong.

Mali thought of the Trekoan stories, and how the jinn could sweep away your soul in a gust of wind if they caught your eyes. She averted her face when it looked at her, but held her head level. Predators went for the weak prey, and Mali did not want to be counted as such.

Azetla set the party on the move, taking an oblique path. Discretion was not easily accomplished with two women, a child, an elderly man, North City guards, a jackal, a Lord, and a devil. Everyone was on foot or on horseback except Anna, whose elation burned hot and bright then promptly flared out. She was asleep inside the cart when dusk stole over the city outskirts.

The soldiers were instructed to walk in pairs—as city-soldiers did—Lord Verris wrapped his head in the Trekoan style, and Mali and Khala wore their headscarves as Makarish women. Azetla forced the greatest possible distance and disassociation, so they might not be thought of as a group, though they never fully left each other's sight.

At the outer roads, Azetla dealt with the rumor-hawkers swiftly and easily. There were many men and women in South City who were known for being collectors and traders of information. Azetla always said that there was no point in paying them to keep silent about something they had seen or heard—they could be bought and sold a hundred times over, and no secret would ever be kept—but if one wanted to *spread* information, this they would do willingly.

He told them that there was "troubling talk" of a violent attack at some South City inn. That there might be a devil in Piarago. Or it might be nothing. He couldn't be sure what was true. Mere rumors, you see.

Azetla gave them the entire falsehood without ever lying explicitly, but he gave it all the same. So much for that jackal piety, if it could be satisfied by a technicality.

Mali's eyes grew sticky, her lids stone-heavy. She dearly wanted sleep, but she knew it would be long in coming. She pressed her fingers against the sides of her nose and underneath her eyes to liven them. Inadvertently, she glanced at the Sahr, which looked back at her with narrowed eyes. That made her start, as if she had turned to find a spider on her shoulder.

From then on, Mali tried hard to keep out from under its eyes, and to think of nothing, nothing, nothing. At some point her feet found a rhythm and soothed her thoughts to a low simmer, though she didn't quite remember when or how that happened.

They made it out of the city without incident, and then past the outlying towns. This was supposed to be a cause for relief. But all Mali felt was an emptiness in her stomach. She had never been this far away from home.

19

The Maurowan road soon began to deteriorate beneath their
feet. Markers grew sparse. Dust became fine, a haze in the air,
drying out the mouth. They had entered the province of Trekoa.

Azetla did not know the land well at all. He knew enough to get
them *to* Areo, but he did not know whether he could do it half as
quickly or safely as he needed to. The Trekoan tribes were famous
for their ruthless inter-fighting, the Rokhs for their implacability.

The march was quiet, heavy as with grief. Azetla could not look
long at Khala and the Colha family without feeling a sting of guilt.
He silenced it, as being of no service to anyone. But the silence bit at
him.

He set a moderate pace as the terrain under the dusty blue sky
began to rise against him. The wind stirred up as the day lengthened, throwing grit in their eyes for almost the entire afternoon. It
calmed just before dusk, giving Azetla a chance to find good resting
ground outside a small Trekoan village. A few Trekoans there spoke
Maurowan, and Azetla was able to bargain with them; that would
not be the case once they reached central Trekoa. Even here, when
Verris tried to hire a guide, none could be found. Azetla took it to
mean none were willing.

The third morning passed quickly. The Sahr caused no trouble. It scarcely said a word. Even when Azetla pressed it on one subject or another, it gave the slightest answer possible. And each time Azetla tried to draw information from it, it somehow turned his words—or his accent—back against him, and he felt he had ceded ground rather than gained it. He was being thoroughly read by a blank page. So he let the silence prevail.

In the heat of the day, Azetla let everyone rest so that he could consult his map. The further they went, the worse the road was, and the more discrepancies he encountered between what the map told him and what he saw before him.

He raised his eyebrows when little Anna Colha came over and began to circle him, eventually sitting down as close as she could. She looked at the map.

"Where are we going?"

With a sigh, Azetla gave up any hope of finding the map's merits, and simply pointed to the symbol that was Areo.

"And where are we now?"

"Roughly *here*."

Very roughly.

The Sahr spoke from its tethered place next to the cart.

"You're a day directly east of the Saav River, four miles northwest of the village of Hamaris, and a half hour's walk from a small Maurowan shrine that marks the old boundary."

Anna peered around Azetla with blazing curiosity; he had not allowed her near the Sahr. But, as with any child, the thing that was forbidden was precisely the thing she wanted.

"What are those marks on her hand?" she asked in a dread whisper.

"I don't know Anna-le," Azetla said quietly.

"But why does she have them?" Anna persisted.

"Anna—"

The Sahr gave a half-smile. "I'll answer the little one," it said, moving its eyes toward Azetla. Suddenly, on its tongue, it carried Anna's particular brand of South City Maurowan, with the same bits of common Makarish slang. The Sahr pulled its sleeve up by dragging it against the wood of the cart, then tilted its head at the marks that circled its upper arm. "This one is for a Trekoan tribe—not mine—and this one," it drummed the fingers of its right hand against the air, "is for a Makarish tribe. Also not mine. Neither mean much of anything to me, but they mean all manner of interesting things to others."

"Why are you marked for tribes that aren't yours?" Anna called out, bold and free and relatively unafraid. Azetla tried not to show that he awaited the answer with as much keenness as the little asker.

"The tribes were never mine, only I was theirs—each for a time," it said in a full, strange voice, all dusty around the edges. Tired, rather. "They ate their fill of me, though I can't say they were satisfied."

Azetla glanced sideways at the Sahr, whose gaze was fixed ahead, across the gray-brown hills to the south which rose to dust and fell to dust and granted very little green life in between. There was no smile on its face now, no mockery in its tone.

Anna's face clouded with the uneasiness borne of not grasping the matter at hand.

"Enough, Anna-le," Azetla said softly. "Why don't you go sit with your sister?"

"All she wants to talk about is how awful and dry and broken up the land is," Anna said irritably, stealing glances at the Sahr. "Why did your God *make* it like this?"

"I don't know. He made the softest green places, and the dry brown ones. He made them all."

"Well *maybe* out *here*, we're better off with your God than ours," Anna said gravely. "I don't think Lyrala or Deyra would last long out here."

Azetla curbed the temptation toward a smile. "I think you're right, Anna-le."

She gave a fierce nod, terribly certain of herself, as most children tended to be.

"And that's why *you* can't hurt us," Anna said, looking around Azetla to the Sahr. Her hand jittered slightly as she gripped the edge of Azetla's shirt, but her eyes were fearlessly bright. "Azetla will call his God down on you first."

The Sahr gently lifted its eyebrows, a strange brightness coming into its expression.

"I hope he does, little one," it said in a quiet, emphatic voice. "I surely hope he does."

Azetla had no response whatsoever, no comprehension almost. He ran the words through his mind over and over as if the meaning might become clear. Mali soon dragged Anna away, instructing her to give the Sahr distance. And give Azetla distance too.

A half hour's march later, they passed a small boundary shrine. Azetla said nothing, but looked at the Sahr sidelong.

"If you cut east here, when you get to the wadi, you'll have the better crossing," it said, no wadi in sight. "Otherwise you'll go the long way around."

"Wadi Arinla?" Azetla said, glancing at his North Trekoan map.

The Sahr gave a grimace as though his pronunciation had a distinct odor.

"*Aharin-yila*," it corrected. "And yes."

Azetla had not realized they were almost to Arinla. *Aharin-yila.* He did not try to say it out loud. He knew he doubly convoluted the name. It came through his Mashevi accent from the even poorer source of the Maurowan version of the word.

"But we can't if—" he began.

"I just told you that you could. After the rains it's the better crossing, and you'll come out at a Lahashet village instead of a Qatlani one. The Lahashet have good wells, and will be less likely to kill you for your women and horses while you sleep."

Its tone was quiet and pragmatic. Azetla looked at his map again, biting the inside of his cheek. The map was made by Maurowans. Markings were oriented toward Imperial interests, and tribal boundaries entirely absent. If the map was even slightly accurate, it would add hours, if not a day, to skirt around the Aharin-yila rather than go through it.

"I'll show you the crossing, and if you don't like it, you may submit to whatever wanderings that map offers you," the Sahr said.

For a moment, Azetla wished he had gone with his first instinct and gagged it. Not because he thought it was lying, but because he suspected it was telling the truth. And he was tempted by it. Far worse the devil that never seems to lie; it became hard to refute.

Azetla almost ignored it for this very reason but, after another long look at the map, he turned in the direction of its tilted head.

Not an hour later, the Sahr proved right. It began to lay out the land before them, mile by mile. It spoke of a sharp rise in the dusty trail, and the rise appeared as if on command. It mentioned a well, and half an hour later, they saw that blessed low cylinder of cut, mortared rock and were grateful to see it. The Sahr became the Trekoan guide they had failed to acquire.

When it marked a more direct way through the River Saav, despite the dangerous rise from winter rains, Azetla stopped looking at the Maurowan map. It was pointless. The Sahr's vivid account of the Trekoan desert became a fixed thing. They were going to catch up to the Black Wren before they reached Areo. Easily.

The Sahr knew how to make itself valuable. A silent barter, Azetla thought. He had sense enough to be wary, sense enough to warn himself. But he chose to listen to it again. And again.

He knew the Sahr might tell the truth a hundred times just so that it could lie once when it mattered. Azetla had no real way to solve that problem. Verris kept asking Azetla if they could try again to hire a guide in the next village, but Azetla knew what the result of that would be. Rokh Bin-Zari of Saqiran and his followers were notorious for their unwillingness to help northerners and any soldier of experience knew that scavenging a guide mid-journey was a ripe chance to be led astray and thoroughly looted.

Yet how did he know that wasn't what the Sahr was doing now? He didn't. He made an assessment, made a decision, and braced for the consequences. That was all that could be done. He could not help how utterly his life in the Black Wren had shaped him; he had seen many times that wavering hesitation was often more dangerous than a mere wrong decision.

When the tiny caravan came to a village or encampment, all of them—from Azetla to little Anna—became wholly reliant on the Sahr devil's tongue, for it was the only one who could speak Trekoan with any fluency. All that was given, and all that was withheld came either by its lies or by its savvy. Who could know which.

By that same tongue, and with subtlety, it began to enforce a hierarchy. It spoke to Azetla. In the villages, it introduced him, translated for him, gave him the lay of the land. It ignored Verris entirely, as if he were cargo.

It was clearly *helping* him, or trying to make him believe that it was. That could only mean that it saw Azetla as useful to itself. An opportunity. He couldn't know its full intent, but it was wise to remember that it must see him as a means to some end.

Well he saw it precisely as it saw him. It was an opportunity. A tool. It was a mere question of who could use who more successfully. Lately, Azetla had found that he was far better at using people than he should have liked to admit. He had loved and respected his Captain; he had used him too.

Azetla mouthed a prayer-lament and laid that grief-guilt mixture in a quiet corner of his mind, alongside its many cousins. He kept his steady pace and his careful watch of the Sahr. And it watched him. Noted every narrowed eye, every clenched jaw, every gesture of the hand.

And, when the next morning came, it watched him when he washed his hands and mouthed his prayers.

"You only pray to the God of the Desert?" it asked after staring long and rather scornfully at him.

"Yes," he said.

"You pray to him because he is God or because you're Mashevi?" it said.

Azetla raised his eyes to it in irritation.

"For both reasons," he replied tightly.

The Sahr clicked its tongue, dissatisfied. "I do have something of a debt to settle with your particular God, over and against my own. Remind him of it for me, since you think he hears you. He won't listen to me."

Azetla stared at the Sahr for several breaths, his lips parted in wordless surprise. He disliked hearing the Sahr talk of the God of Masheva; this was holy and unholy threatening to mix. The Sahr did not smirk at his reaction. It only narrowed its eyes, lowered itself smoothly to the ground, and made quick work of its morning ration of water.

20

I t was late morning when Azetla knew that something was wrong. They were low on water, and he had not seen a well all the previous day. Then there was the sudden westward cant the Sahr had taken for the past mile. It hadn't said anything as to why it shifted direction, but it certainly wasn't for the sake of better ground underfoot. The tribal route they were on narrowed almost to a goat's trail.

Azetla's wary blood awoke. For the first time, he believed the Sahr was pulling them astray. He moved across the caravan until he walked at its shoulder. Before he could say a word, the Sahr indicated the southwestern ridge with a tilt of its head.

He looked up. Several Trekoans crested the low ridge and began to shadow the caravan. Azetla set his left hand, as if to rest, on his hilt.

"What are they doing? Why are they watching us?"

"We're set in the direction of their herds, so they've come to defend them."

Azetla grabbed the Sahr by the back of its overshirt and almost pulled it off-balance. "What did you *do*?"

As Azetla called halt, dozens of Trekoan horsemen began to bleed out from behind the crumbled hills, as if out of shadows. They were

217

all armed but their weapons were not drawn and their advance was slow. The bright white end of their headcloths billowed out behind them as they formed an imposing semi-circle in front of Azetla's tiny caravan.

The Sahr did not tense the smallest bit.

"Greet them, *quickly*," the Sahr said in a low voice. "And let me go."

Azetla called out a simple "blessed peace" in his weak, ill-pronounced Trekoan, but he felt his words fall useless to the ground. Almost certainly the wrong dialect, and badly pronounced. He repeated it again in Maurowan.

"No, by blood, don't use *that*," the Sahr whispered. It hitched its shoulders to try and loosen his grip. "You can get killed here for drinking from the wrong well, and we need their water. And safe passage. Just let me take care of this. You are in no danger unless you ignore me or disrespect them. All I did was draw their attention."

Azetla sucked in a breath through his teeth. The Trekoans made no move to touch their elegant curved weapons. They simply stared, silent in wait. So he let the Sahr go with a forward shove.

He was blind, blind, blind, with an enemy as his eyes.

The Sahr walked calmly and picked out the leader of the band—a short rider who nudged his horse forward in response to its approach—and spoke a few words of Trekoan. Then, inexplicably, the Sahr dropped to one knee and recited something.

The Trekoan leader dismounted and drew his weapon on the Sahr, angling it toward the throat. Azetla cut a swift gesture at the Maurowan guards.

"No, no. No northerners," the Sahr said back to him. "Just you."

Azetla came forward and used a Mashevi gesture of peace; the Trekoans looked at him for the first time.

Slowly, the Sahr came back to its feet, the Trekoan's sword following its rise. The Sahr began to speak in Trekoan. It gestured at Azetla. The Trekoan gave a brisk nod. Then, with an abrupt shift in tone and manner, the Sahr spoke rapidly. Asking questions. The Trekoan gave increasingly uneasy answers. The Sahr scoffed at the answers. Shook its head at them. Said a few simple, calm words. Then the Sahr took three steps forward, bringing itself against the tip of the Trekoan's sword.

The Trekoan almost stepped *back*. Azetla could not fathom it. The Sahr was tied. It looked worn and bruised. What would make the man balk from it?

Without moving or even glancing at the blade-tip, the Sahr curved its voice, expression, and posture down into something new, something strange and gentle and full of gravity.

After a moment of consideration, the Trekoan leader nodded. He looked at Azetla and began to speak.

"All peace and all honor. As you wish us no harm, and only victory, we will do well by you, easterner," the Sahr translated. "I am Rokh Zaid Ihtam of Janbar. Honor, honor, honor."

After Azetla returned the greeting, and the Sahr adorned it with the necessary flourishes. Rokh Zaid sheathed his weapon and mounted. He pointed due west and clicked his tongue. The Sahr nodded. Then all thirty-seven men of the war-party—Azetla had in-stinctively taken a count—departed in the direction of their leader's gesture.

The Sahr looked at Azetla.

"They will permit us to drink and fill from their well. That's the thrice-spoken honor here—greeting, safe passage, water—and the road is dry for a few days from here."

"What did you tell them?"

"What they needed to hear and, as it happens, the truth. In their own dialect, which is the part that actually mattered. Janbari colloquial is so *delicate*. One has to catch one's tongue and reel it in from all the solid, harsh sounds. But you don't have to worry about the Janbaris. If we can keep in their good graces, we've easy movement as far Kahal-dar."

"And then?"

The Sahr shrugged with an indifference Azetla didn't believe for a second. "And then we'll see. Rather depends on the mood hereabouts."

Everyone in the caravan drank from the cool water of a deep Janbari well and then, by the gracious leave of the Rokh, they moved on. The Janbaris treated them kindly, with the famed Trekoan hospitality. They passed through two more herd camps unmolested. They made good time.

But the rising heat sapped the strength of all those who were not of the desert by birth. Mali's father looked unwell, seated at the head of the cart. Mali and Anna, with their paler skin, had both burned a painful red, and Khala sagged at every step. Azetla could do nothing for them. He could offer them no comfort. He could not let them go home. He could give them no assurance of anything, since he himself had none.

All he could do was make them drink their full ration of water and eat their full ration of food, for heat-sickness sometimes deceived the body into feeling revulsion at that which it most desperately needed.

They made camp at dusk, using the last of daylight to start a fire and stretch pallets on the ground. Verris ate in silence with the guards. Azetla hounded Colha and the women to eat once again and it aggravated them. He forced the matter anyway, with less gentleness than he meant. He was used to dealing with soldiers.

He took his portion of the watch each night. The watch was for raiders, and for the Sahr, which made no motion to go to sleep until after everyone else had. It watched the others roll out pallets. Watched them eat. They dropped like stones, momentarily oblivious to the perhaps-devil that fastened its eyes to them. Then it would eat and drink clumsily with tied hands. So it did tonight, and after the last mouthful, it looked across the tiny camp, then up at the clear night.

"You know I'll sleep, by blood. You can stop *waiting* to make sure," it said.

"Why do you want them to think you don't sleep?" Azetla asked.

The Sahr clicked its tongue.

"For the look of the thing. Tell them what you like—that I'm the plainest, simplest nothing of a South Makar. But will they *quite* believe you when you don't believe it yourself?" it said, drawing itself up off the ground in one, smooth motion.

It stood taut for a moment and smelled the air with slow breaths. Azetla's hand slipped to his sagam hilt. He observed it. Not fearful, just ready.

The Trekoan-style shift, hemmed at the knee, wavered in the air over the soft, loose trousers. The sandals, Azetla noticed for the first time, were Makarish. The belt, Sarramai. Again, bits of everything from everywhere. The Sahr did look the stronger for a week's worth of improved rations. Azetla hesitated to speculate its age. Its physical movement and resilience indicated youth, its mannerisms pled otherwise. It at least pretended its joints did not ache, as Azetla's had begun to from years of rugged marching and heavy labor. And he was not yet thirty.

The Sahr's hands strained at the ropes and it rose slightly off its heels, eyes closed.

Then abruptly, the Sahr relaxed, as though whatever scent or thought had drawn it up had passed. It lowered itself back to the ground, taking care as it lay on the thin pallet so that the rope would not catch or twist beneath it.

Azetla waited, as he had done each night. And he was tired. More than that, he was bereft. Bereft of the bits of anger and contempt he harbored toward the Sahr—they would wake tomorrow, but now they slept—and bereft of the ceaseless calculations as to its intentions, its thoughts, its very nature.

"You can sleep, Mashevi." The Sahr raised tethered hands from its chest. "I'm obviously not going anywhere."

"That isn't the worry," Azetla said. He leaned down, just a little, toward the head of his pallet.

"I'm not going to hurt anyone either." Its ink-marked fingers fiddled lazily against its palm, like flickering flames. "I already won against my brother's wager. He said I could kill no more than a dozen before letting you march on into Shihra. I said I would kill more, and you would not make it to the first village. You were in Shihra. My *home*. What could you expect but that I would do as I did?"

Azetla sat up tall, attentive. Anger stirred faintly on its bed of coals to hear his men counted as numbers in a wager. The rest of its words filtered through slowly. Brother. Village. Home.

The Sahr clicked its tongue and turned its head, looking at him through the watch-fire.

"But I forget. You use your sword for northerners and maybe you've forgotten what it is to fight for your own."

It used his own native lilt ever so gently that time and watched his face like someone waiting for a dam to break, *willing* it to break. But Azetla pressed his lips together and slowly breathed away the retaliation that would have been wasted on a creature who was only digging where it could see there were already bruises. He would only be satisfied for an instant if he pushed back, and it would have won something from him.

Azetla knew each time he had failed to fight for his people. He also knew where he had succeeded, and he had learned to be content with small, subtle acts of preservation. Infinitesimal victories. Grain by grain on the scale. Some day, by salt, he would be loosed. He could speak the whole of his mind and not the part, and act the whole as well.

So let the Sahr waste its energy trying to provoke him.

"What did you call it?" he said calmly. "*Shekhara?*" He stumbled over the word.

The Sahr nodded with scornful eyes. "Shihra. Shihrayan is what you actually mean when you say '*Sahr.*' That is just a northern mispronunciation of a Trekoan mistranslation." The Sahr closed its eyes again. "It's interesting to me that you speak Maurowan so fluently, but you don't pronounce it very well. Trekoan either. So try again, Mashevi...try not to destroy my native tongue with that eastern one of yours."

Azetla had no desire to pronounce any word the Sahr threw at him.

"I don't find what you're called to be relevant," he said, feeling his exhaustion pull at him, begging him to lie on the ground.

"Fair enough," the Sahr said. It gave a coarse, coughing little laugh. "It really isn't relevant at all."

It did sleep eventually, closing its eyes before Azetla's watch ended. He was afforded a handful of hours to rest. But the Sahr woke early. It always did.

21

Azetla altered the Maurowan map again and again, until it was so marred it would suit no one but him. On a separate piece of parchment he wrote down the relationships between the tribes; Lahashet allied with Janbar. Numayr allied with Hani. Sub-tribes. Territorial disputes. Shared wells. What the Sahr painted with its mouth throughout the day, Azetla laid down in Mashevi script at night.

He kept waiting for any of it to prove false. None of it had.

"We're in Qatlani territory now," the Sahr said in a low voice, breaking the sweltering afternoon silence.

"Maurow's pet tribe?" he said.

The Sahr nodded.

"They've no reason to trouble us then."

The Sahr smiled. "Ah, I think you misunderstand what it means for Qatlan to be Maurow's authority here; it isn't just license against their own. Those that Maurow deems important can pass with safety. But you have no banner. No courier's livery. Nothing. Qatlanis know what they can get away with." The Sahr gestured westward with its bound hands. "And the other tribes usually end up paying for Qatlani crimes."

"I heard that Qatlan is starting to lose favor with Maurow," Azetla said.

That much he had been able to glean from the southern magistrate.

"Well it's more that they've been losing *ground*. They've been pressed into smaller and smaller pockets. You know how people react when they feel they are in retreat. What bits of ground they have left, they defend all the more rabidly."

As Azetla listened, he began surveying the terrain with an eye to avenues of approach, escape, shelter, and advantageous positions.

"Just so you know," the Sahr said. "If we can get to Yigha we won't have to worry about them from there on. A little less than two days."

Azetla glanced from the road to the Sahr, trying to read what he could from both.

"This is a very small 'pocket' for a tribe that the Emperor still names ruler of Trekoa."

The Sahr smiled brightly. "Yes. Very small indeed. A few years ago, they were the ocean and everyone else little islands in it. Now they are drowning."

That, Azetla believed. He had read reports about the tribal skirmishes a few years ago, had heard court rumblings about the need to build a new outpost in Trekoa to "keep the locals mindful." Much trade had been diverted to the better-built Makarish roads and cities as opposed to the rockier, more rugged routes of Trekoa.

Trekoa had been squirming in Maurow's hands for years, but perhaps more violently than Azetla had realized. The land was treated as so insignificant that even its rebelliousness was almost beneath concern. Trekoa did so little for Imperial coffers, and what were desert tribes before the great and mighty Maurow? Nothing more than petty families with petty squabbles, in which Maurow only need make an appearance if it was to their specific gain.

Azetla wondered if he had let this Maurowan arrogance obscure his own thoughts, thinking of Trekoa as simple, and poor, and weak. A little goat to be herded about.

Maurow had conquered Trekoa more by savvy than strength, with careful manipulation of intertribal fighting. They picked Qatlan as a champion for themselves and gave them all they needed to win. Then they slipped the vestiges of Trekoan autonomy out from under them when no one was looking.

No grand war; just jabs and feints one day, Maurowan rule the next.

But Trekoa was not idle. Not content. Azetla liked to hear that. He walked quiet in thought. He watched the high ground, but felt calm rest on him like the heat of the day. When they passed by a few tribesmen, he greeted them in his weak Trekoan, and they acknowledged.

"Which tribe is the greatest threat to Qatlan?" he asked the Sahr, after a halt and rest.

"Saqiran," the Sahr said without hesitation.

Azetla nodded. "Rokh Bin-Zari's tribe. I've heard of him. He has made Riada very angry lately."

"That he has," the Sahr said. "Most other tribes are holding their tongues right now. They don't know who will win out, and they don't want to pick the wrong side."

The Sahr turned its head and caught Azetla's eye with a strong, earnest look. "But Saqiran is winning."

Abruptly, the Sahr turned its tongue to a Trekoan dialect—a markedly different one than it had spoken to the Janbaris—and it was too fluid and fine a language to be coming out of that unholy mouth. The words had the rhythm of music or chant and the Sahr's voice had a fierce quality to it that came out the stronger in that language than it did in Maurowan.

It returned, almost reluctantly to the northern tongue. "The Saqirani proverb says: 'Offer friendship to reach proximity. Offer drinks to reach the fools. Offer submission to reach your enemy's neck.'"

"Then is that what you're doing, Sahr? Reaching for the neck?"

It breathed a half-hearted laugh.

"Listen, Mashevi, I don't want to kill you anywhere near as badly as you want to kill me. I just want these bloody ropes *off*."

Azetla ignored that. "What are their methods?"

"They prefer to attack while you're on the move. Usually two groups, to flank and encircle. On horseback. They're excellent horsemen. And you can smell it before they go out and feel it in your lungs because they always burn anise and brittlebush resin before a raid." The Sahr twisted its mouth as with a bad taste.

"How do you know that?"

The Sahr did not answer right away. "That's the first time you've asked *how* I know anything."

"I'm patient."

"No, you're worried. You know Maurow because you were forced to know it. And that is how I know Trekoa. Understand?"

Azetla folded his arms and looked back over the ground they had covered. He rolled his jaw, breathed out sharply, and set a course in his mind.

"I ought to assume you're lying," he said calmly, his eyes still searching out the terrain and glancing across the small, vulnerable party of travelers.

The Sahr shrugged its shoulders. "Do as you see fit."

It mimicked his own accent in a subtle, mocking way.

"But you don't think I'm lying."

And he didn't. Not in the least. He had his methods, however, and he was meticulous about them.

"It seems a reasonable idea, though. You being a servant of Qatlan, doing their bidding, bringing them hearty prey," he said, peering sideways.

The Sahr's sloe eyes flashed at him, a hint of real anger slipping through, before cooling just as quickly. Azetla got what he wanted and the Sahr caught it just a moment late.

"Unless you suddenly change your blood, your mouth, and your manner to the northern kind, Mashevi, I am no friend of Qatlan. Satisfied?" it said in a flat voice.

Nearly. All this time it poured the map out before him, feigning neutrality with a deft mouth. But it had favorites here. Saqiran. Janbar. And enemies. Qatlan.

The Sahr settled back into a neutral-faced silence. But soon, it tensed, drew in long deep breaths, and scoured the terrain with its eyes.

"We need to move faster," it said, its tone altered.

It gestured its tied hands to two dark brown scars on the horizon. Two ragged, parallel ridges, with a wide, shallow valley between them.

"We need to make it there before dusk."

⁂

Wesley knew something was awry. The Mashevi—normally obnoxious with calm—was uneasy. His eyes raked over the landscape and he kept circling the little group in a protective manner like a tense shepherd's dog. Then he would go back to the Sahr devil and question it. Even the bloody jinn-thing did not seem so indifferent anymore. It fidgeted at the ropes on its wrists almost to the point of blood.

If that devil was worried, what should Wesley be? He wanted to ask the jackal a thousand questions, but that would make it all too apparent to the imperial guards that Wesley was in command of no one and nothing. He waited nervously as the jackal walked from his place in the lead, gestured to the senior man among the guards, and gave them quiet instructions.

Then he came to Wesley.

"How are you with a sword, Lord Verris?" the jackal said. "Don't exaggerate."

Wesley was taken aback. "I have learned the full course of combat, same as any man of my station."

The Mashevi folded his arms gently, waiting for a more adequate response. It chafed and stung, having to answer to a jackal. But Wesley swallowed the bitterness down his throat. Something was wrong.

"I've not been in battle as you have, jackal. But I have trained with skilled soldiers more than once, and I don't balk."

The jackal nodded, satisfied with the answer; he seemed to respect the honesty of it. For a moment, Wesley felt pride trickle through his chest, which surprised him. Then *appalled* him. This jackal was not the arbiter of courage and cowardice. Or of anything. Wesley should neither need nor want his good will.

But he did need his protection.

"Are you expecting trouble?" Wesley asked.

The jackal did not answer, but his expression spoke clearly. Wesley's shoulders fell.

"What needs to be done?" he said.

"Keep to the inside, my lord; I'll show you where to be if indeed we are attacked. Do you know the standard signals and commands?"

"I'm familiar with them." Gods, that was almost true. He had been with the Black Wren for several weeks, and he had learned more than he'd ever known before.

The jackal glanced around the yellow-brown landscape, toward a gentle ridge to the east. Though he stood tall and looked calm with readiness, his jaw clenched slightly when his eyes settled on the Sahr.

"And what are you going to do about *that*?" Wesley asked.

The jackal didn't answer. He gave a respectful nod to Wesley, turned, and moved back to his place at lead.

Wesley looked at the Sahr. Every so often, it scraped the thin leather slave band on its wrist up and down against the edge of the cart in a way that set Wesley's teeth on edge. It turned its wrists and pressed its palms in a slow, controlled manner, as if by some gesture or jinn-magic it would massage the rope to wax and melt it from its wrists. Maybe it could.

But the jackal wasn't afraid of it.

This was not a perfect comfort. The jackal was a soldier and a commander, so perhaps—But no. He was *not* a commander, Wesley reminded himself, like a teacher rapping the knuckles of his student for an error in rhetoric.

It was easy to forget that the jackal was not now, nor was he ever, the captain of a battalion. Wesley had wondered if pretending to tolerate the jackal's authority would affect him somehow. Now he knew the answer. The jackal was so comfortable—and made others so comfortable—with his authority, that it seemed rational, earned, and unexceptional.

Emperor Riada had that same implacable certainty. The kind that made Wesley question himself, made him feel small and blind and distant. The jackal's confidence was quieter but no less strong, and no less terrifying. Perhaps it did not make Wesley feel as small, for this Azetla told him to put hand to hilt and get ready, as though Wesley could be counted a real soldier. But it did make Wesley question himself.

He curled his palm at his hilt, then dropped his hand. Clenched it, then dropped it again. A nervous habit he had formed in Sahr territory. He focused on the brown, scraggly emptiness of the ter-rain before him. It rustled and whispered and, sometimes, it went impossibly silent, like something sent to sleep, dazed by the heat. It was so bare and worthless to his northern eyes.

Everything about it made Wesley feel isolated. This was not the kind of land he *understood*; it made him feel withdrawn, and it made him want to withdraw. He was cut off, from the place he left and the place to which he had come. He was severed even from his objective. His plans had been badly gnarled by the Emperor's intrusion, and he wasn't sure if he could straighten them out in Areo, or if he would have to start over from scratch.

Amid simmering thoughts, and fidgeting fingers, dusk slunk across the sky. Wesley had almost calmed himself. Almost forgotten why his shoulders were tensed.

But then Azetla shouted halt.

Wesley's heart leapt and pounded. Azetla barked a command, and all the guards began to move to defend against an enemy Wesley could not even see.

He was ashamed that his first instinct was to do nothing. Nothing at all. At best, it occurred to him to hide he knew not where. But he forced his hand to his hilt against every desire of his body and hurried forward in response to the jackal's voice.

22

When the Sahr stopped cold—its spine snapping rigid as a flagstaff, head lifting against the wind, fingers unfurling into the dry, hot air—Azetla already knew exactly what he would do and he was ready for the consequences.

Though he saw nothing yet, he moved as though he had. He sent the women and old Papa Colha to shield themselves behind a small, ragged tower of rock on the far end of the ridge. He set Verris, who shook with terror and determination, as a last guard to protect them.

Azetla turned back to the Sahr. As he drew his knife, it raised its hands, neither of them doubting what Azetla intended to do. He grabbed the Sahr's wrist, dragged the knife up against the rope; it took several pulls to break through. The Sahr turned its right hand upward so that Azetla could dig the taut end out of the remaining knot, then it worked the rest off swiftly.

The Sahr jumped into the water cart, just as brown-swathed figures on horseback began to flutter like a dark wave above the distant ridge. The sound of them, which had seemed like no more than wind at first, rose at last to his ears.

Seven riders. Ten. A dozen. The number kept rising as the figures lumbered over the eastern horizon. The Sahr jumped from the cart,

232

its weapons drawn from beneath the packs and resting easily in its hands. It gestured to its objective and Azetla nodded.

He ordered the guards to hammer their pikestaffs into the rocky ground as fast and sure as they could, forming a makeshift abatis. The sky seemed to grow darker with each breath. Azetla placed the guards in the only formation he thought could hold against a mounted onslaught, trying to force a difficult angle of approach. He didn't have enough men. Just ten, including himself. And a Sahr.

The mounted tribesmen were all in full view now, galloping down the rocks with stunning fluidity and expertise. Their swords were already unsheathed, and the metal flashed faintly with the rhythm of the horses' hooves.

Nimbly, the Sahr pulled itself up a finger of the ridge, angled off the path. It dug its knee into the space between two rocks taking a slight crouch. Then, head gently tilted to one side, the Sahr strung its bow as calmly as would an old woman threading a needle, even licking the tips of the string before it worked them in. It tested the pull in a slow and thoughtful way, tsking its tongue softly at the well-tillered bit of juniper.

Azetla braced. The riders were coming fast and thunderous up the slope. Azetla's heart was loud with the blood-rush of readiness when the Sahr ticked its head straight and drew the arrow. His grip pulsed in response.

There was an airy snap of release. An arrow flew out from the high crevice and the tip of it struck the neck of the frontmost Qatlani horse and burrowed deep. The animal curled and tossed, causing another to stumble in its fall. A second arrow went Azetla knew not where—he shouted an order to the right flank guard—but out of the corner of his eye, he saw a third shaft tear into a man. The fourth brought another horse to writhe and fall, crushing its rider and disordering the raiders just as they breached the ridgeline and barreled into the pikestaffs.

Then all clarity was lost.

Azetla swung at the neck of the first horse, bearing low as he launched forward. A thousand pounds of animal heaved toward the ground and Azetla stumbled, barely escaping the fall. He found his feet and pushed his sagam through the Qatlani's chest the moment he hit the ground.

The gravelly slope plagued Azetla's footing. But the enemy horses stumbled too. He tried to draw the Qatlanis to the highest, most uneven pieces of terrain, biting into the horse's legs with his sagam, and striking upward with his battalion sword, pulling them north. Away from those who could not defend themselves.

It had taken years to learn to use his right hand, but it still could not accomplish what his left could. It was failing him. When he scrambled to block a strike that came down toward his neck, the sagam was bashed out of his weak right grip, and the blade nicked his neck and collarbone. Deep or shallow, he didn't know; he only felt the bite of it.

He pulled his free palm to the other hilt and swung his Maurowan sword across with all the strength of both hands. It cut deep and long across the man's gut. The rider saw his own innards before he slumped over and fell off the horse.

Azetla dragged himself onto the Qatlani mount and gripped hard with his knees. His body had some memory in it still, and the horse was nimble and responsive. Out from beneath the hooves and downward blades, his strikes gained strength.

But the Qatlanis had reached the even ground now. And they held it firm.

Azetla rammed his horse against a Qatlani one until the animals' opposite withers nearly touched. He took hold of the proximity and drove his sword into the rider's ribs, thrusting upward. It was hard to keep his hand from slipping in the blood that seeped over it. The man's eyes were all that could be seen, frantic and glassy, as Azetla jerked the blade out and the man hit the ground in a crumpled heap.

There was a brief and jarring stillness just then which, far from offering relief, made Azetla almost frantic. Where were the rest? There were more. He *knew* there were more. Azetla's breaths were loud in his own ears as he hurriedly looked around. One Maurowan guard was on the ground, still as stone. Another was badly injured. Azetla dropped down, recovered his sagam to his right hand, and mounted again.

He could hear the scuffle of the Qatlanis now; the remnant had shied at stiff resistance and skirted north, to come up where the slope was more forgiving and the angle of attack more to their advantage.

The Sahr. Where was the Sahr? He couldn't see it anywhere. By salt, did that even matter now? The riders came, swooping up and around like a flock of birds to encircle the little caravan and swallow them whole. Azetla raised his head and firmed his grip. He knew how to read a battlefield; this would not go his way.

But then something muddied his view, confusing him utterly. The perfect bird-flock formation of the riders crumpled in an instant, the whole line malformed in its advance. They splayed out, lost momentum. One Qatlani rocked wildly near the base of the ridge. He dropped from his mount to the dust. Another tumbled, he and his horse together. Almost an instant later a third wilted in his saddle, dropping his sword.

It was almost impossible to see amid the dust and the darkening sky, but finally his eyes caught it. Arrows leaped out from a low rocky shelf to his north, far from where the Sahr had been at the beginning.

And then they stopped, all spent.

The Qatlanis tried to right themselves.

A horse with a sheen of blood on its withers bolted out from behind the rocky shelf. The Sahr sat on its back, body and sword bearing low. It flew like a bird of prey against the pack of Qatlanis, and moved through them, fast as fire through kindling. For one short breath that seemed to last a very long time, the eerie light of dusk and the swift, sinuous movement of the Sahr conspired against Azetla's instinct and reason; the sight was surreal, and he could have believed it was almost anything in the whole world.

But the feeling broke away, as if his eyes had adjusted. Azetla drove his own mount against the thinned wave of tribesmen as they gathered together once again. He pulled a Qatlani off his horse by his clothes, lacerating him with the sagam as he fell. His next blow cut into a Qatlani man's knee. He had to let the heavy sword drop; his right hand was betraying him again. He brought the sagam to his strong hand, raised it to protect his neck, and leaned hard to sidle out of range. He almost fell. One of the Maurowan guards cut the Qatlani down in front of him.

He looked around hurriedly, for there were no tribesmen near him. The Sahr had drawn them down the steep end of the ridge. Azetla sat forward, giving pressure with his knees, and his horse responded, hurrying forward over the rocks.

The Sahr fought too *close*, almost against the very skin of the enemy. When a strike came against it, it weaved away from and then alongside the Qatlani, pulling the enemy's hand and slitting his wrist as though it were a piece of rope. The curved sword dropped immediately and the Sahr dug straight into the man's neck.

As Azetla reached the skirmish, the Sahr had already pulled another man from his horse. When the Qatlani tumbled to the ground, the Sahr slipped from its stolen horse and finished the man quickly.

There were two left, but they dropped their swords and dropped from their horses to their knees, speaking rapid and desperate words in their dialect of Trekoan. The Sahr responded calmly to one of the Qatlanis in his own language. He nodded hopefully. Then, with a look that was almost gentle, the Sahr drew the man's own knife from his waist sheath and slit his throat. The other man went silent and lowered his head, lips moving voicelessly as if in prayer.

The Sahr brought the man carefully to his feet and spoke to him. The Qatlani croaked an answer. The Sahr smiled a little. Twisted the

Qatlani around, pulling its knife hard across his neck. For a moment his body hung lifeless in the Sahr's grip. Then the Sahr dropped the man like a sack of meal and walked toward Azetla.

"It would have been better if you had let me free earlier," it said, its voice gritty and breathless. "I could have gone ahead."

The only answer he could give was fast, heavy breaths and a dark look. His left hand must stay ready, even now. He tilted his head toward the others, so that the Sahr would walk on in front of him. It stepped southward without qualm. It didn't *look* tired at all, by salt. It was, though. It must be.

The force of what Azetla had done came to rest upon him. By untying the Sahr, he had taken a step he could not retrace. If they tried to truss it up again *now*, someone would surely pay for it in blood and that would be on Azetla's head. He had to walk the heading he set.

He looked around the field of skirmish; the Qatlanis never fully breached the line, which amazed him. The unarmed among the party had but dimly seen the fight from their sheltered rock. Verris' knuckles were death-white over the hilt of his now christened sword. He had killed two wounded Qatlanis who had fallen from their horses and tried to break through at the south edge.

Mali had one arm wrapped around Anna, and the other hand stroked her father's. They were frightened, but hadn't been touched. Khala's reaction was stranger. She massaged the inside of her palm as she always did when she was nervous, but she was staring at Azetla as though he was from another world, as though she had never seen him a day in her life.

And she never *had* seen him like this. She never had seen a Mashevi fight. Or command.

There was almost as much horror as pride in her eyes, but she didn't say anything. Azetla offered her a soft nod that was meant to be comforting. Khala always said that Azetla's attempts at comfort were irritating and useless, but she gave him a weary, shaken smile.

Azetla turned to the Sahr.

"We can't stay here," he said.

The Sahr shook its head. "They *always* come back for their dead."

Azetla looked at the Qatlani bodies strewn across the ground. Three Maurowan guards were dead and a fourth was badly injured. Two more—Markham and Allaq—had minor wounds. Azetla nodded at Verris and at the two unwounded guards. With dazed, weary looks they followed his lead and began to give all the bodies a hasty desert burial. The symbolic kind all southerners owed to their enemies.

The work did not take long—they could not afford for it to—and the Sahr stood indifferent to their efforts. It could probably have told him what the appropriate rites for Qatlanis were if it wanted to, but it seemed to have no sense of shame, nor any fear of sacrilege. It watched them until Azetla ordered it to help cover the bodies. With a disdainful glance, but without argument, it lent its strength to the task.

Azetla knew it had no intention of relinquishing its weapons; his awareness of its sword hand was almost distracting, like too bright a light, flickering in his periphery. But all it did was carry dust and rocks.

When they finished, the caravan marched all the way through the last of twilight, across the night, toward dawn. When the faintest edge of the sky began to pale, Azetla questioned the Sahr.

"They need rest." He looked back at the rest of the party. The injured men struggled.

The Sahr shook its head. "Not yet."

Morning had broken in hot color before Azetla permitted a brief halt. It was late afternoon when the Sahr said it was safe to stop, and near dusk when Azetla finally sat down for his own sleep shift. He had rinsed and dressed his own injury which, by God's mercy, was little more than a cut. As for the other injured, he had done the best he could.

His body felt heavy as stone and he was exhausted with a mixture of relief that his instincts had allowed the Sahr to fight, and dismay at that same fact.

If the Sahr was even a bit human, it was exhausted too.

He set three of the guards to watch—Markham could still call alert, even though he limped—and told them to wake him in three hours so he could relieve them again. His eyelids had painful weights upon them, and they almost fell as he heard the Sahr sit down a few feet from him in the dust and gravel. It drank water slowly, swirling it around its mouth as though it were Sarramai wine.

Falling prey to habit, Azetla pressed his fingers against the little wooden lion's head below his neck to make sure the leather cord had not broken, then he gripped it tightly. The Sahr watched him carefully all the while. Then it stretched out on its back with its hands resting under its head and shut its eyes.

His own drifted close. *There is a three-man watch*, he told himself. He told them to treat the Sahr like a snake. If it began to slither at all, they were to cut off its head before it could bite. But it was so fast, there was so much he didn't understand, and his thoughts were clouding over.

"What did you say to that Qatlani?" he managed to say out loud, his eyes refusing to open.

"I asked him if he knew what I was; I think he did," it said in a scratchy, sleep-deprived voice.

"And that knowledge is enough to make them fear for their lives?" he muttered.

"Not always. But it's their *souls* they worry about, Mashevi. Only thing worth fearing for."

It seemed to him that there was something else to say, but he was halfway to sleep already, and never brought the words to bear. The conversation fell asleep alongside him. Neither he nor the Sahr had washed off the Qatlani blood, stiff and brown on their clothes.

And the Sahr was never tied that night. It slept deep, free, and armed. Azetla slept better than he should have, sagam hilt under his fingers.

23

Mali woke to the insistent heat of late morning. She lifted her head, trying to shake off the groggy feeling that stemmed both from lack of sleep and from having wakened well after first light. Her body ached. It had been seven days—or eight?—of walking long under the desert sun, dragging her sister away from the Sahr devil, trying to make the girl hold her tongue, and biting on her own as all she knew of life was being destroyed with each step away from Piarago.

Azetla could not understand how driving and cruel his pace was. In fact, he seemed to think he had softened it for them. He spoke to Lord Verris of how he was "slowing movement a great deal" and his Lordship would have to be patient. Given the lowered eyebrows on Lord Verris' face, Mali rather thought that he found the pace as harsh as she did.

Mali no longer had the blazing heat headache that had all but blurred her vision for the first three days. But her feet were raw inside her sandals and, despite her best efforts, parts of her face were burned to the point of stinging pain at the touch. She tested her fingertips gingerly across her forehead and nose, wishing there was cool water to spare for seared skin. It had been days since she had spotted any alloeh plant.

To Mali's left, Azetla was on watch. His dark brows were pinned low over his eyes, his arms folded, and the fingers of his left hand curved tight against his arm. He kept both the horizon and the Sahr under his gaze the way Mali kept Anna and her father under hers. Mali didn't understand why the Sahr devil hadn't been tied up again, or why Azetla had released it in the first place. It sat, calm and free, carefully dressing its chafed wrists.

Azetla saw that Mali was awake. He walked toward her.

"Is your father all right? And Anna?" he asked quietly.

Mali nodded.

"Khala kept her senses and between the two of us, we kept everyone else's for them," she replied coolly. "Papa will probably be less aware for a time. Commotion does that to him. And he needs more water than he's been rationed. I've been giving him part of mine, but I..."

Azetla had opened his mouth to reply when his eyes snapped over to where the Sahr suddenly stood up. He nodded, almost high-blood-like, at Mali. "Keep your ration; I'll take care of it."

Mali watched with half-held breath to see what Azetla would do with the Sahr.

He spoke in a low voice. Mali couldn't hear. The Sahr shook its head. Its fingers were ever tapping the metal of its hilt, like a rhythmic taunt. It wore a faint, cool smile that made Mali feel like it owned the desert, the dust, and the day and could wield any of them howsoever it pleased, so long as its hands were free.

For the sake of your vicious jackal god, tie it or kill it, Azetla! Why they wanted to keep it alive was beyond her. It was the worst of both worlds; it could kill and profane the body and do only the Gods knew what to the spirit.

Mali averted her gaze from both of them and wrapped her arms around herself despite the heat, as if that alone could keep her soul healthy and safe inside her body. She was tired, and that made too many doors and windows for fear.

She had not seen the battle clearly last night, but she saw the aftermath. She felt so useless in the face of it. And Azetla had been so cool and ruthlessly practical; bury, salve, move, move, no rest, consult with a devil for directions. Mali supposed she could not begrudge him being a soldier, but he failed to remember that the rest of them were not.

Mali should not *be* here. Anna should not. Her papa should not. Even Khala. Mali's frustration rose and scuttled about, seeking the proper target. As she watched Azetla talk gravely to the jinn-devil—he still made no move to disarm it—Mali knew she ought to lay every last drop of blame on him. On this *jackal*. Mali never called him that to his face, but she felt the contempt of the word in her throat. This jackal. The one who somehow always managed to finagle what he needed or wanted.

He should have found a different way to go about all of this, one that left Mali's father at peace in his old age and weakness of mind. One where her own sister was not trying to shadow a devil. One where Mali was *home*.

So Azetla had chosen to release the Sahr because it was supposedly *useful*? What a very jackal thing to do: profess piety out loud, then shake hands with demons in the dark at one's convenience. That was what any good Maurowan would have said and Mali, even with her scant Makarish blood, always strove to be a good Maurowan.

And would they really have died otherwise? That was what Lieutenant Markham claimed. But Mali didn't feel like absolving Azetla, especially when she saw that he *still* left the Sahr's sword at its hip.

Who else could bear the responsibility for all this, if not Azetla? Lord Verris? He was obviously not the one in command right now. Moreover, Mali did not quite have the temerity to doubt someone of Lord Colonel Verris' position. He was of a different world, different blood. As far from Mali in one direction as Azetla was in the other.

Mali watched in dismay as the Sahr loosed the string from its bow, wound it carefully about its fingers, and laid it in Azetla's palm.

"Have a token of my good will," it said dryly. "Seeing as I've no arrows left."

Azetla replied in too low a voice for Mali to hear, but whatever he said, it troubled the Sahr none at all. It was Mali who was troubled. Azetla had done nothing to trammel the devil. Confusion and fear twisted into a knot that constricted her chest all through the morning preparations.

When they were ready to depart, Azetla walked up to Mali and her papa. Her papa sat on the ground, looking rather bemusedly into his small wooden bowl of unsalted burghul. Azetla had made good on his word and given her papa a better ration of everything, taken from the mouths of the dead no doubt. But her papa would not eat.

Azetla knelt down and brought his head low in some attempt not to tower over her papa. Azetla had always been very particular about the way he interacted with elders. For him, to disrespect a man of gray hair was tantamount to blasphemy.

"We've freed the packing donkey for you, Father," he said.

Father. That was a southern way of speaking, which Mali usually found softened her toward Azetla. It had little effect just now. Her anger was so strong and savory between her teeth, she simply didn't want to swallow it yet.

"He's very small and docile. Like your old donkey, Keysa. Do you think you could ride him? We have to move quickly today."

Azetla's voice was so quiet and gentle when he wanted it to be.

"Anna?" her papa said.

"Anna will ride in the cart."

"And that one?" her papa pointed to the Sahr, which was obviously listening to every word.

"If it threatens harm to your daughters by even the merest glance or gesture, I *will* kill it. I swear by salt."

Her father's eyes narrowed in confused calculation, flitting from the Sahr to Azetla, but then he smiled slightly, and looked like his old self. His eyes were clever and clear. He gave a contented nod, firm and sure because Azetla was firm and sure.

"Orders be damned?" Mali added quietly.

Azetla did not hesitate in his answer.

"Orders be damned."

Mali didn't know if she believed him. But her papa looked satisfied and was amenable to the idea of riding a very small donkey. Her contempt for Azetla flagged just a little. Azetla had always treated her papa with honor, even when her papa had one of his miry days—the ones where he seemed to forget completely who and where he was. He would see Azetla's jackal band on his arm as though it was a new thing, and shouted for the filthy jackal to *get out of his inn*. And Azetla never said a word. Never got angry. He just waited out the storm.

After being urged to finish his meal, her papa stood and let Azetla lead him to the sturdy little donkey.

The group—smaller now—set off. The heat bore down on them from above and simmered up from beneath their feet. Everyone was subdued by it, except the Sahr, which seemed to draw from it a lively inner fire. It did, however, keep as far away from Mali and her family as it possibly could. Azetla stood as barricade between them, and it made no effort to test his resolve.

Mali thought it strange how the very person who made her feel truly safe just now was the same one she quite justly blamed for all her trouble in the first place, and the exact sort that her own Emperor—honor and peace befall him—would say was the most insidious danger of all.

<hr>

Azetla watched the Sahr's bearing and gestures morph into an almost unrecognizable subservience as it spoke to the tall Bijhali tribesman regarding the use of his well. Azetla understood almost nothing of the exchange, but the result of it was cool water, a short rest, and what appeared to be a warm welcome from the village.

Though the rest was badly needed, Azetla did not like to halt again. They were well out of Qatlani territory now, but he felt the desire to reach the Black Wren driving at his back like a stiff wind. He did not sit down with the others; if he did, the aches and bruises would make themselves loudly known, and then they would not quiet.

Also, he had left the Sahr free, which bound his attention. He stood sentry while the others sat, ate, and drank. When they were nearly done, he said his ritual prayers as quietly as he could. Not for shame or fear of mockery, but because of the Sahr. He worried that if he continued to use Mashevi around it, it might pick it up, put it in its mouth, and swallow it whole.

Azetla ate quickly while the others prepared to drag themselves to their feet. He saw Lieutenant Markham fiddle with the bandaging that covered his wound. He began picking and pulling at it to inspect the gouge in his leg.

"Stop that," the Sahr said.

Markham glanced up, wide-eyed. The Sahr stood up, walked over to one of the elderly village women, and touched its hand to its mouth. The woman nodded, and the Sahr began to speak. Within moments, the Sahr was given blanched cloth rags, fresh water, turmeric paste, and a little bowl of honey.

Shoving the materials toward Azetla, it said, "You know how to do it, don't you?"

When Azetla failed to respond instantly—it did not give him even one breath to clarify its meaning—it tsked its tongue at him in impatience and crouched next to Markham.

It pinned Markham's shoulder back, shoved his hands out of the way, and very carefully peeled away the cloth to inspect the wound. Even though Markham's throat was strained tight and his fist clenched hard against the ground, and even though his whole body braced as for a death blow, Azetla did not stop the Sahr. He had seen it tend its own wounds before. It knew what it was doing.

It washed the wound out, sometimes as coarsely as one washes canvas, and sometimes so gentle it scarcely brushed the skin, as if getting down to the smallest motes of dust. It was so focused on the work that Azetla probably could have gotten a rope around its neck and pulled it taut, if he wanted to.

Markham, teeth gritted, tried with all his might not to make a sound. He fixed his eyes on a pebble in the dust. The Sahr called out to one of the villagers and received a curt answer. The Sahr gave out an irritated sigh.

"This is what abstention and piety will do for you, easterner," the Sahr said, its eyes still carefully focused. "No arak. No wine. Nothing, by blood."

"I don't know why you're saying that to me," Azetla said. "Wine is not forbidden to Mashevis. That's only the western tribes." He handed Markham his water. The man didn't need it, perhaps, but Azetla had needed to give it to him, so that it might be understood: Azetla was present and he would protect him.

The Sahr pressed the skin around the gash to see how ginger it was, always painstaking, not always gentle. It streaked a honey balm on the larger part of the wound, and turmeric paste on the smaller part, then wrapped fresh cloth about Markham's leg.

By the end Markham was shaky. Pain or fear, it was hard to tell.

"Don't touch it again," the Sahr said.

Azetla carefully helped Markham to the cart and refilled his water skin for him. Markham didn't say anything to Azetla, but gave a faint nod of acknowledgment as Azetla situated him. It was as warm an expression as any of the Maurowan guards had ever given him.

As Azetla helped replenish the water barrel, he considered his choice of leaving the Sahr free, inspecting it like an axle or a stitch in cloth. Would it hold? The Sahr made bold with its freedom and, thus far, Azetla found himself amenable to the ways in which it did so.

But it troubled him when he realized what he was actually doing.

He was approaching the Sahr precisely as Captain Hodge had first approached him: untrusting, assuming treachery, harboring a profound disdain, but all the while with a driving need to find out what this pariah would do for him when given a foothold. So the Captain had offered that foothold to Azetla, then stood back and watched. He would have had no trouble, at the beginning, slitting Azetla's throat at the slightest provocation. There was no question about that.

It was a degrading parallel to draw, for although Azetla's people were treated as devils, this Sahr might actually be one. It never quite denied the charge, in any case. It seemed to like keeping itself outside of the usual, workable categories.

It was better for it to be seen as either an obstacle or an asset—like terrain and weather—rather than enemy or ally.

Could he hold it entirely guilty for that? There were times where Azetla would have given his very left hand to be seen as a blank ledger, to be filled in by his own actions, not by tales, hatreds, and histories all established long before he ever opened his mouth. The Maurowan guards, for instance, succumbed to the Sahr's vague devil's reputation very nicely, and held forth against Azetla's specific jackal one with resolve.

Azetla gestured at the Sahr, and it walked over.

"I need you to ask them about the Black Wren," he said.

It canted its head up at him in a calculating way. Then, abruptly, it flicked its slave band.

"I already did. If we bear slightly east and keep on, we'll reach Zadere plain not long after dark. They said that's where your battalion intends to camp for the night."

Azetla lifted his head in surprise.

"And then," the Sahr added with a smile. "You can tell them how it is you managed to catch them up so quickly."

There was a great deal he would have to explain, come to that.

"It won't make any difference, you know," he said quietly. "It won't convince them that you're not what they think you are."

The Sahr smiled at the ground in front of it.

"You misunderstand my meaning, Mashevi. Let's say I'm *exactly* what they think I am. That I'm as unholy as they come. Whatever suits them." Its mouth tightened almost imperceptibly. "But you can't say I'm not useful."

Azetla answered, still quietly, "That won't be enough to make them forget their Captain and their men. Of that I'm confident."

The Sahr acknowledged him only by a squinting glance, then walked smoothly to its position in the caravan. Azetla followed on its heels. It went ahead on foot, guiding, while Azetla and the other soldiers rode their mounts. Once in a while, it fell back toward Azetla to inform him of how close they were or what terrain lay ahead.

As darkness fell, it slowed one last time, walking along the front legs of the mare Azetla had looted from the Qatlanis. He dropped to the ground beside it.

"We should see their camp soon enough," it said.

Azetla nodded. The Sahr's hands hung loose at its sides just now. Its head was erect, its shoulders square, and—if Azetla was not mistaken—it was bracing.

Its newfound freedom was not guaranteed.

Neither was his.

He had many allies in his battalion. But there were some who believed that Captain Hodge's sole failing had been his favor toward Azetla. Lord Verris would side with those and wield his rank among them.

"Why did you treat Markham's wound?" Azetla said, glancing back at the cart.

The Sahr did not look at him as it spoke.

"If you ask, you ruin the illusion. Don't you want me to pretend I did it out of sheer kindness?"

Azetla simply waited.

"You *know* the answer," it said at last. "To keep my hands free and my sword at my side for as long as I can."

Something in its tone stung against his skin. The words had real vinegar in them, and a sharp, aimed point.

Azetla remembered the day, so many years ago, that he had been wounded while saving Captain Hodge's life. He had done so through a combination of instinct and training, but his first conscious thought as he lay in the recovery tent had been: now maybe I will be safe. Now he will trust me. At last, this will serve.

He shied from the memory, cordoning off all that it might bring to the surface. The Sahr had his mind turning where he didn't want it to go, taking his focus off the task at hand. Besides, all this he already knew of himself. Though he put them through the fire, he could never perfectly purify his motives, never get all the dross off. When he was a boy, he had believed with iron ferocity that he was by nature righteous and holy, yet it was being set apart from his people that had shown him how brutally mistaken he had been.

But one had to believe in such a thing as holiness first to know how far from it one was.

Suddenly, the Sahr clicked its tongue and gestured south just as something warm and orange caught Azetla's eye.

Campfires flickered to life on the dark blue horizon.

24

S he moved quickly and quietly over the ground as the sky blackened, as though she was eager to reach Azetla's battalion. Which she was not. But he was also visibly uncertain, steeling himself for the chance that his own might not want him back. She had seen how it was.

His word might be enough. But if not? If they ran at her with their devil-fear which she always found so useful, but which she had been so glad to have laid aside the last two days?

For it had been a little like rest.

Well, it didn't matter either way. Whether she followed in numb silence or thrashed in their hands, the effect was the same. It was like seeking water in a dream while sleeping with a dry, cracked throat; you drank and drank and drank, water spilling over the sides of your mouth, but the thirst never left. Because no matter what these people believed, she was certain that the only hands that could alter her course in any but the most superficial way, were divine ones.

If it were just a matter of being free from this battalion, she could have accomplished that. Taken a Qatlani horse and escaped during the fight, weapons in hand. She considered it, just out of sheer exhaustion. Exhaustion with the ropes that had been on her wrists, the unmapped human terrain, and that irritating word "*Sahr*" by which they always called her. The more northerly the pronunciation, the more grating the sound.

But escape would have been the wrong word for it. Exchange, more like. One uncertainty traded for another, and this one was much easier for her to tolerate. There was more room to breathe in this direction. There was the faint chance of waking up, of feeling the old fire in her gut. It was something she could set between her teeth so as to bite down hard.

And somehow, whether by blood or by blasphemy, she would strike the ear of the desert God and he would be made to contend with her. She didn't even care if she had nothing left for the fight when it came, just that it would come.

For one, there was this Azetla. Devout servant of the desert God, full to the brim with his own quiet fire, and even quieter sense of purpose. *That* was not to be taken for granted.

He had not even tried to make her give up her weapons, which cast her off-balance. She had been ready to parry that. There were several careful and true things she could have said to induce a useful silence in him. With him, silence was thought, and thought was space for words to take root, even against his will.

She even had a few gentle lies she could have drawn out if needed, though with this one, it seemed better to tell the absolute truth. It was more effective. The truth caught hold of him and caged him in, forcing him to pay it mind. You could probably strangle this one to death with the truth, if you wanted, and bury him under it.

But Azetla said nothing, forced nothing. He had, by all appearances, written her down in a certain column in his mind and moved on from there. But she did not know how she had been categorized, nor what caveats he annotated in the margin. Once he cut the ropes, he let her be; there was no conflict for her to read him by. Pressure and doubt and antagonism forced all things—and all people—to reveal their shape. But neutrality told you nothing.

She had absolutely no doubt he would kill her—or try to—should she so much as feint in the wrong direction. But beyond that, he seemed to have read her aright and quickly; she learned through opposition.

And he wished her to learn no more.

Left thus without threat or objective, her mind would quiet, then be filled from its own reserves. That she did *not* want.

She could always try to conjure the old bloodlust that had taken her so long to learn in the first place. Once she had it, it was like flame in her hand. It turned to rot and char, of course, like everything did. Turned her stomach. But it had been fire to stay warm by for a season.

She had tried so hard to wake it. When Azetla closed his eyes in prayer, thinking her asleep. She began running her finger against the knife that rested at her ribcage, like a holy relic against her unholy skin, trying to rouse the instinct to just drag the knife across the easterner's throat and find a new road after. She tried to remember how to make the idea coarse and heady, so that it would rise up through her blood, pour wine-like throughout her muscles, and rest hot and strong on her tongue.

But all she heard were the Mashevi words which she did not understand, but which she could have recited back to him, just to make him flinch. His words were warm and fervent, which left her cold and tired and near to laughter, for she could barely even conjure the desire to antagonize this easterner with his own damn language.

Sometimes she wondered if her tongue was the problem, the real barrier between her and the Gods; it was the only thing over which she felt absolute command. The only part of her that didn't seem like it was petering out. But maybe it would too. Azetla was never quite as staggered—by her words or language or accent—as she wanted him to be.

The corner of his eye was on her now as the outer guard of the Black Wren camp hailed him. The strange assembly of people walked into the camp and, for a few minutes, that strangeness hid her. She was just a figure in the fire-lit night among many.

Azetla quietly instructed one of his Black Wren soldiers to ready a place for the inn people. With respect and immediacy, he was obeyed. That boded well for her.

They had nearly reached the inner tents when the true arbiters of fate arrived: the Nagonan, Joseph Radabe; and the Makarish high-blood, Nimer Sarrez. There was a jumble of gladness and relief in their greeting, until the Nagonan noticed all that Azetla brought in tow. Joy slowly evaporated into confusion.

With bewilderment, the soldiers paid their respects to the northern Colonel, greeted the women warmly, and held back their questions. It took them a long time to notice her. When the Nagonan's gaze found her, it was without clarity, as though his eyes wanted adjusting.

Her pulse livened with readiness and she waited to see recognition snap into his eyes and move throughout his posture. There were many things she no longer cherished about being what they thought—jinn, Sahr, devil, shikk, or any such thing—but it was easy to get a little drunk on their fear, even when it was what she neither needed nor wanted. It always felt like raw freedom before it soured in the gut.

And *there* it was. Wide eyes and horror. Joseph stiffened, and his palm shot to his hilt. Sarrez did the same.

"Stay your hands," Azetla said, looking directly at Joseph, his voice placid.

Sarrez's palm dropped immediately to his side. Joseph was more gradual in his reaction. It stood to reason. His would not be the immediate obedience of a subordinate, but the slow, thoughtful manner of an older brother indulging a younger.

Three weeks of silent observation and she could almost map this battalion down to a man.

For her part, she kept her fingers far from her hilt. That was no way to win this bout. She was still as death and careful with the set of her mouth.

"Lord Verris?" Joseph said, looking at the high-blood.

"Put your questions to the jackal. He's responsible for it," Verris said sharply. "His Highness, the Corra, has commanded that it be kept alive, however."

The two soldiers lowered their heads.

"Of course, my lord," Sarrez said. "Might I escort you to a tent, and have some food brought?"

The northerner gave a short, dry laugh.

"I'll remain with you three, for the time being. There is much to be discussed."

"Of course, my lord," Sarrez said. He gestured for Verris and the others to follow him through the lively, fire-speckled camp.

Joseph held back until the others were a few steps ahead.

"Azetla," he said with a low voice toward him and a blazing look toward her. "We *cannot* allow that."

Azetla glanced at her briefly, then shook his head.

"As I said, Joseph. Leave it be. For now."

"Or set your sword against my throat, Nagonan, if it soothes you. Makes no difference to me," she said.

Joseph stared with a shudder, his step halting as though the terrain had abruptly changed. She forced a cold smile to her mouth; this was less amusing than she had wanted it to be.

"I would carry on the same as before," she added.

Azetla gave her a subtle glance of warning; "*do not test me here.*"

She said it only for the shock of the thing; for the Nagonan to see words come out of a mouth he knew as mute. It wasn't true, though. She would carry on the same as before, but it *did* make a difference when someone pressed metal against her skin. It livened her. It gave her a feeling of accomplishment.

An idiotic reaction, of course. Her brother's doing. If ever he had felt threatened enough to pull a knife on her, she knew she had frightened him—*unnerved* him—and though he always had the advantage, she had that thin bit of victory. To this day, staring in the face of someone who had a blade against her still shot cool triumph to the surface of her skin.

It faded quickly, though, for it was only visceral memory, drudged up by old habit.

Joseph's hand kept to his hilt by instinct. But he did not draw.

"I need an explanation, Azetla," he said in an angry whisper.

"You'll have one. Trust me," Azetla said, giving Joseph a look not too dissimilar from the one he had given her. There was a warning in it.

She slowed her step, crouched low to the ground, and brushed the dust with her fingertips, whispering a greeting in Shihrayan; she did not know for how much longer, but this part of the desert was still her ally. She looked at Joseph then at Azetla and smiled, feeling strangely invigorated. Never had she thought she would be glad to be back here, but she brushed the dust against her palm with affection. It was curious how what had once been reviled could almost feel like home. All it took was coming from something worse.

Savor the feeling while it lasts, she thought, watching the fine Trekoan powder drift back to the ground. It clouded about the ankles, and took a long time to rest.

25

Perhaps Joseph should have felt pity for Azetla, but he didn't right now. After everything he had seen and heard this night, he felt nothing but muddy frustration. And fear. The situation was so dangerously confusing, and much of it was Azetla's own doing. One dread thing piled on top of the other as the night wore on, each coming from Azetla's hand, and set into Joseph's arms. And he was to accept it all as calmly as Azetla gave it?

First, it was troubling to see Azetla act like this again, taking full and unabashed command—perhaps it bit into Joseph's skin, somehow. He didn't want to call it hurt pride, but it would take work to find another name for it.

It could happen to anybody. Watch the jackal boy you dragged out of the dirt. The one you vouched for. Just watch him. He doesn't stay small and silent; he grows till he looks you in the eye, in every sense of the phrase. Watch him partake in the favor you've always received from the Captain, and then overtake it. Watch him walk in with Lord Colonel Verris and a talking devil and tell you—cold as death—that the battalion took the Sahr out from under the Emperor himself. Then he gives you a careful look which tells you there is more—or worse—to come.

Watch him talk like a high-blood and a captain. Watch him firm as iron when he damn well should be shaking.

Azetla used to be so careful and quiet about these things. Even when he had, in the past, commanded on Captain Hodge's behalf, he did it in such a way that the authority didn't seem *quite* his. So it did not rankle or antagonize. One acclimated to it.

But tonight, he had been a different man. The veneer of deference was all but gone. Perhaps it was only Joseph who noticed, for only he knew him well enough to mark it. Azetla did all things technically correct. He used the honorifics and claimed nothing that was not his. He explained how the Sahr had been freed and how the Corra wanted it alive.

He *seemed* as before, but Joseph could feel the lie of it.

There had been a hardness in his voice and a hostility in his manner during the meeting with Lord Verris. Oh, yes, Lord Verris was allowed to speak his piece and berate the "jackal" but, by the end of it, Azetla still managed to firmly gather everyone's words and put them all in his preferred order.

The Sahr was to remain free and would be "put to use," whatever that meant.

The Black Wren was officially subject to the Corra's will. Joseph did not know what that meant either, but there was something in the way it was phrased that made Lord Verris tense.

And the matter of commandership was to be resolved in the old way: by general consensus of the senior men of the battalion. Those senior in both common and noble rank.

This meant that Joseph and Sarrez would have a say, but Azetla would have none. Joseph did not understand why Azetla had put the old way forth. It seemed to his detriment. Yes, most of the men accepted Azetla's leadership, but that had been under the shadow of Captain Hodge's hand, and there were more than a few who had never approved of it.

Lord Verris either countered or assented to Azetla's statements, but try as he might his lordship couldn't take charge. His words seemed to fall from his mouth straight to the ground. Azetla, on the other hand, never once interrupted or raised his voice. But he had no hesitation, and he made no requests. He issued commands.

This alone would have been enough to worry Joseph. To make him grab Azetla by the shoulders so as to jar some sense into him. But Azetla was not done unveiling trouble. He waited until Lord Verris had dismissed the last of the officers and retired to his tent. Then, before Joseph could say a word, Azetla took him aside.

"I need to talk to you and Sarrez right now," he said in the lowest of voices. "Meet me at the southeast of camp, next to the watch-fire."

"You mean next to that devil you saw fit to free?" Joseph said coldly.

"Yes. There exactly."

Pressing his lips together, Joseph reluctantly pocketed his anger. For the moment. There would be time for it later. "I'll get Sarrez."

Azetla nodded and went on ahead. It did not take Joseph long to retrieve Sarrez, for he had anticipated such an order. It had long been the three of them who formed the main arterial lines of authority in the battalion, and this in spite of the technical seniority of Lieutenant Brody, who respected Azetla, and Lieutenant Sable, who despised him with every fiber of his being. Azetla had the most to lose of the three of them, but if he was thrown over, Joseph and Sarrez might follow.

Whatever this game was, Joseph hated it, and he hated that Azetla had already laid the pieces on the board without him.

As they passed the watch-fire, Joseph's anger returned abruptly. There was the Sahr. It sat on the stones of the empty cistern, arms folded loosely, looking to be the most untroubled creature in the whole bloody camp. Azetla stood just across from it.

"I hope this is because we're to be given the honor of killing that devil ourselves," Joseph said.

The Sahr made no acknowledgment of this except to glance at Joseph. It took a long drink of water from the skin beside it.

"I brought you here because I don't know what Verris means to do with me, and I need you both to understand the full situation before I lose the chance to speak. I—" Azetla began.

"Look, just because this devil knows the ground and killed a few raiders—"

"It's not *about* the Sahr," Azetla growled. He closed his eyes and breathed out a short sigh. "It's a coup."

Joseph stilled. There was a moment of fog and then, light broke through.

Gods and devils, Azetla, what have you got us into?

"Azetla, I don't—what do you mean?" Sarrez said.

But Joseph knew already. All the little things said and unsaid in the meeting with Lord Verris fell into place.

"The Corra and Lord Verris," Azetla said. "They are not just bartering with Emperor Riada for some fame. They're planning to oust him."

The Sahr remained sitting and quiet, acting as though this information was either not new to it, or simply not sufficiently relevant to its interests.

"You'd better be damn sure about what you're saying, Azetla, because you of all people can't afford to be caught *talking like that*," Joseph said.

"It's not my treason. It's theirs," he said. "And I am sure."

"But how? How can you know this? And are they *aware* you know this?" Sarrez asked, rubbing his hand across his forehead and down his face.

"If they were, I'd be dead by now. As for how I know…" Azetla glanced at Joseph as if for assistance or succor.

Captain Hodge rarely asked where Azetla got his information. Southern magistrates, Mashevi merchants, records from the Trade and Exchange Council. What difference did it make, as long as the

Captain knew what he needed to know? But Azetla told Joseph nearly all. There were a few undisclosed sources, however, which Joseph had always assumed were Mashevi agitators under assumed Maurowan names. It had been sensible not to press the matter.

Joseph shrugged his shoulders jerkily, as if he knew none of this. Azetla clenched his jaw and went on.

"I have been piecing all this together over the last few years. A list of all the Maurowan nobility that had either reason or tendency to oppose Riada. Certain patterns and alliances emerged. But there were a few crucial holes...which the Corra and Lord Verris kindly filled. I was already quite certain by the time we returned to Piarago but," Azetla glanced at the Sahr, "the discussion around the Sahr confirmed it. They had too much invested in the endeavor to let it come to nothing."

The Sahr rested its palms on the stone, leaning back and looking up at Joseph with a smile that he detested.

"You know, the one you call Corra came to examine me a few days after I was caught," it said. "And, assuming me unable to comprehend—as most of you were so kind as to do—he spoke of all this. To himself."

Azetla turned sharply. "He did?"

The Sahr nodded.

"You never told me this."

"Well most of our words haven't been what I would call leisurely ones," the Sahr said. "It never came up."

The Sahr stood now, pouring its thorough gaze over Joseph and Sarrez. "Your Corra said 'So by *this* I either ascend to power or fall to my death? Pure *madness*.'"

Its lilt changed again; the imitation of His Highness the Corra was disturbingly precise, rife with mockery, and full of the tremulous reluctance for which the Corra was too easily known.

"Then what you mean to say, Azetla, is that this bloody devil knows enough to get all of us killed, and you decided to loose it and let it stand among us," Joseph said.

"I did no different than I always do, Joseph. I did the best I could with what I had."

"Oh, well done then, jackal," Joseph said.

Azetla flinched as if the words were a slap across the face. The anger felt so good right in the moment Joseph uttered it. He would have done it again.

"I'm doing what I can to keep our heads above water, Joseph, and I have no stomach right now for being called that by you too," Azetla said, his voice the fiercest sort of quiet.

Joseph looked askance of Azetla, felt the tension in Sarrez's stance, and gave his best effort at a conciliatory gesture. He hated that he had said that, and yet he still felt justified in it. And he hated that too.

Azetla drew in a long breath.

"The important thing is that you know what we are to them. A token, a talisman. To be owned and used. Sacrificed, even. Also, if I am not mistaken in my reading of all this, the Colonel at Areo outpost is already their ally, which means we are walking closer to the treason, not further away," Azetla said.

He looked coldly at Joseph. "Do you understand?"

Joseph nodded.

Sarrez put his fingers to his temple. "Gods and devils."

Azetla told them all else that he knew or suspected in greater detail—the Sahr did not interject this time for it too was listening—and then Sarrez had to depart to receive the watchmen's reports. The Sahr was left where it was, free but heavily guarded, and Joseph walked with Azetla to the center of camp.

The silence was thick between them, until Azetla broke it.

"You'll need to see that Khala and the Colha family are well taken care of and then—" Azetla began.

"Playing Captain to me now too?" Joseph said. Gods, he could not stop himself.

"I'm not ordering *you*," Azetla said, his voice brier-sharp. "I'm asking. Because I don't know what's going to happen."

Joseph clapped his hand firmly on Azetla's shoulder and looked at him. There were dark circles under his eyes, and worry within them.

"I'll see to them. I'm sorry," he said.

They parted ways with purposeful strides; the agitation in Joseph's thoughts remained. He had not realized how strange and uncomfortable it would be for him to see Azetla making loud the quiet authority he had always had in this battalion. It should have been enough for him, shouldn't it? To have so much of the Captain's favor? Uncloaked, this was all too much, the taste of it too strong.

Joseph tried to assess his own mind and see if this was something he had wanted for himself, or if he simply thought it wasn't something a Mashevi was ever supposed to have, no matter how well command suited him.

He was ashamed to realize, it was probably both.

✦ ⚶ ✦

Azetla felt unsteady when he walked into the lower camp, as if he were finding his way through pitch dark. He was exhausted; both his thoughts and his limbs seemed to grow slack with each step.

One thing he held firm in hand; he would not slip back into the old game of playing the cowering jackal in front of outsiders, ever again. A general consensus should put someone Azetla trusted in command, and would give whoever that was legitimacy. That...that might be enough.

He had been more reckless these last days than he ever had been in his life. There was no choice. He had to keep feeling his way forward until he came to a clearing or high ground. Fourteen years' absence from his people. Seven years debt against his name. Countless silences lying in wait and muddied waters.

And maybe it all comes to nothing.

Azetla set up his pallet and walked toward the privy trenches. He was murmuring rote prayers and, strangely, feeling more isolated now than he had apart from the battalion. He looked out to the east, past the camp, mouthing the rhythmic closure of the prayer. Jagged and moonlit, the desert offered him harsh comfort. It was rough and unforgiving, but it never feigned to be anything else. Let it be brutal and honest rather than gentle and false.

Hearing the watchmen approach, Azetla finished with the trenches and adjusted his sagam and overshirt. One of the men stepped in beside him, turned, and smiled. It was Sergeant Zayfa, a Makar.

"We're so *glad* to have you back, dear jackal," Zayfa said savagely.

Azetla stiffened and looked around just long enough to see a dozen men slipping out of the dark, their faces half shrouded in the West Makarish style. He tried to take a step back. Instantly Zayfa's hand was at Azetla's throat. Another pair of arms grasped his left hand. Lurching to the side, he managed to pull his arm away and throw his elbow into the jawbone of someone behind him. He put his fist into Zayfa's ribs and scrambled for his knife hilt.

He didn't make it. Too many hands gripped him, too many blows broke across his face. He twisted like a snake with its head cut off, to no purpose. They dragged him into the shallow, rank-smelling trench and beat him into it. For one half-second he managed to turn his face and shoulders out of the stench, kicking his boot into the side of someone's knee. Whoever it was buckled to the ground, but Azetla was driven back into the muck and rocky soil.

They smashed their boots against his ribs. Another blow across his face, and his teeth cut the skin inside his cheek. He could taste the blood and the mire together in his mouth. He spat desperately, retching from it. He jerked his arm till his shoulder burned, but he could *not* get free. Someone stuffed a cloth in his mouth and he almost choked on it.

Then all stilled. One side of his face throbbed, dizzying him. It hurt to open his eyes, but he tried to do it anyway. He could not wipe them clean. He could scarcely move, they gripped him so tight. He was wholly at their mercy and his stomach turned over violently.

It would not be the first time it happened to a Mashevi: use, beat, then kill.

God of Masheva, help. *God of Masheva.* He pulled, he jerked, he shouted through the muffling cloth. He arched his back, but they clamped him down like a vise. His chest constricted as shallow, panicky breaths scurried in and out of his body.

"You're no longer sanctioned, jackal," one of the men spat on him. "We owe you nothing."

He recognized the voice. It was Lieutenant Carran Sable, a Maurowan-Makarish noble of Piarago. Behind him stood the Makarish outsider, Haqir. He could guess with his eyes closed who the others might be, but it didn't matter. He could do nothing, say nothing. He could barely breathe.

"You were the Captain's only defect, mercy-be-peace-be," Sable said. "Why should his only mistake be his only legacy?"

Sable knelt across Azetla's ribs and threw his fist into his mouth. The filthy gravel of the trench bit into the side of Azetla's ear and his whole head seemed to grow fire-hot and swollen. The pressure of Sable's knees on his chest made it hard to focus. He strained and strained, but it only made him dizzier.

"Let's have the left hand first, Haqir, before we take the rest." Sable pressed his hand into Azetla's throat.

Azetla snapped his fingers into a tight fist, fingernails burrowing deep into his palm. They'd never gone this far before. They'd never thought they could get away with it. Insults, fists, and cruel jokes, yes, but he'd always been able to fight back.

All of them began to beat, scrape, and tear into him at once. He screamed into the cloth. So little sound came out, so little breath went in.

As two of them pried his thumb out of his fist and brought a knife blade toward the vital tendon, a new shout poured across the trench.

"What the devil is going on here?"

The knife stilled, then jerked away from his palm. Azetla's fingers snapped back, blood inside his fist. Through a haze he recognized the voice. Nimer Sarrez. A good voice. Azetla prayed it was still a good voice. Let it be a good voice. Please.

A few assailants immediately backed away. Others had more conviction, and did not abandon their quarry. Sable's knees were still digging into Azetla's stomach. In the moment of distraction, however, Azetla was able to pull his left hand in and bury it against his chest as if it were all he owned in the world. And it really was.

"Overdue justice, Sarrez," Sable said. "Let us go about our own law, as we always have in this battalion. For the Gods' sake, you of all people should approve. As a man of Makarish blood—"

"Don't tell me what a Makarish man should do, Sable. Step away."

"But he's a jackal and, after all this time, we've a right—"

"Maybe you have and maybe you haven't. But if you abide by our unwritten laws in this battalion, then I am in authority over you and I've said that's enough."

Sable didn't move. Perhaps he thought the tide had turned in his favor. No matter where the consensus fell, Verris could overrule it. His knees were still digging into Azetla's ribs, his hand still at his throat. Sable was not afraid because he felt *justified*. He felt he would win out. If not now, then later.

But Azetla felt others loose their grips on him; he bucked and twisted, trying to free his legs, trying to reach the lip of the trench and pull himself out. He had no strength to strike or fight. He just needed to get out.

There was a sudden scuffle over Azetla's head. Half a dozen other soldiers rushed in—Azetla did not know where they had come from or when and he still could scarcely see—and the others backed away. Sable was pulled off and forced to stand back.

Someone grabbed Azetla's hand—it took him a moment to realize it was Sarrez—and helped him out of the trench. Slowly, he tried to come to his feet, but stopped, resting on his heels, not able to look Sarrez or anyone in the eye. He spat out the cloth and coughed, doubling over. That made everything burn and throb all the more. He began to notice the soldiers who had come to his aid—Nuss, Isilia, Vrai, and several others, all looking like they'd just been awakened, all flush with anger.

"We haven't done anything wrong," Sable said, head held high, looking at Sarrez.

"Then perhaps your men shouldn't have felt the need to cover their faces, Sable. Or flinch at the sound of their own Lieutenant," Sarrez spat back.

Azetla did not even attempt to talk. Even if he had words, his voice would only come out as scraped charcoal. There was such a wretched taste in his mouth. He finally made himself stand up, and stand straight, and it hurt so badly to do it. He pressed his shoulders back. He forced his head to stay up, and forced himself to look Sable in the eyes.

Sable glared back at him with a boundless hatred. "That's because *you*, your despicable left hand, and your jackal tongue all have a history of deceiving good and honest men into trusting you."

Sarrez glanced at Azetla. Azetla's mind wavered.

There were a lot of old and broken things between Azetla and Sarrez, such that even though they had been as friends for years now, all their conversations were shot through with motes of doubt.

Sarrez was Makarish. He was also a just man. Azetla struggled to reconcile these two truths, so they sat there, neither fact quite touching the other in his mind. It was somehow harder to remember how often and how well Sarrez had stood by him of late than it was to remember all the long years that came before.

Azetla had already slogged through half a decade of his debt conscription when Sarrez collected his expensive commission and walked into the battalion with a high-held head and no tolerance for "jackals." Like any well-bred Makarish high-blood, he had assumed Azetla was someone's packing boy and treated him, at first, with mere broad contempt. But when Sarrez realized that Azetla was accorded duties and authorities, he began to deal with him more maliciously. Azetla ached to retaliate. And he could not. The seething hatred between them could have riven the battalion if it had gone on for much longer.

Those vicious years were now passed. But not forgotten. Often it hung over them like a remnant smell they would both very much like to be rid of. Sometimes it seemed that Sarrez was harsher toward his own people in compensation. And sometimes, Azetla allowed him to be.

That was Azetla's weakness. Not Sarrez's. That was Azetla's sense of justice balking at his bruises.

Sarrez was clearly not as infected by the old wounds as Azetla was.

"Lord Verris will decide if this was needed or not," Sarrez said calmly. "Be mindful, though, Sable. If Lord Colonel Verris approves the command order that I, Sergeant Radabe, Lieutenant Brody, and nearly *all* the others have put forth, the next time you attack Azetla, our lawful response will be to execute you, given that he will be your commander."

Azetla had to block his expression as with stone; relief came first, making his muscles feel they were turned to water. Then came doubt on its heels. He glanced carefully at Sarrez who gave a stiff nod.

He kept expecting nothing from anyone, even those that had given to him time and again. Joseph *did* still bristle at any overt sign of Azetla's authority. And Sarrez always balked in front of newcomers when they first saw him take an order from a Mashevi tongue.

But here was the truth. They were ashamed of him to his face; loyal behind his back.

"I don't believe you," Sable growled. "Have you lost all pride?"

Sarrez's face was a mask in the dark. "Believe what you like. I advise you tell your more wary friends what I have told you. You're free to leave."

"You—"

"I said, *leave*. You will be informed of Lord Verris' decision same as the rest of us. And you will honor it, by blood."

Azetla could see Sable straining for a rejoinder. He outranked Sarrez in certain, formal ways. But this was the Black Wren, not the Maurowan court, and Sable knew better than to unsheathe such a merely ceremonial sword as that. Slowly, the rest of the assailants began to retreat toward the camp. As Sable passed close by Azetla, the Lieutenant spoke in a low voice.

"If Lord Colonel Verris is a true Maurowan he'd as soon have your head on a pike as have you command us."

Azetla looked directly at the man, but said nothing. Sarrez too, was silent. Neither said a word until all the soldiers were gone. Azetla started to walk, stumbled, and Sarrez steadied him.

"Thank you, Nimer," Azetla said at last, though he had to drag the words out of his mouth as with a hook. It was the least that could be said, but it scalded the tongue. He couldn't look Sarrez in the eye.

"Is it true, or did you just say it to scare Sable?" Azetla asked.

Sarrez lifted his shoulders half-heartedly.

"It's true. We each went to the Lord Colonel independently, after the meeting. Doesn't mean it's going to work, by blood. I can't guarantee anything right now. Neither can you."

They were both quiet for a moment, walking at Azetla's slow pace.

"But Sable could only scrounge a handful. And that's something," Sarrez added.

"How did you know...?"

"I didn't."

Sarrez glanced toward the eastern side of camp with some apprehension.

"I passed by the jinn-thing to speak with Collory and the devil just stood up and spoke to me—still feels like a slap in the face to hear a voice come out of that bloody mouth—and it...it spoke in *Makarish*." Unease filled Sarrez's voice.

Of course. Of course it spoke Makarish.

"And with the *exact* inflections of my birth-town, I swear by blood. It said, 'In case it matters to you, your jackal has a hunting party right on his heels.' Just like that."

Sarrez shook his head, steering Azetla by gesture to the opposite part of camp.

"There are a few pots of washing water reserved for the officers. I'll show you where they are," he said. "Spare clothes too. A cake of soap, if we're lucky."

"Sarrez, I—" Azetla said, his voice rough.

"Don't worry about it," Sarrez said.

He led Azetla to the privileges accorded the most senior officers, those born from families who supplied their every need, then left Azetla to himself.

Azetla washed the stench off as thoroughly he could, kneading water through the cuts in his face, and the gash on his left palm which, but for a little more depth, could have kept him from carrying a sword for the rest of his life. He rinsed his mouth out dozens of times and spoke prayers of cleansing, his whispered voice trembling slightly. He wanted to collapse to the ground and press his head deep in his hands, resting against the dust; the old ritual posture of desperation and gratitude. Old because it was instinctive.

But he didn't. He felt too distant from prayers and hope and holiness. Unclean, perhaps, and guilty. He walked slowly back the way he came.

He didn't even feel angry. No more than normal. And what tired anger he did feel was heading in all the wrong directions. So let Sable hate him. But Joseph had given him no quarter, jabbing at him, trying to run him aground. And Sarrez? Sarrez had saved Azetla from injury, shame, and—almost certainly—death. And yet Azetla vividly remembered a time when Sarrez would have stood with Sable. He had to knock the memory down hard and put it in its place.

He paused in pain, shuddered in the cool air, then kept walking.

The most direct route was past the southeast watch-fire. Past the Sahr. It lay on a paper-thin pallet—guarded from a distance—sword lying along its body like a mate. It was not asleep. Its head rested on one hand, the other lay softly on its hilt, and its knees were propped up.

He gestured to the watchmen to hold their distance.

"Not out of the goodness of your heart, I don't think," he said.

A tired laugh came up from the pallet. It sat halfway up, staring at him, eyes traveling slowly from gash to bruises to swollen jaw.

"No, I wouldn't put it that way," it said. "If they did that to you, what would they do to me once you were gone?"

There was nothing feigned in its tone. And it was right. They were not allowed to kill it. But they would do everything else besides, all that their hatred and grief allowed. The only reason they didn't now—and the only reason they hadn't since Sahr territory—was because Azetla had set and enforced the rules.

"I couldn't very well come myself; first because these," the Sahr glanced toward the guards, "won't let me go anywhere. And second because if I did anything, it would have harmed your status, not helped it. I can't order people about, I can only kill them at best."

"What do you want?" Azetla said. The stiffness and bruises in his jaw made him sound full of scorn, where in truth he was just *weary*. Weary enough that he could have slept on a jagged stone and slept well. Weary down to his soul and bones.

The Sahr sat fully and squinted up at him, for the fire was at his back.

"Just now? To be able to take relief or a wash without a dozen eyes on me. I think you can find it in your overwrought eastern piety to understand that. Also, I'm still at prisoner rations."

"Because you're still a prisoner here."

"No. I'm not."

Azetla let out a sharp breath.

"You think I can just let you wander around and do as you please? Anyway, it may not be in my hands anymore," he said.

The Sahr put its head back down on the hard ground and closed its eyes.

"Based on the lay of the land, I think it will be."

It was a waste of time to argue with it. He simply shook his head, turned, and left.

Moments later, as he lay down on his pallet and sleep loomed over him, he found a drifting part of his mind wondering what in all the desert the Sahr meant by that remark about his "eastern piety." His bruises ached, and pain fought against rest. He was half asleep when the simple answer came to him. Not what it meant. What *she* meant. The Sahr wanted those privacies that were traditionally due a tribal woman, even a prisoner-of-war, but which no one would have ever deigned to give a devil. Azetla, for his own part, had not once thought of it.

26

———◆◇◆———

"Get up," Joseph said for the second time, giving Azetla a shove.

In all the years Joseph had known him, Azetla was swift to rise. But meager sleep and many bruises do not an easy morning make. No time for pity, however. Or guilt. So he kept telling himself. He should have known that this would happen. If Joseph had been less distracted by the prospect of treason, he might have been prepared. Half the frustration he felt right now was toward himself. But what good did that do Azetla? None.

Azetla pushed himself to a sit in the slow, controlled way a man pushes open a thick iron door. His ribs were green and purpled, and the right side of his face was swollen, but his eyes could open, so that was something. He looked at Joseph and then at the tent entrance, where night still clung to a few corners of the sky.

"I need to talk to you before his Lordship is awake."

Azetla sniffed and rubbed his hand gingerly over his face. He stood—more himself now—dressed, and strapped on his sword. He set the direction of movement, as he was wont to do, walking purposefully toward the southeast of camp.

"You made very bold last night, Azetla," Joseph began.

"Rest easy, then. I paid my dues for that," came Azetla's sharp reply.

"That is *not* what meant. If I could have stopped them—"

"I know." Azetla's tone softened. "I know."

"But might it be better to go back to the old way?" Joseph said carefully.

Azetla did not respond for a moment. He looked out as they approached the makeshift camp stables.

"No. I'm not doing that again. If we are with the Corra and Lord Verris, then we're already outside the Emperor's law. Having a Mashevi command a battalion can do no more harm than has already been done."

"I don't know that Lord Verris sees it that way."

"It was *his* Corra who said that they would not hinder whatever authority the battalion saw fit to give me," Azetla said in a rather flat voice. "So it's down to you, Sarrez, and Brody, for everyone else will follow."

"Sarrez already told you what we've decided."

Azetla stopped, his face tightening. He was not looking at Joseph, but at the tall buckskin dun the battalion had captured in Sahr territory, which had at last been brought back to its master. Azetla set his shoulders. "Then that's all there is say."

"You put yourself in this position and you'll be the first person they blame and discard when things go wrong," Joseph said.

"I know," Azetla replied. "But if not me, then you."

He stepped past Joseph, toward the horses. Joseph stayed where he was.

Devils take him.

Joseph was terrified. Of Azetla. *For* Azetla.

Joseph wanted his battalion, but he wanted it as it had been. He did not want this conspiracy. He didn't want a Sahr devil. He didn't want any of the things Lord Verris had brought to their door and Azetla had let in. It was one matter to grumble against the Emperor with wine in your hand for giving favoritism toward his new Navy. It was quite another to draw a sword against him. But Azetla, as a Mashevi, acted like a man with nothing to lose. And Joseph, Gods help him...Joseph was going to let him do it. He was going to walk directly beside him.

That damned jackal. So silent and alone and exasperating from the moment the boy was dragged into the Black Wren. He was Joseph's little brother as much as his own blood kin.

And he was his commander. The truth was, it had been that way for some time, now Joseph just had to admit it.

The Sahr did not acknowledge Azetla's approach and was likewise indifferent to the assigned watchmen who scarce knew what to do with it. With her. With whatever she bloody was. And what does one do with a charge that is armed and free? Linger and shift and tense the shoulders?

The Sahr inspected its horse in a thorough manner, calming it with whispered words in its own language as the animal flicked its tar-black mane against the Sahr's shoulder. Azetla folded his arms gingerly against his ribs.

"You don't need to do that," he said. "He'll have been treated like a king. He's worth more than either of us bought and sold twice over."

The Sahr smiled as it rearranged the reins and tethered the horse. "Well that's true."

It looked Azetla over in a way he did not like, assessing him now in the light of day where the night had perhaps hidden how severe a beating it had been. He felt keenly conscious of each cut and bruise. And of what they signified. Azetla loosed his arms from their fold and set them akimbo and the Sahr's eyes followed the stiff movement of his left hand and fixed on the bandage he wore. It clicked its tongue at him much like it had done at the horse.

"They went for your hand, then?" it said, as his palm closed defensively over the stained cloth. "The West Makarish tend to prefer the symbolic wounds—one tribe caught a thief who played the oud, so they broke her fingers. And the people of Hushai are great runners, so whenever they take vengeance against that tribe, they sever the tendons in their ankles. But I don't think they would have stopped at your sword hand."

"No," Azetla said.

"A fine, warm welcome for their commander," the Sahr replied.

"Well, as you said, my men would have given you a still warmer welcome, if I'd let them."

"No doubt."

"I do have to consider how long, exactly, I can justify not letting them harm their Captain's killer," he said in a calm, neutral voice.

The Sahr tilted its head to the side. "By blood, Mashevi, is that what you think a threat sounds like? Don't you realize that there's no point in leveraging my life against me, of all things. It's...beside the point. And," the Sahr looked at Azetla's hand again, "it's a false threat. You don't even mean it."

Azetla smiled faintly, which made the Sahr turn wary. He drew out the Trekoan knife he had taken the day it was captured.

"You misunderstand. I am explaining the truth of my position to you. Allowing you free comes at great cost. Even had they not loved their Captain as they did, most think you are capable of evil and magic just by the word of your mouth. That you can bewitch and curse and deceive."

The Sahr gave a quiet laugh and shook its head. "That's an intoxicating thought. I'll admit I like the sound of it, and I'm happy for it to be in as many minds as possible. But that's not how it works, Mashevi."

Suddenly, the Sahr stepped closer and an earnest look showed on its face, which felt far more hazardous than any sneer or cruel grin. "I hear what you say. I see you, your reactions, your mannerisms, and the way your eastern mouth reaches so *far* around Maurowan words. And then, as sure as death, I know what you need to hear. And I say *that*. Some require lies, flourishes, or flattery. But I've found that what you need are the raw facts, even if they're a thousand leagues from what you *want*. Because once you know them, you're trapped by them."

Azetla stared blankly, no words to say, no words to withdraw. His blood felt strange, and his footing, uneasy. He could not scrounge a single thing out of his mouth, and he desperately, desperately wanted to. It was trying to tell him he was being swindled by mere truth. He tapped the flat of the Trekoan knife against his leg at a tense rhythm.

"I'm doing it right now," it continued in an amused voice. "When I speak plain and straightforward like this, you usually let out a long breath and, after a while, your shoulders fall from their tension—they're usually pulled up when you first start talking to me—and each time I do it, you stay your hand and ignore that remaining corner of your mind that begs you to gut me, here and now. Because you *know* I'm telling the truth. I can lie perfectly and without qualm, rest assured. But I have not been lying to you, because it wouldn't work the way I want it to, and it wouldn't do me any good."

He felt the effect even as it was being described; he wanted to relax. Of course it was not jinn or devil or fire; it was just intuitive. It saw that naught but the truth would reach him. Simple. Nothing more than that. No sleight of tongue, certainly not. No clever tricks. Nothing to see here. By salt, it was like having someone say that they were tying your hands a certain way while in the very act of doing so, and you were meant to nod along saying, "yes, you're right, that *is* how you tie a knot. Good job. Thank you."

He almost smiled in astonishment. He could not maneuver around its words, try as he might, but there was such a thing as a percentage of the truth, and such a thing as omission. He knew that better than anyone. So he did let his shoulders relax. Then he curled his fingers securely around the Trekoan knife—the gash stung when he did so—and raised it with a calm gesture.

"So what you mean to say is that if the West Makarish meant to render you harmless, they need only go for the tongue. Without it you would have neither Trekoan, nor Makarish, nor Maurowan, nor any truth or lies," he said.

The Sahr went taut. It pressed its lips together and there was no mistaking the brief and bright flash of fear across its face. It glanced to the side as if to see how many soldiers were about and whether they were closing in. Azetla knew the sharpness of its fear because it was so bitterly familiar to him. The banding of the Trekoan hilt bit into the wound in his left hand.

Azetla turned the knife around in his palm and offered the hilt to the Sahr.

"You do tell the truth, I think. Maybe you don't value your life, but you do value your tongue. Perhaps because that's all you have, and you know it—never mind whether you were telling the truth when you said you don't know what you *are*."

"I'm Shihrayan," the Sahr said flatly. It did not touch the knife.

As if that meant anything to him or anyone. A Shihrayan was a Sahr was a devil was a danger.

"And what else?" he said.

The Sahr narrowed its eyes.

"Ask your God that, Mashevi, not me. The gods are the ones who know what we are."

That was true as well. He breathed out a laugh. The Sahr reached up at last, and took the knife from his palm. It was a simple one, but well made, and worn to fit the palm that owned it.

"I will reduce the watch and alter their instructions. As to privacy, however, none of us here have it entirely, so you can be given no more than the rest of us. No more. No less. And the same rations," Azetla said. "This with the understanding that the less attentive I ask my men to be regarding you, the more vigilant *I* will be. And the less merciful, should you prove me wrong in the slightest."

For once, it looked like the Sahr was the uncertain one, not sure what *he* would do, not even as certain of what he was. That was good and wise of it.

It nodded slowly.

"All right. Then I can force that northern Lord's hand," it said.

Azetla raised his eyebrows faintly and waited.

"I can make them need you," it said. "I can make it so that if he cuts you off, he cuts off his best allies here in Trekoa. It will be all but impossible for them to shake you out."

As impossible as you are making it for me to shake you out, you unholy Sahr?

But this was what he wanted. This was the whole point.

"Very well. Explain," he said.

"Nothing can be accomplished in Trekoa without Rokh Imal Bin-Zari of Saqiran. *Nothing.* If he is made an ally of this conspiracy, and if you are the one with whom he strikes hands, that will get you halfway there."

"If. If," Azetla said.

"I say that because I can make the introduction, but only you can secure the alliance. Surely you understand that."

"Lord Verris doesn't even know that I'm aware of all his plans. He only suspects that I suspect. Not much can be done openly in any direction."

The Sahr had relaxed back to its usual state, and had begun to pick dirt out of the crease at the top of the knife's hilt.

"That I can handle with little cost to you. You can't be an easy target for retaliation if you're merely one of many who know. I mean, it would have to come to light eventually, wouldn't it?"

It smiled and looked at Azetla to see that its meaning was understood in full.

He was playing with fire. He knew that. But, hopefully, a controlled burn. And better risk being singed now, than being turned to ash later.

"But if I do this for you, easterner, then I'm no prisoner here, not even in the mildest form. And I owe you *nothing*."

Azetla nodded.

"And I'll owe you nothing," he said. "Not even protection."

The Sahr narrowed its eyes only a little.

"Then you'll want to take the Pardish road through Saqirani territory today, not the Saav-si. It will add only half a day, and give you everything else you need."

27

She did not give Azetla warning when she laid out the trap. That seemed the most effective tack, for then Azetla would have to feign neither surprise nor anger. He could have them both naturally and whatever retaliation might come from that northerner, Lord Verris, would be directed toward her.

Which meant it would not land, but skitter and stop at her feet, impotent.

Azetla had shown some real capacity for wrenching her wrist when he wanted to, for finding the weak spots in her joints, but regarding this northerner she had not the least bit of concern. He scarcely knew where he was or what to do among soldiers.

There were a dozen officers and ten seasoned men of common rank standing about her when she explained the right respects and protocols for entering Rokh Bin-Zari's village of Bir Herash. Lower the flags as a sign of respect and non-aggression. Do not attempt to engage the women in any fashion. Break marching form and let the Trekoans among them—there were only a mere dozen of distant Trekoan ancestry—walk at the front, just behind the battalion commander, who would represent all.

She gestured at Azetla casually and did not have to wait long for the provocation to induce the necessary reply.

"The Mashevi is not the official commander," the northerner said.

"Oh isn't he? Who is, then?" she said, laying out the sketch map of Bir Herash to Areo which she had dictated, and Azetla drawn up.

This "Verris"—Verris sounded like the Makarish word for mouse, so it distracted and amused her to hear it said all the time—strained. He did *not* like talking to her. Not before they reached the battalion, and not the three days since. Some combination of pride and uneasiness stiffened him each time. But he had no choice.

"I am," he said, with only a little hesitation.

Such an easy falsehood to lay bare and mock in front of the men, and the taste of sarcasm was already warm on her tongue. But she saw Azetla's look of warning, the abrupt tension in his jaw. What was at Verris' expense now, would be at Azetla's later. Humiliating him was not to the purpose.

"That will not serve you, I'm afraid," she said gently, looking down at the map. "Rokh Imal Bin-Zari does not easily tolerate northerners. A Mashevi, he will accept."

"Maurow he *must* accept. And I still have not understood why this tribal chieftain's good grace is of any value to me," Verris said.

She kept her eyes on the sketch-map—a simple little representation, lovely for its accuracy—and kept her voice soothing, calm, and blandly Maurowan.

"Understand, you're in my desert, northerner, and you know as little of its capacity as of my own. If you wish success to your Corra against his brother, you won't waste this chance on formality. This Rokh has opposed the northern Emperor for as long as you've been alive. His authority here is far greater than you realize, and needful. But, until you prove otherwise, you are still *of Riada* to him. You are still the enemy. You have to be patient."

The effect of her words was not wholly unlike a front of cold washing in, with that same, wildly abrupt transition of taste, feel, and smell. As if the Gods themselves were sweeping nature aside with their hands. It was always faintly intoxicating to her when she was able to procure a lightning reaction in the air.

The soldiers murmured. Verris was drained of all his color. Should he try to deny it? The words were already loose. Though he stood stock still, she could almost feel his mind darting, swaying, reeling. And the longer he struggled to speak, the deeper the words rooted, the more the absence of denial breathed out confirmation.

She attended to the map for a few moments longer, as though unaware of the palpable shiver in the air, then glanced up toward Lord Verris with a look of concern. Soft, subtle. As genuine as she could fashion it around her inner mirth.

"Was this not yet meant to be common knowledge? I assumed that was the entire reason for my being here." She flicked her fingers across the map. "If I have misunderstood, then you will be even less welcome in Rokh Imal's tent."

She stood up and adopted her most non-threatening posture: hands held lightly at her waist, shoulders relaxed, head angled a little downward, slow and all but hesitant in her movements as she stepped toward him.

"To one who supports Riada, Trekoa is a wall and then a snare. To one who opposes him, it is a door and even ground. Discuss your intentions with your men or don't—that isn't my affair—but the Mashevi must walk at the head. Do with him as you please, once you have your footing, but at least let him be put to good use first."

"Enough," Verris barked. "I'll grant you your knowledge of Trekoa, but nothing else. And do not speak of what you do not understand in front of my men."

Oh how quickly he had picked up that little token she had of-fered. "My men" indeed.

She had taken great care not to look at Azetla once throughout her little gambit, but feeling the success of it she hazarded a glance. He was stern. Braced from head to foot, waiting for the bite to come.

But it didn't.

Verris immediately called a separate meeting. There was, no doubt, some wrangling, justifying, and many clever euphemisms to be bandied about. She did not know. But a détente was reached. There was grave understanding in the air, and the battalion was ordered to proceed in the manner which she herself had dictated.

It really did seem as if one of these days the game would be up, and no one would listen or bend to her. That her tongue would falter and be routed. But not here. Not yet.

She looked upon the dusty roads of the village of Bir Herash, the fire-pits sending rich smoke into the air, the canopies stretched like patchwork between the stone and clay buildings, the goats and sheep being driven across the road to new grazing. She could not cajole herself into feeling even the least bit of hatred for it anymore. She could barely fend off a sense of rest. And warmth.

The Trekoans had once been nomadic—some still were—but Bir Herash was a settled location long before Rokh Bin-Zari's time. Tributes to wandering ways were scattered throughout the village, but deep permanence was the reality, and it was that—among other things—which used to make her uneasy. It troubled her to be so little troubled by it now.

She stepped forward to meet the young Trekoan man who approached the battalion. Rahummi Bin-Deghan, Rokh Imal's nephew. He was easy to recognize from a distance, for his had always been a buoyant stride, eager like a boy's. He was dressed in commonplace attire: a loose-fitted, long-sleeved linen cloth that fell all the way to his sandals with a simply decorated band about the waist. As he neared and saw it was her, he smiled in astonishment and touched his trim, youthful beard. He had been almost bare-faced when she last saw him.

He tried to speak, but she preempted him.

"What—"

"I'll explain it to you later. I need to speak to your uncle first and foremost," she said.

Rahummi stared at her with bewilderment. "He'll want nothing to do with you, you know that."

"He will see me," she said. She gestured back toward Azetla, who waited at a respectful distance. "Tell him that the *Mashevi* commander of this Maurowan battalion wishes to make an alliance with him."

"What is this, Shihrayan?" he asked, casting a leery eye at all the Maurowan soldiers dammed up behind Azetla's command line.

"Just tell your uncle what I told you."

Not half an hour later, the soldiers were being directed to a plain where they might make camp, and Azetla was beckoned by Rahummi.

"He's to be followed," she said to Azetla. "Just you. He is Rahummi Bin-Deghan, the Rokh's oldest nephew, and someone you want on your side. Him, you can trust."

Azetla looked at her strangely, but then nodded and followed Rahummi into the largest sand-colored structure in the village. It consisted of a two-tiered building, and several elaborate tented sections, for official matters must take place under a canopy. Otherwise disrespect would be implied, and keenly felt by any who knew enough to feel it.

She and Azetla were led through the first canopied room, lined with woven art and paneled with animal skins and richly dyed cloth. Bits of copper, hammered paper-thin, were sewn into patterns, glinting by lamplight across the walls, calling to mind the River Saav shimmering under the sun. She had been dizzied by the sheer opulence when first she saw it, nine years ago.

Rahummi lifted the embroidered cloth door to offer them entry to the formal Great Tent.

She stopped and indicated that Azetla was to go in first. He did so, but glanced back uncertainly when she did not follow him in. She ticked her fingers against her leg and let the cloth door hang against her shoulder. Her blood hurried just a little in her veins when she saw Rokh Imal step forward.

She leaned against that which was the ancient threshold and waited.

Rokh Imal stood with casual authority on a floor of rugs. His beard was full and graying, but he was never one to seem aged or weak. He wore the traditional robe and head covering, the sole distinction from his people being the dye and intricacy of the leather band that kept the linen headcloth in place. The simplicity of the Saqirani band was said to show their "great modesty," a saying which amused her, as they tended to utter it in prideful tones.

Rokh Imal did not look at her or speak to her. Rather, he fixed on Azetla and spoke a greeting to him in Trekoan. Azetla attempted a response, his mouth stumbling over the old, heavy phrase, "God's peace upon you and your family and all that live within your tents." The Rokh beckoned Azetla with a warm and generous gesture.

"I take it he does not speak Trekoan," Rokh Imal said coolly without looking at her.

"He does not," she said.

"You will always force my hand, won't you?" he said, his voice placid for Azetla's sake, his scorn palpable for her better knowledge of him. She wrapped herself in as much coolness and indifference as she could manage and said nothing.

Imal called a serving-man into the room. The man laid a large, dull-colored cloth near the low-set table. With a reluctance that had nothing to do with respect, she stepped fully into the room, grinding her jaw only a little before catching herself.

The cloth laid was an accommodation for those deemed unclean. Unholy. It was used for blasphemers, pagans, and any men who had not been ritually cut clean before the desert God on their eighth day. It was set down as a symbolic protection of the ground on which they walked and the home in which they stood.

And since Rokh Imal did not generally admit any such people into his presence, it had only ever really been used for her. She sat down and told Azetla that he must as well. He threw a questioning eye at her.

"I had to have gotten these somewhere, you realize," she said, flicking the slave band on her wrist and neck. "They speak to the Rokh's ownership of me. Though it has since been renounced."

"Renounced?" Azetla said, his wariness rising close to the surface.

"With a fervor," she said.

"Don't speak aside to him," Rokh Imal said. "He is the one I am here to treat with. You are only the medium through which I must do so."

She forced herself to relax and smile. "I merely explained what I knew he would ask. And he'll need to wash and pray before the meal. He's *your* sort."

Rokh Imal gave Azetla all he needed, and waited patiently, pleased by Azetla's thoroughness.

"What are you doing here?" Imal said quietly in Trekoan, allowing a brief lapse in courtesy while Azetla was occupied with his ablutions.

She clicked her tongue with a soft smile. "Don't you see? I brought you an easterner."

"We presumed you dead."

"Well, I don't seem to have the nature for it."

Rokh Imal pressed his lips together, which made his solemn mouth disappear into his gray beard.

"A truth if ever there was one," he muttered.

She glanced over to the far corner where Azetla scooped water over his hands a second time and mouthed some words in his native tongue. For a moment, he looked almost haggard, and he gripped his hands hard over the drops of water.

"I don't really trust the things you bring to the lintel of my door," Imal said in a low voice. "Who is he?"

She tilted her head faintly to the side. She was not yet satisfied on that point.

"He's a native-born Mashevi. From Rinayim." She paused. "*Devout.* And he's the commander of this battalion."

"Not possible," Imal replied.

"An anomaly, yes, but it's true. And your alliance will solidify the truth of it. He needs a southern ally with clout, and you need a southern ally with a Maurowan uniform. That's why he's here."

"Does he *know* that's why he's here?"

Azetla had finished his prayers and was fumbling through an earnest attempt to thank the head slave, Afir, who bore away the wash-bowl and cloth.

"More or less," she said with a half-smile.

"Why the bruises?"

"There was a brief dispute about his leadership which has been set down, and which, by your word, can be buried entirely."

Rokh Imal pressed his fingers over the embroidered waistband on his thawb, tracing the silky thread. It was the closest thing he had to an anxious habit.

"Nothing has changed, Shihrayan. You are not welcome here as before. You are not taken up again."

She said nothing. The sting was slight, because the words were expected.

Azetla returned to the low table and took the proffered seat on the woven rugs. He nodded deeply at Imal, hesitant to attempt any more Trekoan. So he waited. He held his tension well, but she could see the dark, chary energy in his eyes.

"Is he afraid of you?" Imal said in Trekoan, handing Azetla a cloth that would rest on his knee throughout the meal.

She looked at Azetla as he laid the cloth with some instinctive knowledge—Saqirani Trekoans and West Mashevis shared many practices and beliefs. Although she looked him full in the face, he could not understand what she said. "No, he's not." She paused. "Just careful. Anyway, he calls himself Azetla."

Rokh Imal began to speak.

"Forgive me, my-brother. Forgive my slowness to welcome you and the curiousness of these circumstances under which we meet. And above all, forgive that it is a Shihrayan devil through whom I must speak."

She looked wryly at Rokh Imal, but then she donned his manner, translating his words, his warmth, and every nuance she could glean from his posture. He relaxed almost instantly. Imal's hands fell away from the embroidery and rested on his knees. When she translated, he always found it easy to forget her. He was already tempted by using her as his mouth again, because he spoke only a little Maurowan, and he despised broken speech. Weak discourse gave the unjust impression of a weak mind and Rokh Imal took pride in his natural eloquence. He did not want it marred in translation, and she had always been able to carry everything perfectly intact. It was the reason he had tolerated her for so long, or at all.

"Thank you, my-Rokh," Azetla said. He was still as a stone.

"Rest and take your ease, my-brother. You are my guest," Imal said.

When Azetla heard her translation, he managed a grim smile. He adjusted his hands.

This was going to be interesting, she thought. Azetla could talk a slight dance, if forced—she had seen that proved—but he preferred to be blunt and plain. It was more natural to him, and easterners had a reputation for candor. Trekoans, however, were masters at talking about anything but the matter at hand. They could have whole negotiations without ever overtly mentioning the ostensible subject. *Forwardness*, Rokh Imal had often said, *is in such poor taste. It has no mercy or gentleness. It shows no brotherhood.*

So Rokh Imal meandered his way around the real matter, and it took Azetla some minutes to stop giving excruciatingly straightforward answers and begin making those proper gifts of musing and elaboration that Trekoans so loved. When at last the room began to burst at the seams with the smell of cardamom, that was the sign that the conversation too could gain its flavor, for there would be food and drink at their lips to soften the harsh sound of truth and haggling.

It was Rokha Ayla—Imal's only wife despite the fact that having two or three was usually customary for a man of his position—who brought in the spicy coffee; thick as mud and sweet enough to break the teeth.

For a northerner, only a mere servant or slave would have waited upon them, not the tribal matriarch. Maurowans rarely noticed the subtle discourtesies Imal displayed toward them, and it was possible that Azetla did not recognize the honor given him. But *she* did, and it told her that Rokh Imal was far more excited by the presence of a Mashevi than he pretended.

Rokha Ayla barely glanced at her. She did not show surprise, and she did not break step. The Rokha settled the tray on the table and quickly brought another of a simple meze garnished with a costly eastern lemon—another honor—and a rather subversive third finjan of coffee. Then Ayla was gone without a word, for she would not suffer indignity by speaking in front of foreign men.

The Shihrayan looked at the finjan intended for her. She subtly brushed the back of her thumb twice over her mouth, in an old, wonderfully useful Trekoan gesture showing innocence regarding someone else's error. Rokh Imal *hated* that Ayla should treat her as a guest and an equal, but by bringing the finjan, she did so. Ayla had always been more generous to her than Rokh Imal would have liked.

Ignoring order of precedence, the Shihrayan reached for the tiny cup before Imal did. She lifted the rich scent to her face, breathing the steam in slowly. One hot, soothing sip. Not as sweet this time, by blood. Ayla remembered. She clicked her tongue in satisfaction and rested the cup on the tray with the faintest of smiles offered, just to make Imal bristle. *Just let her warm her tongue first, you will use it for hours, my-dear*, Ayla used to say.

Now she was ready for them to begin negotiations. She would sit back and let them hammer it out themselves, and the less she added the better because they would trust their own agreements more if they used fewer of her independent words.

But every now and again she might gentle Azetla's ungentle phrasing, or tell the Rokh something useful that Azetla was too cautious to say. If necessary. She had promised an alliance and, though she had little interest in honoring a promise, she had great interest in proving her capacity, and keeping her finger close to the pulse.

"So why is your battalion here, Mashevi? And why *you* rather than any of the northern high-bloods who came with you?" Imal said.

She translated faithfully.

"I'm here because I am acting commander of this battalion, my-Rokh. And because this Sahr maneuvered it to be so. Our battalion is bound for Areo by Riada's order, but not for his reasons," Azetla said, his shoulders straight and square. "The battalion rests under the Corra James Sivolne's name at present—and that of his advisor Lord Verris—and we oppose those tribes which Riada's army supports. Namely Qatlan."

As the words passed back through her mouth to Rokh Imal's ear, she watched the Rokh try and conceal his astonishment, his eagerness. He had been fighting Maurow's pet tribe since his youth. So had his father before him.

"You manipulated this." Imal looked at her, folding his fingers at his waistband.

"Which part?" she said with a light Saqirani lilt.

"You bring a Mashevi here as an ally to stir everything up, just so *you* can sink your teeth into some new blooding," he said.

She said nothing in reply. Azetla had his intents. Verris had his. Imal had his. The three intersected just now. She did not know what would happen when they diverged, but that was far beyond her interest or concern. She had simply leapt upon the point where the roads crossed that she might maneuver through it all at will. Rokh Imal could not pretend to be surprised that she would keep her footing.

Besides, his anger at her was for the sake of *his* guilt. He was one step away from having made up his mind already. He longed for the days of his great, great, great grandfathers, the era of the East Trekoan-Mashevi alliance, in which so many Mashevi beliefs—the notion of the desert god himself—had bled into Trekoa and taken root. The only way for the south to survive upheaval in the north was to seize it as an opportunity. Rokh Imal would lament her presence, grind his teeth, and then he would take whatever she brought him with a ready hand. Especially something like Azetla.

"You are not of Riada in any way, then," Imal said at last, turning back to Azetla.

"No, my-Rokh," Azetla replied with quiet emphasis.

"And you owe nothing to Qatlan for the services they've rendered you?"

Azetla was confused by this question as it was translated to him and looked to her for an explanation.

"What services?" he asked her.

She shook her head dismissively and looked at Imal. "I led them to your allies and used your name," she clarified. "They've never so much as struck hands with Qatlan except to defend against them."

Imal nodded slowly, his eyes keeping always to Azetla. "But there are *Makars* in your battalion. Many of them high-bloods."

"Yes, my-Rokh," Azetla replied. "And I have friends among them."

"Cautious friendships, no doubt."

"Even so."

Imal was thoughtful for several moments. He made a surprising decision to humble his tongue to the Maurowan language, and his imperfection in it.

"Careful, Mashevi. Our land with old hates. Old hates, old loves. Stirring air. Have a watch. Just to...have a watch of Makarish. But now, why...why the *Tzal* here? Why our salt-brick by you?"

Azetla narrowed his eyes. "What salt-brick? *Tzal*..."

She looked at Azetla sidelong until at last he turned to her. "Is that your *name*?"

That made her laugh. She could not help it. Devil was her name to most. Unholy. Shihrayan. They were right to suppose it did not matter what a devil called itself; it truly didn't. It only mattered what the Gods called you and if they called you nothing, then that is precisely what you were.

"No," she said. "It's only one of many things I've been called here. To buy a brick of salt in South Trekoa is a euphemism for purchasing a slave that is suspected to actually be Shihrayan. And Tzal is...just a poor way of pronouncing it."

Azetla stared at her a few moments, but corrected himself quickly, turning back to Rokh Imal.

"Very well," he said. "My-Rokh, the Sahr, the...Tzal...was taken captive by us in Sahr territory."

Rokh Imal pressed his hand against his beard with a frown, and returned to his native tongue and her delivery of it.

"You went to Shihra?"

"Yes."

"*You* led them there of your own free will?" Imal said.

"No. We were sent. The Captain who commanded us was a good man, though northern. He was killed."

"By the Shihrayan."

"By the...yes."

She translated every word, enjoying talking of herself as though she were not present. It made them more uncomfortable than it did her. It galled Imal especially.

"But you didn't kill her," he said.

"Should I have?" Azetla asked calmly.

"I have asked myself that question many times."

She translated with a faint smile. It was the truth. How many times had he said as much to her face?

"Riada wanted to make use of the salt-brick...of Tzal, my-Rokh," Azetla said. "So we took it—her. We took the Sahr from him."

"A risky thing for you to have done, my-brother." Imal breathed deeply, extending his hands and pressing them together. He hesitated and she knew why. All the warnings Imal would give Azetla about her must be done *through* her. "You do serve the same God, do you not?"

Azetla gave Imal a look of uncertainty.

"God of the Desert, yes? God of Masheva and of old," Imal emphasized.

Azetla's face cleared. "Yes. I do. I serve my God and my people."

"And your King?"

"My King serves neither," Azetla said.

Rokh Imal's eyebrows shot upward. Obviously that had not been the meaning of his question.

By blood, more effort on her part could have brought no better result than this. Rokh Imal held the Mashevi King in the same contempt as Qatlan. Both, as he saw it, were the hand of Maurow crushing their own people.

For the next few minutes her tongue spoke of what she knew not. Piety and devotion and holy writs. Two men who bowed their heads to a God and believed themselves to be as children to a father. It was all bitterly fascinating, and a thousand miles from her.

The Mashevis had always claimed to be the desert God's favored ones, though many had abandoned this God they used to hoard for the more visible divinities of Maurow and Makaria, or for the convenient nonsense of none at all. Some were said to worship gold, temple pleasures, or to set up shrines to their own knowledge.

Not Azetla. He was the kind that drove the prayers out of his mouth a thousand times a day—like a lashing—hoping it would make him holy. But only the Gods could make and unmake a thing holy, so she didn't understand why these pious people muttered until their tongues turned to dust. It was almost certainly useless.

It took nearly three hours and her voice running hoarse for the treacherous alliance to be forged. Azetla's Black Wren was to stand in direct support of Saqiran, and Rokh Imal was to stand in direct support of Azetla as head of the battalion when they reached Areo. He would accompany them and ease the introduction to Colonel Orde Everson of Areo, who was one of the precious few northerners Imal would tolerate.

She was glad when it was over. Azetla left to see to his men, and she was neither released nor retained by anyone, so she stood a moment adrift. But as she moved toward the back room of the Bin-Zari home, Rokh Imal stopped her.

"Why did you really come back? What do you want from me?"

"I want nothing from you," she said.

Imal shook his head at her.

"It's that vicious Shihrayan superstition of yours. You would make rivers of blood to scrounge for some divine scraps? That's still what this is about?"

"*No.*"

But probably yes. Where there was war, there was plunder, and she meant to strip the Gods bare. Until one turned and *looked*.

Imal's face hardened with frustration. "You think getting your teeth into a Mashevi will make his God give you what your own have withheld from you?"

She had had enough of this. "I think you can gain no more ground against Qatlan without the Mashevi. Hate me, discard me, spit in my face; but remember that I brought you something you *desperately* need."

She stepped to move past Imal to the women's portion of the house.

"Out and around," he said in a cold voice.

"I'm only going to speak to the Rokha," she said.

"I know. Out and around. Don't track your blasphemy through my home."

She gave a breathy laugh.

"You know, I never *made* you do anything, by blood," she said as she turned to walk out. "And you're still standing on the victory I handed you."

She did not wait to hear his reply. Walking around to the low entrance, she sought Rokha Ayla. She clicked her teeth against each other to keep from grinding them and pushed her way through the door, across the stone threshold, and into the slave's quarters. Rokha Ayla was already there, waiting for her.

Ayla's head was covered in pale blue cloth, her graying hair tucked almost entirely out of sight. She looked at the Shihrayan with a sort of gentle moral worry, as if picturing all the blasphemies she had inevitably committed since last she saw her.

The Shihrayan walked in without word or courtesy.

"Will you not exhibit some respect for myself or this home?" Ayla said softly.

"I don't have to anymore."

Rokha Ayla reached out and almost touched her wrist, pointing to the slave band that had been limned with servitude nine years ago. The Shihrayan pulled her hand back. "That's for protection," she said coolly.

"If you take with you our protection, then you can bring back some respect." Ayla's voice softened. "Sit, at least, Tzal."

She did so in one smooth motion, softening ever so slightly at being called Tzal as though it was actually a name, rather than a thing. As though it was actually hers. Imal never used it quite that way and no one else used it at all anymore. It didn't *mean* anything. It was just a sound Ayla had used when she wished to beckon her and wanted something easy and name-like with which to do it. It was also Ayla's Trekoan mispronunciation of the Maurowan word "salt," which ought to have driven her mad, but didn't.

She could easily don the name as she rested, because it had a soft, worn quality. Like borrowed clothing that nevertheless fit just so. She could use it here, as she had used others elsewhere. There was no risk of her forgetting that it wasn't the real thing.

Together, Tzal and Ayla ate the remnants of the meze that had been served to Imal and Azetla. This was what Ayla had always done for her. Imal disapproved, but did not forbid it, for Ayla was not easily overruled.

"You're eating like you've been starved," Ayla said.

"I was on prison rations until a few days ago," Tzal said.

"Where have you *been*?"

She did not answer, because she did not feel like explaining. She just savored each one of the briny olives, the tang and salt of them almost dizzying in their perfection.

"Did you go..." Ayla's mouth tightened over the question. "Did you go home?"

Tzal nodded.

"And?" Ayla pressed.

"It was as I said it would be."

Rokha Ayla's shoulders fell.

"And of the Mashevi?" Ayla said.

"I thought he and the Rokh would suit each other, tactically speaking," Tzal said. "The northerners are trying to bite each other's necks, and regardless of which one bleeds out first, Saqiran can probably get something out of it."

"What difference should it make to you what happens to our tribe?" Ayla said with a soft intimation and restrained smile.

Tzal rested her elbows on her knees and folded her fingers at her mouth. "None. But you know how it is. Bloodlust serves better with an objective and I—"

"Stop that. I used to think you meant it, but the lie of it just wearies me now. And you too, I think," Ayla said.

Tzal laughed. "Still hoping to cure me of my own blood, Rokha Ayla?"

Ayla did not respond but only shook her head, handing her the last of the lamb and a small cup of wine.

When Tzal had first come to Bir Herash, slave bands freshly tethering her to Rokh Imal, she had not understood why Rokha Ayla was so gentle with her, treating her like a runt goat in need of particular care. But she paid attention and learned the truth: Rokha Ayla had four sons and no living daughters. Indeed, she lost her only daughter—a child of two years—scant months before Tzal arrived. That timing proved advantageous to Tzal.

Most of Tzal's work was blood and tongue and falsehood, but Ayla persisted in treating her like a young girl rather than a Shihrayan. The other slaves were from enemy tribes and could never speak Saqirani dialect as Tzal could, nor imitate their manners so precisely.

Ayla always looked at her as though she was something dead, which through kindness she might raise to life—or else something filthy that she might scour clean. If she just worked steady away. It fascinated Tzal, so she indulged her. She let Ayla try her scouring, wasting her time and kindness.

Still. She liked it. Ayla would give her fennel tea during her time—disgusting, anise-scented fennel tea that was nevertheless effective—and ask Imal to lighten her work. A few times he did. Once she gave Tzal her own herbed soap to wash the blood and tar out of her hair after the slaughter at Kabe-dir. Honey and olives. Oil and salt. Small luxuries to Rokha Ayla, astounding ones to Tzal.

It all reminded her of one time, when she was little—so very little she was half afraid she had invented the memory out of whole cloth—and her eldest sister Sereya had drawn swirls of dampened ash along her arm during a ceremonial burning. Sereya had not done it for any purpose, other than to hold her little sister's arm and draw a beautiful thing. That was before the worst of everything, of course, and eventually Sereya would cry mercy of the Gods and cut her palms if Tzal touched her. But in that one uncertain memory, Tzal been half dizzy with the pleasure of having little ashen eddies painted softly on her arm.

So she would let Ayla be as uselessly, foolishly kind to her as she liked. Cool, clean water against the skin it was, and who could say no?

When Uli, the slave girl, came to take the tray, Ayla asked her to fetch something. Uli did as she was told, then Ayla let her leave, because none of them liked to linger around Tzal.

Ayla took the small things Uli had left, wrapped them in a cotton cloth, and pressed it into Tzal's hand. A casp-nut of cedar oil and a small sachet of crushed clove, cinnamon, cardamom, and black peppercorns.

Tzal smiled and, with a mocking half-bow in the northern style that she knew would rankle Ayla, she walked out, massaging the sachet of spices in her hand till the intoxicating scent broke free.

28

There was a knock at the door, gentle and otherwise commonplace, but it startled James. He kneaded his chest with his fist—as though that would make his heart slow down—and waited two, three, four deep breaths before speaking.

"Come in."

He had no doubts as to what was to happen. His old talent for blanking out his mind and choosing to neither see nor understand was weakened beyond repair.

The serving-man entered and bowed.

"His Imperial Highness Riada the Sixth has issued a summons. You are to appear in the court anteroom at noon."

James acknowledged with a tilt of his head, and the servant was gone. He wished the man had rather said "at once," because he was so bone-tired of being afraid. Whatever was to happen, for the Gods' sake, let it happen.

For two weeks James had been walking the halls of the Gray Eagle like a deer in the forest, treading softly, trying to go about his business, jolting at every sound and scent. When would Riada pounce? But Riada had been silent, had spoken not a word to James. The Corra awoke with aches in his neck and knots in his shoulders from the unrelenting worry.

More than ever before, he was alone in Piarago. His court allies were savvy for their own skins and didn't dare seek him out. He, of course, sought no one and attempted nothing. His own servants, excepting one or two, were firmly in Riada's pocket.

James was as a man awaiting trial. Riada was the judge and he was quietly gathering evidence. He had sent men of information down to South City to question its residents, to ask for witnesses, to ascertain what had really happened to the Sahr. He was making his case.

Now the trial had arrived. And since silenced had governed, and all James' sources were cut off, he had not the least notion of the verdict.

He picked at the seams in his tunic as he walked along the blazing-bright columned balcony that lined the western side of the Gray Eagle. He tried to soothe his stomach with deep, steady breaths, but to no avail. James wished that Verris—or *anyone*—would tell him what to say. All he knew to do was act the oblivious fool that Riada and everyone else in Maurow believed him to be. And he was only good at it when it was true.

How he wished it was true.

The anteroom door swung open. Riada sat casually against the pinewood table. The room was flooded with warm, sand-colored light and smelled of agarwood incense; Riada liked to keep the Gods ever attentive—whether by scent, wine, or blood—as if they were the servants, and they too must obey his summons. The incense set a pressure inside James' lungs and set his eyes to watering.

It was a situation calculated to make him feel weak and hazy. He bowed, then straightened himself from head to foot. He offered Riada a grim and tentative smile, then began to try to think.

"You can sit, James."

"Ah," James said. It came out gristly, like a cough. He sat in a rush of compliance. "What do you wish of me, Your Highness?"

Riada waited several moments before replying, but James was able to focus on a gold braid of thread at Riada's shoulder so as to hold himself steady.

"I'm curious," Riada began, his voice calm, his eyes ravenous. "I'm curious as to why you left your Sahr quarry in South City to be stolen out from under you."

James' eyes snapped upward from the gold braid, and he leaned forward in his chair. That wasn't what Riada was supposed to think happened. Something had gone wrong. Gods. Gods and devils.

"It was *stolen*? Did you *find* it?"

His fear burst through his voice and probably worked deceptive wonders for him. He could never have effectively feigned that sort of surprise.

"I had thought...I thought it escaped, Your Highness."

"And why would you think that?" Riada said, folding his arms and seeming to loom over James, though he hadn't taken a single step.

"Because it's *jinn*. And no one knew. I did as you asked. The inn was emptied and closed up even before I arrived. The guards were on watch in the room. All seemed well in hand and I assumed..."

Now Riada pressed off the table and stood his full height.

"You assumed others would manage your responsibilities for you? James, you are actually *astonishing* in your incompetence."

James' shoulders fell. For a moment he half forgot what had really happened, and what his real role had been in the Sahr's "escape." He only felt how unjust Riada's words would have been, had the whole story been true.

"What could I have possibly done had I been there? I heard how the inn was found! I would be nothing but blood on the walls, like your guards, like those innkeepers!"

"And what a loss," Riada said dryly. "You couldn't even do this one thing right."

You mean I couldn't even die.

James hung in a silent, sulking posture, feeling strangely defiant in doing so. Riada assessed James, as though debating whether there was anything worthwhile to coax out of his prey.

Then James had a chilling realization. If Riada would rather James were dead, then he thought James actually presented some danger.

That was new.

New and dreadful. But there was something tantalizing in it too. James, whose mixed blood was so disgusting to his brother and who had always been so decidedly beneath concern, was worth getting rid of.

"Did it ever speak?" Riada said at last.

"No," James said, staring at the curving grains of wood in the table directly in front of him. Since it was a flat lie, he did not attempt to elaborate, lest he give himself away.

"The priests and Augurs gave vague answers. Did it prove itself a devil? Of power?" Riada said, the hunger flashing again in his eyes.

James thought in earnest. "I—I don't think so. I don't know. It killed and mutilated and evaded so many times, it seemed a spirit, but the moment it was caught...it was like a dead thing. And nothing seemed to wake it."

He cleared his throat. His breaths naturally constricted at the least falsehood.

Riada's eyes were vivid with thought. He nodded, not at James, but to himself.

"I heard a troubling rumor, though," Riada began. "There was said to be a Black Wren soldier in South City that night...near the inn."

James flinched, almost in a tic. Better not lie any more than necessary. He cleared his throat again. "I, you see, we had to have one show us to the place...take us through South City, because we didn't know of it. We didn't—I thought it best. The soldier was kept under oath, to be sure, and sent back to his battalion."

Riada seemed to feed on James' stumbling words and skittering eyes.

"But not just a Black Wren soldier, James. A jackal. Can that be explained?"

"He...he was a jackal, yes. But what does that have to do with anything?"

"What was a jackal doing in the Black Wren?"

James might answer that honestly. It didn't implicate him in any way. But the jackal was so inextricably bound up in all he could *not* say, that he did not entirely trust his mouth.

"He was just one of the soldiers. He had no rank. I don't know how he came to be there, but Verris deemed him expendable, which was why we risked him, and let him show us through South City."

"What was his name?" Riada pressed.

For the Gods' sake, he *knew* it, but he could not recall it to his tongue. He had never been much for harboring names after the faces had gone. Even ones of significance.

"Etzel or Zeela or something like that," James said.

Riada looked at him with unbridled exasperation.

Azetla. That was it. Well he wasn't going to say it now.

Another silence followed. James wanted to break it so badly, but he did not trust himself to break it to any advantage. He shifted in his chair. He swallowed and his throat hurt because it was dry.

"Is...is there any chance of finding the Sahr?" he dared at last.

Riada lifted his eyes, as if coming out of a reverie, and looked down at James. James peered upward, feeling almost as ignorant and blank as he was meant to seem, for indeed all he wanted to do in all the world was lie abed somewhere safe and cool and think of absolutely nothing.

"We will see. I want an account. Day for day. Detail for detail, from your initial departure, up until the moment you left the South City inn," Riada said.

And so James gave it. What he saw and experienced. What Verris told him. What the soldiers said. The scattered attacks. Every last thing except those vital facts surrounding the Mashevi and the Sahr. He found himself calming through the telling, since he did not have to lie, he had only to omit, and he was quite free to acknowledge all the parts he did not understand. Riada probed and commented, having turned calm and informal, speaking to James almost as though he was an equal. It had a lulling, fireside-in-winter effect, warming James' stiff bones, feeding a quiet little hunger. To simply be asked questions and for his answers to be listened to as though they had some meaning.

For the moment, he almost felt released from suspicion.

When he was dismissed, he walked out of the anteroom with a heart settled to the usual pace, and a stomach calm enough to express hunger. He did not know if had succeeded. He did not know if he had even survived. If James was condemned, Riada had made no indication of it, but that hardly signified. Why should Riada give him the courtesy of a warning?

James walked in a daze. He sat down and, for a long blank stretch, did not think or worry or do any damn thing. Just ran his forefinger across the top of his thumb over and over, brow furrowed, shoulders stooped.

Finally, feeling unusually cool for himself, he pictured what he would have to do if he wanted out. If he wished to end this whole thing, *that* course of action was the easiest of all. He needed no help to know how to do it. Serve his allies up on a platter, and live the rest of his life unencumbered by the least responsibility.

If he were to go further in, however...what? *What?* What beyond hiding and flinching and waiting for it all to just work itself out on its own?

Sluggishly, as if against a current, he stood up.

First he went to the temple of Serivash and commissioned one of the priests to put pig's blood into Serivash's pool for him and he actually went to the fountain and observed the slaughtering. It seemed the thing to do.

Then he called his old nursemaid and they played two rounds of Arratul while she spoke sweet and proud and motherly to him.

He took a ride across the gardens, where the statues and pergolas lived in delicate, manicured beauty.

He called for wine and music in the early evening.

He listened with real pleasure, and he did not think. His mind was slow as sap, and it was the freest, most wonderful feeling.

Then, when dark fell and the lamps were lit, he let out his last free breath.

Whether he succeeded or failed, that life was forfeit. Perhaps the sword would fall tomorrow. Perhaps a month from now. Perhaps the sword would be taken up by his own hand. Regardless, he had to come to terms with the truth: his time was not his own and it only made him bitter each time he tried to scrimp and save it for himself.

Say he could succeed. In earnest, and in the quiet way. Slow and soft until the whole court was on his side, and Riada would have no choice but to step back or let Maurow break at the seams. No blood was being drawn, no armies surging one toward the other, and no point existed where he was expected to be strong and might falter. No one thought him strong to begin with.

But say it came to war.

No, no. That thought was too unmanageable. He needed something smaller.

Say he needed to flee the city.

How would he do that?

How would he know when to do it?

That was where he would start. He would stand. On his own. Put his mind and muscle—little as they might amount to—toward the Imperial court. And, when the time came, he would be ready to *run*.

Riada was not satisfied.

He had used one of his tried and true methods of smoking out the truth, and he was beginning to think he had obscured, rather than drawn out, his object.

Riada had made James wait, made him sweat, made the fear grow till he was like to burst. Then, handling him gently, he procured a gush of relief. James was usually easier to deal with if he believed himself to *already* have been dealt with. But there had been no discernable difference in any part of their interaction. Riada sat against the pinewood table in his anteroom, bereft. His suspicions were neither fed nor allayed.

His whole mind was fogged over, distracted by other, graver matters. The disappearance of the Sahr concerned him as much because of that with which it *aligned*, as for the Sahr itself. That devil-or-not was merely an unopened box—full of gold or full of ash—so Riada could not know the extent of the advantage he had lost by it.

He had hoped to extract a very real, very otherworldly power; the coarse thirst the idea had stirred in him was heady as lust. It carried the very taste of Serivash in it.

But there was a much harsher salt taste that sat on his tongue lately, and wild unknowns must submit before that which can be held in the hand and seen with the eye.

There were jackals at his gates, circling, growling, snapping at him. Closing in.

"Your Highness?" Lord Noben's voice came from outside the room.

"Enter," Riada said.

Lord Artur Noben stepped in and bowed. Short and gray and sensible, he had been chief advisor to Riada's father and then been passed down to Riada.

"Well?" Riada said, his hands clenching over the edge of the table.

"We caught him. He was alone, but for a few servants."

Riada smiled and let the satisfaction pour through him, warming him.

"Good. Bring him."

"*Here*, Your Highness?" Noben said.

"To the west garden. Sometimes the old ways are best, Artur."

Noben's eyes clouded with worry, but he touched his shoulder and forehead in acknowledgment and left.

A mere gesture in the corridor sufficed to bring two of his personal guards into stride behind him. A scant flick of his fingers silenced and dismissed the General and the High-Lord who waited for him in the assembly room. They must wait longer still.

He knew what sorts of whispers echoed behind him as soon as he was out of earshot. *Riada has become too like his father, worrying that same jackal bone.* As if they themselves were not the same. When their personal profits fell, who did they blame? The jackal merchants. Trouble with the Eastern Navy or shipping? Mashevi portmasters, Mashevi obstruction. And they exulted on the Red River festival with the same fervor as anyone. They wanted to grumble about the jackals, but they shrank when Riada prepared to actually do something about them. No one wanted their daily affairs disrupted, oh no.

His High-Lords liked to talk of what terrible cowards the Mashevis were, and then of how violently subversive, willing to die over trifles. Of how few and weak they were; and then how ubiquitous and forceful. Devout hypocrites. Craven agitators. Dispersed, but a whole. No one seemed interested in rationalizing the contradiction as Riada had struggled to do.

Riada's mind circled round and round, like a vulture over something not yet still enough to invite a landing, trying to make sense of it all.

He knew it must be both, for he had seen the two versions standing side-by-side. Keved, the coward, and Samuel Aver—old enemy and friend—who would have torn Maurow apart with his bare hands.

Riada walked through the late afternoon warmth and sat on one of the crescent-shaped marble benches beside the statues of Deyra, Goddess of fear and strength, and Serivash, of love and blood. The sisters were back to back, both armed and ready to strike. The base of the statue still showed faint discoloration from the old days, when blood flowed freer.

Finally Lord Noben and Captain Geraf approached, a well-dressed jackal pinned between them. The jackal bowed, then was instructed to sit. Noben and Geraf were ordered to stand at a distance, which they disliked, but could say nothing about.

"Would you have wine? A meze?" Riada said, smiling and raising a hand to send for anything.

"No, Your Highness. I am fasting," the jackal said, much too calm. Such calm meant he had already been afraid, and had gone past it.

"You mean you will not eat my food because you think it unclean," Riada said.

"Forgive me, Your Highness."

"You know why you have been brought here?" Riada said.

"I have been told nothing, Your Highness. But I am at your service, of course."

Riada drew a piece of folded parchment from the pleats of cloth beneath his waistband. With a little theatricality in his expression, he rubbed his fingers along the creases, played with the folds.

The very same night the Sahr disappeared, this letter was stripped from the broken body of a jackal and brought to Riada's hand. It had been, by all appearances, sheer luck. A few city guards had come upon the jackal in North City, begun to trouble him, then grown a little too zealous. The jackal's head was bashed against a stone fountain, and the man was brought into custody until he could be made to speak.

The letter was translated for Riada, but it was all obscure poetry and idiom, holy writ and euphemism. There were one or two things Riada surmised, those courtesy of his old acquaintance with the Mashevi King's son, but most of the letter was essentially unintelligible. Where a code could be broken, the whole inner life and literature of a people was far less readily interpreted.

When the jackal courier had recovered enough to be harmed again, two days of firm coercion led to *this* man before him, for the lintel of his door had been the destination.

"What is your name?" Riada said, as he unfolded the letter.

"It is not possible that I was brought here without you already knowing everything about me, Your Highness," the jackal said.

Bristling inwardly, Riada gave the jackal a slow smile.

"You will answer all my questions with your own mouth," he said softly.

"Yonin Atza of Aresh and of Rinayim, Your Highness."

"And did you know, Yonin, that you are accused of treason?"

He handed the letter to Yonin, who seemed indifferent. "This letter was for you."

Yonin read the paper, and Riada watched, hunger in his gut, for a flicker of hope, or fear, or any sign that this man would be of value to him—that Riada could, by means gentle or decidedly otherwise, confirm what he believed he knew, and illuminate that which still eluded him.

There was one moment where Yonin Atza looked struck. A furrow began upon his brow, but he quickly looked up and handed the letter back to Riada. "This is far beyond me, Your Highness. I would have had to study all the scholarly commentaries of the Tusian era to discern what is being said there, and have all the poems and the prophets memorized entirely. I cannot imagine that this letter was intended for a man such as myself, apostate in my youth, and but fumbling through a child's level of study now. There is a chance it is mere doggerel."

Riada accepted the parry calmly, for he had many blows yet to deal this Yonin Atza.

"You mean to say that 'the golden head is not secure' makes no reference to the security of my own head? Your own beloved Samuel Aver told me I was 'nothing more than a golden head.' Twice, actually. Do not tell me I know your scriptures better than you."

The words about the golden head had made Riada's skin tingle with fear and recollection the moment he set his eyes upon them. The "head" was of a great statue in the ancient Tusian Empire which an obscure Mashevi prophet said was doomed to topple. And so it did. Melted, hammered into bits and trinkets, and remembered only for the fact that it was so utterly destroyed.

The jackal shrugged. "I suppose that is what it could mean. You are as powerful as the Tusian emperors were in their day."

"And as ripe a target?" Riada said with a cool smile.

"It was not we Mashevis who broke the Tusian Empire," Yonin said. "They did it to themselves, and it was your ancestors who finished the job."

Riada appreciated the defensiveness in Yonin's voice, for it showed that he was stripping away the man's forced calm, bit by bit.

"You also mean to tell me that the signature at the end means nothing to you?" Riada said.

"'*Written by the goatherd*,'" Yonin quoted. "Yes, I believe that comes from another sacred story, but it does *you* no good, Your Highness. By salt, the story is only a few sentences of one scroll. The man was nobody, and he was asked to entrap certain Mashevi nobles, so to be rewarded. He refused and was beaten. He was told to worship the Tusian gods, so to be left alone. Again he refused and was beaten. He was told he must worship the Tusian emperor as though he were God, so to receive lenience. He refused, and was executed. I don't even know if the story is true. It's written more like a poem."

Memory was stirred, like heat suddenly emanating from underneath ashes. Samuel Aver had spoken of that too, though he may not have realized he had done so. He said that all the kings and all the high-bloods of Masheva were as nothing before "a goatherd." Nonsense to Riada at the time. It was one of the many self-righteous speeches Samuel Aver gave when he and Riada were left to their own devices. Left to spar. Left to prepare for the real fight that would have come.

"I think it's time you stopped playing this game, Yonin," Riada said. "This is not the first such letter you have received. And it is not the first one so signed."

The Goatherd, whispered. The Goatherd, written. The word hovered about Riada's ears like so many flies. Once, the only name he had to worry about was Samuel Aver, shouted with fervor and folly by the desperate and the poor. But lately "The Goatherd" had rivaled that name, or come gently alongside it. It was the mark of something slower, quieter, and far more careful.

"Your Highness, I am not the clever conspirator you think I am," Yonin said.

"Is that so? You were fleeing the city without authorization. You smuggled your family out ahead of you, which means you've long been worried you would be discovered. And I can *find* them, Yonin."

The jackal's veneer of calm broke at those words. The man's shoulders sank, his dark eyes temporarily losing their focus.

"Do not worry, Your Highness. I will save you the trouble of threats and tortures." The jackal glanced at the tall statues of Serivash and Deyra. "I already know how this conversation ends, and never have I been so glad to be of so little importance. I was an intermediary. I barely understood the things that passed through my hands, and thank God for that. I will tell you everything I know, and take fierce pride in how little I can offer. Then, when you ply me with pain, you will only cast doubt on the truth, for I will probably scream out whatever lie you demand of me. I'll not pretend to be stronger than my betters."

Riada squared his shoulders in deepest satisfaction, while the man's posture sank further down. The jackal was at least wise enough to know his own weakness. His actions had been Samuel Aver's boldness; but his end would be Keved's cowardice. Both, and.

"Well. Speak."

"I do not know who the goatherd is," Yonin muttered. "Maybe one person. Maybe several. A scholar, I imagine. It was first thought that he opposed Samuel Aver's followers, but now it seems he merely meant to...redirect their efforts away from inflicting harm on our own. To gather the many factions together and hone them to a point. They no longer talk of killing our King as they once did, or burning the ports. The only thing I know for certain, is that the goatherd opposes the corvee labor drawn from Masheva. And they oppose *you*."

"I will need names," Riada said.

The jackal put his head to his hands and uttered a handful of names through gritted teeth. He told Riada where the letters were sent, and how he had come to be a waypoint. He professed that to be the whole of what he knew. He looked sick with shame afterward.

"And who do *you* think the goatherd is?"

Now Yonin raised his head again, a faint light returning to his eyes.

"I think he is Samuel Aver himself, fighting against all the errors done in his name. He is doing what he was born to do," Yonin said with a sudden fierceness.

Riada smiled. There was nothing so savory, so sating as the pain he was about to inflict. No sword or fire could do as well.

"Samuel Aver is dead."

Yonin flinched. He shook his head. "No. No doubt you have seeded such rumors, and, yes, I have heard them. But *no*."

Riada stood and walked a leisurely circle around Yonin Atza.

"It is my turn to tell you what *I* know, dear Yonin. You know the nature of your King, I imagine?"

"Keved Aver would put his lips to your feet, and lick them till they were clean if you demanded it," Yonin spat.

Riada could almost laugh. "Yes. He would. But do you know who he feared far more than my father, and far more than me?"

Yonin's eyes fell to the ground, his jaw clenched.

"His son," Riada said, his voice soft, the effect like smoke in Yonin's eyes. They began to water. "His son who saw him for the coward he is. And my father was afraid too. So your King and my father struck a bargain. Samuel Aver was a threat to them *both*. You see, I make no boast here, and show no prowess. I had no part in it. I did not even know of it till long after. But I did inherit the sole concession my father ever made to your King.

"King Aver is allowed to pretend that his eldest son is still alive, still heir, still the symbol of whatever absurd holy story you jackals love so fiercely. Samuel is merely 'away.' Studying at Okiziu. Sailing to Bighara. Biding his time. Keeping the story alive has kept your King in hand for me, and your people pacified for him, but mark my words, your great hope is *dead*. No rescue is forthcoming. You committed treason, not for Samuel Aver, but for a charlatan who trades on an empty legend for his own gain."

Yonin crumbled like dirt between his fingers. He sagged, down, down, like one bleeding out. Tears came silently, though his hand moved to erase them. Riada was triumphant and disgusted all at once. All it took to destroy this man was the truth.

"The story of Samuel Aver has served me well thus far, but it is beginning to writhe in my hands. It threatens to bite. I don't know how much longer I should allow the idea of him to live. Your people really do cluster around dead stories like flies around carrion, looking to suck every last bit of meat off the bones. I am waiting for the right moment to lay Samuel Aver at last to rest, so that *everything* in proximity to his name—even your bloody goatherd—will be put to shards."

Yonin seemed to listen no longer. His eyes were closed, his lips traced words. Desperate prayer to a god with no face and an unspeakable name. Riada watched with fascinated disgust, always faintly mesmerized by that which he held in contempt.

"Stand up," Riada said.

Yonin placed his hands on his knees, looked up at Riada in a strange way. He stood. His arms hung loose at his sides, as if all the muscle was gone out of them. He knew.

Don't go for the head, Riada's father had told him. *They will survive. Go for the heart.* Riada had tried. But jackals didn't seem to keep their heart in the usual place, Riada thought—not in their king, in their temple ruin, nor even in their great city. It scattered with them wherever they roamed, and they were *everywhere*. Each time Riada thought he had it in hand, he found he was mistaken. It beat on.

Riada drew his knife and raised his hand that Noben and Geraf would hold their distance. Riada guided Yonin to the base of the statues.

"We shall make this easy, shall we not? For this is a mercy I am giving you. Not to be broken to pieces. Not to be held to the Red River festival. Not to see what becomes of your family."

Yonin almost faltered at the mention of his family, but there was a fixed look in his eye.

"Maybe Samuel Aver is dead, but his God lives. And you are treating me like one of the slain prophets of old, when I am no one. I do not believe you mean mercy, but you manage to do me honor."

Riada hesitated, loosening and tightening his grip on the gold and silver ribbing of the knife handle. He reassured himself. He was not to be manipulated.

"Call it what you like, jackal."

Yonin closed his eyes. He was trembling. His hands clutched his clothes. Riada's own blood raced quickly as he put the beautifully sharpened edge to the jackal's throat, and Riada felt Yonin straining to keep himself still.

Riada pulled back with all the strength he had, and was exultant to see he had done it well. Yonin collapsed. The thirsty stone began to drink. Most went to Serivash, but Riada flung a few drops of the jackal's blood onto Deyra's statue. Deyra did not often get to taste real blood anymore.

The days of high sacrifice were long gone—the jackals had somehow made that most natural practice seem unnatural by the mere pervasive presence of their own beliefs—but sometimes the Gods still needed something fresh to savor. So did the people.

He looked down at Yonin.

Samuel Aver was what the jackals longed for but would never get. He had been the best of them. And how he had *loathed* Riada. How his arrogance had burned beneath Riada's skin.

Riada would let them have him just a little longer, that they would go on making corpses of themselves by shouting protest and dying for that stirring but hopeless name.

He could almost pity them for that, yet the pity had such a satisfying, vigorous flavor. More brackish, like scorn, to be honest.

29

Azetla turned over carefully in the dark, tapping his lion's head at a hectic rhythm. He knew he would not get back to sleep; dawn was too near. He had not rested well since Sable and the others had come at him; the ground was hard, and there was no way to lie which did not dig at some bruise. At least, this time, he had slept through to fourth watch.

Today they would reach the gates of Areo outpost.

Azetla tapped the lion's head again.

Rokh Imal accompanied them, and he believed Azetla was the commander.

The side of his thumb *tic-tic-tic*'ed against the wood.

But Verris did not. Again and again, he refused to affirm the general consensus. Wait until Areo, he said. Wait until I have you outnumbered, he meant.

Enough. Enough of this.

Azetla stood. Dressed. Armed himself. He did not have far to walk among the sleepers before he reached the central fire from which all the other fires were lit. He was not the least bit surprised to find the Sahr there, awake, sitting, and kneading cedar oil into the leather part of her belt and sheath, both items perched across her knees. Her fingertips were yellowed from the task, and soon the sharp, heavy scent of cedar struck him.

The Sahr also traced a scant drop of the oil across the Trekoan slave bands—those worn, ugly strips of hide at the neck, left wrist, and ankle—to keep the material from drying and scraping.

"This is earlier than usual," he said.

"Well, I can't exactly help it," the Sahr said, looking the sheath over. "It's a lesson I can't seem to unlearn. Trust me, I would rather sleep."

Azetla sat across from her, taking careful note of the pattern. She always used those few too-early minutes to do the common things that anyone might have to do. Clean, sharpen, wash, care, stitch, mend. It would have been easier by daylight, but she came to the fire, quiet as dust, waking no one, and did her mundane tasks. If Azetla joined, she took no notice, and she did not speak unless he forced the matter.

Which was what he needed to do now.

Two days after departing Bir Herash, Rokh Imal Bin-Zari had pulled Azetla aside with urgency, attempting to speak to him without using the Sahr as his medium. But unlike their other conversations, which had been conducted with clarity and warmth, this one left both parties with a sour taste in their mouth.

The Rokh advised him to be careful of the Shihrayan—the "salt-brick," as he called her. Azetla nodded, thinking he understood. Yet Rokh Imal was not satisfied with this. He persisted, using all his meager command of Maurowan, but to no clearer understanding. There was anger in his warning, but no specifics. The crux of it seemed to be that Shihrayans were, by nature, unholy and capricious. No doubt. And that her help was an excellent, but dangerous and unreliable thing. Well, of course.

All Azetla could see was that whatever the Sahr had done, Rokh Imal had *allowed* her to do. Perhaps he was concerned for the stains on his own hands. So be it, but that did not alter Azetla's stance at all.

Beyond that, the barrier of language rose high and would not be scaled. There was no accord.

What Azetla *did* understand merely aggravated him. It was much too late for him to be warned away from what he presently could not hope to avoid, and he managed to reach quite a different conclusion than the one Rokh Imal probably intended. Rather than feeling some nebulous worry for a matter he had already firmly resolved in his own mind, he felt a fresh awareness of what was needed…and who could provide it.

And there she sat, wiping her hands on a ragged cloth, and putting it and the cedar oil away in her satchel. She accomplished a few more tedious tasks, and drank a few sips of water while waiting for the oil to set, and Azetla kept quiet. He thought it strange, and strangely calming, that his presence exerted no real influence on her. No wariness or aggressive vigilance. Just silence and work and ease. As if the ground was almost leveled between them.

Perhaps he deceived himself on that score.

"Rokh Imal was very bitter when he cautioned me against you," he said at last. "There is no love lost between you and he, is there?"

She just breathed out a cold laugh, shaking her head as she began to string the belt and sheath back together.

"Why does he allow you back, then?"

"You are the answer to that," she said, looking sharply at Azetla.

The Sahr stood and drew on her weapon, securing and adjusting so that it would rest comfortably for a day's journey. She stepped over the stone that had been her seat and walked toward the outer camp.

"*Tzal*," Azetla said.

She stopped, canting her head toward him with a slight jolt. He had caught her off guard with that name-like sound. A rarity.

"Yes, *Azetla*," she said sharply, as if speaking his name could possess some retaliatory quality.

"My mistake," he said coolly. "The Rokh's wife kept calling you that. If you dislike—"

"I don't dislike being called much of anything, so long as it's pronounced accurately."

Azetla almost smiled.

"Tzal, then."

She gave a loose shrug of assent.

"There's something I would ask of you," he said.

"I thought we were both paid in full."

"We are. That's why I said 'ask.' I need to learn Trekoan."

She gave him a wry look. "In order to avoid relying on my devil's tongue to talk, you're going to rely on it to *teach* you to talk."

Azetla said nothing. He just waited.

"Mashevi for Trekoan."

"*What?*"

"You teach me Mashevi, and I'll teach you Trekoan and all the dialects of it that I know."

Azetla balked. His left hand twitched toward the lion's head hanging on his chest, as if by gripping it he could hold back his native tongue, and rescue it from her mouth.

He had asked for something borrowed. Pilfered, really, from unsuspecting mouths. She was asking for what was *his*, kept hidden preciously under his tongue, tasted through ritual and prayer and almost nothing else. It was not a fair exchange.

Except...if he bartered with his language, he would be *using* it. It would be at his lips always. Not only the odd word with Khala, who knew mere phrases, nor the hundred memorized prayers, but the whole, rich breadth of it. He could dust it off and waken it. This idea had a fiery effect on him, burning past the reticence, for there was more savor in speaking his language than in hoarding it for he knew not when.

"Mashevi for Trekoan," he stated.

"Makarish too, should you want to watch your back," she said, departing up the gravelly rise, toward the mesa. She would climb it, and not return till the camp was awake. Another habit Azetla had noticed since she became free to do as she pleased.

When the sun had nearly crested the horizon, the watchmen gave their chorus of shouts to rouse the sleepers, and a slow crackle of leather and gravel and buckles and dry-throat coughs rose with the light. Azetla went to receive the report from the watch commander. Sarrez hailed him as he approached.

"All clear and sound?" Azetla said the rote words.

"All clear and sound."

Sarrez held a cup of cardamom-spiced coffee with one hand, and waved the off-going watch on with the other, dismissing them for rations without the formal exchange. Azetla and Sarrez stood at the quiet edge of camp, watching the men gravitate toward breakfast. Off to the east, a herd of goats passed to the soft riverbank at the behest of a little girl's clicking tongue. To the west, the sun began sending fresh heat through the air, such that it seemed to pour out around them.

Sarrez's face was clouded in thought as he absentmindedly offered Azetla the still-hot cup of coffee. The rich scent woke hunger in his stomach.

"I can't. I haven't—" Azetla began.

Sarrez nodded quickly, as though he had been thoughtless to offer, and took a sip himself. The men often joked about Azetla's strict adherence to prayer and ritual, but Sarrez never did. Not to his face anyway. Even among Mashevis, Azetla would have been deemed overly rigid in his habits, but he was not among Mashevis. He was the sole representative here, and he felt the burden of it.

"The Rokh's nephew came over and offered this to me," Sarrez said, tapping the cup. He took another sip. "I was a little surprised.

The Rokh himself has made his feelings about we Makarish *very* clear."

"I'm trying to explain our battalion to him, but he doesn't quite understand," Azetla said, staring at the ground, digging his heel into the gravel.

I barely understand, he thought. Never in his life did Azetla think he would have fought so hard against a natural ally to ensure that a *Makarish* man be allowed to enter the meeting tent. Azetla had offended the Rokh with his insistence but, at last, Sarrez had been granted an audience.

This was one strip of terrain where the rule of the Maurowan world seemed to be set upside down. The Mashevi was ushered in with warmth, and the Makarish high-blood waited outside, untrusted.

But today, the battalion would reach Areo outpost. There resided eight full battalions, each with their Maurowan officers, commanded by a Maurowan Colonel who was ally to Lord Verris and the Corra James. The world would be put back on its feet.

"Well?" Sarrez said.

Azetla nodded. "Just a minute."

He took his water. Rinsed his hands. Bowed his head slightly and with a faint rhythm. He whispered a prayer for morning, for gratitude, for the feet far from home. As he did so, Sarrez glanced away, like one does out of a sense of modesty. For was Azetla not stripped bare before his God in those few words? Fervor and mortification and hope were embarrassing to witness when they were not your own.

Azetla had not much self-consciousness left on the subject. The years had eaten away most of his pride, and for that he might well say another prayer of thanks.

Sarrez and Azetla took their rations. The men gathered in clusters; Makarish, Maurowan, Laritonyan, Nagonan. Sometimes by tribe or region therein. Sometimes by nothing discernable whatsoever. The Black Wren was full of invisible lines, halfway honored, halfway ignored, and it had taken Azetla years to learn how to navigate, rather than stumble, across them.

He sat alone with Sarrez today, at a slight remove from the crowd. Both were quiet as they ate, and Azetla felt a strain in it. Sarrez was working himself up to say something, picking at the callouses in his hands, moving his jaw, staring at the ground. Azetla tried to break the silence gently for him.

"I know our Makarish are uneasy being here with this tribe," Azetla said, looking to the east, away from Sarrez. "I'm doing the best I can."

Sarrez waved the comment away as a given. But a moment later, in a low voice, he said, "Our last fight..."

Azetla raised his head and stiffened. That was not what he wanted to talk about today. Five years old, that fight, and the memory was much too vivid. The miserable colors of it needed no refreshing.

"You know, the others still talk about it...even if you and I don't," Sarrez said. He rubbed his hand over his face. "Gods I hated you, with every last drop of my blood."

Azetla said nothing. What good did it do to say "and I you"? Especially when Azetla's hatred was in a slightly shallower grave than Sarrez's.

"And the truth is," Sarrez said, canting his lower jaw to the side in thought, "I was terrified of you."

Azetla furrowed his eyebrows. That hardly made sense. Sarrez could always win. Would *always* win. He was by far the better swordsman and the better brawler.

"What do you mean, Sarrez?"

"I didn't want to chance being bested by a ja—by a Mashevi. I thought that if it got bloody enough, the Captain might step in...and he would've favored *you*."

Azetla had made no such assumption.

"It infuriated me that he was so accepting of you. That," Sarrez smiled unhappily, "and I was convinced that you would prevail, as you essentially did."

Azetla stared, incredulous. "Sarrez...you *won*. Handily. I don't know how in all the desert you could have forgotten that part."

"I couldn't call that winning, Azetla. Yours was the actual victory, moral and otherwise—"

Azetla scoffed loudly. Whatever else might be true, *that* wasn't. There hadn't been a single moral thought in his mind or body. He had wanted nothing but blood. He had hated with such burning ferocity, it all but charred the skin.

Sarrez narrowed his eyes and spoke on.

"You were injured from the battle a week before—I know I didn't say anything, but I *did* see. I might have died if you hadn't dragged me down, and I hated you for it. Your left arm, was it?"

"It wasn't even an injury, Sarrez, it was scarcely a *bruise*," Azetla said. Yes it had been his left arm, it had affected him nowise, and pulling Sarrez down from his horse had been mere battle instinct, *not* kindness.

Sarrez waved that away too. He was still working toward something, and would not let Azetla hinder him or alter his view of their history.

"When I made that challenge, I really imagined it like one of the nursery stories. I was the honorable soldier, and you were the sly, crafty jackal, fooling everyone. I was to be the savior, you see." Sarrez gave a somber grin and shook his head. "For the Gods' sake man, you don't begin to know how you bloodied my pride."

Sarrez's self-abasing honesty pressed, pressed, pressed against Azetla. In a quiet voice, he said, "Well, it's easy for we southerners to do to that each other."

He waited for Sarrez to correct him—to make that subtle differentiation that the Trekoans and the Sahr did between "true" southerners and southerners from the *east*—but he didn't.

"You only had your jackal-knife for some reason—"

"Sagam," Azetla corrected instinctively.

"Yes...that. But you *were* winning. You had me at your mercy and then you just...let me go."

Azetla tried to interrupt, but Sarrez wouldn't let him.

"No, no...Azetla, I saw it. You let me slip away completely. I didn't understand it. But I was going to win now, so I didn't care, did I?" Sarrez shook his head. "If I had killed you right then and there, no one could have said a *word*...not by the law..."

Azetla held the fold in his arms too tightly and looked awry of Sarrez. He remembered seeing Sarrez's livid face and anticipating the final thrust; the tip of the blade had been at Azetla's neck, the onlooking soldiers shouting for or against or to stop the whole damn thing. The misery of that moment, the feeling of failure upon failure, was still too clear and sharp in his mind. And he had *not* lost on purpose. He had lost as plainly and desperately as a man can lose.

Azetla had provoked Sarrez, he thought. He didn't remember the details—insulted him or his gods most likely—but he remembered how satisfying it had been. He had been so rash then. How time did temper one.

"I'll tell you why I didn't kill you," Sarrez said, his voice weary. "It was a terrifying thing; questions came to my mind as though shot in from the outside. What would the men think of me? Would they ever trust me again? Why had Captain Hodge accepted you, when I hadn't? Why hadn't *you* killed me? Why was *I* the one doing this? No, Azetla...*listen*."

Azetla strained to speak, strained to disagree. The humility it took for Sarrez to speak as he did now was almost unbearable. Azetla could not hope to meet it.

"And then I remembered you pulling me down to safety in that battle, and it took the strength out of my hand. Until that moment I knew what I was and what you were, and that knowledge just...turned to mist in my hand. Burned off by the sun. And I couldn't get it *back*. By blood, I wanted it so *badly*. Do you understand, Azetla? That loss of anger when you need it most?"

Azetla shook his head slowly. His anger may have been quiet and regulated, but he never, ever lost it.

"I swear by blood, it was like I'd been struck. There I was with steel on your throat and not a damn clue as to why." Sarrez looked at the ground, pressing his lips together. "I've sometimes wondered if it was your own desert god who doused me."

Azetla's throat ached and his eyes stung. He couldn't have spoken if he wanted to. All he could think of was how, at that time, he had *hated* being shown mercy by a Makar. He had wanted nothing from Sarrez, least of all his kindness. It was still so hard to take.

"I do have my pride, Azetla," Sarrez said slowly. "Proper Makarish pride, and a love for my people as you have for yours. So bear that in mind as I say this. I trust you. But it has not been easy for me. I used to believe that the most unforgivable betrayal to my Gods and my people was to trust a Mashevi. It is a...common belief. Haqir, Sable, and the others. You know."

Sarrez sighed gravely.

"It has taken me nearly every day of my eight years in the Black Wren to look you in the eye and see you as a brother. So you should be patient with *my* brothers. I know my people. Some of my kin are far kinder and wiser. But some are just like me. Anyhow...keep it in mind. They're nervous here. Like this. Scared."

Sarrez fell quiet, staring into the fragrant silt at the bottom of his cup.

He was trying to make Azetla understand his own without speaking too unfavorably of them. So he had sacrificed himself as an example; Azetla was shamed to the bloody ground by it.

At length, Azetla forced his mouth to speak. "I...I was no different then, Sarrez. I was maybe much worse." Undoubtedly, in fact. "But you're hard on yourself. And on your people."

"So says the Mashevi who never fails to berate his own King, nobility, and all 'those half-pagan Mashevis of Maurow.' I think those are your exact words?"

Azetla set his shoulders back and breathed out sharply.

"What I mean is that I understand that being among a tribe that favors Masheva puts you in a difficult position. And I know the others think I'll abuse it. But I swear by salt I will not let the Rokh or his people disrespect or mistreat *any* of our men."

"I know that. I can't say that they do."

Azetla nodded slowly, and attempted a smile. "Swear you'll temper me, then. Knock me down when I'm going awry."

Sarrez succeeded in smiling. "That's what Joseph's for."

"And my arm wasn't injured," Azetla said. "I didn't yield the fight, Sarrez. I *lost* it."

"Of course."

"I *did*."

Sarrez gave one last dismissive glance. "What happens to you when we reach Areo?"

"I'll keep my feet if I can. But, most likely, I'll be brought down to my real rank, drafted for support labor, and cordoned off."

"Then we'll work you back up," Sarrez said. "Like Joseph and the Captain did the first time. And you'll not have the hindrance that I was."

There it was again. Guilt, guilt, guilt, constricting his throat.

"You don't owe me that, Sarrez."

"Yes. Yes I do."

Azetla clenched his jaw and shook his head, but Sarrez was not looking. He rose to ready himself. They had lingered long over their meal, and the day was advancing.

Rokh Imal rode at the head with Verris, Sarrez, and Joseph. Azetla accepted the Rokh's wisdom and generosity; he rode a borrowed horse rather than moving on foot as he usually did.

Tzal fell in silently ahead of them, walking beside her dun, testing the ground before them. Every now and then she traced the dust with her hand.

The gates of Areo struck up from the horizon far too soon, and by dusk the outpost stood tall before them.

30

"They're here, Lord Colonel," Captain Istamo said, standing in the entrance of the library.

Colonel Orde Everson took a sip of his wine and glanced up from the early Tusian epic through which he had been meandering for the last month. Tusian poetry required rather more patience than he was usually willing to give, and frankly, he was glad of the interruption.

"They made unusually good time. What is their report?"

"Black Wren battalion, five hundred and seventy-two heads. Rokh Bin-Zari accompanies with a dozen of his men. He rides at the head with Lord Verris—"

"Came out here himself, did he? Wouldn't have thought it."

Captain Istamo tilted his head and continued, "—and a jackal. Introduced himself as the commander of the battalion. And not a soul contradicted him."

Everson nodded and ran his finger on the rim of his cup. "I suppose that's the one the Corra wrote to us about."

"So it would seem, my lord," Captain Istamo said, scowling.

"Don't look at me like that, Othas. I know it's ugly work. Don't worry, it's to be a quiet affair. Let the man settle his soldiers, put them in order, and then we can take care of him. I don't think there needs to be any ceremony about it."

"There's one more thing, my lord," Istamo said.

Everson gestured irritably. "Go on."

"Bin-Zari's Shihrayan is with them."

Everson set his cup down and straightened. "What?"

That meant...well, he didn't know what it meant except that he could no longer take his understanding of the situation for granted. "Bloody little devil. On whose right was she standing? Bin-Zari's?"

Istamo's mouth pulled into a thin line. Another sharp breath. "The jackal's."

Everson leaned back into his chair and tenderly returned the parchment to its coil. Even the least popular Tusian epic deserved proper care. "Well. This will take a bit more finesse. Go ahead. Let them in."

***

Azetla dropped from his mount as the Lead Captain of Areo escorted the Black Wren down the central road of the outpost. The fortress was enormous and unusually situated; high Maurowan walls to the north and south, deep-cut wadi to the east, and a sharp mountain of rock to the west, thus to be guarded by both nature and nurture. Had he been unburdened by other concerns, the grandeur and strategic beauty of it would have made him pause in admiration.

"Our barracks are full at present, so your men will camp in the east and south training yards until other arrangements can be made," the Captain said.

Captain Othas Istamo, as he had introduced himself. A Laritonyan name. There was no way of knowing the Captain's tradition or upbringing or what attitude he took toward the Mashevi people. Of Laritonyans, Azetla had known all kinds.

"Very well, my lord."

Captain Istamo passed to Azetla the usual sort of information—who the chief officers were, how duties were divided, how meals were conducted, the direction of the stables, and other needful things. He asked Azetla several questions about the Black Wren and looked long and thoughtfully at his system of ledgers. But just as Azetla began to feel kindly toward this Captain, Istamo seemed to stiffen, lock up, and don a fresh formality. For the most part he kept his gaze fixed ahead as he guided Azetla from place to place, but once in a while he set a strange look upon him; Azetla did not know whether to read contempt or merely curiosity thereby.

Regardless, Azetla did not receive the formal summons to the outpost Colonel. A troubling deviation from protocol. Then, upon Istamo's departure, Azetla noticed five Areo soldiers shadowing him. Casual and at a distance, as if they had other tasks in mind, but unshakeable. From the well to the privy, from the north gate to the south stable, they remained fixed upon him.

On the way back up the central road, through the last dull yellow remnant of dusk, Azetla stopped. They slowed. Azetla drew a deep breath, standing taut. The air around him seemed to express what he dared not; the wind cut across the center road in short, agitated bursts of heat, stirring up grit for the eyes, almost as though it did not know where to go or what to do, but that it must act.

Joseph spotted Azetla from the edge of the road and started toward him. The powdery dust clouded around his feet, and the waxing moon showed his features almost as clearly as by firelight but for the cold, harsh angles it forced upon them.

"I think we've done about as much as we can do," Joseph said, looking at Azetla's stillness with mild curiosity. "Should let everyone get some sleep soon. South yard all settled?"

Azetla nodded stiffly. "The Colonel still hasn't asked for me."

"Well..." Joseph sucked in a breath. Azetla could see his face tensing, looking hard for some explanation other than the obvious one. "Well, maybe he just dislikes formalities. We'll wait and see."

"No. I'm going to see right now."

"What?"

"I'm going to request the audience that should have been given. I'll have to force the matter," Azetla said, his mouth twisting.

He did not like the desperate and uncertain sound of his own words, but desperate was what he had become. Uncertain, however, was the one thing he was *not*. The through-line was clearer for him than it had ever been, thrown into sharp relief by the very height of the risk.

"No. Don't even think about it, Azetla. Lord Verris wants you eaten alive, and you'll make yourself a target if you push too hard."

"I already *am* one, Joseph," Azetla said in a low voice, glancing briefly toward the cadre of soldiers that had been set upon him. Their milling about grew more conspicuous, and they must soon give up the pretense.

Joseph flashed his eyes wide at Azetla, pursing his lips, tension curling his fingers. "All the more reason to lay low, then."

Azetla shook his head. "Not this time."

"You've a death wish, you idiotic jackal."

"Stop that," Azetla said, quietly and with a dead calm. Joseph was always less kind when he was more worried, and Azetla had neither thought nor strength to spare for taking offense. A heaviness passed over him, as though his shoulders had been wearing thick iron all this time, and he just now noticed the effect of it.

"Do you think I'm actually safe if I *don't* go?" Azetla said. "If I don't hold my ground? If I find a shadow somewhere and slink into it? Do you really think that will make a difference? It's not just about command of a battalion anymore; it's a matter of known treason. For me, there will be no neutral place to rest between liability and asset."

Joseph shook his head, but said nothing.

Azetla rapped his knuckle slowly against his cedar lion's head, which he had refrained from tucking underneath his clothes as he normally did. He was well past the point of being subtle. "If you can just make sure that the Colha family, and Khala…"

"I'll see them safe and well. Who is on watch command?"

"Carihua. He's at the east well right now. I gave him the supply ledger."

Joseph nodded, his face as mirthless as Azetla had ever seen it, then stepped back to the battalion. Azetla walked across the main road toward the dategrove, which felt an eerie place in the moonlight; curated, empty, grave-silent. Azetla did rest his hand on his hilt. He could scarcely make his hand do otherwise, although the soldiers that followed him made no attempt to close the distance. It was, if not a comfort, at least a signal that "watch" was all they had yet been commanded to do.

A streak of morbid humor suggested he ask *them* the exact way to the Colonel's villa. But, no, he would have to find his own way.

He knew enough to guess. The person of highest rank usually lived central-west in deference to the Maurowan belief that their gods sprang up from beyond the western sea when the sun fell into it and everything burned with life in an ancient dusk. How strange for them, Azetla thought, to believe in gods that were themselves mere accidents of nature, and thus belied by any real knowledge of it.

The villa soon made itself known, not only by size and elegance, but by the abundance of warm torchlight which marked the entrance to the Colonel's courtyard. It was northern in style and reminded Azetla of Piarago city in miniature. The outer walls were low and of a fine gray stone not to be found in Trekoa, and which must have been imported long ago at great cost. For, of course, a northerner must be made to feel that everything around him is yet his.

The guard at the thick wooden gate signaled a casual greeting.

"Name and purpose?" the soldier said, frowning as he took the whole of Azetla into account. Goatskin jackal band on the forearm,

Mashevi lion's head there for all to see. No rank of even the lowest kind.

"Azetla of Rinayim, commander of the Black Wren. I am here to see Lord Colonel Everson," Azetla said.

The man smiled with friendly amusement.

"Ah. No. I don't think so. If he wishes to see you he will ask for you."

"I am putting forth a direct request. I ask that it be delivered, if nothing else."

"He is tending to his guests, I do not mean to trouble him. If you—"

Suddenly, the gate creaked open from the inside, and the Sahr stepped through to stand next to the soldier, smiling as if in friendly warmth. She spoke to him first in a western dialect of Trekoan, then in Maurowan. "By which I mean, the Mashevi's presence *is* wanted. I can vouch for it."

"I'll not take your word by itself," the soldier said with a degree of uncertainty that baffled Azetla. Why should he take her word at all?

Tzal—for she did take that name each time he held it out—offered a soothing, sympathetic glance to the soldier.

"You don't need to," she said. She gestured in the direction of Azetla's five armed shadows. "Send one of them to the Colonel right now. Ask him if the Shihrayan should bring the Mashevi commander to the dining hall. Those exact words. Your man will be back in three minutes with the Colonel's warmest invitation and deepest apologies, rest assured."

There was a look of such untroubled certainty on her face that Azetla probably would have believed her, had the words had been aimed at him. He did not enjoy observing that from the outside.

With a weary glance, the soldier pushed the gate wide and gestured for Azetla to go through. The look on the soldier's face was one of restrained frustration, as if he hardly had a choice.

With a tilt of her head, Tzal bid Azetla follow. She walked several steps ahead without looking back, certain he would keep her pace and take her turns. Azetla was bewildered. He could not make the least sense of it and, watching Tzal, she betrayed no hint of an explanation.

"Colonel Everson cannot be a very careful man if his soldiers yield at a bluff," Azetla said.

Tzal stopped, waiting until he caught up with her. Her expression was, insofar as Azetla could read it, indifferent. "It wasn't a bluff."

"He did ask for me?"

"No. But it wasn't a bluff."

She walked on. Azetla kept in step, holding her carefully in his periphery, on alert, looking for something to glean. He found very little.

She had the travel and grime rinsed off of her, and had fresh clothes, stark white against the night dark. She looked as though she had had hours to rest and refresh rather than merely one, her whole countenance clear and wakeful. Azetla felt as though there was some new mannerism she had donned, or an old one she had sloughed off. But for the fact that her head was uncovered and her ears unadorned, he would have mistaken her for a commonplace South Makarish woman, likely to garner no more than a passing glance. Even her weapon seemed almost to disappear within the loose cloth.

It made him consider that she might be able to coerce the eye as she did the ear—a worrisome thought—and also brought attention to the filth and crudeness of his own appearance. He rolled his jaw slightly. He had not even chanced to wash his face. Grime, dust, and sweat were thick on his clothes, dirt embedded in the lines of his hands. He did not look the role he came here to claim, and he did Colonel Everson no honor thereby.

Tzal wound through the courtyard along a small, manicured pathway. It was lined on either side by stout brittlebush and small desert rose trees, which were in flower. Toxic desert rose, beautiful, and poisonous. A symbol of Maurow in the desert.

In fact, this might as well be Piarago. Might as well be North City on the Red River festival. Even the sturdy portico columns and the granite steps reminded him of the Imperial colonnade. Azetla felt the effect of the gray stone walls wash over him. Maurow *was* here and, in all likelihood, Maurow would win out.

Tzal ascended the portico steps without any trace of the cautious awe southerners usually had when first faced with northern wealth, grandeur, and power. She seemed familiar with it all, and the only acknowledgment she made of her surroundings was to brush her fingers slowly against the slick marble column as she passed it by, lingering on the delicate etching in the center.

Azetla, however, stopped as he put his foot onto the first stair of the courtyard entrance. The entrance was sentineled by two contrasting statues of the Maurowan goddess, Serivash. Each carving represented one of her natures: lust and violence. Or, as the Maurowans so daintily phrased it, "love and blood." Of all the false deities to stand sentry before this place, this one was the worst. It was almost as a placard saying, "we savor the blood of jackals here."

Azetla felt another wave of weariness. He *hated* this pushing, this scrambling, this vying for place. Here he was fighting for a chance to fight more. Working desperately for a chance to work harder still. How much easier it would have been to have stayed hidden in the low corners of the Black Wren and kept his mouth shut and taken whatever little place was given to him as blessing. He was alive, after all, and that was a miracle by itself.

But you can't just take a miracle, hoard it, bury it, squander it. If something was given—even something as simple as breath in the lungs—a meaningful return must be made. It was all right if the return was meager, so long as it was all you had.

The weariness did not depart, but the hesitation did, slipping off at last.

Azetla pushed forward, up the pale steps, through the wide columns, and on into the half-covered courtyard. His eyes took everything in with a focused slowness, undeterred by Lord Verris' look of dismay, or Rokh Imal's casual greeting.

There were translucent curtains for walls on the north and south ends, and full walls to the west and east, leading to the remainder of the villa. There was a raised table in the center, high in the northern style, but laden with southern fare: spiced flatbread, rice, lamb, stuffed grape leaves, dates, honey, olive oil, chuva, coffers of salt, and wineskins enough to set every last one of the command party sickly drunk.

Lord Verris stared at Azetla, lines of tension forming in his face. Azetla saw soldiers settling into position beyond the north curtain. Six or seven of them now, standing attentive in the dark. Everyone had arrived except the Colonel of Areo himself.

Tzal had disappeared; there was no one at his shoulder anymore. He steeled himself with slow, steady thoughts. He had been this one false thing for so long; shedding the role felt like resetting bones. Each bit of boldness made a crack in his own ears, even if no one else heard it.

Verris approached Azetla.

"You do yourself no favors coming here, jackal," he said.

Azetla turned his head to look at Verris. He pressed himself away from the column against which he had inadvertently been seeking stability, drew himself to his full height, and kept his voice soft and clear.

"Don't call me that again."

He walked on to the center of the room. He felt a reckless wind at his back, and a fierce need to steady himself within it.

He looked to the stair, waiting for the Colonel.

31

No one noticed her dip behind the cloth door that the slaves used, not even Azetla. It was made to that exact purpose: keeping out of sight. She felt her way along the cool, rough stones of the dark stairwell until she came out on the balcony of the upper floor. Colonel Everson stood alongside a decorative column watching the strange variety of guests several feet below with a curious mirth in his eyes.

"How long are you going to make them wait?" she said.

Everson drew himself straight and turned slowly. He looked her over as one might a horse that has been brought in after a rough journey; a cursory glance for proof that no further effort was required by him. He made a graceful, dismissive gesture with his hand. "Until I have seen what I want to see. Besides," he added, "you know me. I like to make an entrance."

Colonel Everson looked wryly at her clean clothes. "You've already made free use of all our amenities."

"If you don't want me to do and take as I please, you could tell your people to stop *letting* me, you know. How is it that there is still a standing order in my favor?"

Everson rolled his eyes and gave a sigh of faint irritation. He had every capacity to make things difficult for her, and plenty of desire to do so, but he always held back.

"What are you even doing here, my dear blood-soaked, silver-tongued thing? Looking to put fuel on the fire of our tribal skirmishes again? Or do you dally in Maurowan conspiracies these days?"

She shrugged and looked down. Azetla stood below, half obscured by the smooth coils of the fountain. "I haven't done anything yet. I'm just here to interpret."

Everson breathed a laugh. "Of course. Of course you are." He brushed the gold embroidery of his outer garment as if to dust it off, one of his many fixed habits formed in service of seeming—and being—cavalier. "I was led to believe you were dead."

"You are not the first person to be disappointed," she said.

"And has Rokh Imal taken you up again?"

She rested her hands on the cool stone of the balustrade and said nothing. She ran her thumb over the intricately carved lip, closed her eyes, and listened. Gentle echoes carried across the sandstone and marble surfaces, voices intertwining in fits and starts so as to fill the atmosphere with cordial tension, a sense of unease wafting upward as strong and distinct as the scent of roasted cumin, coriander, and garlic-soaked lamb.

She opened her eyes.

"Very well, be as coy as you like, little devil. I can only assume you know what this is all about," Everson said in a low voice.

She nodded. "I was surprised to find that you would involve yourself in something so dangerous. A coup? You're not normally one to put your shoulder to stone on anything that might break a sweat, let alone risk blood."

Everson flashed a biting grin at her, and there was vinegar in his voice. "I like to keep my hands clean, that's all. The new-bloods have been talking idly about standing against Riada for years now and, given my own position, it's always been good currency to agree with them."

It was a special victory to get a rise out of Everson. Tzal flicked her hand up several times tossing an imaginary coin as she turned back toward the slaves' corridor. "Well, maybe now you have to pay."

"And maybe I'm *willing* to. I can be a man of my word once in a while," he said. His tone was flippant, but it was more of an answer than she had expected. He stepped away from the stone rail and stood against her path. "But that wasn't even what I meant, little devil. The jackal in there. Why was I sent an order to execute him? What did he do?"

Tzal paused at the lintel of the cloth door. This shouldn't be a surprise. The northerners were all so wildly anxious about Azetla, skirting around him as if he was a snake raising its head, even as he bowed before them. She had pulled him across the whole desert, through enemies and allies, straight into the tip of a sword. Well.

She looked at Everson, who was smiling at her. "You didn't know they meant to have him killed, did you?"

"They threatened him several times, but never followed through, so I thought they'd given up on the enterprise."

"By no means. But *why*?"

"Because he's Mashevi."

"And that's the only reason?"

She ran her teeth against her chapped lip and sniffed.

"Well Azetla's capabilities, temperament, and experience would otherwise indicate a rather advantageous person to have around. So, yes, I'd say that's the only reason." She smiled and stepped close. "Have poor Istamo carry out the order. You know how he loves being made to kill a man without any proof of guilt."

"I only made him do that *once*, you bloody snake-tongue."

She shrugged, satisfied. "Silver-tongue when you like what I say, snake-tongue when you don't."

"Enough. Tell me what I'm dealing with. I'll slit his throat with my own hand if I have to, but I need to know what's at stake."

Tzal pursed her lips and tilted her head, weighing her decision. For Everson, it was not a matter of dealing in either fact or fiction, or what alloy of the two. Truth and falsehood were not even the main axes on which he tended to operate, but rather shame and pleasure. He scarcely minded being lied to, provided the lie amused him. And, though his sense of shame was a terribly scant and difficult target, when found it could be pressed till he buckled, as with a wrenched joint.

"Rokh Imal has made an alliance with him. Him, not Verris. His battalion may revolt against you; they are devoted to him in spite of themselves. He kept books and correspondence for the old Captain, and the structure they use is of his invention. No doubt you'll overcome such trifling difficulties," she said with a feigned, flattering glance.

Everson pursed his lips, not yet amused.

"I will say," she added lightly, "that you *might* want to take a glance at the merchandise before you break it."

"Careful, devil, or you'll make me think you have a preference as to the outcome."

"Of course not. I'm just relaying the facts."

Everson laughed. "And you, of all people, have never once used facts like reins and the truth like a bit. Oh no."

She shrugged. "Do as you like."

"It's not 'do as I like.' It's do as I was ordered to do."

"And you, of all people, never sidled delicately around any order, oh no," she said, tsking her tongue softly.

She could see the frustration simmering beneath his calm veneer, the whirring mind behind the wry smile; she watched him ravenously for her own interest, but without concern. To want an outcome was one thing. To need it was another. It was sometimes easier to keep hold of all the threads if they meant nothing to you.

Or meant little, anyway. She fared best when she kept nearest to neutrality. All would sour if she dared slip past preference and into loyalty. Perhaps because that which she gave herself to was then made like her: petering out, breathing blasphemy, losing ground. That was what Rokh Imal believed, anyhow. Everson too.

"You honestly think there's any chance I'll ignore the Corra's order," Everson said, his voice suddenly dry and lofty.

"Not really. A chance of one in four at most," she said, not smiling, a cruel mirth simmering on her tongue. Mirth or anger or blistering certainty. Either way she was glad of it. She felt she would almost burn to the touch.

Everson pressed his lips together and flared his nostrils. He did a poor job of a careless smile. "Enough of *that*. You're here to interpret? Go."

"Very well," she said with a mocking bow. "But if you *do* kill him, keep me in mind for that Mashevi long-knife of his."

"They call it a sagam."

"Yes, I know." She smiled. "I like the length and proportion of it."

"Stop. Stop playing around. You want him alive."

"No, Everson. *You* want him alive," she said. "I already got everything I needed from him. And I really do want the sagam."

She went back to the corridor, stepping down into its soothing pitch blackness, her feet recalling the length and depth of each step. She paused at the base, not in thought, but to silence thought. Then she lifted the cloth, slipping out into the warm firelight and spiced air of the peristyle. She felt a flash of the old ease. During the seven years that she was slave to Rokh Imal, she had always favored his visits to Areo, and did not protest when she was lent to Colonel Everson. Olive brine on the tongue, clean clothes against the skin, soap and hot water. If her mind was quiet, that was enough.

She saw Azetla attempting—unsuccessfully—to talk to Rokh Imal. He marked Tzal's return with a glance that signified relief.

He was not stupid enough to trust her, but he *did* seem desperate enough to lean on whatever wall he could find, even if he expected it to give out. Just so he could catch his breath. Tzal walked over to him, collected the shambles of their conversation, smoothed the jagged edges wrought by misunderstanding, and made all the words flow free and clear once again between the Mashevi and the Trekoan.

Everson took his time. She saw some servants move about, rearranging, taking things away, adding things in. When at last Everson came down the south stair, he wore a manner warm and casual, as if there were no treason afoot, no Mashevi to be killed, and nothing to be considered but the taste of good food.

There was an embrace and kiss to the cheek for Rokh Imal and his relatives—Everson always honored Trekoan customs—then a deep and formal bow for Lord Verris and his officers, which they returned. All the while Everson smiled generously. Then he got to Azetla. The smile remained. Brightened even.

Azetla brushed his forehead lightly: a battlefield version of the formal greeting.

"I'm told you are the Black Wren commander," Everson said.

"Since the death of our Captain, my lord," Azetla said.

Verris parted his lips to speak, but Everson was fixed on Azetla, and his voice won with authority.

"I did not request your presence here," Everson said, still with a smile.

"No," Azetla said. "I came of my own accord to fulfill the responsibilities of my position."

"I've every right to have you thrown out, jackal."

Azetla scarcely reacted. He only took a slightly deeper breath.

"I know that."

"What is your name?"

"Azetla. Of Rinayim."

"Oof, you don't have to say 'of Rinayim.' I knew that as soon as you opened your mouth. No tribe, however?"

Azetla narrowed his eyes slightly.

"Naftal."

He kept dropping the honorific. It seemed strange to Tzal that *now*, of all times, he chose to eschew all those formalities with which he tended to shield himself. He stood, as it were, unarmed. She forced her mind to take a long step back from everyone around her, to glean as ruthlessly and objectively as possible, to watch like a vulture from the sky, indifferent to who became a corpse and who did not, so long as there was something left to pick at.

Everson wanted to play his games. To talk in soft circles and euphemisms. He wanted this to proceed with elegance. But Azetla would not comply. Or *could* not. He was sapped down to the last of his reserves, and all that remained was a desperate candor. It was hard to evade, maneuver, or cast dust into the eyes when your muscles were giving out.

"You see this is all very intriguing to me," Everson said, glancing at Verris. "What a curious circumstance to allow."

Verris looked as though cold water had been thrown at his face.

"Lord Colonel, the Black Wren's informal hierarchy was one the Corra and I unwillingly inherited. I did not approve it, but I did not see fit to tamper with the matter while there were so many things *at stake*."

"Well, naturally," Everson said in a sly voice. "Thorny task, that."

Verris was ready to burst but, once again, Everson refused to give him the room. He clapped his hands twice, smiling again.

"My good guests, I beg your forgiveness. I have been remiss in my duties and you must dine without me. Enjoy yourselves with my blessing and my warmest greetings," Everson said, first in Trekoan—he spoke it better now than he used to—and then in Maurowan. He turned back to Azetla. "You and I will adjourn elsewhere. My captain shall escort you."

Captain Istamo and three other soldiers came around Azetla in a manner that did not entirely denote "honored guest." Azetla must know that he was as a prisoner now, for all that he was being gently handled. Perhaps he had known it before he ever crossed the threshold, and done so anyway.

He was exquisitely calm, though. Clear-eyed and unflinching. He looked at Captain Istamo and followed. Everson apologized again to his guests, then turned to follow his quarry.

Verris stepped in to stop him. With a whisper that did not escape Tzal's ear, he said, "What are you *doing*, Orde? Did you not receive—"

"I received the courier," Everson said softly. "You've no need to worry. I do not much appreciate being left to clean up your mess, but since I must, let me do it *my way*."

"As long as we understand each other," Verris said coldly.

Everson tilted his head in a bow and smiled. "I have the matter in hand."

Tzal rested her hand lightly against the table and watched Everson leave. If he provoked Verris, it was for his own entertainment, and signified nothing in Azetla's favor.

Azetla was going to try very hard not to die tonight. Little good it would do him.

She drew in even, relaxed breaths. Her mind, to the best of her control, was cool and withdrawn. But, looking down at her hand, she found herself leaning a little heavily against the elegant edge of Everson's table. It was a moment before she recognized the exact weight that pulled at her.

A memory of another execution. One that was stayed, though certainly not as a kindness. And the lesson seared into her skin from it, burned across her shoulders and down her spine: *far better to have died*.

That bedrock truth shook under her feet, as it did from time to time. She did not take her hand off the table right away.

32

Azetla followed the Laritonyan Captain up the stairs, along a columned corridor, to an outer terrace. A fresh-made fire was burning in the stone pit on the floor, food was set on the table, and a garden of patterned stone, thornbushes, and fountains was visible below. The Captain said nothing; he would not allow Azetla to catch his eye. The other soldiers lingered at the distant end of the corridor.

The whole thing galled Azetla to the back teeth. The table set as for a welcomed guest, the terrace lit as for warmth and clear sight, Everson smiling as for a friend. And it was all a lie.

"Will you not sit?" Colonel Everson said after he had done so himself, pouring a cup of wine.

"I don't see the point of this, Colonel," Azetla said.

Amusement sparked in the Colonel's eyes.

"If it's a matter of ritual, there is a pitcher of water and a basin in the alcove, just there. Most of the Trekoans I deal with hold to some variation of your practices. All the food here is lawful to you," he said.

The driving wind at Azetla's back had stilled. There seemed a thousand ways he could respond, but he wasn't sure it mattered. Whatever they planned to do with him, they were going to do either way, whether he came knocking down the door to ask his fate, or held back, waiting for it to be sprung upon him.

Better to know. Better to walk than be dragged.

Azetla washed his hands, slowly, slowly, and mouthed a prayer, the words too well known for even fear to interrupt their flow.

He sat, his sagam next to him in the soft chair. His heart beat like a fist in his chest, but his thoughts eddied clear. He instructed his breaths like he instructed his men in the march, and they remained steady.

"So tell me how you came to be the so-called commander of the Black Wren?" Everson said in an irritatingly cheery voice.

"General consensus," Azetla said. "And I'd rather you didn't play with your food before you ate it. You had me followed from the moment I stepped on post. I assume you already know all there is to know. What do you mean to do with me?"

Everson's smile sharpened and he laughed in an odd way.

"I simply want to assess what I'm dealing with," he said. "This is *my* outpost. A man who is responsible for others should be able to understand."

Azetla said nothing, letting the barest nod concede the point.

"The Shihrayan tells me your men are devoted to you."

"They are accustomed to me. Most trust me."

Everson raised his eyebrows. "Not all."

Azetla saw no purpose in elaborating.

"You're not painting the most favorable picture of your value," Colonel Everson said.

"You want me to pretend that I am blindly loved by every last soldier? That my battalion would disintegrate without me in command? It would be no compliment to my leadership," Azetla said. "I'm not going to perform some charade for you in hopes of a good opinion I am fairly certain you have no intention of bestowing."

He had seen it happen to many Mashevis: beg and plead and lie to no gain. Be stripped of dignity, then mocked for having no pride, stripped of all arms, then called cowards.

But, of course, he was something of a hypocrite in this thought. Everything he gained had come of his being so terribly quiet and careful and obedient. Biting his tongue till it was likely to bleed. Walking up to, but keeping just shy of, those invisible barriers. And it could all be taken away in an instant.

That was true when he was a desperate, stupid boy. And it was true now.

Everson leaned back in his chair.

"I have no peculiar hatred for your people, Azetla 'of Rinayim.' I would have you know that. Nor am I ignorant of them: my library, of all things, does not discriminate. But one must contend with reality."

Everson drew a parchment from his embroidered satchel. He set it on the table and pushed it toward Azetla.

Azetla hesitated. "What is this?"

"You like candor? Here you have it."

Azetla picked it up. As soon as he saw the insignia on the outside, he knew. When he saw the official stamp impressed on the inside below the words, he knew. As he read through James' meandering introduction, he knew.

But when he got to the words themselves, they still struck him with cold iron force. Rarely does a man chance to hold the order for his execution in his own hand. Rarer still does a Mashevi have the opportunity to discover what charges have condemned him, only to find that *there were none*. Even those laws that Azetla had broken were not mentioned. Just the order.

Azetla glanced up at Everson, who no longer smiled. His mind was muddied and slow. He was like one standing on the dais in Piarago at the Red River festival.

He could fight. But he would lose.

He should have run the moment he sensed trouble. But the fear of danger and death had been trampled by the fear of failure and cowardice. That old, ironic dread which had been with him all his life. He remembered hearing the word "coward" for the first time and feeling horror before he was old enough to know what it meant.

Somehow fear won even when defeated.

Colonel Everson fiddled with his cup and glanced past Azetla toward the soldiers standing ready in the corridor at Azetla's back, whose presence he could feel without seeing, like a cobweb against the skin.

"So now you understand, Mashevi."

Azetla said nothing. He surveyed his surroundings as he laid the parchment back down on the table. Beyond the Colonel's back, the wide, short columns seemed to go on a long way, slits of moonlight cutting through them, until they ended in pitch dark. Nowhere to go. No good to die running. Prayers of a small child in the dark coursed through his head.

But then he saw. His eye caught her like a shadow or a figment, flickering faintly within a swath of dark, caught between the bands of light, then solidifying.

Tzal leaned like pure silence against one of the etched pillars. There was a look of gentle curiosity on her face. Azetla wondered if Everson even knew of this shadow behind him; she was just a plain texture draped against the dark, arms folded, beautifully still.

Azetla let out a long breath and relaxed his hand where it had tensed at his side. He had not the least notion of her intent, but the awareness of her presence settled quietly over him. It was like something gripped in the hand. It washed out the muddy slowness of his thoughts, faster than fear, or even relief, ever could.

"Why are you telling me this?" Azetla said.

Everson retrieved the parchment from the table and held it up.

"Because, though I am beholden to it, I'm not convinced this is the best possible use of you," he said.

Wary surprise drew Azetla's shoulders up.

"Do not misunderstand me: this will hold until it is stricken and only the Corra can do that. But a delay might be purchased."

Azetla rolled his jaw, which ached. "You must make yourself clear, Colonel."

"There are delicate matters regarding your battalion's presence here which I cannot hope to make you understand—"

"Lord Verris' plan to oust Riada in favor of the Corra," Azetla said.

Now it was Everson who drew taut, but he was quick to smile.

"Well, she would have told you, I suppose."

Azetla glanced beyond Everson to the figure watching in the dark.

"I told her, Lord Colonel."

Understanding passed like light over Everson's face.

"Well. Then they are right to be afraid of you."

Azetla felt the strange freedom of empty-handedness. He had lost all securities. He was wholly abandoned to his God. And his God was wont to throw him the most troubling and unlikely ropes. Ones that calloused the hand to grasp.

"Hand me your satchel, Mashevi," Everson said abruptly. It was the first time he had used a tone of command. "And Captain Istamo, if you please?"

Azetla turned and watched the Captain come from his place in the corridor and reach for Azetla's satchel. There was nothing in it that was explicitly dangerous to Azetla. He always burned incriminating scraps immediately. All that remained were lists, two of his ledgers, and detailed accounts of the Black Wren's battles with extensive analytical and tactical notes. Unusual, maybe, but not damning.

Slowly, Azetla removed his satchel and handed it to Captain Istamo.

The Colonel sifted through all Azetla's careful work in silence, occasionally exchanging a look with Istamo.

"You see?" Istamo said.

"I do. But so much work on the front end. Besides, attempting is one thing. Maintenance is quite another. We've not many literate officers."

Suddenly, Istamo looked sharply into the dark end of the corridor beyond the Colonel. He lowered his head and muttered something in Colonel Everson's ear. A flash of vivid anger passed across Everson's face. He shook his head with exasperation.

"You needn't have bothered, you bloody devil," he said in a loud, cold voice.

Tzal stepped out of her shadow, across the thin strip of moonlight, and onto the firelit balcony.

"I've already made up my mind," Everson added.

She responded in Trekoan and Everson answered in kind. Vicious tones followed, but soon, Everson's Trekoan failed him.

"Do as you please, it has no bearing whatsoever," he said in Maurowan, gesturing toward a seat.

Tzal sat down, took a cup of wine, and dipped bread in garlic oil and salt, full of ease. Her whole manner contradicted Colonel Everson's words. There was no question that her presence was a gently applied pressure, the direction of which could not be known for sure. Though she folded her legs casually into the chair beneath her, and took each bite and sip with seeming disinterest, she sat as one who presided over the whole matter with authority.

It took Everson a moment to regain composure, to calibrate himself against her. Slowly, an air of calculation settled over him, his eyes returning to Azetla.

"So. It never occurred to you to secure your safety by simply...stepping down?"

"No," Azetla said. "By that way, I die regardless, but at a different hour, with a different justification. And I would have behaved in a craven manner to get there. Besides, it's not just my being Mashevi that Lord Verris objects to. It's that I understand his endeavors more thoroughly than he should like."

Everson smiled slightly. "So I gather."

He looked again at Captain Istamo, and at the papers before him. "Well I trust that the Corra will allow some room for my own judgment. I am sometimes a frivolous man, but I am never wasteful."

Azetla cut his eyes to Tzal as though she could translate the real meaning of these words for him. She offered him nothing but a glance.

"Be plain, Lord Colonel," Azetla said. "You keep circling, but you've yet to alight on any point."

"Very well, I shall be as tiresomely direct as any Mashevi could be," Everson said, leaning forward, his posture informal. He took three coils of parchment from Captain Istamo's hand and unrolled them carefully. Then, to Azetla's bewilderment, Everson handed all three to him.

"Take your time. This is the state of my outpost. Glance through and you will begin to understand the difficulty I have been saddled with."

Stiff all through his muscles with a tension he could not fully release, Azetla skimmed through the Colonel's ledgers: the last three years of officer transfers, formal commands, personnel changes, supply deferrals, and numerous Imperial promises of support and relief that proved empty. Azetla began to see the real reason Colonel Everson made common cause with the Corra and Lord Verris.

"Perhaps you can imagine being told to keep the peace in a region as volatile as this, while being handled *thus*." Everson gestured sharply at his papers. "All the quality, trained troops are sent to Hidud, Cozona, or Golmouth. Those we are allowed to keep are mostly debt-soldiers who come to us, at best, with a shirt on their back and a general ability to dig a privy hole. Areo is the tree off which everyone plucks what they want or need, and since I remain a colonel, not a general, I lose every bid, every time. The Emperor has left us as bones to bleach in this hot sun."

Azetla looked up at the Colonel, his mind writing furiously in careful lines and columns. The Colonel could not mean what he seemed to mean. The papers rested in Azetla's hand, almost as jarring to his senses as the execution order, and it was with great restraint that he did not, once again, look at the Sahr for some explanation.

Everson tapped the table.

"Now do not misunderstand me, Mashevi. I have done my job well. When tribal war *has* broken out," Everson shot a look at Tzal, "I have held the effects back from the north with all my might. I have pried open the trade routes. I have soothed grudges. I have coerced. I have bribed. I have suffered devils to accomplish it. All this I have done without ever marching to battle. These men are not blooded. Nor am I."

Azetla pressed his lips together, fingers tightening over the parchment.

"Captain Istamo here is my best man," Everson continued. "You'll deal chiefly with him, but directly with me if and when I so choose. This has not been—was not allowed to be—a true combat outpost for many a decade. Now that you gather my intention—"

"Do I? Lord Colonel, I would ask that you be excruciatingly clear. And then swear by it."

Everson laughed and leaned back in his chair.

"Swear? What should that even mean to me?"

"Precious little, as experience has taught me, but when someone is willing to say the words, there is always a chance they'll be chastened by them. A small chance."

Everson scoffed out loud. "What cookery is it that you Mashevis swear by? Honey? Vinegar?"

The flippancy in his voice needled at Azetla. It was a moment before he could speak again without the hot, bitter taste on his tongue coming through in his words.

"Salt. Mashevi vows to God and men are made with *salt*."

"Odd idea, sealing vows with salt," Everson said. "It ought to be something of color, like wine, blood, oil, or earth. And it's wasteful. Salt is costly."

"As are vows, Lord Colonel."

The Colonel smiled, though barely. "Well seal these words with whatever you think will prove they have savor and can be preserved: I mean for you and your senior men to work alongside my captain to make this outpost what it always should have been. Make these dregs of conscripts what they must be. If they were forced into use now they would be..."

"Food for your gods," Azetla said.

Everson let his silence answer. He took a sip of wine. Whatever else Everson may be, he was not a fool.

"Then you know that their plan is weak and ill-conceived," Azetla said.

"It is incomplete. They have much of the court. More than I believed they could possibly acquire without being discovered. But they have very little support among the Generals. Too few allies who know how to go beyond words and put shoulder to stone. The Corra's plan...it is a good, strong hound actually. It lacks only teeth.

"You and yours are going to help me amend that." Everson smiled and leaned back in his chair once again. He looked for Azetla to speak, but Azetla was sifting, sifting through every word.

"You will keep your battalion. You needn't worry about that," Everson added. "But they will not be your sole responsibility."

Azetla sensed an omission. He looked down and skimmed back over the first curled piece of vellum, then the second.

"There are over sixty officers here, nineteen of which are Makarish. Lord Everson, is this your way of throwing me to the wolves, while keeping your hands clean of my blood?" he said.

Everson's eyes widened and he seemed almost offended. He spoke a little harder and faster than before. "I am Maurowan. I have no qualms about spilling a jackal's blood. I need no immunity and no proxy to do as I wish." He sighed and slowed his words. "My military upbringing may have a more consular flavor to it than yours, but I am Colonel here. *My men will do what I say.* Never mind if they gnash their teeth a little. My spine is not so weak as that."

Everson was not smiling now. But Tzal was. Her calloused, brown fingers tapped against the table so softly as to be almost noiseless, holding some indistinct sway over the room, like heat rising in the air, or wind across the hair on your arm.

"And if I *am* throwing you to the wolves, Mashevi, you have been among them before and survived. It is, to put it plain, exclusively to our benefit," Everson said. "Having a Mashevi commander provides a few unique advantages in crisis. Forgive me if I'm the sort of man who likes to hedge his bets and prepare for things not to go my way."

Now Azetla understood. All confusion cleared away, mist burned off by the sun. He tasted the real meaning underneath all Everson's temperate words, and he actually breathed the faintest, chest-constricted laugh. No relief to be found there.

"I suppose I'm meant to be grateful for your honesty," Azetla said.

"I don't see why not," Everson said. "Would you have preferred something else?"

"No," Azetla said slowly. "No, Lord Colonel. I would not."

Colonel Everson gave a satisfied nod, confident that his seeming act of mercy was understood to be no such thing. Then the Colonel spat several irritable Trekoan words at Tzal and the inflection was so precise that Azetla almost felt he understood: "There you bloody devil, now you have what you want."

She responded in Maurowan.

"I only want to finish this wine," she said with a tilt of the cup.

Her posture and lilt were such that, had Azetla not known better, he would have said she had been soaked in the Imperial court atmosphere from birth. There was mockery in the imitation, and such exactness.

Everson pointed to the tiny, stoppered wineskin at the south side of the table. "Take the whole thing."

She shrugged and pulled the skin to her, standing as she did so.

"Happy, are you?" Everson said.

The northern affectation dropped off her shoulders as she stood, and southernness washed across her mannerisms and back into her voice.

"I just came to observe one thing or the other. Curiosity isn't preference."

Everson's mouth twisted and he breathed out sharply as Tzal departed eastward.

"You may leave as well, Azetla. It is Azetla, right? I heard that correctly?"

"Yes, Lord Colonel," Azetla said.

Everson furrowed his eyebrows and tilted his head to the side.

"That sounds more like an East Tusian pronunciation. In classical Mashevi, it would be Atzil, would it not?"

A trickle of worry ran down Azetla's spine and into his chest.

"It would be, yes."

"No need to look so astonished. I told you my library doesn't discriminate. I have two translated commentaries. Azetla is an obscure pronunciation of an unusual name," Everson said.

Almost holding his breath, Azetla asked, "Do you know what it means?"

Everson waved his hand at Azetla, as if tired or irritated. "No earthly idea. What?"

Azetla's shoulders slowly relaxed. He smiled.

"Nothing."

"Gods, man, if you're going to taunt me like that, just tell me—"

"It means *nothing*. An old slang word for something unnoticed or unimportant."

Because that's what a goatherd *was*. That's what the heroic goatherd in the story had been. No one and nothing, until the classical word for herder-of-goats came to signify "nothing." Then, even the colloquialism had fallen into disuse and oblivion, so that most scholars might struggle to search out the connection.

The obscurity was the whole point.

"Not a very generous name for a parent to give," Everson said with a cool smile.

"You'd be surprised, Lord Colonel. I've seen names so heavy with meaning one can barely stand beneath the weight of them. I'm content to carry something light."

Everson shrugged, looking weary, as if someone had called a draw, and he was no longer required to lob or parry words.

"If you say so," he said, gesturing for Azetla to keep all the coils of vellum. "Those are for your perusal. I'll have you back first thing in the morning, along with your senior men. Just understand, Azetla: there's no rank in this. No honors. No privileges. Just the tools and the work of them. That is all."

Azetla coiled the pieces of vellum with a careful hand and slipped them into his own satchel, maintaining a ruthless focus on each small action of his hands. "Then it is nothing new to me, Lord Everson," he said.

With a nod, he glanced down the corridor, as if measuring the soundness of the terrain. He almost felt that the ground might heave beneath him, that he might need to grasp the wall for support. But he managed to walk steadily eastward, down the stairs, and through the light of the courtyard. When he reached the dark portico steps and the looming statues of Serivash, his fingers were curled deathly tight, knuckles scraping along his hilt.

33

W esley Verris wanted to collapse onto the clean, wool-stuffed bed and let the heavy lids of his eyes fall, but he waited. Everson would send word once the jackal was taken care of. Then Wesley could brush this biting, crawling feeling off of his skin, and finally be done with the growing discomfort he felt with the whole matter.

He had never had anyone executed before. He had never *had* to.

And devils take Orde Everson! He had used Wesley ill, making a game out of everything. Everson was an old ally and one that people were usually inclined to call "clever," but he made Wesley stumble through just for the fun of it.

A quick rap of knuckles on the lintel came soon enough, and it was Everson who pushed aside the portiere door and stepped in. There was a teeming briskness to his manner.

"We're not killing him yet, Wesley," he said. "You didn't think this through."

Wesley was so thoroughly confused, and also so exhausted, that it took more than a few moments for him to focus on what Everson had said, and a few moments more for the fury to whip up its heat till it could be felt on his skin. He stood to look Everson in the eye.

"You're out of your mind, Orde. You have the Corra's order," he said.

Everson breathed a laugh. "Perhaps next time you tell the Corra to give an order, you should watch over his shoulder and make sure he does it with a stronger hand. You give me an order with no charge, not the least opportunity for me to understand your intention?"

Wesley could hardly believe his ears. "My *intention*? What the devil are you on about? He's a jackal. A *jackal*."

"You brought him in as commander—"

"I did *not*," Wesley said hotly. "He was determined to—"

"I don't care what he was determined to do, you *let* him," Everson said. "And if you had done so to real purpose, I might have been impressed, because it's a thousand times as innovative and useful a decision as I could have hoped for. Might have lent me more confidence in this whole endeavor. Confidence I sorely lack—and don't you dare take offense, for you and I both know that *this* is not how you planned it to be."

"You wanted a long, slow game where the tide of new *and* old blood gradually turns against Emperor Riada, where you can create some semblance of renown for James, and then all is achieved with sly talk and gently applied pressure. The new-bloods step into the sun with the Gods' blessing. But that's your court mind speaking. It's not enough, Wesley. You have to do better than that. You need men. And arms. And experience."

Wesley shook his head in disbelief and wanted nothing more than to throttle Everson, to slap the calm arrogance out of him.

"That's what *this* was supposed to be, Orde! That's why James went to Sahr territory, that's why we have that bloody devil, that's why we have the Black Wren."

"You don't really have them if you don't have *him*. His men would acclimate, yes, but they would resent you. They would not forget. And that Shihrayan devil? The one over whom, I assure you, you have absolutely no control? Capricious though she may be, when she tilts her head one way or the other, the whole bloody desert tilts with her. And tonight she set her finger on the scale in the jackal's favor."

"But Orde, you cannot—"

"Forgive me, Wesley, I *can*. My rank came to my shoulder in the old-fashioned way. I have cast my lot into this, but I'll do it my way. Note my contribution: an outpost, five thousand men—who will become better than they are—and a Mashevi upon whom we can *place all the blame* if everything goes awry."

Wesley's lips parted in surprise. Cool air seemed to wash over the heat in his face. How could he not have thought of that? He pressed his hand over his mouth.

"You see?" Everson said. "The Emperor's fervor against jackals means that he sees every evil, every enemy, every inconvenience as drawn from a jackal well. So let his enemy *be* a jackal. I give you a scapegoat and an experienced commander all in one man. Those don't come cheaply, they hardly ever come willingly, and it's a folly to waste them."

Everson inclined his head toward Wesley. "The rest, I'll leave to you."

For one brief second, as Azetla neared the villa gate, he thought he was alone. He drew in breaths and they came back out disjointed as if his lungs didn't want to let them go. He had the instinct to reach up and knead the sore tension out of his jaw, or dig his fingers into the cedar lion on his chest.

He wanted to stop and lower himself to the ground. He wanted to breathe prayers out with those painfully unsteady breaths and, for just one single minute, let everything collapse, out in the open.

But just ahead, there was Tzal. His arm dropped, lead-like, back to his side. He tucked everything away and forced calm as he and the Shihrayan walked unavoidably together on the same road.

For a time there was nothing but the faraway din of many soldiers, and the immediate sound of their own feet moving at discordant rhythm across the dust and gravel of the narrowing path. Tzal's sword rustled at her side and Everson's wineskin dangled in her right hand. The strident satisfaction she had worn only minutes ago had been sloughed off, and all that remained was inscrutable to him.

They veered south toward the Black Wren camp.

"It's not really lenience, you know," she said abruptly.

Azetla nodded jerkily, keeping his focus with an iron grip. He knew exactly what he was to Everson.

"You shouldn't think of him as an ally...but not as an enemy either. It's more complicated than that."

It was all Azetla could do to nod again. And she too was neither enemy nor ally? She played the latter tonight, and it was wearing on him, because he didn't understand why.

By salt. *By salt.* His careful demeanor was breaking, the firm grip he had on himself weakening.

They were almost to the entrance of the camp. Azetla stopped abruptly beside the stone well by the main path. Staring at the stout, shadowy shapes of tents as if they were gates of a city he should not enter, he hesitated. If he was going to do this, he would have to lodge among the officers, not the common men. And if this went badly, none of it mattered anyway.

He stood in strained stillness for several moments, feeling as though his body was locked against his control. At last, released, he turned sharply to the well and drew. Tzal stopped and watched him, but he didn't care. He couldn't. His strength for concealment had worn down till it hit the bone. He focused on the rope, the tethered jar, the trough, his shoulders slumped.

The water was sharp and crisp, for the well was deep. Azetla washed his face and head vigorously, running his palms hard over the grime on his neck. He drank against the cottoned feeling on his tongue. He could feel his pulse hammering under his skin, in his ears, throughout his breath—as if with the blood-rush of battle. It livened every sense. The night air cut through his damp hair and jumped across his shoulders, carrying the smells of refuse, sweat, and privy, but also those of livestock, spices, homes, and hearths. Underneath it all, he smelled cedar oil and smoke.

When he leaned heavy against the lip of the well, head lowered, he saw that his hands were shaking. Hurriedly, he grabbed his cedar lion's head with his left hand and pressed the other gently against his knee, waiting for the sensation to subside. He could not tell what Tzal saw. He did not look at her. All he knew by the corner of his eye was that she also dipped her hands in the high trough, drew water to her mouth, then sat against the cold, hard rim of the well.

She gestured for the empty jar to his left. Thoughtlessly, he passed it across. She took it from him and tied it back.

His hands still shook slightly. The blood still hurtled through the veins. It was a feeling he recognized, usually born of bloodshed or sudden threat. But now it came from a fearful kind of *joy*; it was searing shock and terror wrapped around one small, guarded hope.

It wasn't because he could have been killed tonight, though that fed the fervor. And it wasn't because his pardon could be rescinded as easily as it was given. That was always the case. This had nothing to do with Everson, the Corra, or Verris—nor even with this Shihrayan, who sat quiet next to him, taking sips from the wineskin.

No. This was an old door with a small crack, thrust wide open at last, and a thousand times more dangerous for that fact. For him. For them. That Colonel could never know what an outrageous thing he had just given, and into whose hands he had given it.

By salt and by the God of Masheva, he could use this like nothing else he'd ever had in his life.

His mind was already darting east and west, patching together plans while the rest of him sat there, stunned, almost a bystander.

For a long time he breathed down the blood-rush, let the thoughts steep. He lowered his hands and pressed the heels of his palms hard against the weather-worn stones as if to make sure that his body was still a hale and sturdy thing.

Scattered sounds from the Black Wren camp fell upon his ears. One of the soldiers began playing an oud. The southerners among them hailed the music with claps and ululation. Azetla closed his eyes briefly and focused on the rich, smoky sound of the stringed instrument in skilled hands. He hushed his mind like a mother does a child who is too overwrought to make sense.

The deep thrum of the oud wasn't a sound one heard often in Azetla's part of Rinayim, but the West Mashevis could celebrate neither birth, nor wedding, nor death without it. Mournful and fierce by turns, it steadied him. He was tempted to take it as a comfort from his God, who often seemed so horribly silent, yet could speak through every mote of dust if he wished to.

"Won't hurt to have a bit of wine in your teeth," Tzal said softly.

Perhaps he was too tired, but she did not bother him. It was so dark and she had kept so quiet while he cobbled himself back together. She took a swallow of wine then, without looking at him, raised her hand in the cool night air and offered the wineskin. She did not seem to notice or care as it hung scorned in her grip. Her arm remained outstretched.

"Every victory you have will be theirs and every failure will be yours alone, so drink up, easterner. You've a gauntlet of hells waiting for you tomorrow."

With a slowness that was not quite reluctance, Azetla took the wineskin.

"You look as though you're relishing the idea," he said. His voice sounded even. He took a strong sip of the wine. Maybe it would settle his blood and keep his mind from churning ravenously all night long. Tzal still looked straight ahead. Azetla took another few slow drinks and handed the wineskin back to her.

"Well, all hells are merely my native ground, isn't that it?" she said. "Because no matter what you believe, here Shihrayan means *devil*, and nothing else."

Azetla looked at her. He was not glad of how thoroughly he understood. Here, Mashevi meant *jackal* and nothing else. But Azetla knew what he was, whereas this Shihrayan either did not know or found it to her advantage that no one else did. She held the truth close against her skin like a secret.

Azetla could not even begrudge her that.

He would be long dead now if he had not held his own secrets even closer than that. They *burned*, though. Azetla's throat ached with holding back the truth. He worried that he would forget how to tell it at all. As he tried to shake off the life of a compliant jackal soldier, it might cleave to him because it had become a part of him.

He mouthed a prayer to his God, who sometimes seemed so remote and unknowable, but whose benedictions tasted so warm in his mouth. He rested there, the gentle night hovering over him.

Azetla would put his hands fast to work. He would carve every last bit of this into something he could wield. Even if he had to make good on the foolish words he bragged with as a boy: *if I lose everything, so be it.*

ACKNOWLEDGEMENTS

Thanks to Lottie, for your editor's eye and your timely encouragement. And my thanks also to Jen; you put this manuscript through the refinery and I am forever grateful.

I am incredibly grateful to all my amazing family, who read, or listened, or encouraged, each in their turn.

Thank you to my endlessly and wholeheartedly supportive husband, Philip. Turns out the way to a girl's heart might just be to read her unedited manuscript! You poured yourself into this effort with such joy, enthusiasm, and wisdom. And I am thankful for my kids who make things first harder, then better, and who fascinate me as they grow.

A special thanks to Laura, my dear friend, who has read this book so many times in so many versions, strengthening it in countless ways.

And the greatest thanks to the One who wrestles with this foolish little Jacob, who does not let me walk away so easily, and certainly does not let me pass unchanged.

J.L. Odom hails from Oklahoma. After a five year stint in the Marine Corps as an Arabic linguist, she graduated from George Washington University with a degree in International Affairs with an emphasis on Conflict and Security. She lives with her husband and five children wherever it is that the U.S. Army happens to send them. Her hobbies include running, jiu jitsu, and cooking to feed a crowd. She can be found online at jlodomauthor.com.